"PEOPLE OF BRISBANE—WE ARE
THE FUTURE. ONLY THROUGH
ADAPTATION TO THE VIRUS CAN OUR
RACE EVOLVE. DO NOT FEAR IT.
JOIN US."

Did the message come from a madman?

Or a bizarre cult?

Or, as some believed, alien invaders?

Only one unthinkable truth was certain.
This was no fantasy. The mounting horror
astounding the nation's medical experts was
real. The murderous hysteria sweeping the
town was real. The hopeless, helpless dying
was real.

As real as the

VIRUS

VIRUS

PETER CAINE

AN ONYX BOOK

NEW AMERICAN LIBRARY

A DIVISION OF PENGUIN BOOKS USA INC.

PUBLISHER'S NOTE

This is a work of fiction. Names, characters, places, and incidents either are the product of the author's imagination or are used fictitiously, and any resemblance to actual persons, living or dead, events, or locales is entirely coincidental.

NAL BOOKS ARE AVAILABLE AT QUANTITY DISCOUNTS WHEN USED TO PROMOTE PRODUCTS OR SERVICES. FOR INFORMATION PLEASE WRITE TO PREMIUM MARKETING DIVISION, NEW AMERICAN LIBRARY. 1633 BROADWAY. NEW YORK. NEW YORK 10019.

ONYX TRADEMARK REG. U.S. PAT. OFF. AND FOREIGN COUNTRIES
REGISTERED TRADEMARK—MARCA REGISTRADA
HECHO EN DRESDEN. TN. U.S.A.

SIGNET, SIGNET CLASSIC, MENTOR, ONYX, PLUME, MERIDIAN and NAL BOOKS are published by New American Library, a division of Penguin Books USA Inc., 1633 Broadway, New York, New York 10019

First Printing, September, 1989

1 2 3 4 5 6 7 8 9

PRINTED IN THE UNITED STATES OF AMERICA

Prologue

The invader moves jerkily through the host fluid. It has no power of self-locomotion. Instead, it is bumped along by the incessant, random movement of the molecules surrounding it.

Neither animal nor vegetable nor mineral, it inhabits a strange shadow world between life and nonlife. It can reproduce itself, like a living creature, yet in most other ways is an inert lump of matter. It is unimaginably small. If people were its size, the entire population of the United States could inhabit a pinhead; so little does it weigh that nine quadrillion of its kind could be mailed to California with a single first-class stamp. In no sense of the word does it possess intelligence, yet it is . . . seeking something.

Specialists call it an obligate intracellular parasite, meaning that it must reproduce within a living cell; outside that cell, it can do no more than a stone. Most others—nonspecialists—call it a virus.

Once it arrives at its destination—the one particular cell among all the thousands of cell varieties that it has been "looking for"—its journey will still not be over. It must next find a properly receptive spot. When it does, it will clamp on and, ever so slowly, infiltrate its way through the cell wall.

Inside, it will take control of the life of the cell, and the cell will become dedicated to producing exact clones of the original invader.

In time the cell will die, replaced by a multitude of these clones. Each in its own turn will ride the fluid, searching for another of the target cells.

Only moments before, the invader's home had been an entirely separate host organism. But there had been a transfer of fluids. It had changed hosts, though it could in no way have been aware of what had happened.

As it ricochets here and there, a floating cell looms large in front of it. A complex cell whose numbers in the organism are not large, but whose role is critical. Is it the type of cell the invader seeks? There is a moment of contact. Yes, this is the one.

It bounces off the cell, once, twice, a hundred times before finding its toehold. It attaches, and begins to do the only thing it knows how to do.

The cell is a *helper T-lymphocyte*, whose purpose in the organism is to direct the production of antibodies that will ultimately attack and destroy hostile microorganisms. But this cell has never encountered anything like the invader before. There is panic. Even as the invader is killing the cell, the *helper T-lymphocyte* continues to try to function. Function becomes malfunction. Antibodies are directed against the normal, healthy cells of the host. The host begins to eat itself alive.

The host organism is a human being. The host fluid is human blood.

The invader belongs to a category known as Human Immunodeficiency Viruses.

It is called HIV-4.

1

The piedmont town of Brisbane was founded in the seventeenth century and has grown steadily ever since, until today it is home to some seventy thousand souls. Assuming everyone in town to be in possession of a soul.

Like all early American settlements, the focus of Brisbane's existence involved water, in this case the Squier River. The Squier was dependable. It flowed year-round, yet rarely overflowed. In addition, it had over the centuries carved out a valley filled with dark, nutrient-rich soil. Then, when the factory became more important than agriculture in the scheme of things, the Squier's banks provided ideal industrial sites.

Foremost among those companies who chose Brisbane was the Claymore-Perkins Chemical Corp., whose life mission was the manufacture of the broad-spectrum pesticide BiChlorothane. Claymore-Perkins' model operation employed over eleven hundred of Brisbane's men and women, in shifts working around the clock to meet demand for the product.

No one could say for sure what long-term effects this activity was having on the Squier River. What *was* certain was that upstream from the plant's chemical doings, the Squier ran relatively clear. Below, the river turned a dark reddish-brown, the color of dried blood.

Claymore-Perkins had selected for its operation a prime spot on the eastern edge of town. No businesses had subsequently located along the river beyond it. So today the factory squats there by the water, its steel towers and vast holding tanks and high chain-link fences announcing either the beginning or the end of the town of Brisbane, depending on the point of view.

The frenzied, unceasing process of pesticide making is, however, the exception. For the most part, Brisbane is a quiet place. Not as quiet as when the area was mostly given over to horse farms and tobacco plantations. But by late-twentieth-century standards, and for a town of its size, it is very quiet indeed, almost rural.

Toward the end of a long, particularly hot and dusty summer, Brisbane, surrounded by green woodlands and gently rolling hills, seems an oasis, still cool and refreshing despite the heat. A very pleasant place to be. Its people are as gentle as the hills, friendly and gracious and helpful to a passing stranger in trouble. They are the essence of what is best about old-fashioned Southern hospitality.

Or have been. . . .

2

Thursday, August 9

Brisbane Hospital was still a madhouse.

Two mornings earlier, there had been carnage on the Interstate south of town. A small plane, stalling out short of the airport, had tried to land on the highway. There was some fog. A multivehicle accident was the result. Eighteen-wheelers had jackknifed, cars had piled up. And then a gas truck had slammed into an overpass and exploded.

Six people had died immediately. Dozens more were injured, many of them seriously; bodies were badly burned and mangled. They arrived at the sprawling U-shaped brick hospital building by the truckload.

The call had gone out for blood donors, to help replenish supplies that were being rapidly depleted. And the citizens of Brisbane responded, as they always had—generously, without a moment's hesitation.

In normal times, standard operating procedure at Brisbane Hospital was to prescreen potential blood donors. Those with infectious diseases or poor-quality blood could then be politely asked not to give. Time and effort were thereby saved, and no one donated whose blood would not be used.

When there was an emergency, however, it was more efficient to skip the prescreening. All blood was still tested, of course, but after it had been donated. Lab personnel worked long hours to deal with the massive influx. Blood was tested, typed, and stored as quickly as possible. Any found to be unacceptable, for whatever reason, was just as quickly destroyed.

The Interstate tragedy had been just such an emergency.

Two days after it happened, Clayton Husch was waiting for the last pint of Batch 342-B of donated blood. Husch had been a lab tech for a year and a half. Unlike many of his coworkers, he was not at this point a walking zombie. His metabolism was such that he could go for weeks on two hours' sleep a night, and be none the worse for it.

"Rough couple of days, huh?" Husch said to Janet Willen, who was preparing Batch 342-B.

Each pint of blood was in a sterile plastic bag, tagged as to type and ultimate destination. The bags fit into slots in a special tray.

Janet Willen groaned. "God, don't remind me," she said. "I think I'd kill for eight straight hours when the phone didn't ring."

Husch smiled. He leaned back against a stainless-steel table, resting his knobby elbows on it, and folded his hands over his belly. There wasn't any flab around his middle. In fact, he had no excess pounds anywhere on his six-foot-two-inch frame. That—combined with his pleasant, clean-shaven baby face—made him look even younger than his thirty years.

He waited, watching Janet with eyes that were so perpetually bright and watery, they gleamed. Though not by nature a patient man, he was good at waiting. Anything could be controlled if one had the will for it. Anything.

"Done," Janet said finally.

She managed a faint smile as she looked over at the lab tech. Not a bad-looking guy, she noted, not bad at all. Those intense eyes played off the innocent face. Fine light brown hair that she really wished he wouldn't cut so short. And a nice trim body. But still just a lab tech. The hospital was full of more desirable men.

"One bad one," she said to Husch. She indicated a bag that had been tagged DESTROY IMMEDIATELY.

"What is it?" Clayton asked.

"HIV-4," Janet said. "Fortunately, we don't see a lot of *that* around this town. *Yet.* Sign here."

"I'll take it down right away," Husch said.

He signed the form accepting responsibility for the pints of blood in the tray. Then he transferred the tray to a rolling steel cart, nodded to Janet Willen, and wheeled the cart out to the lab. Behind him, Janet slumped into a chair and closed her eyes.

Out in the corridor, various hospital personnel rushed past Clayton Husch without even noticing him. To those who did see him, he was just an anonymous technician pushing a cart full of blood bags. He seemed calm, and conscientious about what he was doing.

Inside, though, Clayton's heart was pounding. The palms of his hands were slick with sweat. So much depended upon what happened during the next few minutes. He felt as though he was walking along the rim of the universe, with the glory of the stars on one side and infinite emptiness on the other.

First, he pushed the cart to the blood bank. There, the clerk signed for Batch 342-B. Except for one pint.

"I'll get this right down to Hazardous," Husch said.

The clerk nodded his dismissal of the lab tech. The clerk was a busy man.

Husch went back out into the corridor and walked purposefully to the nearest men's room. He locked himself in one of the stalls long enough to slip the plastic bag inside his crisp white uniform shirt and secure it in place behind his belt. He flushed the toilet as he left the stall.

Then, instead of going directly to Hazardous Waste Disposal, he took the elevator to the basement. He went to his locker. Inside was a large brown lunch bag. He took it with him to another men's room.

This time he took longer in the stall.

From the brown bag he removed the two items he'd been carrying to work every day for months now, while waiting for this moment. One was an empty plastic blood bag. The other was a thermos containing a mixture of beet and tomato juices, blended so that it closely resembled whole human blood.

Husch poured the contents of the thermos into the empty blood bag and sealed it. He wiped out the open thermos with a paper towel, then set it on the stall's tile floor. With great care he removed the identification tags from the bag containing real blood and transferred them to the one containing the simulation.

The next step was the nerve-racking one. He took a small pair of scissors from the brown bag. He wedged the plastic bag containing the infected blood between his thighs, being extremely careful not to force the blood level up so high that the stuff would spurt out when the seal was broken.

Ever so slowly he snipped off a corner of the bag. He lifted the bag gently, using both hands. They were trembling slightly; a slip here, and who knew what might happen. He spread his feet and lowered the bag toward the floor. Then, without losing a drop, he poured the blood into the thermos. He capped the thermos very tightly.

It was done. He held the thermos in his hand, turned it around once, admiring its smooth finish, wondering in how many ways the fluid it contained was going to change all their lives. For a moment he was almost overcome with pride. He had fulfilled his purpose. His eyes stung with tears.

No time for sentiment now. He had to finish the job. Hastily he went about it. The used blood bag went into a plastic bag that he wrapped in paper towels, securing them with an elastic band. That packet went into the brown bag, along with the precious thermos. Except for the thermos, the whole mess could go into a dumpster on his way home. The bag of phony blood went under his shirt.

Husch returned to his locker and put the brown bag away. Then he left the changing area. He took a small subterranean corridor across the hospital basement to Hazardous Waste Disposal. At one point he found himself alone and quickly reached under his shirt. Nobody came unexpectedly around the corner. By the time he arrived at Hazardous Waste, the counterfeit blood bag was in his hand.

He presented it to the woman in charge of Hazardous. She was a petite blond with perfect teeth. The name on her tag was "Ms. Joanna Feene." He smiled at Joanna.

She smiled back, until she saw what he'd brought her. Then she immediately put on a pair of plastic gloves. She handled the bag as though it might at any minute rupture and contaminate her.

"Man, this stuff really gives me the creeps," she said.

"No danger," Husch said, plinking the bag with his forefinger.

"Don't *do* that!" Feene said.

"Ah, these things are tough," Husch said. "Besides, it won't go through your skin. You'd have to shoot it up to get it."

The young woman shivered slightly. "No, thanks," she said. "Got the paperwork?"

"Sure."

He handed Joanne Feene the forms and she signed for the one pint of HIV-4-contaminated blood from Batch 342-B, received by donation two days earlier.

"Thanks," Clayton Husch said. "Actually, I think you better incinerate that stuff right away."

"Don't worry," Joanna said. "It's outta here."

Husch gave the woman a thumb-and-forefinger circle and left. He returned to his post at the lab by way of the hospital's main lobby, where there was a row of old-fashioned phone booths. He closed himself inside one of them and made a call.

"It's Husch," he said when a man came on the line. "I've got the item we've been waiting for."

There was a pause.

"Of course," the man said. "I had a dream last night that this was going to happen. It's the fulfillment of the plan."

"I know."

"All right. Bring the item to the house tonight. I want you to arrive at exactly nine-fifteen. Go to the communications room and walk straight in. We'll be expecting you."

"Yes, Glorio," Husch said. "As you say."

3

When Clayton Husch called, Dante Glorio and Sandy Fraim were lounging on some oversize pillows in the entertainment room. An old episode of *The Sands of Time* was running through the VCR.

The episode was drawing to a close. Rebecca was about to reveal to her financé Jonathan that she was pregnant by Blake, the man she really loved. Lynette had locked herself in the house against the intruder, only to discover that the phone was dead. And Old Man Howards was in the process of telling his wife about a minor change he intended to make in his will.

The handsome, dashing Blake was played by Dante Glorio.

It's doubtful that the casual observer would have immediately connected the character on the TV screen with the person watching it, though in many ways they were quite similar. Both were short, but strong and physically fit. Both had thick dark wavy hair, without a trace of gray, and penetrating black eyes. Both had liquid tenor voices that seemed to caress the listener.

There was a difference in age, of course. The flesh-and-blood man was in his late thirties, the flickering image about five years younger.

That wasn't it, though.

It was the face. The face of the Dante Glorio who was playing Blake was a face most men would kill for. It was smooth as the surface of an apple, free of any suggestion that there might be pain in life. The features were symmetrical, the eyes pleasingly spaced, the nose straight and slightly flared without being prominent, the lips full and sensuous, the jaw square and strong. With such a face, the actor needed little talent. He would be a star.

And then there was the face of the man on the pillows, the Dante Glorio who lay watching his previous incarnation. The casual observer would look, then look again. Surely it couldn't be the same man. It couldn't be.

Yet it was.

The face of the living Dante Glorio was a convoluted mass of overlapping scar tissue. It was a horror from which most people would turn away, a topographical guide to the very darkest nights of the soul.

The man on the pillows, of course, did not think of himself in that way as he watched the glowing cathode-ray tube. His image of himself was what he wished it to be. He thought of Bobby Drew, a nice-looking boy growing up among the wealthy and privileged of Brisbane. Or he thought of Dante Glorio, the devastatingly handsome TV star young Bobby became.

He didn't think of a particular night in New York City, nor of an actress long since forgotten by the public, nor of a frying-panful of scalding oil. He didn't think of futile plastic surgery or an agent who no longer called. He didn't think of taking up residence once again in the Brisbane estate that had been slowly decaying since the death of his parents.

In his mind there was the immutable image of Blake, father of Rebecca's unborn love child.

And there were no mirrors in Dante Glorio's house to contradict him.

The Sands of Time's theme image appeared on the screen. It was a naked dune, with the wind whirling sand up its flank and over the crest. A congregation of violins bemoaned the sadness of this short life. Against the sand background, the afternoon soap's credits flashed past at the rate of two per second.

As the credits flickered, Glorio said, "I was good."

Sandy Fraim said, "You were good. You were the best. *Nobody* had that kind of screen presence."

Fraim was in her early twenties. At five-two, she was four inches shorter than Glorio. Her figure was curvaceous or, as she perceived it, plump. She had brown eyes and dark curly hair that brushed her shoulders. The hair framed a face that was pretty by most people's standards, though even as she handed Glorio the compliment, her expression was barely animated. There was no hint of emotion. The look she presented to the world was as serene as that of a monk or a heroin addict.

She curled up next to Glorio, fitting herself to his body, and kissed him on the neck. He lay on the pillows, staring at the ceiling as the tape rewound.

"Something's happening, Sandy," he said. "I can feel it."

"Uh-huh. You mean with E.T.?" *E.T.* was Sandy's personal term for the Polarians who spoke through Glorio.

The phone rang. The private, unlisted number. Glorio gave Fraim a knowing look. She answered, then passed the phone to him.

"I've got the item we've been waiting for," Clayton Husch said.

Glorio's whole body quivered. This was it. His mind sorted quickly through the various possible scenarios, settled on the one that would be most effective.

"Of course," he said. "I had a dream last night that this was going to happen." And he gave Husch his instructions.

Afterward, Sandy Fraim asked, "What is it, Bobby?" She was the only one in the world still allowed to call him that.

Glorio's eyes were bright. He was looking at his companion, but what he was seeing was far away in distance and in time.

"They have provided," he said.

"Provided what?"

"The blood."

He said the word as if it were a term of endearment. Fraim looked at him uncomprehendingly. Then he seemed to snap back into the present. He rubbed his hands together. A smile split his full lips and lit a fire behind his eyes.

"We've got a lot to do before tonight," he told her. "I want the whole HIVe here. We need to put on a show they'll never forget." He rested a hand lightly on her shoulder. "I'm going to need you to help me, Sandy. I do depend on you."

"Sure, Bobby," Sandy Fraim said. "Whatever."

4

The brief ceremony was timed to coincide with the changing of the shifts. Evening cops coming on duty, day cops going off.

A wooden lectern had been set up at one end of the room. Metal folding chairs, maybe forty of them, had been laid out in uneven rows. Perhaps half were now holding up cop butts.

Howard Kyser—known to everyone as "Kip"—the chief of the Brisbane Police Department, stood behind the lectern and rapped for attention.

When Kip Kyser wanted attention, he usually got it. In his late fifties, he was still a commanding presence. He had thick forearms, and large hands capable of a crushing grip. His legs were heavy and powerful. The pale blue eyes had unassisted twenty-twenty vision.

Kyser's body had seemingly made but two concessions to age. He was completely bald, the skin of his head darkly blotched in random spots. And he had a hard, protuberant belly by Budweiser that had been in place for years and was never going to leave him. He carried the belly proudly.

"All right, men," Kyser said. "Y'all know I'm a rotten hand at speechmaking, so let's keep it short. We're here to honor one of our own. Twenty years this man's been on the force. Twenty years. Think about it, you young guys. That's a deal of service to the town of Brisbane. So now I'm real proud to make it official. The department hereby promotes William Grant to the position of detective lieutenant. Come on up, Will."

Will Grant shuffled to the front of the room.

"Good job, Will," Kyser said.

"Well, thanks," Grant said. "It's been a long time coming."

"Long time, hell," Kyser said. "You'll be after my job most any day now." He laughed. "But say a couple of words, will you? Then we can get back to work around here."

The new lieutenant turned and faced his fellows, some of whom had clapped, others of whom had hooted at him.

Grant was, in a word, plain. He was just over forty, just under six feet tall, just a little too heavy for his height, as evidenced by the slight soft bulge that encircled his middle. He wore horn-rimmed glasses; behind them was an unremarkable pair of gentle brown eyes. His brown hair was flecked with gray and thinning just a bit at the front. He wore a lightweight plaid jacket over a white short-sleeved shirt open at the throat, rumpled cotton twill trousers, and scuffed brown tassel loafers. The jacket seemed cut for a slightly larger man.

"Well, thanks, guys," Grant said. He talked slowly, with a noticeable drawl. "I didn't have no speech prepared, so I guess I'll just say I hope to hell I'm not still here twenty years from *now*." Scattered laughter from the boys. "But meantimes I'll give Brisbane my best."

He looked at Chief Kyser and shrugged. Kyser asked the boys to give him a hand. There were more applause and more catcalls, and the little gathering broke up.

"Just one other thing," Grand said to his chief. "I'd like to keep Jeffers as my partner if I could."

"Sure thing, Will," Kyser said. "No problem."

"And my old office. Hell, it's plenty good enough for me."

"Sure."

"Thanks."

Grant walked back to the office he shared with his partner and two other detectives, the team of Pound and Worth, sergeant and lieutenant respectively. Along the way he was joined by his partner, who was carrying two coffees in paper cups that would be soggy and useless within five minutes. Jeffers presented one of the cups to the new lieutenant.

"Congratulations, boss," Jeffers said.

In marked contrast to Grant, his partner was dressed in a charcoal-gray poplin summer suit, burgundy-and-green tartan tie, and polished black wing tips.

Grant took the coffee. "You must want my job bad to be bringing me this stuff at the end of the day," he said.

Jeffers grinned and stood aside to let his partner through the office door.

It was a cramped space. Each officer had room for a desk and a filing cabinet. There was an old-fashioned wooden coatrack in one corner. The only potential source of fresh air was a window set high in the far wall, above a copy of the *Sports Illustrated* swimsuit calendar. The window had never, in Grant's experience, been opened. Or washed. It was crusted with grime.

Since the entire police department was climate-controlled, the lack of access to the outdoors shouldn't have made a difference, but it did. Because neither Grant nor Jeffers smoked. Both of their office-mates did, so they might as well all have. There was no exhaust fan in the ceiling.

This afternoon, however, the air was relatively life-supporting. Pound and Worth were out on a case. Grant and his partner sat at their desks, Grant with his feet up and Jeffers with his elbows rested on his knees.

Martin L. Jeffers was five-foot-eight and wiry, his body seemingly composed entirely of flat slabs of muscle. His pencil mustache made him the only cop on the force to sport any facial hair. Not that that was particularly daring. Jeffers probably could have grown a beard and a full-fledged Afro if he'd wanted. The truth was, the department needed a few highly visible blacks, for the good of community relations. And Martin Jeffers was not only indisputably black, he was good. He'd made detective in less than four years.

"Well, how's it feel?" Jeffers said.

"I asked Kyser to let us stay together," Grant said.

"Oh, yeah? I appreciate that."

"We're a good team."

"I reckon."

"Don't let it go to your head. You're about the only man available who doesn't smoke. Or fart your brains out. And it don't feel a damn bit different, except that I stand to be twenty years older now."

"Must of been a long twenty years," Jeffers said. "Slow as you talk. But maybe now you're lieutenant we'll get a few interesting cases our way. You think? Any less action and I won't be able to tell my butt from my shoes."

Grant raised his coffee cup. "Twenty down," he said. "Five more to full pension and I'm outta here. Far as I'm concerned, they can be the slackest five years I ever seen. And I pray to God this is the only weapon I ever have to use."

He patted the Security Blanket flashlight that he wore clipped to his belt. It looked like an ordinary light, but it produced a single high-intensity flash that would blind a person for three minutes without causing permanent damage.

"You might be itching for some action now," Grant went on. "But wait till you actually have to fire your gun on the job. Believe me, after that you'll do your shooting down to the range. Hopefully by then I'll be long gone."

"Come on, Will," Jeffers said, "I known you a year now. You always gonna be a cop. What else you gonna be?"

Grant laced his fingers behind his head and stared up at the fiberboard ceiling that continually shed little flecks of itself, leaving a perpetual coating of white dust on everything in the room. Grant wondered if he might be breathing asbestos. He didn't want to ask.

"What do *you* want to be, Jeff?" he asked.

Jeffers chuckled. "I believe I settle for Kyser's job," he said.

"When I was twenty-five years old, I suppose I would of too. But look at him. That really what you want?"

"I ain't like him."

"Yeah, you're not white and you're not an alcoholic, but if you want to be chief you best kiss the mayor's ass just like he does. Even you."

"No way."

"Well, good luck *to* you," Grand said. "And damn me if I don't send you a postcard from Nashville."

"Aw, man, you still talking that trash?"

"You don't know, Jeff. You don't know can I write a good song or what."

"Oh, I don't doubt you can write a song, Will. Anybody can write that hillbilly shit."

"Country and western. And that's where you're wrong, my friend. *Not* everybody can write that stuff. What the music's about is life, wrote up so the people can understand it, so it makes them laugh and cry about their *own* life. And there's no one seen more of life than a cop has."

"Will Grant," Jeffers said dramatically, "the cowboy in blue."

Grant smiled. "Laugh if you want," he said. "But I won't be but forty-five. I'll have my pension, so what I make off the songs will just be gravy on the roast. I'm gonna have a very good time."

"I believe it the day you leave Brisbane. Hell, you can't even *spell* Tennessee."

"Don't have to. Long as I can spell the name of my bank. So what do you say we log out. I don't believe there's anything nasty happening in Brisbane today."

Jeffers groaned and rolled his eyes. "Tell me what I know," he said. "There's *never* anything happening in Brisbane."

5

Clayton Husch was missing, but otherwise the HIVE was complete, gathered together in the communications room. Dante Glorio stood on the gold-carpeted dais, with Sandy Fraim seated cross-legged on the carpet next to him. And in front of them, in a semicircle of chairs on the parquet floor, were the six others.

They were divided equally by sex. One of the men was in his mid-thirties, one of the women close to forty. The rest were young. One girl was just nineteen, and none of the remaining three was over twenty-four. All the members of the group were clean, neatly dressed in casual clothes appropriate to the season. The only common denominators were their gold or yellow shirts and blouses.

There was little interaction among the people on the floor. They smiled a lot to themselves. Whenever Glorio spoke, he had their total attention, and they smiled a lot at the things he had to say.

Glorio was dressed in a pale yellow silk shirt with puff sleeves and no buttons between his throat and his navel. His saffron polyester pants were so tight that his manhood was sculptured in bas-relief. He was barefoot.

Sandy Fraim, as always, was wearing blue jeans and a well-worn man's dress shirt—pastel yellow, in her sole concession to HIVe fashion—with the cuffs pushed back to her elbows and the tails hanging out. She was shoeless as well.

The room, the *communications* room, had been built to Glorio's specifications shortly after he began having spontaneous trance experiences. It was one of the few modifications he'd made to the family mansion after moving back. And it was a magnificent achievement.

The room was the inside of a perfect sphere, or as close to a perfect sphere as construction techniques would allow, and it had been painted pale gold. The floor bisected the sphere, so that those inside perceived themselves as simply being under a domed ceiling, but the sphere did complete itself beneath their feet.

The room was lighted by recessed indirect lighting, masterfully arranged so as to be invisible. The ventilation grates were hidden as well. Even the electrically operated door was flush with the wall and had no inside knob. Nowhere were the soft curves of the room noticeably broken.

In the center of the dais was a single, simple straight-back chair of stained and polished walnut, the room's centerpiece. As desired, Glorio could bring the general lighting down and the spotlight on the chair up, until the walnut gleamed within an ovoid of buttery yellow light. It was his channeling chair. When he was seated in it, and the lighting was properly set, he seemed suspended in a golden capsule that floated between worlds.

The room as a whole was a divinely inspired creation. Glorio had begun with the well-known theorem that a perfectly curved space allowed for the focusing of various types of wave transmissions, and put that theorem into practice. And it worked.

"Last night," Glorio said to his followers, "last night I had a dream. As you well know, the Polarians rarely speak to me in my dreams. But equally true is that when they do, the messages are invariably as important as, if not more so than, those I receive during channeling.

"This is what they made clear to me: the HIVe's time is at hand. As if, indeed, any of us ever thought it wouldn't come."

General shaking of heads.

"We are about to become active agents of the greater cosmic plan, the first link to the beings of the Polarian system. We are, as we have long suspected, the vanguard of their contact with Earth. Working in concert, the human and Polarian races are set to form an interstellar union. There can be no greater purpose to our lives."

More murmurs of assent.

"And now, by the light of my dream, it is time to begin

forming that union. The Polarians are going to actively
assist us, donate to us the means by which we may act.
You have noticed that Brother Clayton is not among us
right now."

Puzzled nods.

"That is because in my dream I learned that Clayton
has been chosen to be the Polarians' messenger. It is he who
will deliver to us their instrument of goodwill. *If* we are
ready. *If* we are worthy. Are we ready? Are we worthy?"

"We are ready, Glorio," came from the nineteen-year-
old girl. General assent.

"Then let us will it to happen," Glorio said. He sat
cross-legged on the mat, next to Sandy Fraim. "Let us
concentrate our energy. Let us bring Brother Clayton
through the door with the means to attain our goal."

Glorio rested his hands on his knees, palms up. He
closed his eyes. Members of the HIVe followed his lead.

The room was silent. Then, slowly, the curved walls
began to pick up the deep breathing being practiced by
the eight people within, and to amplify the sound. The
HIVe members' long familiarity with one another soon
brought the varied breaths into unison. When that happened, there was an eerie change.

The golden walls began to breathe. In and out. In and
out.

For the very air had subtly altered. One floor down, a
timer in the control room had gone off, and what was
now flowing through the hidden vents had an artificially
heightened concentration of nitrous oxide.

It seemed the room itself pulsed with life. A life far
greater than the mere sum of the few fragile human lives
it enfolded therein. A life that, ultimately, joined those
present with Polaris, the Pole Star, the distant, glittering,
age-old beacon for mankind. A life that drew breath, and
soon would come out of the darkness of interstellar space
and take its first tottering steps on the earth.

At precisely nine-fifteen, Clayton Husch walked through
the door. He cradled a shiny silver thermos in his hands.

The HIVe's collective head turned. Sandy and Glorio
stared at the lanky man as he made his way to the dais.
He moved with a purposefulness that was evident in
every step. His eyes shone even more than usual.

Husch stopped in front of Glorio and held out the thermos.

"For the fulfillment of the mission," he said.

Glorio got to his feet. He took the thermos from Husch. Then he kissed the lab technician on the lips.

"You are the messenger of the gods," Glorio said. "Your name will be remembered forever." He held the thermos aloft. "The blood," he said. "Our blood."

The rest of the HIVe swarmed around Husch, hugging and congratulating him.

And as they did so, each of them could plainly see, deep within his eye, the cold, glittering North Star.

6

The humidity level in the warm spherical room rose rapidly. HIVe members began to kiss and fondle one another. Tongues moved in and out of mouths. Bodies swayed to the silent music they all heard. The women vied for the attention of Clayton Husch, messenger of the gods.

When he felt that the energy level was properly pitched, Glorio commanded the group's attention.

"My friends," he said. "Brother Clayton has brought us the blood, the instrument of our destiny. Now the fullness of our mission must be revealed to us. I feel the Polarians are ready to speak once again."

A quiver of anticipation ran through the group. Looks of longing were shared, fingers intertwined.

Sandy Fraim had brought a small mahogany table into the room, placed it at the front of the dais, and set Husch's silver icon on it.

Glorio closed his eyes. "I am ready," he said.

Fraim led him to the channeling chair and saw to it that he was comfortably seated. As if guided by astral hands, the room's general lighting lowered, while that around Glorio's chair came up.

The HIVe found its seats in the golden half-light. Once again a semicircle was formed, facing the dais. The group's collective breathing fell into its natural rhythm, its attention focused completely on its leader, suspended in his yellow capsule of light. Sandy Fraim stood by his side, one hand on the controls in the pocket of her jeans.

There was a low tone, just at the edge of hearing, which seemed to come from all directions at once. Glorio began to hum softly, matching his pitch to the tone.

26

Fraim imitated him; then the rest of the HIVe joined in too.

The volume rose. Individual voices were raised along with it, until a certain level was reached. Then, simultaneously, everyone fell silent.

Glorio spoke.

But not in his own voice. It was a deep bass voice, rich and resonant, somehow otherworldly. The voice of the Polarian who had chosen the HIVe to be his point of contact.

"I bring you greetings from Polaris," the voice said.

"Welcome, Joseph," Fraim said. "We are all gathered to hear from you. We have received the gift you sent us."

"We are pleased with you," Joseph said. "You have shown your worthiness by your patience and your dedication."

"We are ready to fulfill our purpose. Help us to understand it better."

The people leaned forward slightly in their seats.

"You were originally called here," Joseph said, "by your common interest in making contact with other worlds. There are many like you on your earth, but it was the strength of your desire that brought you to our attention, a beacon in the stellar night.

"You are also fortunate in having as a channel that man to whom you now give your allegiance. On your planet, he has no peer in this ability.

"Through your association with us, you have learned of the greater cosmic family. Now you wish to join it. We feel you are ready. And the rest of your race is poised to follow the HIVe's courageous lead. The way is hard, make no mistake about that. But with our assistance, all is possible."

Joseph lapsed into an unknown language and continued for about two minutes. Behind their lids, Glorio's eyes were darting about as if he were deep in dreaming sleep. Sweat had beaded up on his forehead, and Fraim carefully wiped it away.

"We cannot understand you, Joseph," Fraim said. "You must speak to us in our language."

There was a pause; then Joseph said very carefully, "In order to join the cosmic family, your species must be capable of change. That which you know as *virus* is the universal agent of change, the connecting link between the living and the dead, the created and the formless. And the virus your scientists call HIV-4 is the most important of these agents.

"It is the one sent to your planet across the vastness of space, and the one that has come into your hands tonight.

"A fundamental change in your species consciousness is now needed. You must not listen to your doctors, who will try to eradicate the virus. You must instead recognize it as the agent of positive mutation. Without HIV-4, you will not be able to take the next step along your proper evolutionary path.

"This virus requires your blood, the very fluid of your life, for its host. Accepting the change it brings will be difficult; many of those exposed will die. But those few whose blood *is* purified, their whole beings will be transformed. They will acquire the power of interstellar communication. They will be the avatars of the *new* race, and their numbers will grow.

"You have no choice. As long as you adapt, then your species and ours will become as one. You will join the greater family. If you fail, however, if you succumb to the virus or prevent it from doing its work, then your evolution will be at an end."

There was another pause. Fraim broke the silence by saying, "We must evolve or perish."

"Yes. HIV-4 is the universal cornerstone of *all* evolution. It is that upon which you either build or founder."

"How long will the process take?"

"Many lifetimes, perhaps. You must be patient. Those who would destroy the virus will have the upper hand at first. They will appear to have reason on their side. But they must not prevail, or you are all doomed."

Another pause. The muscles in Glorio's face twitched and contorted as if there was static in the transmission. When Joseph began to speak again, the words were garbled for a moment before resolving themselves into clear, precise English.

"The HIVe has been chosen to facilitate the process whereby humanity will eventually be initiated into the cosmic family. You have received a seed supply of blood containing HIV-4. The rest is up to you. You must ensure that this fluid receives the widest possible dissemination."

"By introducing it into the bodies of our fellows," Fraim said.

"Yes."

"Human beings fear this virus, Joseph. I don't think anyone is going to willingly inject himself with it."

"Then they must be made to unwillingly. Remember, your entire species' future is dependent on the outcome."

Sandy Fraim paused. She looked out at the semicircle of people hanging on every word. None had spoken, but they were obviously filled with their sense of purpose. *We are one*, Fraim thought, *we are truly one.*

"We understand," Fraim said. "And should we then begin with ourselves?"

Again there were twitches and convulsions on Glorio's face. His eyes were rolling wildly behind their lids. His jaw quivered, clenched tight, then released.

"No!" The word shot out of his mouth, startling his listeners. Then, more calmly, Joseph went on. "There will be death, much death at the beginning, but you of the HIVe *must survive*. You cannot risk severing your line of communication with us.

"For now, do not attempt to mutate yourselves. Your day will come. You will be admitted into the cosmic family, and you will be heroes when you are.

"Your purpose is to assist the initial spread of HIV-4, and to generate publicity that will draw attention to its significance. In time, the tide of opinion will swing in your favor. When that occurs, you will no longer need to take the virus to the people. The people will come to you. They will beg you to transform their blood.

"And then your mission will have been completed."

Glorio's body had begun to shake violently.

"We must break off communications now, Joseph," Sandy Fraim said. "Our channel is highly stressed. Thank you, and we will speak with you again soon."

There was no response. Glorio's facial muscles had tightened until they were taut over the bones of his skull. With lips drawn back over the gums, he was a grinning mask of death.

Then his eyelids opened to reveal the whites of eyes dancing in their sockets. The color of his face became a deeper and deeper red. Veins in his forehead stood out prominently, especially one on the left side.

The people came up out of their seats and crowded close to the dais, their expressions ranging from concern to horror. This was the most violent trance they had ever seen. Sandy Fraim held up her hand, motioned to them to keep a safe distance away.

The light that enfolded the channeling chair increased in intensity, until it seemed as though it might sear Glorio's flesh. Every feature, every hair, every wrinkle in his clothing stood out starkly in the glare. People shielded their eyes from the light.

Glorio shook as if about to explode. The vein in his forehead was standing out like a purple snake. The tension in the room was palpable. The group was on the edge of collective hysteria.

Then the vein popped. Blood streamed down Glorio's face. The people gasped as one. Again they tried to get to him, but again Fraim kept them away.

"No!" she screamed. "Don't get near! Don't touch him!"

The blood flowed down Glorio's chest and was absorbed by his shirt. A dark stain spread across his front.

He stopped shaking, let out a long plaintive moan, and slid off the chair onto the gold carpet. Simultaneously, Fraim killed the spotlight. The room was illuminated only by the soft glow that seemed to come from the walls themselves.

Fraim knelt next to Dante Glorio. With her own shirt she sponged the blood from his forehead. Faces above the two of them peered down.

"Is he all right? Is he all right?"

"He's fine," Fraim said. "Please stand back. Please give him air to breathe."

The crowd shuffled backward.

"Thank you."

Fraim cradled his head.

"Glorio," she said. "Glorio, can you hear me?"

There was a mumbled affirmative. Glorio's eyes opened. He looked around, obviously having difficulty in focusing. There were smiles on his people's faces.

"Have we learned our purpose?" he asked.

"Yes," Fraim said. "We know."

"Good. That was a . . . a difficult experience."

Holding the shirt to his head, Fraim got him to his feet and helped him from the room. The group waited, buzzing about what had happened right there in front of them all and what it meant to their lives. The indirect lighting came up slowly.

One floor below, in the control room—a room that was always locked except to the master of the house and his mistress—Dante Glorio was cleaning up as he listened to Sandy's account of the channeling session.

The control room was a state-of-the-art special-effects center. With the equipment he had, Glorio had total mastery over the communications room. He could reproduce many of the illusions of the movie or TV screen.

Sandy removed the thin wire taped to his back, along with the small plastic pouch that had been filled with the chicken blood that now soaked his shirt. He peeled off the artificial skin—with its prominent purple vein—that had been seamlessly applied to his forehead. She returned the small remote-control unit that had been in the pocket of her jeans.

Glorio sat in a chair, wiping sweat and chicken blood from his body. With his other hand he fondled the remote. The unit had several dials on its face, for fine tuning the communications room's environment, and a number of switches, for such things as triggering the electrical impulse that had ruptured the artificial vein.

He looked up at Sandy Fraim. "It was real, you know," he said.

"Yes," she said, "I could tell."

"It's never been so intense." He tossed the control unit into the air and caught it. "All this other stuff, it's for the people. They expect it. They love it. But I'm not cheating them. I'm *not*. I had no idea what the Polarians said through me until you told me. Sandy, it's begun. Cosmic change, and we're the point of contact."

"We mustn't fail," Fraim said.

"We won't. The HIVE believes." The slightest smile creased his lips. "*I* believe. You realize that, don't you?"

"Of course."

"You really don't mind helping me with . . . ?" He gestured around him at a room filled with the trappings of the actor's trade, as well as the electronic gadgetry.

"I will do what is necessary, Bobby," she said. "The means are not important. What is important is our part in the greater plan." She leaned down and kissed him lightly on the mouth. "Come on," she said. "If we wait too long, the energy will be lost."

Fifteen minutes after they had left the communications room, Fraim and Glorio returned. He had changed into clean clothes, and there was no sign of a wound on his forehead, no indication that only moments before he had been in the clutches of a life-threatening seizure. The group was elated. Each member beamed love at him and hugged him close.

Glorio made his way back to the dais and spoke to the HIVe. Fraim left the room again.

"Sister Sandy has told me of the message that was passed through me tonight," he said in a clear and steady voice. "We have our mission and we have been given the tool with which we may fulfill it. Let us begin with a celebration."

At first, the music was just at the threshold of awareness. Slowly the volume rose. It was music by the Skulls, an avant-garde rock group.

"We are the first," Glorio said, "the forefront of planetary awareness, but we will not be the only ones. As we have known for some time, the Skulls are our brothers. They in turn know of us, and they speak directly to us in their music."

The song was called "Virus." It had been a minor national hit in the spring, without ever receiving so much as a minute of air play. It did the band no harm that there had been a concerted effort by health officials, politicos, and nervous parents to ban the record on which the song appeared.

Death Aims, lead singer of the Skulls, sang:

Fathers wait and mothers pray
This is not their passing day
America has dug her grave
Survivors carry
  Ahhhhhhhhhhhhh   THE VIRUS!

"They will soon come to visit us," Glorio said. "They will bring the music to us. We must recognize our common goal and welcome our brothers with open arms!"

The lighting pulsated and bodies began to move in time to the music. The bass line ricocheted off the curved walls of the spherical room. The incessant power chords of the lead guitar rammed the song home. It was musically simple, but there was no denying that it tapped the primal urge.

The room's door opened and Sandy Fraim came in with a rolling metal cart piled high with food and drink. The group cheered.

It wasn't long before the humidity level began to rise again. The champagne flowed and the steady pulsation of the music seemed to draw people together, to encourage touching and fondling. As more clothes were loosened, and then discarded, more of the celebrants exchanged the parquet floor for the soft gold carpeting of the dais.

And at the front of that dais stood the mahogany table with the silver canister perched atop it.

Within, there was the blood.

Floating in the blood, being bounced haphazardly by the random movement of adjacent molecules, was the virus. Each virus waited, would continue waiting for as long as it took, waited inertly for a chance encounter with the *helper T-lymphocyte* cell, waited for the opportunity to take that cell apart in the cause of its own proliferation.

The encounter would take place. The inert virus would come to life in the only way it knew. It would multiply. Its offspring would multiply. There would be nothing on earth strong enough to halt or even slow the process. The outcome was inevitable.

It had already happened with this particular blood. And as soon as the opportunity arose, it would happen again with someone else's.

7

Friday, August 10

Wesley Thomas fidgeted in his chair. He hadn't been able to contain his excitement since the afternoon mail had arrived. He wanted to share the news with his partner. He wanted to make the call that was going to change the face of Brisbane.

It was three o'clock when Dewayne Rhoades finally returned to the Thomas Building, a three-story Brisbane landmark that had been the tallest structure in town when Wesley's granddaddy had snipped its ribbon seven decades earlier. Through all those years it had served as home base for Thomas Realty and the First Commercial Bank of Brisbane.

When Rhoades appeared, Thomas grabbed his elbow and steered him into the conference room. He slapped the papers into Rhoades's palm.

"We got it, Dusty," he said.

Rhoades looked down at the papers. A slow smile spread across his face.

"Environmental approval?" he said.

Thomas beamed and nodded. "In the afternoon mail," he said. "The commission gave a green light to the whole project."

Rhoades let out a whoop, put a meaty arm around his partner, and clapped him roughly on the shoulder. Thomas winced, but never stopped smiling.

"Wes," Rhoades said, "I believe I'd kiss you if you weren't a single man."

Thomas blushed.

Together they looked fondly at the model laid out on the table in front of them. It was an intricate piece of work, the factory a perfect facsimile, the land contoured as it was to be, everything to scale. The Gustavia Brewing Company, Brisbane branch. Their greatest achievement.

The two men had been born on the same day of the same year. They were both forty-five years old. They had been friends since first grade.

Thomas was of medium height and thin. His gray hair was very sparse on top, only a little thicker elsewhere. He was nearsighted and wore a pair of old-fashioned glasses.

"Shall we call them now?" he asked his partner a little hesitantly.

"Hell, yes," Rhoades said. "Let's get a hump on, Wes. The sooner we break ground, the sooner Brisbane's gonna love us for the jobs we're bringing in."

"You do it," Thomas said.

"You bet."

Rhoades went to the phone. He was six feet tall and heavyset. His salt-and-pepper hair was still as thick as ever, a matter of considerable pride, and he sported a bushy mustache and sideburns as well. He looked like a nineteenth-century politician. His eyes were dark brown behind his contact lenses.

"Get me Gustavia," Rhoades said into the receiver, and they waited while the call was put through.

"You've done a good job, Dusty," Thomas said.

"Couldn't have done it without you, partner. If your family hadn't owned that little parcel down to the river, it wouldn't of mattered how many damn options I took on the rest. That was the linchpin, no mistaking it. You done good yourself, holding on to it all these years."

"You really think they'll go for it, Dusty?"

Rhoades laughed. "Well," he said, "if they don't, I might's well oil the pistol. I got so much tied up in the thing, my life'd be right down the chute."

"Don't say that."

"Ah, hell, Wes, there's no sense to worrying about it. Look at it this way: there's no damn reason in the world why they *shouldn't* want to locate here." He ticked his points off on his fingers. "We got reliable year-round water. The stuff's about as pure as it gets. Least it is above Claymore-Perkins, which is all they care about.

And we don't have a bunch of whiny unions around here, so their labor costs are manageable. *And* we got people want to work. *And* we're situated good for the Eastern market. And that's all the fingers I got. Damn straight they'll come to Brisbane."

"Well, I hope so."

The intercom buzzed and Dusty Rhoades picked up the phone.

"Yeah."

His secretary said, "I have the Gustavia Brewing Company on the line."

"Put 'em on. Neir, that you?"

A female voice said, "This is Vice-President Neir's executive assistant. Please hold."

Rhoades silently and sarcastically mouthed the woman's words.

Then a deep male voice said, "Wilson Neir, Mr. Rhoades. What can we do for you?"

"Build us a brewery," Rhoades said.

"Ah, you have approval."

"You bet. The state environmental commission just put the gold star on it today. All the local greasing's long since took care of. Why don't you come down here and we can start talking profits."

"That sounds fine. Excuse me for a moment."

There was a pause. Rhoades flashed Thomas a thumb-and-forefinger circle.

"Yes," Neir said, "I believe I could make the trip next Wednesday. How's that suit you?"

"Hey, I'm ready to sign the papers tonight. But if it's Wednesday, it's Wednesday. We'll be here. And we'll be sure Brisbane's got its happiest face on for y'all."

"Fine. See you then."

Rhoades hung up and said, "Wes, I believe I'll go on home and see if Rhonda Jo remembers what she married me for. You reckon you can celebrate without getting in any serious trouble?"

"I'll try," Thomas said.

8

The Inferno was the place to be on Friday night.

Outside, it looked like a warehouse. Gray cinder-block walls, metal roof, no windows. But inside was Brisbane's hottest singles bar. Fire, in fact, was the primary decorative motif. The walls were painted with brilliant red and orange and yellow flames. The ceiling glowed blood red. For contrast, chairs and tables and the bar were done in black. The music was loud, programmed by a DJ perched in a glass booth high above the dance floor.

From the night it opened, the Inferno had been a success. There was a large crowd of young, relatively affluent people in Brisbane who had apparently been waiting for just such a gathering place. On weekends it was jammed.

Wes Thomas rarely went to the Inferno. For one thing, he was significantly older than most of its patrons. For another, he basically lacked the courage to strike up an acquaintance with an unknown woman.

He'd tried, and had failed.

Nevertheless, after putting himself in position to swing the biggest business deal in Brisbane's recent history, he felt he had to celebrate in some way that would mark the day for the rest of his life. So he did. First, he went to the finest restaurant in town and ordered pheasant, the most expensive entrée on the menu.

Later in the evening, he went to the Inferno. He paid his ten bucks to get in the door and went immediately to the black-and-chrome bar, settled himself onto one of the black leather high stools, and ordered a toasted almond, a lethal drink concocted of amaretto, Kahlua, and cream. He swiveled on his stool to watch all the little birds perform their intricate mating rituals.

As he watched, he couldn't help thinking how small and insignificant they all looked, especially compared with someone who was currently negotiating with Gustavia Brewing, one of the most powerful companies in the country. Their fields of vision were so narrow, their needs so simple, their intents so transparent.

Wes Thomas was feeling good about himself. There was a warmth radiating from his stomach and a pleasant tingling in his legs. Whatever happened tonight, he wasn't going to have to lift a finger. The game would come to him, as befitted a man of his stature. He was in control.

Two hours and five toasted almonds later, nothing much had happened. Then the man on the bar stool adjacent to Wes Thomas went staggering out of the night-club, bitching and moaning about his lack of good fortune.

He was replaced by a young woman. The woman's hair was platinum blond and dead straight, with the front cut in bangs. Her skin was stark white, her eyes set off in blue. Her lips were bright red and glossy, and her long pointed fingernails were painted to match.

Thomas looked at his new barmate. She looked right back at him, making what seemed like a very frank appraisal. It was difficult to tell how he had done, but she did raise her right eyebrow slightly.

Without taking her eyes off him, the blond woman laid a small shiny black handbag on the bar, snapped open the clasp, and took out a silver cigarette case. From it she withdrew a hundred-millimeter filtered cigarette. She propped her elbow on the bar and waited.

Thomas hesitated. The first thought that came to his mind was that he didn't smoke. But that was irrelevant. The Inferno had placed boxes of tiny wooden matches all along the bar.

The woman still waited. Thomas decided there wasn't much to be lost. He snatched up one of the boxes of matches and lit the woman's cigarette. She left a minia-ture crimson mouth on the filter.

"Thanks," she shouted over the music.

Thomas shrugged as if it was the least he could do.

"My name's Linda," the woman said to Thomas.

"Wes," Thomas said.

"You don't look the type, Wes."

"Uh, what type?"

"Come on, the Inferno type. You see anyone else in here with a suit like that? What do you do, Wes?"

"I'm a . . . sort of developer."

The woman smoked. "Oh, yeah? Are you pretty well-developed?"

Out on the dance floor, the people were gyrating to the unmistakable sound of Michael Jackson. The kid, he was assuring them, was definitely *not* his son.

"I do all right," Thomas said. "I've had a good year. Our position is strong."

"Um-hmmm. Mine too."

"Really? Are you also in real estate?"

"Jesus," the woman muttered. She sipped at her Scotch and water.

"I don't understand," Thomas said. "What do you do exactly, Linda?"

The woman looked at him closely again, shrugged, tossed off the rest of the Scotch, and came up all smiles. She stubbed out her cigarette. She leaned close to him and pitched her voice as low as was possible, considering the competition from the Jackson boy.

"Look, Wes," she said, "I spend all day with the vertical markets, you know? I get out on a Friday night, what I want to do is explore the horizontal ones." She raised the right eyebrow again.

"Oh, that might be interesting. It's sort of the way we're trying to restructure Brisbane. We're entirely too much of a one-horse town here."

"Right." The woman sighed. "Do you think we could continue this discussion elsewhere?"

"Uh, sure. Let me just finish my drink."

Thomas slurped down the remains of his toasted almond. Part of it dribbled onto his shirt. He blotted at it with a cocktail napkin.

"You want to go someplace a little quieter?" he asked.

"Just get a bottle to go," Linda said. "Make it champagne."

"Champagne, sure. Hey, bartender!"

Outside, the air was warmer and muggier than it had been in the nightclub. The disco beat boomed out through the block walls. A few people were in the overflowing parking lot, smoking and talking and drinking next to their cars. Some were hoping for action without having to pay the cover.

"Do you have a car?" Thomas asked the woman.

"Let's take yours," she said.

"Okay." Tentatively he took her arm and started her moving. "What's your pleasure?"

"I'm at the Green Brae. We can go there."

The Green Brae Inn was situated on a knoll overlooking the Squier River. It was expensive and discreet, favored by politicians from the capital who wanted to spend a weekend romping with a mistress or cutting a quiet deal with a patron. There were no rooms, only suites, and every suite had its own private outside entrance.

Linda had Suite 6-B, on the ground floor.

Thomas took a look around the suite's lavishly appointed sitting room and said, "The market must be doing well."

The woman smiled. "Of course," she said. "Sit down."

She got a pair of wineglasses and an ice bucket. She popped the cork on the champagne bottle, wrapped it in a towel, and placed it in the bucket.

"Dinner is served in three minutes," she said.

She moved behind Thomas and rested her hands lightly on his shoulders. He shivered slightly at her touch. She ran her hands down, over his chest, and back up.

"You're not afraid of me, are you, Wes?" she said.

"Well, actually, this isn't the sort of thing—"

"You usually do. I know. I could tell that about you right away. You're a real Southern gentleman, aren't you?"

"Is there anything wrong with that?"

Linda kneaded the back of his neck. He was surprised at how much stress had accumulated there during this momentous day.

"No," she said, "of course not. I *like* that."

"The South is full of men who might just as well have come from New York," he said. "Used to be you could tell the difference. Not anymore."

"Relax that muscle right there. That's better."

"Where do you come from, Linda? What are you doing here?"

She traced a fingernail along the line of his jaw as she moved away from him.

"Champagne's ready," she said.

She poured two glasses of the bubbly, handed one to Thomas, and sat facing him. She raised hers in toast.

"What shall we drink to?" she asked.

"Well," he said, "I don't know as *we've* got that much of a future, so how about to the future of Brisbane. May it grow and prosper."

Linda grinned. "Okay, to Brisbane." She drank. "And you're right about us. The future is definitely now."

"Thomas drank half the champagne and belched. "Ahhh, that is fine," he said jauntily. "And where might the bathroom be in this joint?"

"Through the bedroom," she said, raising her eyebrow. "Don't be long."

Thomas got up and made his way to and through the bedroom door. He was weaving slightly.

As soon as the bathroom door closed behind him, Linda opened her handbag and took out a large capsule filled with white powder. She broke open the capsule and dumped its contents into Thomas' glass. Then she refilled both her glass and his with champagne. In a few minutes Thomas returned.

"Another toast," she said.

"Why not?" He picked up his glass. "I see you've been busy in the meantime."

"Have you ever been completely satisfied by a woman?" she asked.

Thomas giggled.

"Don't spill your drink," she asked.

He made a conscious effort to balance the glass in his hand. In the end, only a few drops fell to the carpet.

"Sorry," he said. "But it's not the sort of question a man could possibly know the answer to, is it?"

Linda smiled coyly. "To satisfaction, then," she said. "And the ability to answer questions."

They drained their glasses. Linda got up and took Thomas by the arm. She steered him to the bedroom, sat him down on the edge of the bed.

Then she began to dance. Her body was young and limber. She moved slowly, sensuously, suggesting the pleasures in store for anyone who was able to hold her. She closed her eyes and hummed a tune as she danced.

Thomas watched. He felt himself drawn into the rhythm generated by her body, as if he was a part of her, though they were separated by four feet of empty space. The room, too, seemed to dance with her. The air was hot and damp with promise. Thomas loosened his tie.

His eyes were riveted to the woman's body. It swayed and shimmered in the subdued light of the bedroom. Then it appeared to go in and out of focus. The woman was a wraith, as insubstantial as the fog that rose each morning from the surface of the river a hundred yards away.

Thomas reached his arms out to her, but his arms didn't move. He tried again, and nothing happened. He couldn't move his arms or his legs or any part of himself. Linda was smiling, beckoning to him. He wanted to touch her more than anything he'd ever wanted, but he was immobile.

She ran her hands slowly, suggestively up her body, cupping her youthful breasts.

He tried to speak, and couldn't.

Deep inside, he knew something was terribly wrong. This was the most wonderful day of his life, and he could feel it descending into nightmare. He summoned all his will and forced it into a single piercing scream.

His mouth opened slightly, but no sound came out.

Someone was lowering the lights, too. Where was Linda? She had disintegrated, and the night was coming on. Thomas tried to force himself to remain awake. There was too much that could happen in the dark.

Darkness descending.

And then the night. The long, silent night. . . .

When Wes Thomas awakened, he didn't know where he was, and he was afraid. He lay on the bed, staring at the ceiling, forcing down the panic.

Slowly it came back. The Gustavia deal. The pheasant. The Inferno. Linda. The Green Brae Inn.

Calm down.

He raised himself onto his elbows. The pain hammered

at the inside of his skull. His mouth felt as though it was stuffed with cat hair.

Too much to drink. That's all. Nothing to worry about. Passed out from too much amaretto and champagne. Hold it together here and everything's going to be fine.

"Linda," he said aloud. His voice came out as a croak. The croak of a very sick frog, he thought.

There was no answer.

"Linda," he called again, this time louder. The effort set the hammers pounding in his head. Tiny pinpoints of light danced in front of his eyes.

No answer.

God, he thought with disgust. *The oldest trick in the book. My money'll be gone, of course. And all my credit cards. How could I be so stupid? I just hope she left the rest of my wallet.*

Cautiously he got himself out of bed. First into a sitting position, then legs over the side, then up onto his feet.

When he was upright, he was hit with a wave of nausea. He sprinted for the bathroom on rubbery legs, wrapped the toilet with arms that belonged to someone else, and emptied his stomach. He threw up until there were only the dry heaves left.

The spasms subsided.

Drained, he pulled himself up to the vanity and turned on the cold tap. He bent over. Cupping his shaking hands, he splashed water up into his face. He did it over and over, until he at last began to feel life flow once again in his blood.

He turned off the tap and raised his head.

There was a small hypodermic needle taped to the bathroom mirror. Beneath it, written in block letters with a bright red lipstick were the words:

HIV-4 is the virus of change
Welcome to the HIVe

Wesley Thomas screamed. It was all of the scream he had not been able to force from his lungs hours earlier. And more.

9

Monday, August 13

Dr. Craven's waiting room was half-full, but Wes Thomas was shown immediately into the doctor's office. Thomas didn't look directly at any of the other patients.

The office was a pleasant book-lined room done in dark wood paneling. It was a place designed to put the patient at ease, no matter what had brought him there. Thomas settled himself onto the edge of a heavy oak swivel chair.

There was a ten-minute wait. Thomas didn't read any of the certificates on the wall or the captions to any of the photographs. He stared at the air conditioner wheezing away beneath the window. It was a meaningless piece of machinery.

The thick door opened and Craven came in. The corpulent white-haired doctor sat in his own chair, on the other side of the desk. He folded his hands in front of him and looked down at them. His face was grave.

"Tell me," Thomas said.

Craven shook his head slowly. He looked across at the man who'd been his patient for thirty years.

"I don't know, Wes," he said. "I honestly don't. This is such a new thing. A couple of months ago, the *only* things we could've tested you for were HIV one, two, and three. And you don't have any of those." He shrugged. "But the HIV-4 . . . well, frankly, no one knows how accurate this test is going to prove to be."

Thomas' voice quavered. "I've got it, don't I?"

"Your blood tested positive, yes," the doctor said. "But as I told you on Saturday, that doesn't necessarily mean the worst."

"Oh, God . . ."

Thomas began to cry. Craven knew that there was nothing he could do, so he waited until the sobbing subsided.

Then he said, "I'm sorry, Wes. But you have to consider that even if the test result is correct, you may not come down with it. Some people don't. There *is* hope."

"How . . . how long before I know?"

Craven looked him in the eye. "There's no latency period, Wes," he said. "Not with HIV-4. You'll know soon."

Thomas wiped his eyes with the palm of his hand. "If I'm going to get it, how . . . long do I have?" he asked.

"It'd be better if you didn't think that way."

"How long?"

The doctor rocked back in his swivel chair. "To be honest with you," he said, "we still can't say for sure. But most likely, it's a matter of weeks."

"Weeks . . ."

"The only advice I can give you, Wes, is to think positively. No one knows for certain what's going to happen tomorrow—especially with this type of virus—so why not assume the best? That in itself may have a therapeutic effect."

"Yeah, sure."

"But of course, if you *do* start to feel weaker, see me immediately."

Thomas got up to go, but Craven raised his hand.

"Just a sec," the doctor said. "Ah, have you decided to tell me how you were exposed to the virus yet?"

Thomas shook his head.

"I really wish you would. It's entirely confidential, of course. But any information we can get will ultimately help us to control the spread of the . . . of the disease. I'd appreciate your cooperation."

Thomas sighed. There was a long pause. Then he told it all, beginning with the Gustavia Brewing Company and ending in the bathroom at the Green Brae Inn.

"My God," Craven said when he'd finished. "You can't be serious."

"I am."

"That's the most evil thing I've ever heard of. Have you been to the police?"

"No."

"You have to. I know how you're feeling, Wes—"

"You don't know shit."

"All right. I'm sorry. I can't know how you're feeling, but I know you've had a terrible experience. I know how *I'd* feel. But if there's someone out there doing this, she's got to be stopped. You have to go to the police."

Thomas chuckled without humor. "Or what passes for the police in this town," he said.

"They may not be the best," Dr. Craven said, "but Brisbane is still small enough that a woman like that won't be able to hide out for long."

Thomas got up. "I'll think about it," he said. "Anything else I should know?"

Craven just shook his head, so Thomas walked out of the office. When he'd gone, Craven picked up a ball-point pen and tapped it against the blotter on his desk. He stared at the pen without seeing what he was doing.

"Jesus," he said to himself. "Jesus the living Christ."

Wes Thomas crunched his way across the gravel of Dr. Craven's parking lot. He walked past his car and into the street. A pickup truck swerved to avoid him. The driver swore out the window, but Thomas didn't hear him.

He walked all the way from the doctor's office to downtown, to his own office in the old business district. There was only a single thing on his mind.

I'm going to die, he thought. *I am going to die, going to die.*

Oddly, as he walked, the despair he'd been living with for three days lifted. It was replaced with a cold, hard anger.

Linda.

The betrayer.

She must pay.

He found himself standing outside the Thomas Building, staring at its stern granite facade as if for the first time. His granddaddy was dead, and he would be too. Maybe soon.

And then there was nothing. The anger was gone, the

depression was gone, and in their place there was only a hollow emptiness, a slight ringing in the ears, the impression of a damp heat that penetrated the bones.

One of the employees of the First Commercial Bank came through the revolving door and said, " 'Morning, Mr. Thomas."

Wesley didn't respond. He looked at the man blankly. Who was this man? This man had nothing to do with his life. This building had nothing to do with his life. The man was puzzled, but he backed away discreetly and went about his business.

The corner on which Thomas stood was a busy one. People in shirtsleeves and lightweight summer suits streamed past him. He stood there, studying faces, looking for . . . What was her name? The woman. Dark hair. No, blond. Linda. If he could find Linda, everything would be all right. She'd make everything all right. She was really a very nice girl.

He tried to remember where he was going. Someplace that would help him find Linda.

What was it that Dr. Craven had said? It was . . . The police. Yes, that was it. The police would know where Linda was. They knew where everyone was.

Thomas turned and very deliberately set one foot in front of the other. Then again. In this way, he walked the three blocks to the police department.

The duty officer asked him what he wanted.

What *did* he want? "I want to find someone," he said.

"Is this a missing person?" the officer asked.

"Yes, missing," Thomas said. "Her name is Linda. She's a very nice girl."

10

Dr. Craven intercepted Dusty Rhoades in the corridor.

"I think we'd better talk before you go in and see him," the doctor said. "Come on."

The two men walked together to the sun room at the end of the third floor.

"I came over as soon as the hospital notified me that the police were bringing him here," Craven said.

"Just tell me what it is, Doc," Rhoades said. "What's Wes got to do with the police?"

"You'll have to let me do this my own way, Dusty. It's not a simple matter. The police just said he came in to report something, then couldn't remember what it was he wanted to report. He started acting strange, so they brought him here for observation. I took the liberty of having him admitted immediately and placed under my care."

"I just saw him on Friday. He was fine, damm it."

"He's not fine now. He's having spells of complete amnesia, alternating with periods of what appears to be total lucidity. At times, he becomes close to catatonic. It's unpredictable. I've called in the best psychiatrist in town, but frankly . . . I don't know what we'll be able to do."

Rhoades was very agitated. "But *why*? What's going on? I don't understand this."

"I'm almost certain he's reacting to what happened to him over the weekend."

"For Christ's sake . . ." An old man in a wheelchair turned to look at Rhoades. The man had fluids running into him through one plastic tube, fluids running out through another. Rhoades lowered his voice, took the

48

doctor by the arm, and led him to the far corner of the room near a window that overlooked a graveyard.

"For Christ's sake," Rhoades said, "what happened to him over the weekend?"

Craven thought about it, then said, "Dusty, I'm in a terrible ethical bind here. Wes Thomas has been my patient for more years than I care to remember. He's entitled to confidentiality."

"Wouldn't you tell his *family*?" Rhoades demanded. "I'm the closest thing to family Wes's got. You know that."

"I do know that. That's why I called you. I suppose I've known what I was going to do all along. But that doesn't make it any easier, believe me."

"Please, Doc, what's going on?"

The doctor sighed. He placed a hand on Rhoades's shoulder and looked the other man in the eye.

"Wes Thomas has been exposed to the HIV-4 virus," Craven said.

Rhoades shrank away from his touch.

"No," he said. "That's impossible. Wes couldn't . . ."

"Yes, he could. He has."

Rhoades revulsion quickly turned to fury. "I don't believe this!" he said. "There's no way. How do you get it? Prostitutes? Blood transfusions? Wes didn't go to *prostitutes*, for Christ's sake! He hasn't gotten any *blood*!"

The old man in the wheelchair looked over at them again. He smiled. What teeth he had left were little more than yellowed, rotting stumps.

"Let's sit down," Craven said, indicating a vinyl-covered couch under the window.

"I don't want to sit down."

"Come on, Dusty. This is as difficult for me as it is for you. I've got to try and put it together as much as you do."

The two men sat.

"All right," Rhoades said. "Now tell me what the hell is going on."

"You're going to find this hard to believe," Craven said.

"Try me."

Craven sighed again. "Someone deliberately injected your friend with the virus," he said.

"What?"

"That's what Wes told me this morning. In the absence of evidence to the contrary, I think we have to believe him. That's why it's a police matter."

Rhoades looked as though he'd just seen someone long dead.

"I . . . I don't understand," he said. "Why . . . why in God's name would . . . ?"

Craven shrugged. "I don't know."

There was a long pause. Rhoades had been completely unprepared, and had nothing to say.

Craven waited, then said, "It was a woman. The circumstances suggest a psychotic. She must be found before . . ."

"I see," Rhoades said woodenly. "Of course. Can you tell me how it happened?"

Briefly Craven told him of Thomas' deadly encounter with Linda. Rhoades sat stunned.

"That's unbelievable," he said. "No one could do that. It's . . ."

"It's evil," Craven said. "Look, you're his best friend, Dusty. Which is one of the reasons I've told you. But the other reason is this: Wes needs to tell his story to the police, in his own words. It's our best hope of catching this woman. I think if you were there, he might be able to do it before he lapses into one of his silences. It's worth a try." He paused, then added, "This is not going to be easy for you. But it's important. You have to help."

Rhoades gritted his teeth. There was a cold anger in his dark eyes.

"No," he said, "it isn't going to be hard. Someone is going to find this Linda. The police just better hope they get to her first." He got up. "Now let's go see Wes."

Craven got up wearily. "Okay," the doctor said. "But remember, he might not know who you are. Be prepared for that."

"I'm prepared for anything," Rhoades said.

The two men started back down the corridor.

*   *   *

An hour later they were shaking hands with the newly minted detective lieutenant, Will Grant. Dr. Craven had commandeered an examining room where they could talk privately.

"Now," Grant said, "I've been told you want to report an attempted homicide and the department has assigned me to the case. If you don't mind my saying so, this is kind of a funny place to meet, but I understand it was at your insistence, Doctor, so I'm all ears."

"Thank you, Lieutenant," Craven said. "I think you'll see that this is a very . . . unusual thing that's happened, and . . . well, frankly, I just didn't know how to proceed."

"The story itself will be fine," Grant said. He got out a small pad. "I'll want to make a few notes." He nodded. "Whenever you're ready."

"Go ahead, Doc," Rhoades said. "It's the right thing to do."

Craven took a deep breath and ran through the story again, as much as he knew of it. When he'd finished, even Grant was stunned. There had been nothing remotely like this in his experience.

"Jesus. This is unbelievable," he said.

"I want that woman caught," Rhoades said.

"I think you can see what kind of potential disaster we have here," Craven said. "I'm hoping, Lieutenant, that we can keep it a little quiet, for my patient's sake, but Mr. Rhoades is correct. The woman must be stopped."

Grant thought. He had no idea what exactly he ought to do next. One thing was certain, though. Something as bizarre as this couldn't be kept quiet for long.

"Where is Mr. Thomas now?" Grant asked. He knew Wes Thomas by reputation, of course, knew the family, but not well enough to call the man by his first name.

"Room 310," Craven said.

"And what is his condition?"

"I'd say right now he's pretty lucid."

"You believe his story?"

"Now, look here, Lieutenant—"

"Please, Mr. Rhoades," Grant said. "I know he's your friend, and I know you're concerned about his condition, but this is a very serious matter here. If he's telling the truth—"

"Of *course* he's telling the truth. I *know* Wes Thomas."

"Here, Lieutenant," Craven said.

He handed Grant a small brown paper bag. Grant opened it. Inside was a sealed plastic bag. Inside that was a syringe.

"The one that was taped to the mirror?" Grant asked.

Craven nodded. "My prints are on it, of course. And Wes's. But no one else's that I know of. I've had it locked up since he gave it to me Saturday morning."

"Was there anything left in it?"

"A trace of blood. That's it."

"Enough to test?"

"No, I'm afraid not."

Grant stared at the syringe. A simple tube and a hollow needle. A medical implement, in itself neither good nor bad. So important in its many uses. And so easily abused.

He closed the paper bag. "Thank you, Doctor," he said. "You have good presence of mind. I doubt that we'll get much from this, but you never know."

"Now, what do you think's the best way to handle it? I'd like to get someone over here to take down Mr. Thomas' statement. And the police artist to make a sketch of the assailant."

"All of those people at once might spook him," Craven said. "Personally, I'd rather you talked to him alone first. Then you can try bringing in the others."

"I'll have to tape it, then."

"That would be fine."

The three men went up to Room 310. They found Wes Thomas sitting up in bed, alert and rational.

"I'd like to go home now," Thomas said.

"Soon, Wes," Craven said. "I've brought someone who'd like to talk to you. This is Lieutenant Grant."

"Is he going to find Linda?"

"I think I can do that, Mr. Thomas," Grant said.

"Pleased to meet you, Lieutenant," Thomas said. "What can I do for you?"

Grant turned on the tape recorder. "I'd like you to tell me what's happened to you since Friday last, as completely as you can, and I'm going to tape it if you don't mind."

"Oh, I don't mind. Let me see . . ."

And Thomas told the whole story, up to that morning's interview with Craven in his office.

"So when I went to see Doc there, I was a little nervous, you understand." He laughed. "But he told me there was nothing to worry about. There's nothing wrong with me. So I tell you, Doc, I don't know why you've got me in the hospital here. Dusty and I've got a lot of work to do. Brisbane's counting on us."

"You bet," Rhoades said. "We need you back at the office, old buddy."

"Just a couple more tests, Wes," Craven said. "You'll be out of here before you know it."

"Right," Grant said. "But while you're here, Mr. Thomas, I wonder if you could describe Linda for a friend of mine. You know, we can't have people going around scaring other people like this. Even if they're not doing any real damage. My friend would like to make a sketch of Linda, so we can find her and ask her to stop."

"Sure," Thomas said. "If it'll help find Linda."

"Good. I'll send my friend round straightaway. Now, there's just one other thing. On Saturday morning, after you woke up, did you look around the suite to see if Linda had left anything behind?"

"Sort of. I looked to see if there was anything of mine, but I didn't find anything of hers either. You'd think she might have left her phone number or something. But it looked like no one had been in the room at all."

"And what did you do with the syringe?"

"Oh. I gave it to Dr. Craven. Dr. Craven has it."

"And what about the message on the mirror?"

"I washed it off. Um-hmm, I scrubbed it off good."

"Why?"

"I made it go away."

"Okay. And the champagne? The glasses? The ice bucket?"

Thomas looked puzzled. "Well, they wouldn't be there," he said. "Not if no one was staying in the room. would they?"

"No, I guess not," Grant said. He held out his hand. "Well, thank you for your time, Mr. Thomas. I'm sure with what you've told me we won't have any trouble locating Linda."

"You come back, Lieutenant. You're a nice lieutenant. You're from around here, aren't you?"

"Uh-huh. My daddy knew your daddy."

"I thought so."

Out in the corridor, Grant asked Craven, "You're sure he's been infected?"

"Goddammit, Lieutenant!" Rhoades said. "The doctor told you—"

Craven silenced him with a raised hand. "The test says so," he said with a shrug. "But we can't be absolutely positive. The test is new and there's a margin of error. If you want my professional judgment, I'd say yes. A story like that, and then the test result to confirm it. It's too improbable not to be true."

"And his story, the way he told it to me, that's the same way he told it to you?"

"Yes, the same."

"Okay, you two sit on this for the time being, while I look into it. See if you can get him to cooperate with the police artist. I'll have the tape transcribed and someone can bring it over. If he's got his wits to him, have him sign it. In the meantime, I'm gonna do some poking around. But I tell you, I need help on this one. From the chief or the D.A. or somebody. I don't even know what the hell kind of crime we *have* here."

"You find the woman, damn you," Rhoades said. "That's all you have to do."

Grant looked at him coolly. "I know you're concerned," he said, "but don't tell me my job, Mr. Rhoades."

Rhoades's jaw clenched but he said nothing.

"Good," Grant said. "And please don't talk about this with anyone else until you hear back from me. Gentlemen."

Grant shambled off down the corridor.

"God, where did they find that one?" Rhoades asked.

"He's been on the force for twenty years," Craven said. "It was in the Saturday paper. He just made lieutenant. Didn't you see the article?"

"If I did, it didn't register. I don't think I'd trust him to find his own nuts with a flashlight."

"Supposed to be a good cop."

"Well, he better be. He don't find whoever done this to my partner, there's gonna be some hell to pay in this town."

"There may be some hell to pay anyway," Craven said.

Grant took the elevator down to the lobby and put in a call to the department. He got his partner on the line.

"Jeff," he said, "I've got a weird one. Get a techie and meet me at the Green Brae Inn. . . . Yeah, right away. . . . No, I'll tell you when I see you. You're not gonna *believe* this."

11

"You shitting me?" Jeffers asked.

Grant shook his head. "I wish I was."

They were sitting in the parking lot of the Green Brae Inn, waiting for the crime technician to arrive.

"This could shake the town up bad," Jeffers said.

"I know."

The man from the lab arrived. The two detectives told him only that they'd had a tip a suspect had spent the previous Friday night at the inn and that they were trying to get confirmation. The techie didn't much care who it was. He waited for them while they went inside to clear things with the management.

Grant flashed his badge and a few minutes later he and Jeffers were in the office of Robert Cismont, general manager of the Green Brae Inn.

Cismont greeted the cops with smiles and hearty, pumping handshakes.

"Welcome, gentlemen, welcome," he said. "Please sit down. How may we be of assistance to Brisbane's finest? I assure you the fish was fresh when we bought it . . ." He chuckled. "But seriously, we're not involved in a crime, are we?"

"It's hard to say, Mr. Cismont," Grant said. "We're interested in someone who stayed here last week. Friday, to be exact. Suite 6-B. Could we see your register, and perhaps talk to whoever might have checked this person in?"

"But of course, I have it right here in my pocket. *Voilà*. No, just kidding, of course." He punched a button on his intercom and repeated the detective's request to someone. A few moments later a young woman in a

spotless tan uniform came in with a single white card.
She handed it to Cismont and stood next to his desk.

Cismont produced a pair of reading glasses and looked
the card over.

"Yes," he said, "a Miss Lynette Forbes. Home address
in Atlanta. No car. Representing self. Stayed only the
one night. Paid in cash. Lucille here checked her in, I
believe."

Lucille nodded nervously. Cismont handed the card to
Lieutenant Grant. He looked it over, noted down the
information it contained, and passed it to Jeffers, who
glanced at it and gave it back.

"Thank you," Grant said. "Now, Lucille." The young
woman stiffened. "Relax, please. You're not a suspect
here. I'd just like to know if you remember Lynette
Forbes."

"Yes, sir," Lucille said.

"Can you describe her for us?"

"Yes, sir. She was about my height, about my age, but
blond, shiny blond, the fake kind I think, and she wore a
lot of makeup. She didn't say much, just took the room,
paid in advance, and left. The key was in the room
Saturday at checkout time."

"Nothing else unusual about her, in the way she looked
or acted?"

"No, sir."

"Okay. Now, what I'd like you to do is describe the
woman for a police artist and see if he can make a sketch
that you recognize. Do you think you could do that?"

"Yes, sir."

"I'll have him come around later today, if that's all
right with you, Mr. Cismont."

"Of course," Cismont said. "May she go back to work
now?"

Grant nodded and Lucille left the office.

"I assume the suite has been cleaned since Friday
night," Grant said.

"Yes, of course," Cismont said. "You think we're
running a Holiday Inn here?" No one laughed. "Just a
joke."

"And did the person responsible for cleaning report
anything unusual about the condition of the room?"

"What kind of unusual?"

"Anything at all. Anything left behind by the guest. Anything that wasn't there the day before."

"I don't think so. I get a report every day on the condition of the rooms. For theft and that sort of thing. So I'd know. I don't recall anything out of the ordinary on Saturday."

"All right," Grant said. "I'll want to talk to the cleaning person, though. And I need to know if the room has been rented since then."

Cismont made another quick call. The cleaning person wasn't on duty, but Cismont passed along his name, address, and phone number. Yes, the suite had been rented on Sunday for a week.

"Can you move them somewhere else?" Grant asked.

"Now, just a minute, Lieutenant," Cismont said. "I'm trying to be cooperative here, but I can't go bouncing my guests all around for no good reason. Would you mind telling me what this is all about?"

"I'm afraid we would," Jeffers said. "We can do this nice and quiet or we can crawl your precious hotel with cops, either way you want it. You dig?"

"Martin," Grant said, then to Cismont, "I'm sorry. My partner sometimes gets a little carried away. I'd appreciate it, though, if you could clear the room. We're going to have to let our technician go over it, so whoever clears it should touch as little as possible. Okay?"

"I suppose," Cismont grumbled, then made a call to get it done.

While he was on the line, Grant added, "And the relevant information about the current occupants, please."

Cismont got Grant the requested information. He said that the present guests in 6-B were out at the moment and would be informed when they returned that they'd been moved to 5-B. When he'd finished, he said wearily, "And what else?"

"That should do it," Grant said. "I don't know how long we'll have to be in the room, but we'll let you know when we're done. Thank you, Mr. Cismont. You've been most helpful."

Grant and Jeffers went back out to the parking lot,

where Grant instructed the technician to dust 6-B for prints. Then he took Jeffers aside.

"I still don't know how much we should tell the techie," he said. "I'm gonna have to go back to the Block and get some guidance on this. You baby-sit him. Have him dust the place and see if he can bring up any lipstick or anything on the mirror. By that time we oughtta know how fine a comb to drag through the room."

"You want anyone else printed?" Jeffers asked.

"Let's wait on that too. What I will do is have the artist come over here first and get a sketch from the desk clerk, before he goes to the hospital to work with Thomas. And I'll get the lab to start work on the syringe. Later on we can do the Inferno if it looks like we should."

"Okay."

"I'll be back to you as soon as I can. Hold down the fort, partner."

"No problem." Jeffers paused, then said, "And you was right, by the way."

"About what?"

"I *wouldn't* of believed you."

12

Kip Kyser, chief of the Brisbane Police Department for just over ten years, was red in the face. Or, to put it more accurately, he was redder in the face than usual.

"Grant, that's the craziest goddamn thing I ever heard of!" he said.

"I know," Lieutenant Grant said, "but that's the story. And I believe him."

The two men were in Kyser's spacious office in the Brisbane City Office Building, a forbidding granite structure in the old business district that overlooked the pools and fountains and shady trees of City Plaza. Among those who worked inside, the building had been nicknamed the Block. For one thing, it consumed an entire city block. More to the point, perhaps, it was widely thought to bear a strong resemblance to a maximum-security cellblock.

The Block's three massive wings housed the entire apparatus of local government: the Brisbane Police Department, district court, offices of the mayor and city council, and so on, down to the animal-control officer and Parks and Rec softball director. Law enforcement had one wing to itself, including, in the basement, a few temporary holding cells. The city jail itself, or "security complex" as it was now known, was the only thing off-site.

The chief had gotten out of his chair halfway through Grant's retelling of the tale and begun pacing behind his desk. He hadn't stopped yet.

"We better get the D.A. in on this," Kyser said. He picked up his phone and punched a three-number combination. "Yeah," he said, "this is Kip. Is Sleeth around?

Uh-huh. Tell him to stop down to my office. Sure right away, if it ain't all that much *trouble*."

Kyser hung up the phone and muttered, "Damn pansy."

Grant shrugged. "He's a decent D.A., though."

"You say."

The district attorney's office was only two doors down from the chief's, but the D.A. made the two cops wait for seven minutes before Kyser's secretary showed him through the door.

Durwin Sleeth was dressed, as always, in a Brooks Brothers suit, the result of one of his semiannual trips to the Big Apple. Today it was a gray three-piece suit, with the inevitable gold watch chain stretched across his flat belly.

The man was in his mid-thirties, medium height, slender and with the physical fitness that came from a thrice-weekly workout, combined with daily jogging. He might have been a star athlete in one of the major sports if he'd only been a little taller, a little heavier. He'd settled for soccer.

He greeted Kyser by name, nodded to Grant while smoothing down the expensively cut grayless wavy brown hair that helped him look like he might yet be on the near side of thirty.

"Have a seat, will you, Sleeth?" Kyser said. "You're gonna be ass-glued for a spell. We got one bitch of a problem here."

The district attorney sat. "Legal problem?" he said.

"You might say." Kyser finally stopped pacing and sat down too. "Tell him the story, Will."

As straightforwardly as he could, Grant once again repeated what had happened to Wes Thomas.

"Whew," Sleeth said when the lieutenant had finished. "That is one *hell* of a thing."

"Yeah, we know," Kyser said. "The question is, what the Christ are we gonna do about it?"

"Unprecedented," Sleeth said. "Absolutely unprecedented. There's not much doubt about the intent, what with the message on the mirror. I don't know, though. As long as Thomas is alive, all we have is attempted murder."

"Goddammit!" Kyser said. "At *least*! That's what the

sonofabitch is. Unless Thomas comes right down with it and dies. Then we got murder One."

"That we do. But if he doesn't . . . then I don't know what we have, except a very sick mind that we've somehow got to put away forever. This is really one of a kind here."

"Jesus," Grant said, "we're supposed to hope Wes Thomas *dies*?"

"Of course not," Sleeth said. "But I'm just preparing you. If she gets a good lawyer and a sympathetic judge, she may be able to walk out with simple assault and battery."

"Shit," Kyser said. "That ain't good enough, and you know it. The way people feel, they're scared pissless of weird viruses these days. Something like this is really gonna get their blood up. They ain't gonna be satisfied with no A-and-B."

"I agree with you," Sleeth said. "And I wouldn't be either. Let me think about it and see what I come up with. You know, if we don't have a murder, this case could end up a precedent. I want to think about it very carefully.

"In the meantime, of course, there *has* been a crime committed. I suggest we find the perpetrator and *then* worry about how we handle it in court. And I'd also suggest we give it as much priority as we would if Thomas were already dead."

"Then it'll get in the papers," Kyser said.

Sleeth shrugged. "With something like this, that's inevitable."

"And there's something else," Grant pointed out. "It may not be a murder, but it's that kind of case. When it gets public, I'd go ten to one we're gonna have every loon for twenty miles around confessing to it."

"Shit," Kyser said. "You're right."

"Better plan now on something to hold back from the press," Sleeth said. "To weed out the phonies."

"Well," Grant said, "count on the lipstick message getting out. But we might could keep a lid on the syringe."

Kyser looked at the D.A. "It's fine by me," Sleeth said.

"Okay," Kyser said. "When we're ready to go, we

release everything else but we sit on the syringe. Will, you make sure everyone who gets sucked into this case knows that."

Sleeth got up. "Anything else you need me for, Kip?" he asked.

"Naw, just get back to me as soon as you've got some of your brilliant legal ideas. No matter what, we're gonna have to work close on it."

"I'll do that," Sleeth said, and left.

"You agree with him about top priority?" Grant asked. "Treat it just like an actual murder?"

"Yeah, I guess so. An RW murder." Kyser meant *Rich White*, the category that commanded the department's fullest attention.

"That means we've got to fingerprint everyone who's been in that hotel room since Friday night. We'll need more crime-scene techies out there to comb the place. Once we get all that moving, we won't be able to keep the lid on the story. If it hasn't leaked already."

"I know, I know. Jesus." Kyser massaged his temples. "All right, just don't take any action until I check with the mayor. I'll go over there right now."

"Okay, Kip. I think I better start the lab to work on the syringe, though."

"Yeah, do that, but keep the damn thing quiet. I'll get with you directly after I talk to Brad."

"Yes, sir."

Grant left the office. Wearily Kyser got up, climbed the stairs to the top floor of the Block, and walked over to the central wing, where Mayor Davis had offices commanding the best view of the Plaza below.

The chief was shown in without waiting.

"What the hell, Kip?" Davis said immediately as he came around from behind his desk to shake hands, limping slightly. "You look like you got hit by the night train." His manner was friendly, and his tone suggested a genuine concern for the well-being of his longtime friend, and colleague for the past four years.

"Close to, Brad," Kyser said. "You best sit down for this."

The two men sat with the oiled walnut desk between them.

Bradford Davis was fifty years old and exactly six feet tall. He was the most famous athlete in Brisbane's history, a star fullback at the state university and a blue-chip pro prospect. He'd even been tagged "Jimmy White" by a hometown columnist who thought he was the equal of the other guy up in Syracuse. Then a vicious sandwich tackle had torn up his left knee beyond repair, and the dream had gone down the hole. He'd limped back home to Brisbane, unable to finish school without the benefits of an athlete's curriculum.

Since his college days, the years had been less than kind to Brad Davis. His playing weight of 205 had been augmented by fifty pounds of flab. His hair, though still thick, was completely white. He had heavy, sagging jowls. His dark, deep-set blue eyes looked out at the world from a face whose complexion was permanently ruddy, courtesy of Mr. Beam.

"Shoot," Davis said.

Kyser shot. He didn't hold back anything. During the telling, Davis' expression reflected curiosity, then horror, and finally serious concern.

When Kyser was done, Davis said, "This could have a very negative effect on the town, Kip."

"Not to mention your chances in November," Kyser said.

"Well, let's don't let that enter into it. Let's just get this woman in the nuthouse where she belongs. And keep me up-to-date on your progress, if you would."

" 'Course, Brad. Think we should break the story tomorrow?"

"If the lab folks have gathered all they can, I don't see why not. Better if it didn't look like we were withholding it for some reason."

Kyser nodded and returned to the police wing. He told Grant what had been decided. Grant said that he'd work straight through until all the preliminary spadework had been done. He'd report to the chief the next day on how he planned to pursue his investigation.

Kip said that sounded fine and returned to his office to do some serious thinking.

Down the hall, Durwin Sleeth was completing his journal entry.

He'd been keeping the diary since he'd first been hired as an assistant prosecutor. On page one he'd written: *Journal of a Justice.*

Sleeth had a master plan for his life. It involved a steady progression from job to job, with each one being more prestigious than the last. From prosecutor to district attorney. From there to a district-court judgeship. From there to the state supreme court. And then, naturally, the capstone: an appointment to the United States Supreme court.

The details of such a career begged to be preserved for eventual sharing with the rest of the country. And Durwin Sleeth was nobody's fool. He realized that by the time he reached his ultimate goal his memory of how he got there might have a few gaps in it. So, from the very beginning, he had been meticulously recording the high points. Someday, he knew, *Journal of a Justice* would be one of America's most precious legal histories.

Monday, August 13, would almost certainly prove to be a very important day indeed.

Sleeth looked over the first details of the HIV-4 case, as he'd recorded them. Then, satisfied, he placed a call to the local TV station.

13

Tuesday, August 14

Kip Kyser was livid.

He slapped the morning paper down on his desk. The headline read: "HIVe Witch: Virus Killer on the Loose." Inside, the paper editorially demanded that the police provide more details than had been revealed in the previous night's sketchy TV newscast.

"This is not the way I wanted it done!" he shouted. "God knows what the public thinks now! I warn you, you better not have leaked the sonofabitch!"

"No, sir, I sure didn't," Lieutenant Grant said.

The chief ran his palm over his bald head.

"All right, Grant," he said in a little calmer voice. "Hell, I believe you. How many people knew about it anyway?"

Grant ran down the list. What with doctors and lab people and detectives and D.A.'s men and the mayor, it was lengthy.

"Probably somebody's secretary," Kyser muttered. "Or that oily little bastard Sleeth. Thinks he's slick as bat shit. I don't trust him for a minute. I wish to hell we didn't have to work with him."

"I'm afraid it's important to keep him informed," Grant said.

"Yeah, I suppose. You turn up anything last night?"

"Not really. We got sketches of the woman out of Thomas and the desk clerk at the Green Brae. Except for the platinum hair and the bangs, they're two different people. Which I'm not surprised, considering the witnesses. Plus who knows how many oars Thomas has got in the water at this point."

Grant consulted his notes. "Then," he continued, "Jeff and I tracked down the guy who cleaned Suite 6-B on Saturday. Nothing there. The mirror was clean when he arrived, the wastebaskets were empty, et cetera.

"Everyone who's been in the room since Friday morning has been printed. It's just a few hotel employees and the two new guests. The techie got a load of prints from the room, but frankly, I don't think much'll come of it. I think our perp was too smart to have made that kind of mistake, and then there's no telling how many different prints are in there from earlier. We can't possibly chase down everyone who's used the room since Jesus in the straw.

"Then, around nine we visited the Inferno. We talked with the bartender who was on duty Friday, showed him the sketches. He drew a big blank. There's about a thousand pickups going on around him every weekend, and he says he doesn't even look at faces anymore. He thought he remembered the hair, but that's it, and he wasn't even dead sure of that.

"And I'm afraid that's all there is, sir."

"Hmmph. That ain't much," Kyser said.

"Well, we *are* just out of the chute."

"Uh-huh. You got any kind of a plan on this one, Grant? You or either your partner?"

"Uh, no, not really. Other than the obvious stuff. Follow up whatever the lab gives us. Try to trace the syringe. After that it gets leg-tired. We can try to interview everyone we can find who works at the Green Brae or was staying there that night. But that's not likely to give us much we don't know. If she had a car, maybe throwing the net like that would get us a description, but her registration card said she didn't.

"We can also try to find out how she got to the Green Brae. She take a cab or what? After she got there, a lot of people must of noticed her. We find out who the regulars are, see if they tried to hit on her, or saw anyone who did, before she got to Thomas. Then again, how'd she leave the Green Brae? If she took a cab, where'd she go? That's a promising one. *If*.

"Another thing would be to make the bar circuit, those places she might of gone if the Inferno wasn't her first stop. That's one way we could try to establish if she was just cruising.

"Because there's another possibility. Maybe Thomas wasn't a random choice."

"He didn't know her," Kyser put in.

"He says. He could be lying, for some reason or other. Even if he isn't, she could still have picked him beforehand, for reasons we won't know till we get her.

"So we really oughta look into Thomas' life. See what we can find by way of enemies."

Kyser nodded. "Worth a shot."

"The other thing I'd recommend is to run the sketches in the paper. Now the story's broken, there's no need to hold back. Brisbane's still a small-enough town that *some-*body's bound to know her."

"If she's from here. If she's not in Oregon by now."

"If she ain't local," Grant said, "then God himself'll have to give us a hand."

Kyser sighed. "Yeah, okay," he said. "It makes sense to use the paper. TV too. Circulate the sketches. And talk nice to the bastards, will you? See if you can't get 'em to stop this 'HIVe Witch' shit. They get the people all spooked out, and who the hell knows what could happen in this town."

"I'll see what I can do, Kip, but you know them . . ."

Kyser rolled his eyes heavenward. "*Un*fortunately," he said. "Okay, you and Jeffers get back to work on it, but leave word where you are. There's no way in hell we're gonna be able to handle this without a press conference. Probably sometime this afternoon, and I want you to be there. I'll let you know as soon as I set it up with Brad and Mr. Slick."

"No problem," Grant said.

After he'd gone, Kyser called a meeting with the mayor and the D.A. They agreed with him and scheduled the press conference for three that afternoon.

Long before three, a crowd began to gather in the Plaza. The people were there specifically in response to the story, which had quickly spread to every corner of the city. It was a strange mix. There were street preachers talking about chickens coming home to roost. There were representatives of committees who wanted HIV-4 victims quarantined from the rest of society. There were civil-rights activists who sensed some hard rain was about to fall. And there were fearful citizens of no particular group affiliation who simply wanted more in the way of facts.

Some carried signs, some distributed medical pamphlets, some just stared up at the offices of their elected representatives. And high above, nervous officials looked down on them.

At five minutes past three, Kyser went to the large room that was used for press briefings, hearings, and other public events.

Media representatives had been allotted spots in the front rows. There were people from the town's five radio stations, the two TV stations, the daily newspaper, and the two weeklies. Reporters, photographers, video-camera operators. Other local-government officials had been given some seats. And a scattering of places had been reserved for some of the concerned citizens who'd earlier been out in the Plaza. Large numbers had been turned away with the reassurance that the proceedings would be well-covered by the various media.

Kyser detailed for his audience the facts presently known to the investigation, omitting only what was being held back to help weed out crank confessors. He introduced Lieutenant Grant as the investigator with overall responsibility for the case and provided figures on how much additional manpower had been assigned to it. He stated that the perpetrator would not be able to hide for long in Brisbane, and promised an early arrest.

After Kyser, Sleeth spoke briefly. He assured those gathered that, when arrested, the perpetrator was going to be prosecuted to the absolute fullest extent of the law. This might be an unprecedented case, but they could be certain that he'd use every ounce of his energy and every bit of his legal expertise to see to it that the woman was properly punished for what she'd done.

When Sleeth sat down, there was applause from the audience.

Then came the questions.

What exactly were the police doing to catch the perpetrator? What plans did they have for preventing her from striking again? Were there any leads? How was the infection of the victim accomplished? Did the perpetrator somehow have a bottleful of the virus? If so, what were the ways in which it could be spread? Should people beware of touching doorknobs or using public toilets? And so on.

The three men did their best, trying not to prejudice the investigation or wander into medical areas where their command of the facts was insubstantial. Above all, they reassured. There was no way the perpetrator could remain at large for long. There was nothing to indicate that she intended to do this again. There was an overriding need to resist the sort of panic an isolated episode such as this might induce. The media in particular were urged not to blow the whole thing out of proportion.

HIV-4 was a scary thing, sure. But an epidemic of it was *not* coming to Brisbane.

A woman in the third row stood up.

"Ah, I don't believe I recognize you, ma'am," chief Kyser said.

"Dabney Layne, *AmericaNews*," the woman said.

That was bad. *AmericaNews* was one of the largest-circulation weekly newsmagazines in the country, and here they were already. If the national press glommed onto the story, the investigation was going to turn into a three-ring circus quicker than a bunny hump.

"Yes, Miss Layne," Kyser said cautiously.

"I was wondering why you think something like this happened first in a place like Brisbane. My impression is that this town is about as all-American as they get."

"Yeah, we like to think so. And I have no idea why it happened here. I'd give anything if it hadn't."

"Do you think this incident is finally going to alert the rest of the country to the realities of HIV-4 and related viruses?" Layne asked.

"Beats me. I would hope we don't get a lot of national publicity."

"It would certainly put the town on the map."

"We are already on the *map*, Miss Layne. We don't need to become famous because of some lunatic." Kyser turned toward another raised hand. "Yes, sir?" he said.

Dabney Layne sat down and made some notes.

The editor of one of Brisbane's weekly newspapers asked what effect all this would have on the upcoming election campaign.

Sleeth said he didn't see why it should become an issue.

The press conference wound down. The TV journalists left first; there was precious little time in which to write copy and edit videotape before the six-o'clock anchors had their scripts loaded into the scanner. Then the radio people slipped out. They'd still hit the air with the story before anyone else.

Finally, Chief Kyser terminated the proceedings.

Dabney Layne went immediately to the front of the room. She walked up to Will Grant and looked him right in the eye.

"May I interview you, Lieutenant?" she asked.

14

Dabney Layne was in her mid-thirties. She stood halfway between five and six feet, and had a slender, slight-hipped build. Her dark-reddish hair hung straight down to her shoulders. It seemed lifeless no matter what she did with it. She had a narrow face, with a sharply pointed jaw and gray eyes set a little too close together for the effect to be pleasing. Because contact lenses irritated her eyes too much, she wore large circular gold-rimmed glasses that gave her a look of perpetual surprise.

Will Grant had never before spoken to a representative of the national media.

He and Layne were using one of the interrogation rooms, because Pound and Worth were in his office. Grant didn't feel comfortable asking them to leave. But then, neither did he want to conduct this interview in their presence.

Kyser had told him to play it very cool.

"Welcome to Brisbane, Miss Layne," Grant said. "What brings you down here?"

"Come on, Lieutenant," she said. "One of our stringers called in this story last night and I was on the first plane. You know perfectly well this is national news."

"Frankly, I don't know much of anything yet, ma'am."

Layne sighed. "Look," she said. "How about if we skip all the Southern-gentleman stuff, the 'ma'ams' and the 'Miss Laynes,' okay? I'll try not to be the obnoxious big-city reporter. Just call me Dabney. And I'll try to treat you like a fellow human being with a job to do. Call you whatever you wish."

"Will would be fine," Grant said carefully.

"Will, this is a big story—"

"I'm afraid it isn't *any* kind of a story yet, Miss . . . Dabney."

"And I'm afraid it is. I've been in this business for fifteen years, Lieutenant. I'm good at it. I'm good enough that the senior editor at *AmericaNews* lets me choose my own stories; he trusts my instincts that much. You're sitting on one of the major stories of the year. I'm not going to be the *only* one down here; what I wanted was to be the *first*.

"Will, you're right in the middle of this thing. Your life is about to be turned inside out. I don't believe you even begin to realize how much.

"First off, the TV people will come swarming around. You'll have cameras and microphones shoved in your face until you feel like taking a swing at the next person who asks: 'How's the investigation *going*, Lieutenant Grant?' " She put on a whiny nasal voice that had Grant smiling. "You'll have so-called journalists profiling your life in fifteen-second spots so full of lies you won't even recognize yourself. You won't be able to so much as take a leak in peace.

"Fortunately, the TV people's interest span is about as long as their stories. They'll bug you for a few days, but if nothing dramatic happens, they'll move on to wherever the next big thing's breaking.

"I don't suppose you expect to solve this case in two days."

Grant shrugged. "You never know," he said. There was a pause; then he added, "So who are you? You're just another part of the circus, ain't you?"

"Yes and no." Layne smiled. "I'm here for the show, I'll admit that. But I'm going to stay. There's a story behind the story here. And I won't be able to get it unless I stick with you right through. What I'm saying is, I want to do something in depth. About the town, about how it reacts to this extraordinary thing that's happening, about the people whose lives are affected. It's a story about the criminal, whoever she turns out to be, and the D.A. and the mayor and the chief of police. And about you."

"You want something from me?" Grant said innocently.

"I want to do a fair and accurate story, and believe

me, there's going to be plenty that won't care a tenth as much. It'd help a lot if I had your cooperation."

Grant sighed and folded his arms across the top of his belly.

"You want me to be your source," he said.

"Only to the extent that it doesn't interfere with your job," she said quickly.

"But you'd rather I shared more with you than the next person who asks."

Layne grinned. "Hey," she said, "that'd be nice. But I know I can't ask for that. I'd just like you to let me in on what's happening from your personal point of view. You're the one. I watched the three of you up there today. The others like to talk, but they aren't going to break this case. *You* are."

"With some luck."

"With luck and skill and perserverance and a dozen other things. I've covered crime stories, Will. I know the kind of sweat that goes into your successes."

"Well, we'd better be successful on this one. God help us if the woman stays on the streets for long."

"You will be." She winked at him. "A hunch. That's what makes it such a great story."

"Thanks for your confidence, uh, Dabney. I'm sure it's well-meant, and I don't doubt but what you know your job. But you may find here in Brisbane we do things a mite . . . different."

"I'm willing to learn," Layne said.

"And I ain't sure I rightly know what you're getting at. Just what is it you want me to do?"

"Talk to me, that's all. Help me discover the human side of the story. In return, I intend to write some stories that you and the rest of the town will be pleased with—you have my word."

Grant smiled. "Around here," he said, "we figure a newspaperman's word is about as useful as a saddle on a bullfrog."

Layne let her eyes wander over his body. She raised one eyebrow and let the hint of a smile touch her mouth.

"And a newspaper*woman's*?" she said.

"Well-took," Grant said. "I got no cause to mistrust you."

"Thank you."

"So like I said, what can I do you out of?"

Layne took a small tape recorder from her pocketbook and held it up.

"These spook you?" she asked. "If they do, I can take notes."

"That's fine," Grant said. "Might's well get it right."

Layne punched the Record button.

"August fourteenth," she said. "Afternoon. Interview by Dabney Layne of Lieutenant William Grant, detective in charge of the investigation.

"Lieutenant, tell me how you first became aware of the strange events of last weekend."

15

The little girl walked through the front door of her house at five-thirty in the evening. She was six years old and had long golden-blond hair. There was a confused expression on her face, a dazed look in her eyes.

Her mother saw her look and rushed to hug the little girl.

"Lorene," she said. "What are you doing here alone? Where have you been? Are you all right?"

The little girl nodded dumbly.

"What happened to you, girl? You wasn't supposed to walk home from the playground 'less your brother was with you."

"Well, Scottie went behind the school with the boys to have them a smoke and *I* knew what they was gonna do. So I come home to tell you, but I didn't have to walk 'cause the man give me a ride home."

Mrs. Greene held her daughter at arm's length, by the shoulders.

"What man?" she said. "*What* man?"

"Oh, it was okay, Mama. I remembered what you told me. About not letting no man give me rides, but he didn't try to do any of them things you told me about. You know . . . He didn't tell me to take my pants off or nothing."

"Who is this man? Did you know him?"

"No, Mama."

"Where is he now?"

The girl looked at her mother dazedly. "Well, I don't know, Mama," she said. "He brung me home, but not all the way home. He kinda let me out over by Sueann's house. And then he . . . drove away. I axed him to bring me home, but he didn't."

Mrs. Greene still held her daughter tightly.

"Lorene, I want you to tell me," she said slowly. "Did the man do anything to you? What did the man do?"

"Nothing like you told me, Mama. He didn't want to see any of my private things or nothing. He just oncet made me lie down on my face and I thought maybe that he was gonna do something, but he didn't. I just felt a little sting, like a bee stung me on my bum, and then he let me sit up again, and he didn't try to do nothing else."

"Like he pinched you on the bottom?"

"Uh-huh. Like that, but more like a sting. And he give me a paper to take home."

"What paper?"

"This here." Lorene took a folded slip of paper from her pants pocket and handed it to her mother.

Mrs. Green unfolded the paper and read:

The young are the future
Welcome to the HIVe

"What's it say, Mama? Huh?"

The woman bit down hard on her knuckle and somehow managed to keep the scream trapped deep inside her.

16

Dabney Layne was at the desk in her suite at the Brisbane Arms Hotel, working on her Compaq lap-top computer. She'd completed her first story, which included background on the town and the sequence of events up to the story that had broken over the radio earlier in the evening. In a few minutes she'd hook up the modem and download the whole thing to a PC back in her office. Her assistant would make a printout, her editor would edit, and the copy on the edited diskette would be fed directly into the typesetting machine. By morning the story would be formatted and ready to roll.

She was tight on weekly deadline, and she knew the other newsmagazines would be too. TV would get it first, of course, but in terms of print the net result would probably be an exclusive for *AmericaNews*.

What with the latest development—the attack on the little girl—preempting the field was particularly sweet, because it was now obvious that the story was very, very big. She smiled to herself. She still had the best nose in the business.

She hurried to wrap it up. The news story was done, but she wanted to include a letter to her editor, so he would have a little better understanding of its background and where she was expecting to go with it:

The cast of characters is fascinating, Sam. I decided to zero in on Grant, the detective lieutenant who's going to be in the middle of it. Though I don't think he's an intellectual giant, he seems like a bulldog type who'll never let go of something once he gets it in his mouth. He's a little trapped in the Southern-gentleman

78

thing, but otherwise very straightforward. He may be exactly what's needed to go after these people. And he's kind of cute, in his own way. I think I can probably get him to respond to me as a woman, if that will help us keep the inside track.

Kyser, the chief of police, is a caricature of the alkie cop. My take is that he's risen to his maximum level of incompetence. I'd say he's probably more interested in not screwing up than in getting any particular job done. He's the one I think will be most susceptible to pressure.

The mayor and I haven't met yet, but he's a good old local boy and he's up for re-election. Plenty of glad hand on the exterior, but inside I expect he's street smart and tough as they come. He's up for reelection in November, so I imagine everything he does will be to keep his best image in front of the voting public.

Then there's Sleeth, the D.A. He's a slimy one. I interviewed him after I talked to Grant, and I had to wash my hands afterward. He's as devious as the lieutenant is straight. He's aware of the publicity that's coming, and you can see the wheels turning inside his head. But he's going to be right there when the case comes down, so he's useful. I found myself carefully considering what I said, to let him believe he was controlling the conversation and that I was succumbing a little to his imagined charm. He'll probably give me anything I ask for if he believes I'm going to write a flattering article. Also, someone is leaking this story bit by bit, and I wouldn't be surprised if he's the one. So if we need a quick fix in the future, this might be the place to go.

Now, about the strange turns this thing is taking. After the attack on six-year-old Lorene Greene this afternoon, this town's going to be in a tizzy. Instead of one crazy woman out there, we've got a woman and a man and God knows what else. And child victims. There's a chance that the man was just doing a copycat, but it's a damn slim chance. And if the virus does show up in the little girl, then it's no chance at all. The only conclusion would be that the two people are working together.

This is a story and a half. Who are these people? More to the point, why in the hell are they doing this? And what's the town's reaction going to be? We'll know a little more about that last question in about twelve hours, but the first two . . . The whole country's going to want to know, and when we find out, the truth's bound to be more shocking than anything we could have imagined.

Sam, I think I should stay on this for as long as it takes. I'm in on the ground floor, I'm developing solid sources, and the damn thing is going to blow like a ten-meg nuke. My instincts say we can frontline it for at least three or four issues.

And then there's always the possibility that I could be in on the bust. Tell me what you think of this: if they're going to do another bar-pickup scene, this time it might be a man on a woman, instead of the other way around, like with Wes Thomas. So I start cruising the upscale bars at night, hang my scrawny butt out as bait. I sniff hard at anyone who comes on to me. Maybe I get lucky. Eh, amigo?

Layne scrolled the computer back to the beginning of her letter to Sam and read it through. When she came to the last paragraph, she paused and stared at it for a long moment. Then she deleted it.

"No," she said to herself, "you wouldn't approve of that, old friend, would you? Best I do that on my own."

17

Wednesday, August 15

The people of Brisbane will not tolerate this kind of terrorist activity among them. The perpetrators of these hideous crimes must know that when they strike at our children they will meet with a united citizenry that is tougher and more determined than they could ever have imagined.

This paper calls upon our law-enforcement authorities to redouble their efforts. We call upon the chief of our city police department to turn every available person loose on the trail of these malignant monsters. We demand a more visible police presence in our streets. If our own manpower is not sufficient, we call upon the country and state to pitch in. And we call upon the law-abiding men and women of Brisbane to keep their own vigil. It is your duty to report *any* suspicious activity immediately.

No matter who you are, the next victim could be *you*. It could be your mother, brother, or even, as we have seen, your own precious child. The HIVe killers must be stopped, and stopped now, *before* they have the opportunity to strike again.

We must stop them and, one way or another, we will.

Kyser slammed the newspaper down on his desktop.

"God damn them!" he shouted. "What kind of shit *is* this?"

"Now, calm down, Kip," Mayor Davis said.

"Calm *down*? I thought we agreed to keep the Greene story out of the paper for a while."

"Lay it off on Grant. He's the natural one to take the flak."

"Right," Kyser said sarcastically. "Right. Look at the goddamn editorial, Brad! You see where they say someplace, 'We call upon Lieutenant Grant'? Fuck no, you don't. 'We call upon the *chief*.' Like I'm sitting here picking my nose, for Christ's sake! And did you take a look at the Plaza this morning?"

Davis nodded. The Plaza had begun to fill as soon as the newspaper was on the streets. It was an angry mob, demanding more protection from its police department. There were signs calling for the immediate arrest of all known sex offenders, others begging the sinful to repent.

"I'll speak to them," Davis said.

"You better. I'm not gonna have this department run by a damn lynch mob."

Davis made his way to the door. "You don't get to the bottom of this mess soon," he said as he left, "you might not have this department at all."

Kyser banged his desk so hard his eyes watered.

"You sonofabitch," he muttered to the closed door. "Don't you threaten me, you sonofabitch."

Then he called Will Grant in.

"We're in a shitload of trouble here, Grant," he said.

"Yes, sir," Grant said. "But the people don't know how difficult our job is. They never do."

"I don't give a crap about difficult. I want some results, like maybe yesterday."

"Jeffers and I are working on it as hard as we can. We'll get results, but it won't be yesterday."

"I want everyone on double shifts. From now until we get the bastards. Borrow as many men as you need. The people want to see our men out there working."

"All right," Grant said. "I'm afraid we just don't have that many leads, though. Here's where we are as of this morning: I'll see if we can coax a usable sketch out of the little girl. If it's any good, we can run it in the paper tomorrow. And the lab should have their report on the note pretty soon. Other than that, it's still leg time."

"So move your legs. What about some kind of link between Thomas and the Greene kid? Or her family."

"I thought of that. It's a long shot, but worth a try. We've also got two descriptions now. If the man and woman ever appear together, they'll stick out more, and there's that much better a chance of nailing them. Also, if they're married or something, it's likely someone'll know who they are."

"I really don't like this," Kyser said. "There being two of them."

"Yeah, I've thought about it. I don't know what in hell it means. Let's just hope there ain't more yet." Grant got up. "That it?"

Kyser fixed his gaze on his lieutenant. "One other thing, Grant," he said. "You best watch what you say to who from now on."

Grant folded his arms. "And just what's that supposed to mean?" he said slowly

"It means that horse-faced woman shows up from the city, and next thing, we got stories leaking out like we're running a boat-sinking contest. I can't use that."

Grant's expression was cold. "Are you accusing me of being a leak, Chief?"

"I ain't accusing nothing. Just see you keep your mouth glued up till I tell you to open it."

"I didn't leak the goddamn story, Kip. You oughta know me well enough for that."

"Good. You find me who did. I want his ass in a suitcase. You with me?"

"I'll do what I can. Is that all, *sir*?"

Kyser just stared at him, then finally motioned with his head for Grant to leave the room.

When the lieutenant had gone, Kyser paced back and forth behind his desk, swearing and muttering to himself, trying to think of some good way for all this to resolve itself.

While Mayor Davis tried to reassure the crowd in the Plaza, Will Grant was plotting his activities for the day. He was alone. Pound and Worth were out pounding and worthing. Jeffers was running down a couple of anonymous tips they'd received that morning concerning the HIVe killers.

Dabney Layne walked in.

"Hi, Lieutenant," she said.

Grant looked up, then back down at what he was

doing. "I don't believe I'm talking to the press just now,"
he grumbled. "How'd you get in here, anyway?"

Layne walked over to his desk. "You arranged a pass
for me, remember? What's the matter?"

Grant looked her in the eye. "You know goddamn
well what the matter is," he said. "We didn't want that
poor little girl's story splashed all over hell today. How
do you think her family feels?"

"Hold on, Will. Just a minute here. You think *I* did
it?"

"I don't know who did it, and I don't care. It's done.
Now, if you don't mind, I've got a couple of maniacs to
catch."

"You know, I really don't appreciate this," Layne
said. "I heard that damn story on the radio, just like
everybody else. It hadn't even happened when I left here
yesterday. When I told you I'd work *with* you, I meant
it."

"Yeah? Well, that was yesterday. As far as I'm concerned, you're all dogs in the same pack today. Why don't
you go find another crippled deer to run down."

Layne went red in the face. "I suppose *you're* holy
enough to throw stones, Mr. Grant. Well, let me tell you
something. You wait until you see what's going to happen the next few days. You're going to *wish* there were a
few more like me!"

She turned and stalked out of the office.

Grant stayed at his desk. He worked doggedly through
the pile of paper in front of him, sorting leads and tips
and ideas, searching for the best approach to take at this
point. As he worked, he hummed a tune he was trying
out with some lyrics he'd written. He tried the tune this
way and that, but he just couldn't get it to fit.

18

At one o'clock that afternoon Wilson Neir strode into the offices of Thomas Realty.

Neir was a large barrel-chested middle-aged man with tiny blue eyes sunk far into his head and heavily greased black hair. He had a loud, deep bass voice. He wore, as he always did during the summer months, a blue seersucker suit.

He was immediately shown in to see Dusty Rhoades.

"Mr. Neir," Rhoades said, taking his visitor's hand warmly. "A pleasure."

"My legal assistant, Miss Mapes," Neir said, introducing a diminutive young woman with a large moon face and oversize glasses with pink plastic frames.

"Miss Mapes," Rhoades said, taking her hand and letting it go almost immediately.

After getting some iced tea for his visitors, Rhoades showed them into the conference room. He did a mock trumpet fanfare as he switched on the lights.

"May I present the new Gustavia brewery," he said.

The model laid out on the table seemed almost to shimmer in the soft fluorescent light, Rhoades thought. Damn, but it looked good. Neir and his assistant walked slowly around it, leaning in to examine more closely its intricacies, poking at its movable parts.

Neir nodded. "Pretty," he said.

"And you've seen the site," Rhoades said. "It's got everything you need. In addition to which, you put the whole package together and you got a damn nice environment, a place people are gonna be *happy* to work in. You're gonna get loyalty, count on it."

"I don't doubt," Neir said. "It's a pretty-enough

picture. Now let's see some of the paperwork. You have everything in order?"

"It's all there except the ink. Come on back in my office and we can go over it."

For the next hour the three of them examined permits and other background material, explored legal ramifications, discussed the support the town was ready to put behind the project.

At the end of it, Wilson Neir said, "You've done a decent job there, son, and a week ago it might have gone through without a hitch. But now you've got this problem here in Brisbane and, well, it won't do any good not to talk about it."

"You mean the virus thing," Rhoades said.

"Uh-huh. Folks are spooky about that. Including folks like the directors at Gustavia. I'm not going to pull any punches. This is the sort of thing that could tip them right toward the other fellers."

"We're making a much better offer than Greenville."

"As may be. But you're getting some bad publicity. There's no denying that."

Rhoades reminded himself that this was not something to lose his temper over. In fact, it was not something to even appear agitated about.

"Mr. Neir," he said easily, "we have crime here in Brisbane, yes. A lot less than they have in any big city, or even Greenville for that matter. And we have a few people running around with their lug nuts loose. Just like every other place in the world. But on the average, you're not gonna find a better lot than the people of Brisbane. And when we get a problem like this one, we take care of it. Our police are solid professionals. Our district attorney is plenty tough on crime. You can tell the brass at Gustavia, and this is gospel, that we'll have this thing straightened out in no time. And believe me, it's not the sort of thing that's likely to be happening again, not in our lifetime. We got an aberration, and that's all it is."

"Perhaps," Neir said. "But then, there is the other thing. It's your partner who isn't here today." He raised an eyebrow and gave Rhoades an interrogative stare.

"My partner, Wesley Thomas, is a victim, yes," Rhoades

said evenly. "It is a tragedy, and poor Wes is still in the hospital. But I visited with him just this morning, and let me assure you, Mr. Neir, there'll be no problems if Wes . . . if he can't carry on. Not with the land, or anything else. In fact, we're drawing up the papers now, giving me full powers should something happen to Wes. Believe me when I say that Gustavia has absolutely nothing to worry about on that score."

"I do believe you." Neir shrugged. "But those who make the ultimate decisions are a thousand miles away. I cannot predict what they will believe."

Neir got up, and his assistant followed his example. He shook hands with his host.

"I sincerely wish we could spend a few days in Brisbane, Mr. Rhoades," he said. "But alas, I'm afraid we have to leave in the morning. It's been very enlightening. I expect that you'll be hearing from us in a week or so. The decision must be made soon."

"Thank you for coming," Rhoades said. "I look forward to working with you."

Neir shrugged. "As may be," he said.

When the brewery representatives had gone, Dusty Rhoades told his secretary to hold all incoming calls. He sat at his desk for half an hour, thinking his way through the potentialities of his situation.

Then he walked downstairs to the street-level floor of the Thomas Building, which was entirely occupied by the First Commercial Bank of Brisbane.

He was immediately shown in to see Phil Atherton.

"We have to talk," Rhoades said to the bank vice-president.

"Sure, sit down," Atherton said. "You look a bit spooked, Dusty."

Atherton was fifty-four years old. He grew his gray hair long on the sides, then combed it up over the top. His beard was short and professionally trimmed. He was tall and statesmanlike, and moved with a natural grace. No one had ever seen him in anything but a suit.

He made sure he and Rhoades wouldn't be bothered, then gave the other man his full attention.

"Let's don't turn the truth," Rhoades said. "We got trouble."

"The brewery."

"Yuh. And we can't sit on it, Phil. They're gonna make their decision in a week or so, and we got to get the sonofabitch, you know that. I got so damn much money in the pipe now I won't be able to stand it if we suck air." He paused. "Hell, you ain't gonna do so good yourself if we lose it."

Atherton nodded and Rhoades said, "It's the damn HIVe thing, Phil. It's got 'em worrying their butts."

"I don't understand."

"Me neither. But it seems like they read some of the publicity and now they don't know is Brisbane a safe place or something."

"We can't take a dive just over that."

"I know," Rhoades said with determination. "We've got to do something about it."

"Talk with Brad and Kip? What . . . ?"

"No, I mean really *do* something about it. If the cops can't catch these loonies, then maybe they need some help from the private sector."

"What are you saying, Dusty?"

"I'm saying that we can't afford to lose the Gustavia project because of some damn crazy people. I'll do *anything* to save it."

"I see," Atherton said.

"Are you with me?"

"I don't know. I agree that we need to—"

"Good. Then come to my house tonight. We'll get a group together, the right kind of people. Just to supplement police activity. It can't hurt, Phil. The more of us are trying to resolve this thing, the quicker it might happen."

"Yes, I suppose so."

"Make it around eight. Invite somebody else, if you know what I mean."

"I know what you mean. I'll see about it."

"Thanks," Rhoades said, and left.

Atherton tended listlessly to business for the rest of the afternoon. Then, at five sharp, he got into his car and drove south for six miles, to the Paradise Motel.

Dorothy Pritchett was already there, in Room 12, as they'd agreed, when he arrived.

Pritchett was a severe, prim-looking unmarried woman of thirty-two. She had brown eyes and close-cropped brown hair. The latter, combined with the figure-concealing clothing she habitually wore, caused many people to imagine her a lesbian. She wasn't. She simply couldn't bear the thought of actually living with a man.

There were no phony preliminaries. Atherton immediately began to strip off the restrictive clothes that Dot had worn to her job at the police station. He marveled, as always, at the softly rounded body she kept so determinedly hidden away. That, in fact, was one of the things that so inflamed him, that this treasure was locked away from everyone else. That he alone would kiss these lovely breasts, or run the tips of his fingers over her trim belly. That she would arch her back and with a muffled moan draw him deep inside her. Only him.

With Dot Pritchett, Atherton was young again.

For her part, Pritchett had stumbled upon the best of all possible worlds. She had a skilled, experienced lover, but one who never troubled her with his personal problems or pressured her for a more serious commitment. A man who could bring her sexual satisfaction and then be sent home to his wife and children. And, equally important, a man who willingly lent her the benefit of his financial expertise so that, over the years, she had put together a solid investment portfolio.

Though now, as she kneaded the heavy muscles of her lover's lower back, her portfolio was far from her mind.

Atherton rose to the occasion as he first had four years earlier, on the eve of his fiftieth birthday, and every time since. Their sweat-slick bodies locked together as they thrashed on the cheap motel-room bed in oblivious abandon, the proper banker and the equally proper police clerk, moaning and screaming, clawing and biting as if they were no longer rational human beings, but had somehow regressed down the aeons and been transformed into primitive creatures of a far more instinctual and violent nature.

Miraculously, they climaxed together, something neither had experienced with any other partner, and then they lay huddled and shaking, sweat drying in the artificially chilled air, as their pulse and respiration rates slowly returned to normal.

Atherton was the first to speak. "It still works," he said.

"Mmm-hmm," she said.

"I don't know what I'd do if I didn't have you."

She put a finger to his lips. "Don't," she said.

He kissed her finger, then fluffed his pillow and propped his back against the bed's headboard.

"How're Jane and the kids?" Pritchett asked.

"Oh, fine. What about you? Everything okay?"

"Sure. Except the department's nutso over the HIVe thing. I've never seen Kyser so uptight. I don't know what's going to happen if they don't catch those people soon."

"Well, I'll tell you one thing that's going to happen. We're going to lose the brewery."

"What?"

Atherton shook his head slowly. "It's bad news, Dot," he said. "Dusty was in to see me today. The Gustavia brass is getting spooked over the thing. Somehow they think it means that Brisbane is an unsafe place. It's crazy. But we've got to take it seriously. If they decide against locating here, Dusty's going to be down the tubes. The bank's going to take a beating." He turned his head so he could look her in the eye. "And you're going to lose a pretty stack too."

"No," she said. "Goddammit, *no*! You said this was a terrific investment—"

"It is. But I told you it was also a gamble, Dot. If it comes through, you make a pile of money. If it doesn't . . ."

Neither spoke for a while; then Atherton said, "Dusty thinks some of us should get together, form a citizens' group to help the police find these loonies. He thinks the more people are working on it, the better chance we have."

"How long before the brewery decides?"

"I don't know. A week, maybe a little more."

"Then Dusty's right. We can't let a stupid thing like this bung up the works."

"He's having a meeting at his house at eight tonight. It'd be good if you were a part of it. So we'd know what progress the police were making and all."

"I'll be there," Dot Pritchett said.

19

Rhonda Jo Rhoades was applying her makeup.

There'd been a time when she hadn't needed any. She'd been the Brisbane town beauty, tall and curvaceous, with cornflower-blue eyes and long dirty-blond hair that suggested an untamed feline. She'd won a string of competitions, and been fourth runner-up to represent the state in the Miss America pageant.

Now, though still striking for her age, she was thirty-five years old. Some of the curvaceousness had gone to plump. And her face could benefit from a little discreet cosmetic help.

Rhonda Jo had been married for twelve years, to a man ten years her senior. She'd made the decision to tie the knot when she began losing competitions to willowy teenagers and realized it was too late to start college again at the point she'd dropped out.

She'd had her pick of the local boys. And had chosen Dusty Rhoades, who was widely regarded in Brisbane as a comer. Dusty Rhoades was still regarded as a comer.

"What're you doing?" the comer was saying to his wife.

"What does it look like?" Rhonda Jo said. "I'm goin' out."

"Dammit, I told you I was having an important meeting here tonight. It's something you oughta come to. These are your friends, your neighbors, people concerned with what's happening in Brisbane."

"They are not my friends. And I'm not interested in your meeting."

"Well, you oughta be."

Rhonda Jo examined herself carefully in the mirror, got the blue eye shadow just the way she wanted it.

91

"Well, I'm not," she said. She looked directly at her husband. "You work your days away, Dusty, every day. You want to work your evenings too, you go right ahead. *I* still want to have a little fun in my life. And if I can't get it from you, I'm damn straight gonna get it someplace else."

"Please, honey—"

"Don't *honey* me."

"Look," Dusty pleaded, "the meeting's due to start at eight o'clock. Just give it a half-hour. See if you don't think it's important. I could use your help, Rhonda Jo. Just give it fifteen minutes, for Christ's sake. Is that asking too much? Jesus, the bars'll hardly be open at that hour."

Rhonda Jo sighed. "All right, Dusty," she said. "All right. I'll stick around for a few minutes. If you'd rather have people see me leave in the middle than not be there at all, okay. It's your show."

"Thanks, honey."

Dusty Rhoades bent over to kiss his wife on the cheek. She pulled away slightly at the last second so that he didn't do anything damaging to her makeup job.

At five minutes past the hour, there were nine people in the living room of the Rhoades house. Rhonda Jo knew Phil Atherton, the bank vice-president, and Dot Pritchett, who worked in the police department. She recognized the others by sight—the proprietor of a hardware store, the Brisbane Mall manager, a pizza-chain owner, a lady realtor. And there was Edna Clint, the registrar of voters.

For twenty minutes Rhonda Jo filed her nails and listened as Dusty briefed the group on the threat to the Gustavia brewery project and laid out his plan for a citizens' committee to help the police round up the HIVe before any further damage was done.

The energy level in the room rose steadily. There were expressions of anger and outrage. In the end, all agreed: Dusty was right—the more people became involved in the case, the better.

All were agreed, that is, except Rhonda Jo. She'd finished her nails and had been following the conversation, looking in shock from one face to the next. Now she got up.

"Y'all," she said, "this is the absolute stupidest thing I ever heard of."

"Come on, Rhonda Jo," Dusty said. "This is necessary."

"Necessary my hind end. Look at yourselves. You're a bunch of clerks and shopkeepers. You ain't cops. You start messing in cop work, you're gonna get your buns burned." She glanced around the room, shaking her head. "And that's all I got to say on the subject. See y'all later, after you come to your senses."

She started for the door.

"Rhonda Jo," her husband called.

"*Vigi*lance committee," she muttered over her shoulder, and she chuckled as she left the house.

Everyone turned and looked expectantly at Dusty.

"Don't worry," he said. "She'll be all right. I'll take care of Rhonda Jo. Now, let's adjourn this meeting and go find the bastards."

20

For Rhonda Jo Rhoades, it had been a slow night at the Skyview Lounge, which featured a cocktail pianist, leather bar stools, and a revolving mirrored globe, but nothing remotely resembling a sky view. So far, none of the men who'd hit on Rhonda Jo had seemed the least bit interesting. Maybe she was getting pickier as she got older, she thought.

Whatever the case, she hadn't minded when the slender woman with dark-reddish hair sat next to her at the bar. They were about the same age, though the woman didn't do all that much with herself. She wouldn't be any kind of competition if someone attractive did show up. And if someone didn't, perhaps the woman would provide a little decent conversation to help salvage the evening.

Rhonda Jo had introduced herself and found out that the woman's name was Dabney Layne. Now, there was a name for you. Dabney was obviously from up North. Probably went to the finest schools and all that.

But drinkers can't be choosers, Rhonda Jo thought, and she silently drank to that. A White Russian, her favorite. And not her first.

The Layne woman drank white wine. It figured.

"Just passing through, eh?" Rhonda Jo said.

"Uh-huh," Layne said. "Pretty country."

"And what do you do, Dabney?"

"I'm a photographer. Free-lance."

It was what Layne always said when she was working. It wasn't entirely untrue; she took photos when there wasn't a professional available to do it for her. And it didn't cause that instant clamming-up that often happened when you said "journalist." People knew that a writer might write any damn thing about them. With a photographer, they felt safe as long as they didn't have their picture taken.

"You?" Layne asked.

Rhonda Jo raised her glass. "Party girl, can't you tell?"

"Married party girl?"

"Ah, is it obvious as that?"

Layne shrugged. "Just a guess. Someone who looks like me always figures that someone who looks like you has to have landed the handsomest man in town. If not the wealthiest."

Rhonda Jo laughed. "That's a good one," she said. "But thanks, anyway. I did used to been a model. You shoulda seen me then."

"You look like you could still model to me."

"Oh, here we go. You best watch it, girl. You're trying to bullshit a bullshitter now, and there's no future in that. Why, you do that kind of photography?"

"No, I've done a lot of things, but I never worked much with models. Mostly men do that, it seems like."

"Faggoty men, I'll bet." Rhonda Jo leered like she knew something most people didn't.

"Not always," Layne said. "It's like anything. All kinds of people doing all kinds of jobs. Some men get into fashion photography because the women won't be a distraction; some do it to try to make everyone who steps in front of their lens. It all depends."

"Well, my modeling career never got too far off the ground," Rhonda Jo said wistfully. "Let's face it, I was a little too . . . curvy, you might say. But you can bet I won a few bathing-suit contests in my time. And a lot of people wanted to go to bed with me." She grinned. "Maybe if I hadn't of said yes so often they would of wanted to take my picture instead."

"I don't know. It's a rotten business, believe me. I've seen too many women get drugged out and trashed by the time they're twenty-five."

Rhonda Jo chuckled. "Yeah," she said, "but wouldn't it have been fun to take the ride?"

Layne shook her head emphatically. "Not for me. How about kids? You have any?"

"I can't have children."

"Oh, I'm sorry." Layne drank some wine. Sometimes the easy questions went hard on you. But sometimes that did you no harm in the end.

"Don't be," Rhonda Jo said to her White Russian. "Think of how much fun I'm having otherwise." Then she looked up. "What about you?"

"I tried marriage, and six months later I untried it. He got bent out of shape because my paycheck was bigger than his, so he found himself a teenager who was long on bod and short on brains. No kids for us, fortunately, and I haven't found anyone since then I'd even consider. Guess I'm just not the type. Marrying or childbearing."

"Now, ain't that the familiar story. Mine's the other way round to your teenager. He's long in the brains department but he's kinda let the body stuff slide. It's that older-guy thing, I suppose. We keep on falling for them, and they do look great when you're twenty, but ten years later they're already on the down side and you gotta come to places like this to pick up the slack."

"You're still with him, though."

"Yeah, there's times I think about getting quit of Dusty. God knows, I don't believe he'd care that much. But I gotta admit, he takes care of me good. And what I'm gonna do at my age, start over again? Go back to school?" She laughed. "There's a joke. No, I got nothing anybody wants."

"Don't sell yourself short, Rhonda Jo."

The blond looked sharply at her drinking companion. "What do you know about it?" she snapped.

There was a pause. Then Layne said, "I'm sorry. I usually try not to give advice, but sometimes I stick my foot in it anyway. You're right, it's none of my business."

She looked away, caught the bartender's attention, and ordered another glass of wine.

Rhonda Jo touched her on the forearm.

"Ah, forget it," Rhonda Jo said. She grinned. "Maybe I really like my life. And what's not to like? I don't have to work, I've got a new car every year, the house is paid for, and my husband doesn't care what I do on my own time as long as he doesn't have to hear about it. . . ." She grimaced. "Of course, the one time he did find out about the guy, he near to killed him. But other than that, it's not so bad."

"Don't I know. Take it from someone who works seven days a week, with no paid holidays or health insurance. There are a lot of times I'd trade places with you in a heartbeat. So what does your good provider do?"

"He's in *real* estate. I always wondered if that meant that there were people in *phony* estate."

Layne laughed. "Well," she said, "I can see how he keeps you in the style to which I could become accustomed. Brisbane looks like a real boom town to me."

"Yeah, it's growed a whole lot since I was a kid, like you wouldn't believe. Dusty's been a goodly part of that. And the place is about due to grow some more, if we can get out from under this HIVe business."

"I heard about that. It's horrible."

"You're telling me. People are getting about afraid to walk the streets alone. Used to been, that was one of the things about Brisbane, the streets was always safe."

The women sat alone with their thoughts while another round of drinks was served.

"As if it ain't bad enough we got to contend with these maniacs out there," Rhonda Jo went on, "it's getting us a bad image in the rest of the country as well."

"Maybe so," Layne said. "But in the trade there's an old saying that all publicity is good publicity. It can't take forever for the police to catch these lunatics. When they do, the frightening part of it will fade away fast, but people will still have that curiosity about Brisbane, since they've seen it on TV."

She stopped herself when she realized what she was saying.

"I'm sorry," she said. "I don't mean to sound callous. I wouldn't wish something like this on my worst enemy. All I'm trying to say is that, awful as it is and as much as we wish it'd be over with tomorrow, it'll bring a lot of people down your way in the long run."

"Yeah, I know what you're trying to say. No offense took. Unfortunately, most folks got a lot tied up in the *short* run around here. Like we got some new business that's dying to move to Brisbane, and now the virus thing

is getting them spooked out—ain't it just like some damn
Yankees? 'Scuse my French.''

"What kind of business?" Layne asked casually.

"You heard of the Gustavia brewery?"

"Sure. It's one of the biggest."

Rhonda Jo raised her glass to toast the air. "That kind
of business," she said.

Layne whistled softly. "They want to move here?"

"Part of them do. But *part* of them is like the *entire*
somebody else. It'd mean a lot to the town."

"And to you?"

"You're a sly one," Rhonda Jo said, chuckling. "You
figure Dusty stands to make some money out of the
deal."

"If he's in real estate, he'd have to. New jobs. The
demand for housing goes up. It stands to reason."

"Hnnh. Well, I suppose so. I hadn't really thought of
that, but you're absolutely right." She lowered her voice.
"And we're also in on the deal itself," she said with
whispered pride. She nodded to confirm the point.

Rhonda Jo gulped at her drink, then added in a more
normal tone, "Everything's pure hundred proof, unless
those sonofabitch loonies put a match to it all, or either
my crazy husband gets himself in the middle of it."

"The middle of what?"

"Oh, the whole damn thing. He's got a bunch of people
together, people who'd be unhappy—to say the *least*—if
Gustavia changed their mind, and these people are gonna
form some kind of damn citizen vigilance committee,
supposed to *help* the police out to find the nut cases.
Look around for clues or some weird shit, to get to the
bottom of it quicker. Now, ain't that the dumbest thing
you ever heard of?"

"Yeah, pretty foolish," Layne said. "Not to mention
dangerous. It doesn't sound like the HIVe nuts are people to be fooling around with. My experience is that if
you're trained for police work, that's what you do, and if
you aren't, you're best off leaving it alone. There are too
many ways to get burned that you'd never even think
of."

"Exactly. That's what I tried to tell them. But Dusty

gets these ideas sometimes, and there's no reasoning with him. He's so damn stubborn."

The women finished their drinks in silence. Rhonda Jo looked first at her watch, then at the bartender, who went immediately to the bar phone and made a call.

"Ah, hell," she said, glancing around the thinly populated bar, "there ain't nothing gonna happen in this place tonight. Slow as it is, I'd be just as well off at home. Long as that stupid committee meeting's broke up, which it ought to've by now. It's been a pleasure, Dabney Layne."

"Are you okay to drive?"

Rhonda Jo dismissed the thought with a wave. "They know me here," she said. "The cab's already on its way."

Rhonda Jo dropped a couple of bills on the bar and slid off her stool. She was a little unsteady on her heels.

"Dry land," she said, laughing. "Always tough."

"Well, it's been a pleasure for me too," Layne said, taking the other woman's hand. "I've learned a lot about your town. You watch out for yourself, Rhonda Jo."

"Hey, me I always land on my feet. You don't have to worry about that, sister."

21

Thursday, August 16

At ten-thirty in the morning, Dusty Rhoades was shown into the office of Mayor Brad Davis.

Davis was standing at the window that overlooked the Plaza, his hands clasped behind his back. He was gazing down at the commotion below, shaking his head slowly. After the door closed behind Rhoades, Davis sighed and turned to face his guest.

"That's an ugly scene out there," Rhoades said.

Despite Davis' efforts at reassurance the previous day, the crowd in the Plaza had not dispersed. The area had become the focus of the town's feelings about the HIVe killers: Frustration. Anger. Fear. The mistrust of one group for another. The damning of everyone's soul to everlasting hellfire by some.

Leafleting and picketing continued; speeches were made and sometimes people listened. Free-lance opinion-mongers harangued whoever would sit still for their rap.

The hot, humid dog days of August weren't helping any, either. There were occasional flare-ups of temper as differing points of view came into conflict. Chief Kyser, despite the manpower being drained by other aspects of the case, had decided he had to keep at least one uniformed officer in evidence at all times. He hoped that would be enough.

And through it all moved the invading army, the swarming media army that had descended on Brisbane from every corner of the country and not a few places beyond its borders.

That army, spearheaded by foot soldiers with exceptional instincts, like Dabney Layne, had begun arriving when the Wes Thomas story had hit the wires. But few would have predicted what would happen next. For the slow trickle of advance troops had, overnight, given way to a flood of regulars.

After the attack on little Lorene Greene went public, the army arrived in full strength: The national TV networks. The major daily newspapers. The wire services. The legit newsmagazines and the supermarket scandal rags. Foreign press stringers. Anyone and everyone with the least interest in turning news into money. And all of them scrambling for an edge, that crucial interview or overlooked fact that would give them a one-hour lead on the rest of the pack.

By Wednesday night there wasn't a room to be had in the Brisbane Arms or the Ramada or the Green Brae Inn or anything short of a fleabag. Downtown restaurants were doing their best business of the summer. The hotel lounges buzzed with half-soused journalistic chitchat, the swapping of lies about L.A. and New York and London and even Beirut.

In the Plaza at midmorning, men and women with notebooks and tape recorders and microphones scurried among the picketers and leafleteers. Others had Nikons strung from their necks or portable vidicams balanced on their shoulders. No citizen of Brisbane was safe from the army of questioners. And the questions were the same, over and over, always the same.

Because there were no answers.

A full-time clerk had had to be posted in the lobby of the City Building, to screen visitors. Those wanting to interview either the mayor or the chief of police or the detective lieutenant were asked to place their names on a list. The list was growing longer and longer.

"It's a stewpot waiting on the boil," Davis said. "I'm afraid this whole damn town is. Sit down, Dusty."

The two men took chairs on either side of the mayor's desk.

"This is a damn shame, Brad," Rhoades said. "I almost had to show my birth certificate to get in to see you."

"It's some kind of bad," Davis agreed. He rolled his eyes heavenward. "I really don't know what's worse, having half my own people mad at me or having to sneak in the back way so I don't get a damn mike shoved in my face." He looked back at his guest. "So what can I do for you?" he asked. "And please don't say you got any worse news for me."

"Well, we'll see," Rhoades said.

Davis groaned.

"But hopefully not. What we got is a situation getting away from us here, Brad. And we got to take steps to make sure it don't happen. There's some things you ought to know about."

22

At one o'clock, Will Grant did a summing-up for Chief Kyser in the chief's office. The lieutenant had an open spiral notebook in his lap.

"It's pretty close to a zipper," Grant said. "The lab ran every test known to God on that syringe Thomas found taped to the mirror. The only prints on it were his and Dr. Craven's. It'd been washed out good, so we can't be sure what was originally in it, if anything. And as far as tracing it goes, I made the rounds of the drugstores and medical-supply outfits, just to see if there were any recent purchases that might've been the least bit suspicious. Nobody could remember any. If the thing came from the hospital, we're looking at hundreds of employees who could've boosted it. I don't think there's much point to pursuing that.

"The techies lifted a slew of prints from the suite at the Green Brae. So far we've identified about ten of them, all people with good reason to've been in the room. That only leaves a dozen to go. I ain't holding my breath there.

"They was also able to find a trace of lipstick left on the mirror, which all it tends to do is corroborate Wes Thomas' story. Not that we've got any reason to doubt him. The color appears to have been bright red, but they couldn't get enough to tell us what brand or anything.

"Next, me and Jeff have now tracked down everyone who was working at the Green Brae that night and talked to them. Nobody remembers anything about the blond woman or anything else out of the ordinary.

"We did locate the cabdriver who took the woman from the Green Brae to the Inferno. He identified her from the sketch we got off the room clerk at the motel. He said *that* one looked more like her than the one from Thomas, so that's the one we're leaning most on now. Anyway, he thought she was nice-looking, but that's about it. She didn't talk to him in the cab. She paid him in cash, threw in a fair tip, and he drove off and never saw her again.

"That's not too helpful, except it does establish that she wasn't cruising before she went to the Inferno, but doesn't particularly establish that that was the one and only place she was bent on going that night.

"Then we questioned as many of the regulars at the Inferno as we could find. She seems to have walked into the place that night and gone straight to the bar and sat next to Thomas. It's hard to tell if she had her eye on him particularly, because there happened to be an empty seat next to him at the time.

"The guy on the other side of her was thinking of giving her a whack, but Thomas beat him to it. Thomas lit her cigarette for her, and that was all she wrote. They was God's friendliest creatures after that. Guy at the bar did remember that she took the cig out of a silver case, and he described it fairly good, which may be of some use to us later on. We showed him the sketch and he said it was a pretty good likeness, near as he can remember."

Grant paused and Kyser said, "I don't think none of this amounts to doodly-squat."

"It don't," Grant said.

"Jesus. I got about a three-ring circus outside breathing down my back, not to mention the mayor and the D.A. and the Brisbane Ladies' fucking Auxiliary. We got to come up with a sight more than doodly-squat."

"We will, Chief. But it's gonna take time."

"Time I don't have. What else you done?"

"Well, next," Grant said, "we followed on the possibility that the woman might of known Thomas beforehand. We talked to a lot of his friends and business associates and whatnot. We got the picture of a guy who was kind of a milquetoast but pretty much well-liked. No enemies that we could turn up. Lately he was heavy involved in the plan to put that brewery down on the

Squier, but I don't see how that could have much to do with it.

"I also went through the story another time with Thomas, see if maybe there wasn't something he left out the first go-round. But I'd say he lost a few cards from the deck in the meantime. I didn't get nothing useful.

"Then we tried to find some connection between Thomas and Lorene Greene or any of her family. There wasn't none.

"So we checked all the kids who were at the playground that day. We found one, an eight-year-old boy, who saw her getting into the car with the man. He couldn't describe the man at all. The car, he said, was a big one, looked old and beat-up, and some dark color, which is no better than Lorene could do. None of the people in the neighborhood where she was dropped off saw it happen, unfortunately.

"Other than that, we been following leads that come in over the phone. People who seen the sketches in the paper and are sure they spotted the man or the woman or both together. We check out every one, but so far nothing's come of it.

"We've run down all the anonymous tips so far. Nothing's come of that either.

"Then there's the confessors. We got three so far, but I imagine that number ought to up itself now the TV people've arrived. All three're men, naturally. So far no ladies have come forward to say they done Thomas. And all three guys flunked the interrogation. I put them down to two wackos and a publicity hound.

"And that's where we are up to right now."

"Nothing," Kyser said.

"Nothing," Grant agreed.

Kyser sighed. "Well," he said, "we just got to do better. What do you think next?"

Grant scratched at the edge of his receding hairline. "Run down the tips," he said. "I think if we're gonna get a break, that's where it's apt to come from. I'm also starting to bring in all the known freaks and weirdos. Just ask them a few questions.

"Thing is, since Lorene's test come back positive, that

kind of eliminates the guy as a copycat who's just getting some fun out of scaring people. So I ain't expecting a lot.

"Still, we gotta check. So I got that boy, let me see, David Eye, the one lives out in the woods there and we caught him playing naked with kids a couple of times, I got him coming in later this evening." He looked at his watch. "About after we get through here. He seems like a harmless type outside the exposing, but you never know with that sort. He's got a old beat-up black Ford. And he's got that long hair, like the guy Lorene Green described. It's possible he coulda gotten weirder over the years."

Grant shrugged. "It ain't much," he went on. "Now we know that Lorene really was contaminated, we got at least a two-person conspiracy going here. In which case the freaks won't help us any. They ain't gonna cooperate with each other long enough to get it done. So then we probably got crazies, but organized ones, and I don't like that at all.

"But operating on that assumption, me and Jeff'll make the rounds tonight, check out the bars, show the sketches, see if anyone can pin down the woman for us. And the guy. He might be out for big girls too.

"Then tomorrow I got an appointment with a doctor over to the hospital. See if I can't get a handle on where the crazies are getting the stuff in the first place. This guy's supposed to be an expert in the field." Grant closed the notebook he'd been referring to. "And then we'll see from there."

"You ain't exactly a fountain of good news," Kyser said.

"We're doing our best, Chief," Grant said evenly.

"All right, get back to work. And bring me something soon, will you?"

"Sure," Grant said.

After the lieutenant had left, Kyser jabbed viciously at the desk blotter with his ball-point pen.

Grant went directly back to his office. He was alone there when David Eye was shown in.

Eye was twenty-eight years old, tall and somewhat fleshy, soft-looking. He had dark brown eyes that were always wet, and straight light brown hair down to his shoulders. He walked deliberately, as if where he placed his next step might be of critical importance.

"Hello, M-Mr. Grant," Eye said.

"Sit down, David," Grant said. "How have you been?"

"I been fine. Ain't been in no trouble, n-no sir."

Grant spread some papers from a manila folder around on his desk.

"I've just been looking at your record," he said.

"No trouble," Eye repeated.

Grant nodded. "Not in four years. Not since the Wilshetts give you that corner of their land. You been raising rabbits back there, right?"

"Yes, sir."

Eye looked jerkily around the room, his nose twitching a little.

"It's them damn smokers," Grant said. "Always smells that way, even when they ain't here."

Eye smiled, slightly out of synch with Grant's remark. The smile vanished as he focused on the *Sports Illustrated* swimsuit calendar. The August model was jumping up out of the sea, her arms flung above her head, crystal droplets of water frozen by the camera's strobe flash, her blond hair swirling, her upflung breasts threatening to rip the thin Lycra of her canary-yellow one-piece suit. Her head was tilted back and she was biting her lower lip with flawless front teeth.

Grant noted where Eye was looking and said, "You like girls, David?"

Eye swiveled his head to look at the lieutenant. There was incomprehension in his face. "Huh?" he said.

"Nothing," Grant said. He looked down at the papers, then up again. "This last report," he said, "your doctor said you should be released from the hospital on account of you're not likely to hurt anybody. That true?"

"Th-that's true," Eye said. "I ain't been in no trouble."

"You still have that black Ford?"

"Uh-huh. Why? What's it done?"

"The report also says you're not to be playing with any little girls. You haven't been playing with any little girls lately, have you?"

"N-no, sir. I have my bunnies now." He nodded with satisfaction.

Grant leaned toward the young man. "Now, David," he said, "this is a serious matter. I want to ask you again. Have you been down by the Walker schoolyard in your car lately?"

"No, I sure haven't, Mr. Grant. It's been such pretty days, I just been to home." He shook his head, then smiled innocently, the water in his large eyes looking as if it might spill over any minute. "I used to like to play with the children, but the judge told me I couldn't do that anymore, which is when I got the bunnies. But I d-do miss them."

"Did you ever hurt any of the children, David?" Grant asked.

Eye looked at him in horror. "Oh m-my, n-no," he said. "Hurt a child? What a terrible thing to say."

"I mean, maybe just in fun. You know, pinching and stuff."

"I usedta played with the children." Eye shook his forefinger at the lieutenant. "I wouldn't hurt, or either let anybody else. It's not right to hurt other people. Everyone should have b-bunnies at their house, then there wouldn't be any hurting."

"How about Tuesday evening, David? What were you doing?"

Eye's brow furrowed as he thought about it. After a few moments he shrugged.

"I don't know, Mr. Grant," he said. "I surely d-don't. But mostly I just been to home these pretty days. Is that okay?" He smiled expectantly.

"Yeah, sure, that's fine," Grant said.

Suddenly David became agitated. His eyes opened wide in surprise and he squirmed in his seat.

"What's g-going on?" he asked. "Is someone hurting the ch-children?" His hands were fluttering, so he rested them, fingers interlaced, on top of his head.

"Calm down," Grant said. "No one's hurting the children. We just want to make sure it stays that way."

"Those are strange questions."

Grant held out one of the sheets of paper. "Doctor's orders," he said. "We make sure you stay out of trouble and you won't have to go back to the hospital ever."

Eye let his hands fall to his sides and stared at the lieutenant without expression.

"Okay, David," Grant said. "You can go. Come on, I'll walk you out."

Grant got up, took the young man's arm, and helped him up from his chair.

"All those people outside," Eye said. "What are they all doing there?"

"Oh, you know," Grant said. "Politics. People always got to protest something, when it comes to politics."

Eye nodded and let himself be ushered out of the detectives' office. The two men walked down the hall in silence. They stopped just before the hall opened out into the main waiting area. To their right was a clerical office. Its door was open.

Grant rested his hand on Eye's shoulder. "Some men have been looking at your car while you were talking to me," he said. He indicated one of the long wooden benches in the waiting room. "I want you to wait here until they're finished, okay?"

Eye looked at the lieutenant suspiciously. "What's wrong with my car?" he asked.

"Nothing. Just routine. They'll be done in a few minutes and someone will come and get you. Don't worry about it, okay?"

"I need to get home."

"You will soon. I'll get in touch with you if I need to talk to you again. In the meantime, you just stay out of trouble, y'hear?"

"I ain't been in no trouble."

"Good. Then there's nothing to worry about."

Grant turned and walked back down the hall while Eye settled himself uneasily onto the wooden bench. The young man looked around as if everything in sight was unfamiliar to him.

In the clerical office, Dot Pritchett had stopped typing. She'd scrutinized the long form in her machine, as though checking for errors. But she'd actually been listening to the conversation taking place a few feet away, between the lieutenant and the queer-looking boy.

After Grant had left, she fished around in her desk drawer and pulled out the police artist's sketch of the man who'd abducted Lorene Greene. She stared at it for a long moment, then put it back in the drawer.

Five minutes later she got up from her desk, took her purse, and told her office mates she'd be right back. She paused outside the door and stared at the young man in the waiting area. Then, very purposefully, she walked up the stairs to the second floor. The ladies' room was up there, along with a pay phone set into the wall.

Dot Pritchett made a call to Dusty Rhoades.

23

Thursday night, Grant and Jeffers were out in the unmarked tan cruiser. Though it was past dark, the heat of the day had failed to dissipate and they were running the air conditioner. Jeffers was driving, Grant looking out the window and humming to himself.

"What's that?" Jeffers asked. "One of your hillbilly hits of the future?"

"Thought you'd never ask," Grant said. "As a matter of fact, it is. Want to hear it?"

Jeffers groaned. "No, but I got the distinctive feeling I'm gonna anyway."

"This is a good one, you'll like it."

"Will, this is entirely the wrong man you talking to, you know? I go into some hillbilly bar and all I got is trouble from one end of the place to the other."

"Well, you're safe here. Listen up."

And Grant sang. He had a pleasant if uneven baritone voice, with just the right timbre for an aspiring country star. The melody was based on a simple three-chord progression.

'Cause she's a tired mama
With a fam'ly on her hands
Waitin' for that mis'rable
Excuse she calls a man

Yeah, she's a tired mama
With no prospective rest
So she don't try to do it all
She just tries to do her best

"That's just the chorus, of course," Grant said. "But that's the most important part. You gotta have a hook in the chorus there, or nobody's gonna walk up and down the street singing your song to theirself. But you get the chorus right, and you got a hit. You see what I mean."

"Man," Jeffers said, "that's the worst sound I heard since my dog broke his tail and it hurt him so fierce when he had to raise it up to take a shit."

"You're jealous, Jeff. That's God's awfullest truth, right there."

"Yuh-huh. How come my eardrums got a mind to arrest you for assault, then?"

Grant laughed. "Say what you like. 'Tired Mama' has just got 'hit' wrote all over it."

"I don't wonder, them rednecks that listen to it being about as half-bright as the ones who think it up."

"Yeah, it ain't Lionel Ritchie, you got that right at least."

"I think we better change the subject, partner. What'd you get out of that goony boy, anything?"

"Nah," Grant said. "It was a long shot. He looks some like the sketch, but some not. He's simple enough, I figured if I tossed him some questions he'd give it away if he was the one. He didn't. His roof may be nailed on loose, but otherwise I think he's clean. We got no evidence he's been fooling with kids for pretty long now."

"They lift any prints from his car?"

"Nothing but his."

"So you think we oughta keep after the sex freaks?"

"I guess. Somehow, though, it don't feel like a pervert thing, you know? It's too . . . I don't know, *cold* or something. And the people got too good of a disappearing act. Perverts, they *want* to get caught most of the time. They wouldn't of been able to do this twice and not left a clue behind."

"Well, there can't be nothing," Jeffers said. "I don't believe that."

"Then you tell me what there is," Grant said.

"What there is, is the Skyview Lounge." Jeffers gestured at the big green sign dead ahead.

"Next stop, if I am not mistaken."

"And bound not to have that terrible music, either."

"Hey, don't forget Charley Pride," Grant said.

Jeffers shook his head as he turned the cruiser into the bar's parking lot. "You're a muddle-headed human being, Grant," he said.

"Ready to do some muddle-headed police work."

Jeffers parked the cruiser and the two men went inside.

"All right," Grant said as he and his partner surveyed the Skyview, "this is it. I don't have another one left in me tonight."

"I thought you'd never quit, brother," Jeffers said.

"This look like a yuppie bar to you?" Grant asked.

"I thought they all died when the stock market crashed."

"Not in Brisbane. Didn't you know, we're about five years behind New York here."

"Oh. 'Scuse me, boss. I jest a country boy."

Grant chuckled and the two of them went down the stairs to floor level and walked to the bar. The lounge wasn't crowded, and a lot of the trade was obviously from out of town.

The two cops talked with the bartender, but he just shook his head to every question. When they'd finished, they gave him copies of the sketches and asked him to keep his eyes open. He said he would.

Grant looked down along the bar. Near the end, a woman raised her glass to him. "Lieutenant," she said.

He tipped his imaginary cap to her.

Next, he and Jeffers covered the waitresses and whichever regular patrons of the Skyview happened to be around. None could provide any leads on the people they were looking for but all agreed to keep watch for the police.

After they'd covered the entire lounge, Grant said to Jeffers, "You go ahead home, Jeff. I can walk over to the Block and pick up my car."

Jeffers grinned. "You settin' up to hit on that reporter?"

"Yeah, sure," Grant said wearily. "Just what I need. But she might of turned up something. Might's well ask."

"You do that. See you tomorrow, Will."

Grant walked back to the end of the bar.

"Miz Layne," he said.

" 'Evening, Mr. Grant," Dabney Layne said.

"Bourbon and water," he said to the bartender. He raised his eyebrow to the woman.

"I'll have another white wine," she said, then to Grant, "Is this by way of a truce, Lieutenant?"

"We'll see," he said.

When their drinks arrived, Grant said, "Let's sit someplace has got a back to it."

Layne smiled. "Fine."

They carried their drinks to a heavy butcher-block table and sat in some sturdy captain's chairs.

"Well," Layne said, "to what do I owe the honor?"

"Look, Miz Layne," Grant said, "I been busting hump all day on this case and I'm tired and I want to have a drink in peace and that's what it is."

"Don't be touchy, Will. I've been trying to cooperate with you all along, remember? I'd still like to."

Grant drained his bourbon and signaled for another. He didn't say anything until the waitress brought it. He took another hefty swallow, then breathed out heartily.

"All right, Miz Layne—"

"Dabney."

"All right, Dabney—"

Layne giggled. "Though back in school my friends used to call me Penny."

Grant looked puzzled.

"You know," she said, and in a voice just slightly tipsy, she sang a couple of lines from the Lennon-McCartney tune.

"Oh, yeah." He chuckled. "The Beatles. Can I call you Penny?"

"Why not? Can I call you Willie Boy?"

"Now, wait a minute—"

"Forget it. Old Robert Redford movie. But you don't look like him, anyway."

Grant settled the second bourbon in place, said, "Now, that's more like it," and ordered another.

"You have a nice voice, Penny," he said. "You ever do it professionally?"

Layne rolled her eyes and shook her head.

"Reason I ask is, I'm kind of a musician myself."

"Let me guess," she said. "You play guitar and sing country and western."

"How'd you know that?"

She toasted him. "I'm good at my job, Will. Remember?"

"Hnnh. Well, I reckon you are. But what you probably didn't know is I write my own songs too."

"Sing me one."

"Uh, I don't know. Right here?"

"Right here."

"Well, usually I only sing to home or in the car with my partner, one. I don't usually . . ."

"Come *on*," Layne said. "I won't be too critical, I promise."

Grant took a healthy hit of the whiskey, cleared his throat, and sang:

Well, she's prob'ly drinkin' coffee
In some burnt-out Texas town,
And thinkin' how to work her ways
On ev'ry man around,
I saw only what she wanted me to seeee . . .
But exceptin' in the darkest hours
It don't bother me

And ohhh ohhh, money and pain,
Ahhh ahhh, money and pain,
And all of the years don't come again,
Lost in the sound of the fallin' rain . . .

"And there's a couple more verses," Grant said. "But that's the general idea. That's one verse and the chorus."

Layne had cocked her head and was staring at him with a slight smile.

"What's wrong?" he said. "You don't like it. You don't like country music." He soothed his vocal cords with a swallow of bourbon.

"No," she said, "not at all. I do like country music, at least at times. And that's a *damn* good song. I'm surprised."

"Not bad for a hick cop?"

Layne laughed. "That's not what I mean," she said. "It's just . . . You have to understand, the business I'm in, people are all the time wanting to show me their writing or their photos or whatever, thinking I can somehow help them with their careers, and ninety-nine times out of a hundred it's crap. But that's not. That's a good song." She shrugged. "So I'm surprised. Pleasantly, I might add. *My* turn to buy *you* a drink."

"Well . . . thanks," Grant said.

Layne paused, then added, "I'll be honest with you, though. I'd get somebody else to sing it for you."

"So I've been told."

"Waylon Jennings, he'd be a good one for that song. Or Hank Williams, Jr. Got to be somebody with a rough edge to him."

They both laughed.

"So," Layne said. "You're a songwriter of the future. Is that what you always wanted to be?"

"Hmmm," Grant said, "I don't think so. At one time the police looked pretty good to me. It's got security, and it's not all that dangerous around here. Wasn't much I could of done better. Then I found I could write songs people liked, so, well, when I retire I believe I'll move to Nashville."

Layne nodded. "And what else about you? You married?"

"Used to been, but my wife didn't like the hours." He smiled ruefully. "Party girl, you know? And I haven't been able to talk anyone else into it since. You?"

"I tried too. Yours probably lasted longer than mine."

Quickly she ran through the story of her failed marriage. As she did, she removed her gold-rimmed glasses, breathed on the lenses, and polished them with a cloth from her handbag. Grant watched as if he'd never done it to his own.

"It's not as bad as New York," she said. "There's so much grit in the air up there, you wouldn't believe. You clean your glasses and the cloth comes out black."

"I would of thought you'd wear contacts."

"Allergic. And speaking of which, those things you wear make you look like Clark Kent."

They laughed. "It helps," he said. "Makes me look harmless. That gets people to talk to me, which is half of what being a cop's about."

Layne raised her wineglass and looked at him conspiratorially. "We going to be friends, Will Grant?" she asked.

"Might could," he said.

"Good. You're an interesting man, personally. And professionally, I think we can help each other."

Grant stiffened a little.

Layne touched his arm. "Relax," she said, "please? I'm not going to get in your way. But I'm out digging around every day, and maybe I can come up with something of use to you. I'll share whatever I get. All I ask in return is that you talk to me from time to time. You don't have to tell me anything that compromises your investigation. Just talk, like we're doing now. I may be a journalist, but that doesn't mean I'm totally burned out on other people." She smiled her most winning smile.

"Well," he said, "I don't know. Just don't push on me, okay?"

"Great," she said enthusiastically.

"And it'd probably be better if the chief didn't see us hanging around together. He already suspects me of leaking stuff to the newspapers."

"I'm the soul of discretion."

He stared down into his bourbon and sighed. "It's an awful thing, the way it's all happening," he said. "Gets me down sometimes to where I wonder if the town will ever be the same again. Hell, I suppose it wouldn't hurt to have someone on the outside to talk to."

"I appreciate that," Layne said, touching his arm briefly again. "And to prove it, let me tell you something I found out last night."

"You don't have to prove nothing."

"Right. Let me *share* something that I believe you will find most interesting, if you don't already know about it. And I don't think you do."

"This have to do with the case?"

"Uh-huh."

"Okay," Grant said, "but let's just get something straight. If you come across *any* information of value to us, you're *required* to let us know. It ain't a matter of do you feel like sharing it or not at that particular moment. If you withhold evidence, not only am I not gonna be your friend, I'm gonna throw your ass in jail so fast Herschel Walker won't be able to grab you. We understood on that point?"

"Will," Layne said, "you're a hard man. But I tell you, I don't withhold evidence. Period."

"Good." There was a careful pause; then Grant said, "Ah, let's lighten up. I'm sorry. It's just I don't want to see you wind up on the wrong side. Not that you *would*, or anything. I'm a tad hard where the law's concerned."

"Especially here, I'm sure."

"Yeah, especially here. This damn thing is the worst experience of my en*tire* life. I got crazies running around trying to kill people by delayed reaction, the chief and the mayor on my back to catch them when I don't have a clue who they are, half the population of Brisbane in a panic and the other half getting a shave and a haircut so they look good on TV. It's the damnedest . . ." He stopped, shook his head, and drank some bourbon. "Ah, forget it," he said. "What was it you wanted to talk about?"

"I'm sorry for you, Will," Layne said. "You've got a tough job to do. You're doing your best. I'll make sure my doing my job doesn't interfere with you."

Grant grunted acknowledgment.

"Okay," she went on. "You know a woman named Rhonda Jo Rhoades?"

Grant smiled. "Sure," he said. "Rhonda Jo. She was a few years behind me in school, but that didn't matter none. Wasn't a boy of any age around here didn't want to peel her pants. Begging your pardon."

"Don't apologize. She's very attractive now. She must have been a knockout when she was eighteen."

"She was. I don't know how Dusty lucked into her. Hell, he's older than I am."

"He's a big-time realtor, I understand."

"Yeah, I suppose. One scam or another, Dusty's been into it, every one since he got back from the war. He's done all right, or he must have, to keep Rhonda Jo in fancy clothes and BMW's or whatever the hell foreign thing it is she drives. How do you know her, anyway?"

"She doesn't like to drink alone," Layne said. "I ran into her right at this bar last night. She felt like talking. I'm paid to listen."

"And what'd Rhonda Jo have to say that would interest me, Miz Penny? She better not be involved with this HIVe thing."

Layne shook her head. "Nothing like that," she said.

She leaned forward, resting her forearms on the butcher-block tabletop. She spoke softly, as if not wanting anyone else in the bar to hear.

"It seems," she said, "that you've got some people in this town who want to deputize themselves."

Grant stared at her. There was a very bad feeling starting to crawl up his spine.

"What exactly is that supposed to mean?" he said evenly.

"It means that there are people outside the police who want in on this investigation."

"Who?"

"I don't know, Rhonda Jo didn't want to talk about it a lot, and I think she regretted having brought it up. But her husband is one of them. Some of his friends—I'm sure you'd know who they are."

Grant took a notebook from his coat pocket. "You don't mind?" he said. "I can't trust my brain after this many bourbon and branch."

"Of course not."

"Dusty Rhoades," he said as he made his first note. "I guess that figures. And some of his friends. How'd Rhonda Jo know about this?"

"They had a meeting last night at the Rhoades house. It has something to do with the brewery that's getting set to build a plant here."

Grant smiled. "You do work fast," he said appreciatively.

Layne nodded. "Apparently these people are worried that Gustavia might change its mind if the case isn't cleared up soon. So they want to work behind your back, to try to hurry things up. Rhonda Jo told them they were crazy and walked out."

"Well, I'll be damned," Grant said. "Good for Rhonda Jo."

"I think she used the words 'vigilance committee.' "

Grant snapped his notebook shut. "Shit!" he said. "God damn them. That's all I need right now, a bunch of half-baked civilians running around not knowing what they're doing."

"I told Rhonda Jo I thought she was right to stay out of it," Layne said.

"Thanks," Grant said. He fumbled some money out of his wallet. "And thank you for the tip. This we gotta take care of right away. Damn thing's enough of a circus already."

Layne offered her hand and Grant took it. She held on to it for a moment.

"I'll be checking in with you, Will," she said.

"Fine," he said. "Anything you get, you bring it to me first. And I'll . . . I'll make it up to you. I owe you one."

Layne smiled. "I'll remember you said that."

24

Trance rammed his guitar through a succession of power chords that had the Jersey Shore crowd screaming. Bodies rococheted off one another. Several of the younger members of the audience had already opened veins with razor blades and were offering their blood to friends and strangers. The aptly named, motionless Trance heard and saw nothing but the sound of the band and the glare of the spotlights.

It had been a pretty good night, all things considered. The crowd was enthusiastic, the Skulls had played well. A few more followers were bound to have been added to the Empty Sockets, who traveled from town to town in the Skulls' wake.

Out under the number-one spot, Death Aims, the Skulls' lead singer, was preparing the show's climactic moment. And the screaming intensified as the fans anticipated.

Slowly, seductively, Death Aims pulled from beneath his skeleton suit a plastic hospital bag filled with blood. His other hand held the cordless mike, into which he shrieked the lyrics to "Floating Death," the band's second-most-popular song after "Virus."

But no one was listening to the words.

As the band careened into the song's final instrumental break, Death Aims tore the blood bag's seal with his teeth. He raised the bag high over his head, tipped it, and poured blood down over himself. Then he drank.

The act seemed to transform him, and he spun into a dance of spastic fury, howling nonsense syllables into the mike.

He whirled over to the edge of the stage and the real ritual began.

Death Aims got to his knees. His body jerked and quivered like a marionette gone berserk. Somehow, though, he managed to draw mouthfulls of blood from the bag.

And he passed it on to the fans. Mouth to mouth. They clamored for the sacrament, shoving and elbowing, trampling underfoot anyone too weak to hold his or her ground. It was the mystical moment of every Skulls concert, when performer and audience were joined in physical and spiritual union.

It was the transcendental act of faith in the lives of those who had no other.

When the blood was exhausted, Death Aims hurled the bag out into the crowd. Two young skinheads fought over the precious icon. They gave no quarter.

The band slammed into the terminal power chord and the stage went black. People clambered up after their idols, but by the time the lights came up, the Skulls were long gone.

Backstage, the band's four members draped themselves exhaustedly over chairs, dripping sweat and blood and whatever alcoholic liquids had been thrown their way during the performance. They drank beer and ate from a tray of sandwiches that had been waiting in the dressing room for them.

As usual, they had to wait for their ears to stop ringing before they could have a conversation.

Finally they could hear again, and Trance said, "So what's next?"

"Tuesday," Death Aims said. "That hick college down in redneckland."

"Great," said Bloat, the bassist.

"No, it really is," Death Aims said. "I got a letter from some people down there today. You'll love this."

He rummaged around in a black nylon bag and came up with a sheet of paper. He cleared his throat portentously.

" 'We welcome the visit of our brothers the Skulls to Dunmore College on August 21,' " he read. " 'We are flesh of the same flesh, blood of the same blood, and will make ourselves known to you. Our forces will be joined.' "

"Who's that from?" Trance asked. "The Jaycees?"

"No signature," Death Aims said. "But you gotta love it. If the message is reaching hicksville, there's no stopping it."

25

Friday, August 17

"I don't like it," Mayor Davis said. "All those damn people out there. It makes it look bad on us."

He and Kip Kyser were in the mayor's office, morning coffee in china mugs on the desk between them. The scene in the Plaza below them was every bit as crazed as it had been the day before. Perhaps more so. Now vendors had made their inevitable appearance, selling everything from overpriced food and drink to souvenir T-shirts.

"We got us another problem," Kyser said.

Davis groaned. "I don't believe it," he said. "What in the hell now?"

"Maybe nothing, but maybe something. Grant's been pulling in some of the local freaks, and yesterday he brought in this kid, David Eye, you know him?"

"No."

"He's a young guy, kind of simple, lived by hisself in a shack out the edge of town. Thing is, he sorta fit the description Lorene Greene give us, and he drove an old black Ford besides, which might be the kind of car we're looking for. And he had a past history of exposing himself to little kids.

"So we had to at least question him, which Grant did yesterday afternoon. And after which, Grant decided that the boy didn't know a virus from his asshole."

Davis looked at his watch. "So the idiot kid wasn't involved," he said. "Is that it?"

"No, that ain't it. David Eye's dead."

"Huh?"

"Last night. His cabin burned to the ground before the fire boys could even get near it. He was inside. Right

124

now, it looks like a accident. The kid didn't have no electricity, used kerosene for light, he coulda spilled it. But then, how'd he get trapped inside?"

"What're you trying to say, Kip?"

The chief stroked his chin. "I don't know," he said. "It just strikes me as a strange coincidence. Grant brings the kid in for questioning, he looks like the guy who attacked the little girl, and the same night he dies under kinda peculiar circumstances. I'm a cop, Brad, and the damn thing stinks.

"Let's suppose something. Let's suppose that Rhoades and that damn committee you told me about got wind of this Eye being a suspect. And suppose they got a hard-on to go out there and scare him a little or something, and suppose maybe things got a little out of hand . . ." Kyser spread his hands and looked the question at the mayor.

"That's a lot of supposing," Davis said tersely.

"Yeah, but it's got a feel to it."

There was a pause; then Davis said, "This idiot boy, he have any kin or anything?"

"No, just some people who gave him a bit of land to help keep him out of the hospital."

Kyser let Davis think it over, which the mayor did for a long silent minute.

"You can get a ruling of accidental death?" Davis asked finally.

"I don't think that'll be a problem," Kyser said.

"All right, do it. But you're gonna have to assign somebody to investigate, to make it look right.

"So let's look at what we have to do.

"One, let's keep it as far from the HIVe thing as we can. That means don't put Grant on it." He looked at Kyser and Kyser nodded.

"Two, make sure whoever you do assign knows not to make a big issue of it. And to wrap it up as fast as he can. We don't have any men to spare as it is, if you need an excuse." Kyser nodded again.

"And three, there's Rhoades and his bunch. I'll handle that. I won't get specific with this Eye thing. But whether Dusty's involved or not, he's got to understand that we can't have any cowboy shit going on out there. I'll call him in here today and tell him that personally. Does that cover it?"

"I think so." Kyser got up. "For what it's worth, Brad, I don't like this any more than you do. Maybe less so. But sometimes you got to do things as cut the wrong way. There just ain't no choice."

"Yeah, sure. And keep leaning on Grant, will you? I got a bad feeling that the longer this thing drags on, the more we're gonna be doing things we don't want to do."

Kyser nodded and returned to his office. He sent out word that he wanted to see Grant, then took care of the details in the Eye affair. About an hour later, the lieutenant was shown in.

"Sorry I'm late, Chief," Grant said. "Been out running down some possibles."

"Anything?" Kyser asked.

"Dead ends."

"Well, Will, that's sort of what I wanted to see you about. I don't mind telling you, the mayor's getting antsy for some results on this thing. Not to mention . . ." He swept his arm in a wide semicircle to indicate the carnival going on outside the building.

"I wish," Grant said. "But I'm afraid we're still putting up zeros. Jeff and I covered near every bar in town last night, it feels like. We talked to about forty-eleven bartenders and waitresses and regular drunks and we couldn't get even close to an ID on the faces, neither one."

Kyser grunted. "Well, we need to come up with something. I hope you got some alternate lines of investigation in your head."

"I've got some ideas. But there's something I wanted to talk to *you* about, Kip."

"Ain't the investigation enough for you?"

"This *is* about the investigation, and it's been bothering me. Last night I heard from a pretty good source that Dusty Rhoades and a bunch of his buddies are putting together a vigilante committee or some damn thing. You hear anything about that?"

"Who's your source?"

"Rhonda Jo," Grant said casually. "She apparently

thought it was nutso and walked out on them. What about it, you think it's true?"

"What I think is that Rhonda Jo's got her facts twisted around some. I know Dusty's pretty worried about what all this might do to the chances of the Gustavia people coming to town. He wants the crazies caught as much as we do. And he said him and some of his friends would be keeping their eyes and ears open and report anything suspicious to us. I don't believe there's any more to it than that. I told him I thought it was a good idea. We can use all the help we can get."

The lieutenant looked coolly at his boss for a moment. Then he said, "Well, I still don't like it, Kip. The last thing we need is folks taking the law into their own hands, which is exactly what could happen with this. If it does, we got ourselves one hell of a mess around here. I think I ought to have a word with Rhoades and make sure we get a lid on it right from the git-go."

"Let it be, Will," Kyser said with authority. "I'm sure Dusty and them ain't intending to take the law into their hands. I'll have a word with him next chance I get, just to make sure. In the meantime, though, let's remember that we're all on the same side here. He wants the bastards caught and so do we, and maybe if we cooperate it'll get done that much sooner."

"Could be, but I don't like it," Grant said. "I don't like the whole idea of it."

"Well, it ain't your worry. Clear?"

"Yes, sir."

"Now, what else you got the intention to do?"

Grant looked at his watch. "Jeff and me have got an appointment with Dr. Mendez, over to the hospital, in half an hour. He knows more about HIV viruses than anybody in town. I thought he might have some idea where the crazies are getting it. If he gives us a track, we'll take it. And we've still got a few tips and one new confessor to follow up on."

"All right," Kyser said. "But I tell you, Will, I don't want these bastards to have to strike again before we make any progress on this."

26

When Will Grant returned to his office, Detective Pound was the only one there.

Pounds, he ought to be called, Grant thought. *That'd be more like it.*

Pound and Worth were a pair of matched bookends. Both were squat and overweight, ate too much artery-hardening food and smoked too much, wore the same kind of rumpled brown or gray or blue suit, smelled bad, and bored everyone but each other. Each was, however, an adequate detective, and together they managed to get results, sometimes. Grant got along fine with Pound and Worth as long as he wasn't stuck in a car with one of them.

"Anything new come in this morning?" Grant asked.

"Nah," Pound said. He was poking between his yellowed teeth with a flat-ended toothpick. Judging from the condition of his gums, it was a practice he'd taken up way too late.

"Hey," he added, "sorry about your buddy."

"Who's that?" Grant asked distractedly.

"The Eye kid. You was pulling on his tongue yesterday, wasn't you?"

"Uh-huh. Why, what happened to him?"

"Oh, you ain't heard? He's dead."

Grant turned his full attention to the other man. "What are you talking about?" he said.

"I'll be kiss my ass if it ain't true. Idiot boy burned down his own house with him inside of it. Don't that cap the stack?"

Grant sat down, a dazed expression on his face. "I don't understand," he said. "How . . . ? What . . . ?"

"Beats me." Pound shrugged. "They think he was playing with some kerosene and catched the place on fire. Don't nobody know how he trapped hisself in it, but with a idiot boy, 'bout anything can happen."

"Anyone from here investigating?"

"Yeah, Kyser put Maupin on it this morning, wouldn't you know? So it's gotta be pretty open-and-shut. If there's anything to find out, Maupin'll sure never find it. And he can take his time not finding, far as I'm concerned. He ain't no good to us to find the HIVe killers."

"Jesus," Grant said. "David Eye."

"What'd you think from yesterday," Pound asked, "was he one of the ones we're looking for?"

"I guess if that's the end of the attacks, he was. But I didn't think so. He was just a not-too-bright boy, I think. I don't believe he ever heard the word 'virus' in his life. He sure didn't seem the type that reads the newspapers. . . . What a damn strange thing to happen."

Pound got up. "Seen a lot stranger," he said. "I'm gonna have a whack at this new confessor, Will. If that's okay by you."

"Sure, that's fine," Grant said mechanically.

"Later, Lieutenant."

Grant sat at his desk and stared at the far wall. There was something *damned* strange about this. What if Eye *had* gotten involved? What if other people had been using him for their own purposes? Would there have been a reason to kill him? Or was it nothing more than a coincidental accident?

"Hey, anybody home?" a voice asked.

Grant became aware that someone had laid a hand on his shoulder. He looked up and saw Martin Jeffers.

"Sometimes I don't know anymore," Grant said. "You hear about the fire at David Eye's?"

"Yeah, I heard."

"Strike you as strange?"

"Uh-huh. But if there's anything suspicious, we sure never gonna hear about it with Maupin on the case."

"I know," Grant said. His expression was puzzled. "Only thing I can think is, Kyser must of thought he couldn't spare anyone better, or that he didn't need to. But you and me better keep our eye on whatever comes out of that. There's a couple weird ways it could connect up."

"Believe we should. But right now we got things to do, partner. You about ready to go over to the hospital?"

"Yeah, let's go."

Grant slipped into his jacket. It was another plaid that didn't quite go with the slacks he'd chosen, nor with the shirt he wore open at the collar. When he'd turned his back, Jeffers eyed the outfit and shook his head sadly.

Fifteen minutes later they had an audience with Dr. Jorge Mendez. Mendez was a short, dark-complexioned man with intense eyes and a perpetual five-o'clock shadow. Professionally, he was a hematologist and a specialist in viral afflictions of the blood.

"Gentlemen," he said after the cops had introduced themselves, "I'm glad you've come to me. This is a terrible thing that's happening in Brisbane. How may I be of service to you?"

"Well, we're kind of at the end of our rope here, Doctor," Grant said. "I thought it might help if we learned a little more about the disease. I gotta confess I don't know all that much about it, and I think Martin here's in the same boat."

Jeffers nodded his agreement.

"Of course," Mendez said. He leaned back in his swivel chair and steepled his fingers. "The most important thing about HIV-4 is that, like other immunodeficiency viruses, it's *not* very contagious. You can't get it from doorknobs or kissing or somebody sneezing in your face. As far as we know, the only way of becoming infected is through sex or exposure to contaminated blood. So we're not going to have the kind of epidemic you can get with the flu. Okay?"

Grant made some notes in his spiral notebook. He and Jeffers nodded that they were following along so far.

"Okay," Mendez continued. "The other thing to remember is that there are some important differences between HIV-4 and HIV-1—that's the original AIDS virus—even though we suspect that the one may have evolved from the other. But since HIV-4 was only discovered eighteen months ago, we can't be sure of much.

"In any case, both viruses have the same target cell,

the *helper T-lymphocyte.* Where they differ is that with HIV-1 there's a latency period, after which the target cells simply lose their ability to do their job. The body becomes unable to fight off a whole list of diseases that normally would never get a foothold. People die because they can no longer fight them off. But it takes a while.

"HIV-4, on the other hand, is much faster. There's no latency period. If you're going to get it, it's apparent within a couple of weeks. And, unlike HIV-1, we can detect the presence of the virus within hours after someone is exposed, as we did with Wes Thomas.

"All of this makes us wonder how the damn thing got started in the first place." He shrugged. "It's a mystery. As is how HIV-4 manages to keep spreading. It acts so quickly and is so difficult to transmit that we *should* have brought it under control by now. Not that we should have a cure yet. But we haven't even been able to contain it, and I can't tell you why. The thing just keeps cropping up."

Mendez paused, then said, "And there's one other thing you need to know. When the *helper T-lymphocyte* is attacked by HIV-4, and is in the process of breaking down, it sort of, I don't know, goes crazy. Whereas normally it directs antibodies that attack specific invading organisms, after exposure to HIV-4 it causes the antibodies to turn on the body's *own* cells. The victim essentially . . . consumes his own flesh."

Grant cleared his throat. "Thank you, Doctor," he said. "That was very informative." He looked at Jeffers.

"Yes, thank you," Jeffers said a little nervously. Then he added, "So you die pretty fast with HIV-4."

"Yes," Mendez said. "Normally, the life expectancy of a victim is going to be a month or less. But here's the oddest thing of all. When it was first discovered, we thought it was a hundred percent fatal. Now, however, we know there is some small percentage of people who *do* survive. I'd say it's under one percent, though."

"Not very good odds," Grant said.

"No," Mendez said. "But *if* you survive, the virus disappears from the blood. Entirely. We have no idea how or why this happens. It's almost as if there's some tiny part of the population that develops an immediate immunity to HIV-4. When we discover the mechanics of *that*, well, I don't think it's an exaggeration to say that the whole science of immunology will change overnight."

"All right," Grant said. "Now for the sixty-four-thousand-dollar question. What in the hell is going on in Brisbane? Someone has deliberately infected two people in the past week. Do you have any idea how they'd be able to do that?"

"I'll try to help," Mendez said. "But I'm at the mercy of what passes for our local newspaper." Grant and Jeffers smiled. "Which I confess I don't read that often or that thoroughly. Could you just give me whatever details of the case you're allowed to?"

The two cops filled him in on what was known of the attacks on Wes Thomas and Lorene Greene. They included information on the syringe that had been taped to the motel-room mirror, after swearing the doctor to absolute secrecy in the matter.

"Thank you," Mendez said when they'd finished. He thought for a minute about what he'd heard.

Then he said, "Okay, in the case of the gentleman, there are two possibilities. Since he can't remember much about the night in question, it may be that he had intercourse with an infected person, and that she transmitted it to him. The other way would be that he received it by blood transfer. You see what I'm getting at. The hypodermic might have been used, or it might have been left there to mislead you.

"As far as the little girl goes, there was no evidence of sexual molestation, right?" The detectives nodded. "So she couldn't have gotten it that way. She'd had no transfusions recently?"

Grant and Jeffers shook their heads.

"Then I'd conclude that she received it by injection at the time of the incident."

"Say they were *both* injected," Jeffers said. He shrugged. "How? I mean, people don't carry bottles of this stuff around with them, do they?"

"No, they don't," Mendez said. "In fact, to my knowledge there is no such thing as a *bottle* of HIV-4 virus. There is, however, infected blood. The most likely scenario is that your perpetrators are injecting the victims with it."

Grant noted this down. "And where could they be getting it from?" he asked.

"That's a tough one," the doctor said. "All hospitals and blood banks screen for the virus now that we have a reliable test. They don't even accept blood that tests positive. If they do accidentally get some, it's immediately destroyed. And if a patient infected with HIV-4 loses blood while in the hospital, great care is taken to dispose of it quickly and properly. Frankly, I doubt that that's your source.

"My best guess would be that one or more of your perpetrators is contaminated himself. Or herself. And is using his or her own blood."

Jeffers grimaced.

Grant felt nauseated as well, but he said, "That might explain why, too."

"Yes," Mendez said. "Someone who contracted HIV-4 could conceivably decide to spread it to innocent people, perhaps if he thought he himself had only a few weeks to live. It's a truly horrible thought, but stranger things have happened."

Grant closed his notebook. "Well, I think that's it, Doctor," he said. He looked at Jeffers, but his partner shook his head. "The only other thing is, I'd like to talk to the people in this hospital who handle contaminated blood. Just in case."

"Of course. I'd be glad to set that up for you. Would you like to do it now?"

"Yes, right now if you don't mind," Grant said.

27

Grant and Jeffers found Janet Willen in her lab. She was dressed in her white smock, sitting on a high stool peering into a microscope. Her long brown hair was tied in a tight bun. Next to her on the stainless-steel table was a plastic tray filled with tiny test tubes full of a yellowish liquid.

The cops waited until Willen had finished what she was doing, then introduced themselves.

"Police, huh?" Willen said. "I was kind of wondering when you'd be showing up here."

"We've just been to see Dr. Mendez," Grant said.

Willen nodded. "Good choice," she said. "He's the best. So what can I do for you gentlemen?"

"We're curious as to how you'd handle blood that was contaminated with the HIV-4 virus," Grant said.

"Well, normally we don't get any. We prescreen everything, and if the sample tests positive, we don't accept the donation."

Grant had his notebook out. "What happens to the samples?" he asked.

"We incinerate them immediately."

"You keep records?"

"Yes, of course. There's a record of every drop of blood that's passed through this lab."

"How many samples have tested positively in the past, oh, let's say six months?"

"Only one," Willen said. "Fortunately, we haven't had many cases of the disease around here. But that one was kind of a special case, as it turns out. We actually ended up with a pint of that blood."

Grant and Jeffers looked at one another. "Uh, whose?" Jeffers said.

Disposal. Joanna Feene was on duty. The top half of the divided door to Hazardous was open; the bottom half was securely locked.

Husch introduced the detectives and said, "These men are interested in a pint of blood I brought you last week. Batch . . ." He turned to Grant. "What was it?"

"Batch 342-B," Grant said. "Thursday, August 9."

"The HIV-4 blood," Husch added.

Feene shivered visibly.

"Sure, I remember that," she said. "Who wouldn't? I put on the plastic gloves before I ever touched the bag. Clayton made fun of me, but *I'm* sure not going to take any chances."

"You have records?" Grant asked.

"Absolutely." Feene went to her filing cabinet and removed a folder, then showed the chart for the ninth of August to the lieutenant.

"See," she said, "here's a list of everything brought to me that day for disposal. Here's my check and initials for receipt of 'Blood Batch 342-B, One Pint, HIV-4-Contaminated.' And here's my check and initials for proper disposal."

"What'd you do with it?" Grant asked.

"It went right in the incinerator. Before I ever took my gloves off."

"You supervised the disposal yourself?"

"Yes, sir."

"Was it ever out of your sight?"

"No, it sure wasn't."

"Thank you, Miz Feene," Grant said.

"Anytime," she said. "If this is about those people in the newspaper, I hope you catch them soon. The whole thing gives me the creeps."

"We will," Jeffers said. "Soon."

"Anything else, gentlemen?" Husch asked. "I really ought to get back to work."

"No. Thank you for your time," Grant said.

"Brisbane has the best safety record of any hospital for three states around," Husch said proudly. "You can look it up."

"I'm sure," Grant said.

The two cops left the hospital.

In their cruiser, Grant slumped in the passenger seat and said to his partner, "Shit, Jeff, that damn blood, if that's what it is, could of come from any state in the goddamn country. Not even counting straight out of somebody's arm around here. I don't know. Christ, I don't know how we're ever gonna find out what we're dealing with."

"That's great," Jeffers said. "You giving up, Will?"

Grant sighed. "How could I? I was there when the Greenes come in. I won't forget that little girl as long as I live. It's just, we need a break so bad, and every lead we run down takes us smack into a brick wall."

"Maybe not. We learned a lot today. I did. Don't you feel like you're getting inside the heads of these people?"

"Yeah, I suppose so. God damn the crazy bastards. I just wish I wasn't so damn tired all the time. I ain't thinking as straight as I oughta be."

"You're putting in a lotta hours. And this McKey is a lead, I think. You want me to check him out?"

"Nah, I'll take it," Grant said. "You get with Pound and see what he makes of our latest confessor. You have a session with the guy too. Dealing with Pound, I want a second opinion. I'll track down McKey."

28

From his office, Will Grant put in a call to Andrew McKey. Considering that it was midafternoon on a weekday, Grant was mildly surprised to find McKey at home.

"Lieutenant Grant, Brisbane Police Department," he told the man. "I'd like to speak with you for a few minutes, Mr. McKey. What would be a convenient time?"

"Police?" McKey said. "What about?"

"I'm afraid I can't discuss it over the phone. May I come out and see you?"

"Get lost," McKey said, and hung up.

Grant looked at the dead receiver in his hand for a moment. Then he checked the address Janet Willen had given him. He decided to drive out to the man's house.

McKey lived on the affluent southwestern side of town. It was an area of rolling hills overlooking the Squier River in the distance. There were still a few horse farms about, and some country estates. And a couple of pricey developments.

Grant drove through the stifling heat to one of these. It was called Castlereagh, and the homes in it, if not exactly castlelike, were nevertheless regal in their own way. Each was set in a beautifully landscaped five acres of grounds. Hybrid poplars had been planted at the development's inception and they were now tall enough to screen many of the homes from the road.

The houses themselves were more or less in the Tudor style, with dark-stained exterior wall posts that weren't really structural, white stucco finishes, brick chimneys through which smoke never passed, red tile roofs, and stained-glass windows with leaded panes.

Andrew McKey's place was on a knoll at the end of a

long, curving asphalt driveway. There was an area set off
for parking, and Grant slipped the cruiser into it, right
next to a black Mercedes sedan.

The lieutenant walked to McKey's front door. Off to
his right were a paddock and small stable, neither of
which looked as if it had been used for some time.
Behind the house, Grant could see a pool glinting tur-
quoise under the merciless sun. He was sweating heavily
by the time he rang the doorbell.

The door opened to the width of its chain and two eyes
peered at him out of the interior gloom.

"What?" a voice said.

"Lieutenant Grant, Brisbane Police. Mr. McKey?"

The door slammed.

"Mr. McKey," Grant shouted. "I wish you wouldn't
make this difficult. If you'd just talk to me for a few
minutes, I won't have to come back with a search warrant."

The door was flanked on either side by tall, skinny
windows. Grant stepped to the right-hand one. He took
out his wallet, flipped it open to his police credentials,
and pressed them against the window. He rapped on it to
get McKey's attention.

There was a pause. Then suddenly the door popped
open and McKey was behind him, pressing a gun to his
skull. In the silence of the hot afternoon, the sound of
the hammer being cocked itself seemed like a gunshot.

"Lemme see that," McKey said.

Cautiously Grant handed his wallet behind him. He
waited while McKey looked it over. After a few moments
McKey grunted and there was the sound of the pistol's
hammer being relaxed. Grant turned around.

"You greet all your visitors like this?" Grant asked.

"Nothing against you," McKey said as he handed the
wallet back. "I defend myself from my enemies."

Grant found himself looking at a small man dressed in
an elegant silk robe that hung slackly on his body. The
expensive robe was in contrast to the rest of the man's
appearance. His long hair was uncombed and it was
obvious that he had given up shaving about ten days
earlier. His skin was pale, his face gaunt, as if he'd
stopped eating about the same time he threw away his
razor. He was barefoot.

He slid the pistol into one of the robe's pockets.

Grant wiped his brow with his jacket sleeve. "Could we step inside?" he asked.

"Here's fine," McKey said.

"McKey, you just assaulted a police officer who clearly identified himself. Maybe you got a permit for that thing and maybe you ain't, but I could take you downtown just for pulling it. I'm not in no mood to hassle with you. We can go inside and you can answer some questions and we can call it squared off even. Or we can get in my car and take a ride, either way. You take your pick."

McKey looked at the lieutenant with mistrustful eyes, but finally shrugged and opened the door for him. Grant walked into a gloomy mahogany-paneled foyer and was shocked by the air that hit him. It was hot and musty. He'd been expecting the pleasant chill of central air conditioning. Instead, the inside temperature seemed even higher than the outside's ninety. Grant's throat dried and he began sweating even more profusely, but he gave no indication of his discomfort.

McKey closed the outside door and led him into a room on the left, apparently a study or library of some kind. There were built-in floor-to-ceiling bookcases, a large desk, roomy leather chairs.

Grant sat in one of the chairs, McKey on the edge of the desk. McKey swung his foot back and forth. Grant pulled out his notebook, then took a hard look at the man he'd come to interview, and was unable to get his first question out. It was the first time he'd seen someone with the full-blown disease. McKey was dying, and it was obvious.

"Never leave a man alone," McKey said to the air. "He hasn't got enough problems, there's always the police."

"I'm interested in some blood you donated to the Brisbane Hospital ten days ago," Grant was finally able to say.

McKey laughed. It was a loud, hollow, ugly sound.

"Blood," he said. "That's a good one." He held out his arm. "You want some? Grade A." And he laughed again, spraying spittle. "Grade A useless. I don't have blood in here anymore, mister. I've got some miserable red stuff that's going to eat me up from the inside out."

"I understand that you have HIV-4." Grant said. "I'm sorry."

McKey mimicked Grant's sentence without actually saying the words.

"Did you know you had the disease before you gave blood?" Grant asked.

"What does it look like?"

"I don't know, Mr. McKey."

"Of course I didn't know, you goddamn moron! When *they* found out, *I* found out. Happy birthday, Drew."

"I see," Grant said.

"Sure you do."

"I'm sorry, but I have to ask you a few more questions."

"No *problem*. Support your local police. Go out as a public-spirited citizen."

"Do you know how you picked up the virus?" Grant said evenly.

"Ask my wife, why don't you? Louise," he yelled, "are you here?"

The house was silent.

"Gee, I guess she must've stepped out," McKey said. "Well, to hell with her. Who knows how you get the thing? You bang someone who's banged someone else—who bothers to trace it back? Somewhere in there, somebody got it and that somebody gave it to me."

"I understand that this is painful," Grant said. "I just have one other question. If you don't mind, where were you on the afternoon of the fourteenth? That was Tuesday."

"Hey, where am I every day? You think I go to work anymore? Why bother? I was right here. What'd you think, I was out selling my blood?" McKey laughed hysterically at that, ended up gasping for breath.

"What kind of work did you used to do, Mr. McKey?"

"Oh, investment broker, you bet." McKey's expression became wistful. "Clarkston-Wythe. I was the best. You just ask, anyone in the business'll tell you I was the best." He gestured vaguely around him. "As you can see."

29

Back in the bad old days, Brisbane had been a strictly segregated town. Negroes lived on the east side, whites everywhere else. When Claymore-Perkins had elected to locate their new pesticide plant in Brisbane, it was no accident that they'd chosen to build on the city's eastern edge. Land there was cheaper, of course. And, in addition, if there was ever a serious accident, the first people at risk would be black. That suited the white power structure just fine.

In the aftermath of the civil-rights movement, all that had changed somewhat. Blacks were now theoretically entitled to live anywhere they could afford the housing. So, in theory, Brisbane's neighborhoods had become multiracial. And there *had* been movement of families from one part of town to another. A lot of movement.

On the other hand, there were economic barriers to black penetration of certain areas. There were also some covert agreements among homeowners as to whom to sell to, and among realtors as to whom to show property to. The result was that certain enclaves, particularly in the west and southwest, remained exclusively white. The east stayed almost entirely black. Other sections integrated, to a greater or lesser degree.

The Jefferses lived in one of these integrated sections, to the north, on the far side of the Squier River. They had just finished dinner. It was one of the few times they'd eaten together since the day Wes Thomas collapsed in front of the desk officer in the Block.

Over coffee, Martin said to his wife, "We ain't had much chance to discuss this, but I think this case could be a big shot for me."

"I think so too," Clarice said. "If you and Will breaks it, the whole town'll be beholden to you."

"Well, I tell you, Clarice. I'm thinking something else. I'm thinking what would happen if I broke it myself."

"What you talking about?"

"I'm talking about what a black man can expect out of the Brisbane Police Department. Which is second cousin to nothing. Sure they feel like they got to hire some of us. But that don't mean they gonna promote us. You think when I got twenty years in I'm gonna be a lieutenant like Will Grant? I be lucky if somebody died and left me sergeant."

"Martin, don't do this," Clarice said. "You smart and you got the drive. You gonna get ahead." She patted her stomach, which wasn't beginning to show yet. "The boy gonna be proud of his daddy, you see."

"And that's another thing," her husband said. "We come a ways from where *we* growed up, but I want my son to have it even better than this. Which we ain't gonna do on my present salary. Anything better that happens, it's gonna happen because I make it. When I do something they *got* to recognize. And this is probably my chance to do it."

"I don't know what you're saying, baby."

Martin leaned toward her, his eyes intense.

"What I'm saying is," he said, "this is the biggest thing ever hit this town. If I come out on top, *I'm* gonna be one of the biggest things in town."

"You and Will Grant."

"Maybe, maybe not. I think there's the chance I can do some investigating on my own."

"Wait a minute," Clarice said. "What you saying? You gonna go after these . . . these HIVe people by *yourself*?"

"I got some ideas."

Clarice stared at him in horror. "Oh, no," she said. "Martin, no. Them people killers!"

"I ain't talking about nothing dangerous," Martin said hastily. "Ease up, girl."

"I can't help it. The whole thing gets me churned up inside. I don't even want to *think* about you out there alone. If something was to happen to you, what would I . . . do?"

Martin reached over and gently massaged the back of his wife's neck.

"Easy," he said. "I'm not talking about taking on these people by myself. I'm just talking about doing some poking around on my own, following my hunches. That's what's gonna break this case. Soon's I find out anything, don't worry, I get the whole of the police behind me."

"Poking around, like what?" Clarice asked suspiciously.

"Like today, for example." A little excitement crept into his voice. "We went to the hospital, talked to some Mex doctor about this kind of virus. We found that some guy donated a pint of infected blood week before last. Well, that was some news. So we tracked it through the hospital from when they discovered what it was to where they destroyed it. Another dead end, is what Will Grant thought. But you know what I think? I think that pint of blood somehow got out of the hospital and that's what's causing all the trouble now."

"How you come to think that?"

"Hunches, like I said. Will's a good cop, but he's white. Other white people, he don't necessarily know when they telling him the truth or lying through they teeth. But *we* know. We got to deal with that stuff our whole lives."

"So what?"

"So this," Martin said. "What I figure to do is keep my eyes open and see can't I tell when we getting a phony story. And that's what I think happened today. I watched these people that handled the pint of blood real careful. I believe one of them's lying."

"You didn't tell Lieutenant Grant?" Clarice said.

"No. He wouldn't've put any stock in my hunches. He just don't understand. Besides, the hospital got all these *records*, and white people *believe* that stuff. No, this one I think I go after myself."

"What's that mean?"

"Well, I was thinking I'd do it on my own time. Just investigate very quiet. If I turn up something weird, then I can go to Will with more than my hunch, and we can take it from there."

"I don't like it," Clarice said firmly. She folded her

arms across her chest. "I got our baby to think about, and I just don't like it."

"It'll work out, Clarice, you'll see. Don't you think I'm gonna be careful?"

"I don't care how careful you be, you get mixed up alone with them HIVe people, no good's gonna come of it."

"Well, I gotta do it," Martin said. "Don't you see? It's our *chance*, for us and the boy both."

"No, Martin. *You* the one don't see. I'm *scared*."

30

The HIVe had gathered together in the communications room. The lighting was subdued, and Glorio was standing on the dais, facing them. He'd tried to generate a positive trance state, but had failed.

"The message was there," he told them. "It is just that Joseph was unable to speak through the etheric disturbances tonight. But that only means there was no vocalization. His message was imprinted in my brain. I can retrieve it for you. Let me try."

He closed his eyes. The muscles of his face contorted with his efforts, then suddenly relaxed. When he opened his eyes, there was a slight smile on his lips and he wore an expression of contentment.

"Joseph wishes us to know that we have done well." There were murmurs of self-approval. "Our selection of those to whom we have passed the viral gift has been flawless. We must continue to concentrate on bringing members of the same two groups into the cosmic family.

"There should be those in positions of prominence, for they will inevitably draw attention to our cause.

"And then there should be those of youth, who will help the spread of knowledge through their potential for mutating and passing the seed on to their own children."

More self-congratulation.

"And by now," Glorio went on, "our brothers the Skulls will have received our letter. They will be coming to join us. Together, our message will be irresistible."

The HIVe cheered.

31

Saturday, August 18

The heat had abated with the arrival of a high-pressure system from the north. It was still seasonally warm, but the haze was gone from the air and the humidity had dropped off markedly. The sky was cloudless.

It was only two-and-a-half weeks before the beginning of the new school year. The weather was perfect for one final celebration of summer.

The chosen spot had been known for a hundred and fifty years as Lynch Sycamore. It was a bend in the Squier River, five miles west of Brisbane. The water there pooled up against the south bank, forming a natural swimming hole.

In the early 1830's, a plantation owner named Harper had been pursuing three runaway slaves and caught them at this bend in the river. One had jumped into the water and tried to swim across. He had drowned. The others had surrendered to their master, thinking they would be returned home and, at worst, beaten for their misconduct.

Instead, Harper and his men had thrown a rope over one of the branches of a large sycamore growing by the riverbank. The remaining two slaves were lynched and the site of the deed received a name it would carry down through the years.

The murder of the slaves was the last episode of intentional violence that would be committed at Lynch Sycamore, though it would continue to witness its share of death. Accidental drownings primarily, as the spot became popular with picnickers, lovers, and youngsters just out to beat the heat. There had been, in addition, one case of fatal snakebite, and in 1987 a terminal cocaine overdose.

150

For the most part, though, Lynch Sycamore was a place of fond remembrance in the hearts of most natives of Brisbane. It was the place one had learned to swim, or tasted one's first kiss, or become acquainted with the pleasures of alcohol abuse.

Physically, it was a picture-perfect setting. It was a ten-minute walk from the nearest road, down a well-worn path. Thus there was privacy. There was a flat table of land, mostly open, leading up to the riverbank. The earth had been tamped down hard by the feet of generations. All around was a mixed forest of poplar, oak, and sycamore, a number of traditional trysting spots hidden within it.

The riverbank itself fell a sheer ten feet to the water. Naturally, there was a rope swing so the more adventurous could fly out over the river, then drop into the pool. But the bank also sloped gently off to the east. The more cautious could reach the river by walking down this slope to a small pebble beach, and enter the water at ground level.

On this Saturday there were a dozen teenagers at Lynch Sycamore. Seven boys, five girls. Three couples and six free agents. There was a keg of beer and a pit fire and the smell of burnt hot dogs.

Ten of the kids—the boys dressed in boxer-style swimming trunks, the girls in bikinis or high-cut one-piece suits—ringed the fire, chugging beer, engaging in mock shouting matches, playfully antagonizing one another while building the feeling that this was going to be one hell of a senior class.

Mary Terry and Brian Sites had separated themselves from the group. It wasn't that they didn't share in the camaraderie. They'd rejoin their friends later. For now, they just wanted to be alone. So they'd come to a small open area surrounded by a thick clump of mountain laurel. They were within easy earshot of the party, but at the same time in their own little world.

Mary was a petite brunette cheerleader with a trim figure, oversize brown eyes, and a 4.0 grade-point average. Brian was a hunk, tall and blond and muscular. He quarterbacked the football team.

Brian was sitting cross-legged on the ground. Mary lay

with her head in his lap. They were having a conversation similar to several they'd had before.

"I just don't understand," Brian was saying. "The state university is one of the best in the country. What's wrong with it?"

"There's nothing wrong with it," Mary said. "For whoever wants to go there. It's not what I want."

"You think you're better than the rest of us."

"Brian, please. You're not going to change my mind on this. You've got a full scholarship; for God's sake, use it. But I *want* to go to Dartmouth, and with Daddy's help I'm gonna make it. State's not right for me, Brian. You know that."

"Dammit, Mary, it ain't fair. You know I can't get into no Ivy League school."

Mary gazed fondly up at her boyfriend. She reached up and stroked his cheek.

"I know, baby," she said. "I'm sorry. Let's just try to enjoy senior year, okay? When you get to State, you'll find somebody else. But I'll always be with you. I'll be there cheering for you every game, if you listen real close."

"There ain't nobody else," Brian said, "and there never will be. That's what *I* know."

There was a silence between them, and into the silence came a strange man's voice. The voice was loud and commanding, and it raised the hair on the young lovers' arms.

"Everybody freeze! Right where you are!" the voice said.

Brian was the first to recover. "What the hell . . . ?" he said.

"It's from over by the fire," Mary said.

Then there was a single piercing scream, cut short, as if in its middle. Mary rolled roughly off Brian's lap as he rose to hands and knees and began crawling toward the mountain laurel that screened them from their friends. As soon as she'd regained her balance, she came scuttling after him.

"Down on the ground! Facefirst! All of you! *Now!*" came the voice.

There were scuffling noises as Brian and Mary made

their way cautiously through the dense bushes. And there was a steady, low whimpering.

"My God, that's Amy," Mary whispered. "What's going on?"

"I don't know yet," Brian whispered back. "I can't see any . . ."

Brian stopped. He now had an only slightly obstructed view of the area around the fire pit. He gaped in horror.

His friends were lined up on the ground, facedown, their hands clasped behind their heads. Standing over them were four figures in khaki clothes with stocking masks over their heads. There were three men and a woman. The men were all carrying pump shotguns. The woman had a large leather bag slung over her shoulder.

"Jesus Christ," Brian said softly.

"Brian, what is it?"

Brian just shook his head. Mary scrambled up next to him so she could see what was going on. She stared at the scene, uncomprehending. Were they going to shoot all these defenseless kids in bathing suits? Why?

"Brian—" she said. "Brian—" And she grasped onto his forearm, her grip like the jaws of death. "What—"

Brian was equally mystified. But within him there were other competing emotions. Anger. And fear.

"Sister," one of the men with shotguns said.

As Brian and Mary watched, the woman set down her leather bag. Very deliberately she opened it and took out a pair of plastic gloves, which she put on. Then she took out a hypodermic syringe and a bottle of dark red fluid. She jabbed the needle through the bottle's rubber top and pulled back on the plunger, filling the syringe. The bottle went back into the leather bag.

"Oh, my God, Brian," Mary said. "It's blood. Do you think . . . ?"

The woman bent over one of the prone teenagers. The needle went into his left buttock.

"What are you doing?" the boy cried out. "What are you *doing* to me?"

"Next person who says a word gets shot," one of the men said. His voice was flat, emotionless.

The whimpering noises became more general, but no one spoke. Quickly, efficiently, the woman moved down the line, giving each of the victims precisely ten milliliters of fluid.

Brian was hyperventilating. His emotions had clashed, and rage had won out. He rose as if being drawn up by the plunger in the syringe.

"Brian, no!" Mary whispered frantically.

He never heard her. Grasping a stone that was the only weapon that had come to hand, he went through the screen of mountain laurel without a word and raced toward the fire pit.

Brian was fast. He almost made it to the closest man before the man heard his footsteps.

The man turned. He was tall and skinny, and he seemed unperturbed at the sight of the athlete bearing down on him. He remained calm even as Brian threw the stone, which grazed his forehead. The blow, though a glancing one, rocked him and cut him deeply. Still, the man held his ground.

As he threw the stone, Brian could see the man's eyes behind the stocking mask. They were bright and moist and didn't blink as he pulled the trigger.

Brian took a full load of double-ought buck in the chest. The force of it stopped him in mid-stride as effectively as if he'd hit a wall. He fell backward, blood geysering from the massive wound before his heart stopped beating seconds later.

The scream rose in Mary's throat, but she bit down hard on the inside of her lip and stifled it. She moved backward like a crab until she could stand upright. She crossed the little clearing, found the half-hidden path through the mountain laurel, and made her way into the deeper woods. Then she ran for her life.

The man who'd shot Brian said to one of the others, "See if there's anyone else up there."

The other man did as he was told. After a hasty search, he returned and shook his head. All of the teenagers were sobbing now.

The woman had completed her injections and returned her equipment to the leather bag. She nodded to the others.

The man who'd done the shooting said, "Don't even think of raising your heads."

The four masked figures went silently back down the path to the road. Before they left, the woman took a stick and cut words into the dirt:

The seed will spread
Welcome to the HIVe

32

The sun was nearly down before Grant and Jeffers drove away from the hospital. Their faces reflected the anger mixed with weariness that each man felt. For a while, Jeffers drove the police cruiser in silence.

Then Grant said, "So now we got four of them." He shook his head. "Jesus Christ, how many more?"

"Three men, one woman," Jeffers said. "They ain't afraid to shoot anyone who gets in their way. And they still could be anybody."

"I don't suppose there's any doubt all those kids have been infected."

Jeffers shook his head. "All but the one who got away."

"Goddammit, Jeff!" Grant banged his fist on the dashboard. "What are we gonna *do* about this?"

"I just don't know," Jeffers said. "Them descriptions we got, I don't think they gonna do us much good. The kids were pretty much in shock from the git-go."

"Especially the one who ran. Mary Terry."

"Yeah, but I got a hunch about that girl. She's the only one *saw* much. The rest had their faces in the dirt most the time. Once she comes out of it, she might have something more for us. I believe that girl can help us."

"I don't know. Maybe. Okay, you keep in touch with her, Jeff. She comes around, we'll see." He sighed. "God, I don't even want to go into town anymore. This thing with the kids is gonna be on the street by sundown if it ain't already. There's no way to keep it quiet."

"You thinking panic?"

Grant shrugged. "Who knows?" he said. "By tomorrow morning we might have people shooting their neighbors over a funny look. I wouldn't want to bet against it." He paused, then added, "Jeff, I'm afraid. There're so many guns. If a war breaks out around here, I ain't sure the good guys'll be able to win it."

33

Janet Willen preened herself in front of the mirror.

It might not be the most important date of her life, but then again, it might be. She'd never been invited anywhere half as luxurious as Pennington's estate.

A very rich, very powerful man, and he was sufficiently taken with her to have her to dinner at his home on the second date.

Little did he know what kind of woman he was linking up with.

Janet worked her magic with makeup and perfume, spent a full half-hour deciding on the perfect undergarments, completed the effect with a stunning black dress.

She pondered whether she ought to pack an overnight bag. No, a bit too forward, she concluded. It wouldn't do to give Pennington too many clues.

In the end she took only a small handbag and the little leather case with her syringe inside.

34

Sunday, August 19

The man in the stocking mask was standing outside the window, peering in. It was dark inside and light out, so Grant could see him plainly. But Grant was helpless. He lay in his bed, paralyzed with fear. The man was *that* close, and Grant couldn't get up and go after him.

And the man was laughing. Somehow, though he couldn't quite make out his mouth, Grant knew the man was laughing. Laughing at *him*. Laughing at his inadequacy. The laughter was soundless.

Then the man raised his arm. And there, in his hand, was a huge syringe full of blood. It dripped from the needle. The man pointed at Grant through the window. *You*, the man seemed to be indicating. *You're* next. Grant's whole body flushed and the hair on his arms stood straight up. He threw himself violently from side to side, but still he couldn't get out of bed. He tried to scream, and there was not even a squeak.

The man raised the syringe, higher and higher, holding it aloft like a gold medal. And then, with a violent crash of cymbals, the window exploded inward. . . .

Grant came completely awake in an instant. Instinctively he reached under the pillow and pulled out the small pistol he'd lately taken to sleeping with. He rolled off the bed and came up kneeling, the pistol's hammer cocked, ready to fire. His eyes took in the whole of the bedroom at a glance. If there'd been anyone there, he would have been able to shoot, and accurately, without thought.

There was no one.

The tiny room. The unshared bed. The single worn

dresser. The dirty clothes here and there on the floor. The closed closet door. The intact bedroom window.

The rest of the house was silent as well.

But the dream vision of the man in the stocking mask still played with Grant's imagination. And the sound of shattering glass—that had been too vivid. The lieutenant had an experienced policeman's mind. It was telling him there was something wrong.

Cautiously he got to his feet and edged to the bedroom door, which was ajar, the way he always left it. He hugged the wall next to the door and peered through the opening. He saw nothing but the empty bathroom across the hall.

Grant flung open the bedroom door and leapt out into the hall, facing the living room. His arms were extended, the gun in firing position, one hand wrapped around the grip, the other supporting it. But there was nothing more than the familiar sights and sounds of early morning.

He began to relax a little as he walked slowly down the hall, though he kept the pistol close to his chest. There was no one there. It had all been a dream.

But it hadn't.

As he stepped into the living room, he saw what had happened. The splintered ruins of his front window lay on the carpet. The air conditioner grumbled as it strained to meet the challenge of this unexpected blast of heat.

In the center of the mess was a brick. Grant set his gun on the coffee table and started in that direction.

The pain shot up his leg.

Cursing madly, he hopped over to the couch and flopped backward onto it. There was blood on the sole of his foot. He reached out and, very gingerly, extracted the sliver of glass. What an idiot. There was glass everywhere, and he was still barefoot. A barefoot middle-aged man in his underwear, he thought. Alone in his house on a Sunday morning, sitting on his couch with blood staining his carpet, staring at a brick that some dick-head had thrown through his front window.

It was even funny, and Grant chuckled to himself for a moment.

Then, skirting the circle of imploded glass, he went back to his bedroom. He deliberately went through all his usual morning rituals. Shaved, showered, poked around until he found some clean clothes. Only when he felt prepared for the day did he return to the living room.

First thing, he switched off the mightily laboring air conditioner. Then he crunched across the broken glass and picked up the brick. There was a note taped to it, of course. The note had been printed in a childish scrawl, perhaps on purpose. It read: "We want action, not talk. If you can't protect our children, we'll do it ourselves."

Grant shook his head sadly. It was not, he knew intuitively, the worst thing that was going to happen. He put the note into his pocket; there was the slim chance it would someday be evidence.

Then he set about cleaning up.

Three hours later, Will Grant was crossing City Plaza on his way to his office. It was Sunday, but he knew the case was going to be a seven-day-a-week affair from here on out. And it was easier to think about police matters in his office.

At ten in the morning the Plaza was already jumping. It had become, Grant thought, as garish as any carnival sideshow. He walked quickly and kept his head down, hoping none of the freaks would recognize him. There was no way of telling how violent the feelings against him might get.

Everywhere people were clamoring for one another's attention. A lot of people. They were there to protest or to inform, to maintain silent vigil or to blow off steam, to panhandle the big-city visitors or to market the inevitable trinkets of tragedy.

There was a haggard preacher, probably self-ordained, standing atop an apple crate, screeching his message out to the crowd. The sins of Brisbane were coming home to roost, he cried. And its people would suffer in their very blood if they did not repent. The coming of the Gustavia brewery was evil and should be immediately repudiated. For example.

Grant hurried along and made it into the Block without being spotted. He cleared the tight security checkpoint and went up to his office. He was grateful when he found it empty this morning. With meticulous care he arranged the case file on his desk, putting everything in chronological order. Then he went over what he had. He'd been studying the material for a while when his phone rang.

"Will, it's Dabney. Somehow I figured you'd be at work today."

'Yeah, for all the good it'll do."

"Can I come over?"

Grant thought about it, then said, "Ah, why not? You still got that pass I give you?"

"Sure do," Layne said. "Thanks. Be about twenty minutes."

Half an hour later, Grant and Layne were alone in his office.

"Whew," Layne said. "This town's on high simmer, my friend."

"Tell me something I don't know," Grant said.

"Have you seen some of the stuff they're selling out there?"

"Like what?"

Layne opened the large shoulder bag in which she carried the portable tools of her trade. First she took out a bright red T-shirt. She held it up for Grant's inspection. Printed across the shirt's front, in black, was a skull and crossbones. Below that was the message: "I survived the Brisbane HIVe."

Grant shook his head.

"And look at *this*," Layne said.

She pulled out a clear plastic water pistol filled with a dark red liquid.

"A *novelty* item," Layne said. "You use it to fight back if you're attacked. There're kids having water fights with this stuff."

"Jesus," Grant said.

Layne returned the souvenirs to her bag.

"Really brings out the worst in people, doesn't it?" she said. "But I suppose it's the only way a lot of them can deal with it. Turn it into a big joke."

"I don't know, Penny . . ." Grant began. He stopped, feeling awkward.

Layne grinned. "It's okay, Lieutenant. Whatever you want."

"I was just going to say that I feel like I don't even

know my own town anymore. It's like there's this whole ugly underside to it that I never knew was there."

"I know what you mean. I've been doing some poking around. Did you know that the gun shops can't fill the demand?"

"I would've guessed."

"And here's the scary part. People are harassing the gun-shop owners for instructions on how to convert semi- to full automatic. The owners are telling them to get lost, of course. But you can buy that information through the mail."

"I know," Grant said disgustedly.

"And I'll tell you one more thing. I've never seen so many loaded gun racks in the back of pickup trucks. I've even noticed them in a few cars."

"Yeah, church is out. But I sure don't see what we can do about it."

"Except catch these maniacs."

"Except that. You think we ain't doing our dead level best?"

"Hardly," Layne said. "I'm sure you're trying in your sleep. Anything new?"

"Uh-uh. We thought they was one, then two, now we got at least *four* to deal with. Sometimes I'd rather it was a gang of Colombian drug lords."

"What about those poor high-school kids? They give you anything to go on?"

"Nah. We got three men and a woman, half of which we knew about anyway. And for all the kids could tell, they looked like any three men and a woman you'd meet on the street."

"Damn."

There was a pause, but not an uneasy one, as the two sorted through their thoughts. Grant felt ill whenever anyone reminded him of the teenagers, but they weren't the worst. Lorene Greene still cut him the deepest.

Then Layne said, "You know, it's got to be some kind of cult."

"Beginning to look that way," Grant said.

"Well, how about this? Investigating local organiza- tions. There must be a good number of clubs and such, people who get together out of some kind of shared interest. Fringe religious groups, maybe. A lot of cults begin in innocent ways."

Grant nodded. "It's possible. But what in hell are we looking for?"

"I don't know," Layne admitted. "Something that . . . doesn't seem quite right?"

"Outside the ladies' garden club, who *is* gonna seem quite right these days?"

"Just an idea."

Grant made a note. "It's not a bad one," he said. "Be a lot of legwork, though. Every damn hobby's got its little core of fanatics. And I'm sure there's dozens that most folks've never heard of. Half a dozen people meeting in someone's living room on Thursday nights.

"Now, the hate groups, the KKK and whatnot, we got on them right away. But the problem there is, the victims aren't any particular race or religion or anything. So I don't really think it was them people. They've all got their alibis, anyway. And tell you the truth, the ones we've talked to, they seem as nervous about this thing as anyone else. Not nervous like they was *involved*. Just nervous."

"I'm getting a little that way myself."

"We all are."

"Okay, look, Will," Layne said, "maybe I can be of some use to you. I'm interviewing people all the time, anyway. I'll see if I can pick up word about any local 'club' that seems to be more secretive than it ought to be."

"That's fine. Don't go doing no cop work, though. Okay?"

Layne mentally crossed her fingers and said, "Okay."

35

Jim Teague unpacked his bags in his room at the Brisbane Arms Hotel. He was a stocky, athletic-looking man in his early thirties, with thick dark curly hair and a beard. He liked to work in his shirt sleeves, with the knot of his tie hanging two buttons down his neck.

In other ways, he was a neat, meticulous man. Within a few minutes his traveling clothes were folded in drawers or hung in the closet, his bottles and other equipment were lined up on the long dresser top. His notebooks were arranged on the table the hotel provided for meals taken in the room.

An hour after the plane had landed at Brisbane Airport, Teague was ready to begin.

36

Will Grant sat on his couch, alone, drinking a beer. He'd been able to persuade a carpenter friend to come and rig a temporary screen where his window had been. That'd help keep the bugs out. But until some replacement glass was installed, he'd have to live with the heat. At least it wasn't as muggy as it'd been a few days earlier.

Small favors.

Grant's TV was on, but he couldn't have told anyone what show was playing itself out across the tube. He was thinking about the case, and about all the useless leads he'd spent his afternoon running down. Maybe Martin was having more luck, if he wasn't taking the day off. Being a family man, Jeffers *should* take a day off once in a while.

What'd Grant have better to do?

The lieutenant sucked on his beer. He was drinking it for its coldness rather than for the alcohol. As he did, he tried to get his mind to switch subjects. He thought about the great country drinking songs he'd been listening to all his life. "Hey, Bartender" and "Whiskey River" and "Don't Come Home A-Drinking with Loving on Your Mind." He hadn't written a great drinking song himself yet, but he knew he needed one in his repertoire. That was one thing that never changed.

He thought about the legendary hell-raisers, from Hank to George Jones to Jerry Jeff. To Hank's own boy. A second generation of craziness, as if it could be passed down in the blood.

Blood . . .

And the phone rang. Grant twitched involuntarily. The sound seemed ominous in the hot, stale night.

Jesus, he thought. *Well, goddamn Sunday started out for shit. I suppose it's only right it oughta end that way too. How many more we got* this *time?*

He answered the phone.

"Lieutenant, it's Dick Fain." Fain was a uniformed patrol officer in the Brisbane department.

Grant cringed, but said, "Sure, Dick, what is it?"

"Uh, I'm out on Route 680, just past the Hudgins place. I think you better get out here. There's been . . . there's been a shooting."

"I'm on my way."

Twenty minutes later, Grant arrived at the scene. It was a relatively quiet state road. There were several vehicles pulled off on the shoulder. What traffic there was was being moved along by an officer with a flashlight.

As soon as Grant got out of his car, a man rushed at him. Reflexively Grant reached for his gun. Then he recognized the man as Treat Richards, a Brisbane CPA. He didn't know Richards personally, but he'd seen him around.

"Lieutenant!" Richards said breathlessly. "Boy, am I glad you're here. You'll understand. These guys have been giving me such a hard time, when they oughta be *thanking* me!"

"What's going on, Mr. Richards?" Grant asked.

Richards seemed to grow an inch or two on pure pride. "I *got* one!" he said. "I got one of them *HIVe* killers! Me!"

"Treat, what in hell are you talking about?"

Richards' words came out in a rush. "Well, I was driving down this road 'bout an hour ago. And I seen this car stopped." He indicated a dark sedan back down the road. "Lady was down with a flat tire. 'Course I pulled over myself, without even thinking about it. I try to help someone in trouble. But then quick I got to thinking, well, there's been so many strange things gone on of late, maybe I best be a little extra careful. So I took out this little gun I keep in the glove compartment. For emergencies? And then I went to see could I help her.

"Well, she had her a flat tire, sure enough. But there was something about her, you know? I kinda kept my distance there. She said she didn't have no spare and she wanted to know could she catch a ride into town, deal with her car in the morning. I said okay, but I'm still kinda keeping my distance. I got my hand around the pistol inside of my pocket.

"Then she said just a minute, she had to get something before we left, and she reached inside her car and took out this little box. That really put me on my guard, of course. 'What's in there?' I asked her, and I made her open the top of it. 'Just my hypo,' she says. And there was this needle and this little bottle. I knew right away what I was dealing with. She woulda stuck me too, but I was too quick for her. She didn't realize I had the gun.

"So I blew her away."

"*What*?"

"Quick thinking, huh? Is there a reward, Lieutenant?"

Patrolman Fain had joined them. Grant shot him a look of disgust, which Fain returned.

"Richards," Grant said, "your reward is gonna be some jail time."

Richards looked stunned. "But . . . but . . . *Lieutenant*, I got one of the *HIVe killers*!"

"Don't test my patience, Treat. We got laws in this state, and you just broke one of them. Where's the woman you shot?"

Richards just stood there. Fain motioned to Grant, who followed him along the shoulder of the road. Grant moved Richards in front of him, gripping him just above the elbow.

They walked to the farthest one in the row of cars, the dark sedan with the flat tire. There was an ambulance standing by close to it, waiting. There was no hurry.

The body had been covered with a blanket.

"Let me see," Grant said.

Fain hesitated.

"What's the matter?" Grant asked.

"Uh, nothing," Fain said. "It's just, well, we got an I.D. on the victim and I think maybe you, uh . . ."

"Oh, for Christ's sake, Fain!"

Grant reached down and pulled the blanket away from the dead woman. She was lying on her back, wearing a slinky black dress.

"Janet . . . Willen," Grant said. Confused, he looked over at Fain. "One of the HIVe?"

"Uh, I . . . I don't think so, sir," Fain said, and he handed the lieutenant a small leather box.

Grant opened it. For a moment he just stared, his face registering a mix of shock and disbelief. Then came the anger. It came from somewhere deep inside him and it picked up all of his recent frustration on its way to the surface. The first sound that came out of him was the roar of a wild animal.

He spun around and grabbed Richards by the shirtfront.

"You son of a *bitch!*" he screamed. "That's a diabetic's outfit! You killed a defenseless diabetic, you bastard! God *damn* you!"

And then he threw a punch that knocked Richards flat. Yelling incoherent obscenities, he pounced on top of the man, yanked his head up, and was prepared to hit him again when Fain and another uniformed officer grabbed him, one on either arm. He struggled against them.

"Leave me *alone!*" he shouted. "Leave me alone, and that's an *order!*"

"Ease up, Lieutenant," Fain said. The two men held him as he continued to flail wildly. "Come on, now, ease up."

Slowly the fight went out of Grant. The officers were able to get him to his feet. Richards lay where he'd fallen, out cold.

"You okay now, Will?" Fain asked.

"Sure, I'm *okay*," Grant said wearily. "The whole goddamn town is coming apart around me, but I'm *fine*."

Fain looked down at the unconscious man. "Hell of a mess, ain't it?" he said. "Turns a wimp like Treat Richards into a killer." He shook his head. "Good thing he didn't resist arrest more than he did. Who knows what we might've had to do?"

37

Clayton Husch lived in an apartment on the southeast side of town, in an area that had been slated for "renewal" for a number of years, but which no one had yet had the time, money, or inclination to renew. The apartment building was a pre-World War II white frame house, two stories, with two apartments on each floor. Husch was on the second floor, front.

Access to his apartment was from the outside. Stairs ran up along the side of the house to a landing, then a door let onto a tiny hall which separated Husch's rooms from those of Marie Tarrant, his neighbor.

It was almost eleven when Husch returned home on Sunday night, but as he was getting his keys out, the door behind him opened.

"Hi, sugar," Marie said.

Husch felt his body stiffen, as it always did automatically when he ran into Marie Tarrant. Or any woman who showed an aggressive interest in him, for that matter. Men were the natural hunters; women should allow themselves to be taken. That was his belief. He turned around slowly.

"Hello, Marie," he said.

Tarrant was dressed in a velour robe cinched only loosely at the waist. The front of it was open enough to suggest that she didn't have anything on underneath. The cleft between her large breasts was like a standing invitation.

Husch didn't like breasts much to begin with, and he was especially repelled by large ones. When he found himself staring at Marie's, he looked away.

Once, months earlier, Husch had invited Tarrant to a

channeling session, thinking she might be a potential recruit. She'd laughed, said she didn't believe in "that flying-saucer stuff." And that was that, except that Marie had apparently taken his invitation to mean he was interested in her in other ways as well. Though he'd never encouraged her at all, she still tantalized him occasionally with glimpses of her body.

"Hot date?" Marie asked, well aware of what had drawn his first attention.

"Yeah, sure," Husch said. "What're you doing up so late?"

"Waiting for you."

Husch just laughed. This was a scene they had played before. Marie knew she probably wasn't going to get anywhere, but that didn't stop her from trying.

"Come on, Marie," Husch said.

"You run into an angry husband, honey?"

Husch reflexively reached up and touched the still-raw wound on his forehead.

"Argument with a door," he said. "Might look bad, but you oughta seen the door."

Marie laughed.

"You're cute," she said. "And you got a sense of humor. I like that in a man."

"I'm also tired," Husch said. "So if you don't mind . . ."

Marie pouted. "I told you I was waiting up for you. Why you think I was doing that?"

"I give up." Husch sighed. "Why were you waiting up?"

"Bet you'd like to know."

"Look, I'm not in the mood, Marie. Okay?"

Husch turned and started to slip the key into his lock.

"Guy was here asking questions about you, that's why," she said in a sly voice.

Husch froze. He turned back around to face his neighbor.

"Who?" he said.

"Bet you'd like to know."

"Don't play games with me, Marie."

There was something in his face that Marie had seen before, once or twice. It gave her chills. It was scary, yet it was one of the things that attracted her to this man, that he could have that spooky side to him.

She felt a little brave this night. "Want to come in and have a drink with me?" she said.

"Who?"

"Okay, okay. Some black guy. A cop, he said."

"Cop?"

"Yeah, Jeffers. Martin Jeffers. Said he was a cop, he had I.D. and all, but I never know to believe those people or not."

"He's a real cop," Husch said. "What'd he want?"

"Just to ask some questions."

"What *kind* of questions, Marie?"

"Well, let's see. Questions about you, like I said. How long had you lived here, what'd I think of you, how long you been working at the hospital, what you do there, that kinda thing."

"What else?"

Marie thought. "Mostly what sorta guy did I think you were," she said. "You know. Cop questions. Who your friends are. Do you have any strange . . . habits, I think it was."

"Do I?"

"Nope, I told him. I don't know what he does around here, I said, but he sure as hell don't do it with me."

She offered a smile that Husch didn't return.

"Anything else?" he asked.

"Let me see . . . yeah, he wanted to know did you belong to any organizations, have any hobbies, like that."

"And what'd you say?"

"I said not as far as I knew. I didn't really tell him *any*thing about you, Clayton. I don't like cops. Especially black cops. What've you done, anyway?"

"Nothing. I . . . It's probably the hospital. They're thinking of promoting me so I'd have access to the drug cabinet. They do an automatic background check on anyone who handles narcotics."

"Oh. Well . . . did I do good? You know, he asked me not to say he'd been around."

Husch smiled for the first time. He leaned over and kissed Tarrant on the cheek.

"You did great, Marie. You're my friend."

Tarrant smiled shyly. She gathered the robe at her throat.

"Look," Husch continued. "You're doing the right thing. Cops got no right to go sneaking around in people's lives without telling them. If that nigger comes again, or any of his buddies, you'll let me know, won't you?"

"Sure, Clayton. You know I will."

"Thanks, Marie. And . . . good night." The two looked at each other for a long moment. "Maybe another time."

38

Monday, August 20

Glorio and Sandy Fraim got up late and did nothing for most of the day. Glorio was tired; the previous night's channeling had been a particularly difficult one. But he was also restless beyond what might be expected from simple fatigue.

Sandy recognized the signs. There had been, and were going to be, those inevitable times when the burden of Glorio's *possession* became so heavy that he struggled visibly with its weight. That was part of the curse of being who he was.

So she was not surprised when he suddenly switched off the episode of *The Sands of Time* they'd been watching. He threw the remote control at the TV.

"Screw you, Rebecca!" Glorio said. "You don't deserve him anyway!"

"No one can have Blake," Sandy said. "No one deserves him."

"I'll take her on *my* terms!"

"Of course, Blake."

"I'll have to set the house on fire. Fire is the only way to cleanse the soul."

"Do what you have to do."

Glorio brooded for a while. Sandy was silent, having long since learned the value of knowing when to speak. And in which voice.

Glorio put his hands to his temples and pushed on them, as if trying desperately to hold something in. His head moved violently from side to side. He seemed to be wrestling with it. His scarred face contorted with the effort.

Then, abruptly, he relaxed.

"Sometimes," he said in a monotone, "I turn the corner in the upstairs hall and I see Bobby Drew walking in the opposite direction. I don't think: *That's me.* I don't think: *That boy's going to have the best of everything.* It doesn't seem possible that anyone could have grown up to become me. I see that little boy and I realize that he died a long time ago, I mean literally died. And that somehow I *replaced* him. A different man . . ." He chuckled without humor. ". . . with a different face."

"I know what you mean," Sandy said. "I think the same thing sometimes, maybe when I'm riding in a car and I have what looks like a near-accident. I think, well, maybe I actually did have the accident and the person that used to be me is dead and the person still driving is someone else."

"That's not quite what I mean."

"I know that, too."

There was a pause; then Glorio said, "God, that was a hard night, Sandy. It's real. You believe that, don't you?"

"Yes. Why, are you worried that I don't?"

Glorio shrugged. "Sometimes I . . . The tricks . . ."

"The effects are important," Sandy said. "They serve to strengthen people's belief. But they're not the content, I know that. The Polarians' words are the content. Whatever helps those words to be heard is the right thing to do."

"The other voices have been strong. I . . . have doubts."

"You *will* have doubts. Joseph warned us of that. The other voices are the voices of your past conditioning. They're strong. What you're being asked to do goes against all that. You can do it, Bobby."

"Clayton killed that boy, as you continue to remind me."

There was a pause. It was a subject they'd gone over and over and been unable to put to rest. Sandy pulled one of the pillows into her stomach and wrapped her arms around it.

Sandy finally broke the silence. "That was wrong," she said. "He had no choice, but it was still wrong. There must be no more killing. It will poison the minds of the people against us. And rightly so."

"I can see that boy," Glorio said. "Even though I wasn't there, I can see him. He was in the way. The other voices *tell* me it's wrong, *you* tell me it's wrong. And I can *feel* it's wrong. But it isn't wrong. The voice of the Polarians is clear. The only wrong is to hinder the taking of the next evolutionary step. Killing someone who does that is not wrong."

"No. There must be no more killing. If death comes because the person cannot adapt, then yes. But cold-blooded murder, no."

"If that is the way it happens. I need you to stand with me, Sandy. I don't think I would have made it through last night without you. If I can't count on you, it's over."

It was a question. A question Glorio wouldn't even have thought to ask a few days earlier.

"You have my support," Sandy said. She started to add a qualifier, then thought better of it.

Later that evening, the HIVe gathered informally in the entertainment room, which they often used rather than the communications room when there was to be no channeling. Glorio had recovered his spirits, and his enthusiasm concerning the upcoming Skulls concert was infectious.

The group discussed the concert, scheduled in the nearby town of Dunmore, which had a college and an auditorium large enough to handle the expected crowd. Glorio was excited by the idea of the Skulls playing their music so close to Brisbane. Among the people who turned out, there were bound to be potential recruits for the HIVe.

And then there were the Skulls themselves. Their songs seemed to confirm that they were also in contact with the Polarians. It was time for the HIVe and the Skulls to link up.

There was also the question of how the Skulls should be approached, and everyone agreed it should be done cautiously. There was always the possibility that anti-Polarian agents were operating in the world. If there were, they would behave much as the Skulls were behaving, hoping to lure Polarian contactees into whatever trap had been set.

When all details relating to the concert had been settled, Husch asked for the group's attention. He then told them what he'd learned the previous evening from his neighbor, Marie Tarrant.

"What do you think this means?" Glorio asked when he'd finished.

"I don't know," Husch said. "This Jeffers and his partner interviewed me at the hospital, but I don't think they suspected anything then. He does now. And if he's investigating my life, sooner or later he's going to end up here. The question is, what are we going to do about it?"

"What do you suggest?"

"Well, our best hope is that he's working this on his own. He told Marie that if she had anything further to report she was to call him. She said he made a point of it, that it was specifically him she was to call. That sounds like a cop who's trying to keep something to himself. Which means we oughta be able to cut him out of the pack like a sickly dog."

"What do you mean, 'cut him out'?" Sandy Fraim asked.

Husch gave her a long, cool look. She represented a possible problem, he thought. He had lately come to feel that she might lack the strength of conviction required to carry out the cosmic plan set forth by the HIVe's Polarian contacts. The plan must be carried out *by any means necessary*. Sandy Fraim, quite possibly, didn't understand that.

For her part, Sandy thought of Husch as someone who always followed the shortest path between two points. And that was not always the most effective thing to do.

"I mean, cut him out," Husch said. "Those who get in the way must suffer the consequences. Our mission is more important than any individual."

"You think we should eliminate him," Glorio said.

"Before he has a chance to spread any misinformation. Yes, I think we should."

Sandy looked at Glorio, but couldn't read his face. She turned her attention back to Husch.

"We can't just kill people," she said.

"A lot of people will die from the virus," Husch said. "Even the Polarians admit that. It's a necessary part of the adjustment process."

"That's different."

"Not really. The goal is the same. So is the death."

"It's not. It's . . ." Sandy searched for the words, but the ones she found didn't do what she wanted them to. "It's cold-blooded," she said finally. "And counterproductive."

"Glorio?" Husch said.

"I don't know," Glorio said. "I think we need higher guidance, so let's put it off until after the concert." His expression brightened. "Which is what we're here to *celebrate*."

And the celebration began.

39

Tuesday, August 21

Will Grant was returning to the Block from his visit with Dr. Craven.

The news was bad. Wes Thomas was sick and getting sicker. The virus had taken hold and was spreading fast. Like Andrew McKey, Thomas had responded by retreating to his home and locking himself in.

Pretty soon everyone in Brisbane will be hiding behind locked doors, Grant thought.

The scene in City Plaza was bad too. There had been some theft. With the failure of the police to apprehend any of the HIVe killers, plus the continued hot weather, tempers were getting very short. The previous day there had been a minor scuffle, with only a few punches thrown before the participants were rounded up and jailed until they cooled off.

There had also been an attempt to build some shanties in the Plaza, so those demanding action could keep their vigils through the night. Kyser had immediately ordered the shanties dismantled and anyone not cooperating arrested. An emergency midnight-to-dawn curfew was put into effect. Civil libertarians squawked and threatened suits, but Kyser ignored them.

Grant crossed the Plaza, as he always did these days, quickly and without looking directly at anyone. He'd almost reached the Block when he stopped short. He retraced his steps. There, fixed to a lamppost, was a poster that had just barely caught his eye.

The poster was an advertisement for a concert. It featured a grinning human skull and below it the words:

See the Skulls
With Their Hit Song "Virus"
In Concert at Dunmore College
8 P.M.—Tuesday, August 21

Something clicked in Grant's mind. As it did, he heard someone shout, "Lieutenant!"

Grant turned. There was a woman running toward him. He didn't know who she was, only that she had a microphone in her hands and was trailed by a man with a video camera. That was all he needed to know.

Grant ran too, in the opposite direction. He wasn't in top shape, but he was fast enough to beat the woman and her colleague to the Block. He made it inside without having to field any stupid questions.

After clearing the checkpoint, Grant paused to catch his breath and let some of the sweat he'd generated dry. Then he went upstairs to his meeting.

Chief Kyser and District Attorney Sleeth were already there.

"Sorry I'm late," Grant said. "But I just got out of a meeting with Dr. Craven. Wes Thomas is dying."

Kyser and Sleeth looked at one another.

"Well," Sleeth said, "the charge already turned into murder when they shot Brian Sites. But I guess this is what we got to look forward to."

"Damn," Kyser said. His face was at least as florid as usual. "Don't we have *anything* yet, Will?"

"Not much, Chief. I'm sorry. And we're gonna have the awfullest time *getting* anything if people start shooting at the drop of a hat."

"Heard you blew your cool the other night, Will," Sleeth said.

"Richards ain't about to make a big deal of it," Grant said evenly. "He's looking at trouble enough as it is."

Grant didn't want to admit it to anyone, but he *had* blown his cool. For the first time in a long, long while. He didn't know if there was a connection, but the following day he'd had a blinding headache, the worst of his life. He'd had a lot of responsibilities in the aftermath of the shooting on the highway, but he'd done little more than go through the motions. As soon as he reasonably could, he'd returned home and gone to bed. He'd slept for twelve hours without stirring.

He felt bad about losing his temper, but not about slugging the trigger-happy Treat Richards. And he had to wonder what else was going to happen to him before this was all over.

"I'll buy that," Sleeth said. "I'm pretty sure his lawyer will agree to forget the incident if we agree not to add resisting arrest to the charges."

"Yeah, but you better nail the bastard good, Sleeth," Kyser said. "We need to make a example out of him, and now. Or we're gonna wish we had."

"I intend to do my job," Sleeth said.

"And how about your investigators?" Kyser asked the D.A. "They come up with anything yet?"

"Nothing usable."

"Y'all are working together on this, right?" Kyser looked from Sleeth to Grant and back again. "You better had be, or the mayor's gonna be royally pissed."

The two men nodded.

"He wants results," Kyser said. "If Thomas is dying, the little girl's next. And when *she* dies, the lid on this town's gonna blow sky high. We better get *some*body in custody before that happens."

The other two nodded again.

"Okay," Kyser said.

"There's something else, Chief," Grant said. "I saw a concert poster on my way in here. The Skulls are playing over to Dunmore tonight."

"Who in Christ are the Skulls?"

"They're that hard-rock group, they had a song called 'Virus' that none of the radio stations would play but it was still a hit. It was in the papers a while back."

"Never heard of them," Kyser said. "So what?"

"The song's called 'Virus,'" Grant repeated. "I believe they associate it with Satan worship or some damn thing. They're about the last folks in the world we need around here right now. You see what I mean?"

"Yeah, I do," Sleeth said. "There could be trouble if the notion gets around that the HIVe killers are devil worshipers. We could have a holy war, with a lot of innocent people caught in the middle."

"Jesus Christ," Kyser muttered.

"Him too," Sleeth said, but nobody laughed.

"Well," Kyser said, "what in hell are we supposed to do about it? We gonna close down concerts? Then what? Bookstores? Movies? Get the governor to put the national guard in the streets? The damn thing ain't even in our jurisdiction."

"I know that," Grant said. "We can't take any direct action. But people from Brisbane are going to go to the concert. And if there's trouble, they're gonna bring it back here. Let me try to convince the folks in Dunmore to cancel on their own."

"Fine," Kyser said, looking at Sleeth.

"Sure, give it a shot," Sleeth said.

"And if they won't do it," Grant said, "I want to go to the concert myself. Me and Martin. It's an odd coincidence, them being here right about now. We might pick something up."

"Sounds like a waste of time to me," Kyser said. "But go ahead. Just make sure you don't step on any of Dunmore's toes in the process. We got good relations with their department, and I'd like to keep it that way."

"I'll be careful," Grant said.

The meeting broke up.

Sleeth walked back to his office, where he sat in thought for a while, then made an unnamed-source call to his contact at the newspaper.

"There's dissension in the HIVe investigation," he said. "Questions are being raised about its lack of progress, even within the police department. . . ."

Grant returned to his own office, where he immediately put through a call to Dunmore College. His call was transferred three times before he got to someone of authority.

"I'm sorry, Lieutenant," the spokesperson said. "But this is an important event to the college. These guys may not be artists to you, but they are to a lot of the young people around here. And they bring in money that we badly need for our other cultural events."

"I'm warning you that there may be trouble," Grant said. "You understand that?"

"Yes. We plan to have a wholly adequate police presence. And consider this, Lieutenant. The amount of violence you'd see if you canceled the concert might be a lot higher than what'll happen if we go ahead with it."

"I see. Perhaps you're right," Grant said, though he didn't for a minute believe it. This thing was about money, pure and simple. All the rest was idle speculation. "Thank you, and I hope I'm wrong."

Next Grant tried the Dunmore police. They were courteous, and concerned about what was happening in Brisbane, of course, but they'd had experience with rock concerts before, they said, and they felt the officers assigned to maintain order would be fully capable of doing so.

Fine, Grant told them. Would they object if he attended the concert? Strictly in an unofficial capacity, naturally. No problem, they said. They'd see that he was admitted as a guest of the town of Dunmore.

Martin Jeffers had come into the office during the conversation. Grant thanked his Dunmore counterpart.

"Jeff," Grant said after he'd hung up, "what do you think of the Skulls?"

"Who?"

"They're a rock group. I think what you call heavy metal. They baaad and they nationwide."

Jeffers grinned. "I still never heard of them."

"No reason you should've. But if you think *my* songs're lousy, wait till you hear the Skulls."

"All right, I'll bite. Why would I want to hear the Skulls?"

"I didn't say you'd *want* to," Grant said. "But you're going to."

"Uh-oh."

Grant explained why he thought they should go.

"Aw, shit," Jeffers said when he'd finished, then added, "You got a extra set of earplugs you could bring?"

40

The Dunmore College auditorium doubled as the athletic field house. It wasn't huge, but it could still pack over five thousand people into its bleacher-style seats. When Jeffers and Grant arrived, it was beginning to fill.

"You know, I thought it was a good idea to check out who was coming to this concert," Grant said as people began to arrive. "Now I'm not sure I wanted to know."

"Say it again," Jeffers said.

The crowd was not like any the two policemen had ever been in the midst of before.

The dress code seemed to dictate either denim or leather, or some combination thereof. Hairstyle ranged from mohawk to skinhead to long and stringy and moussed. Hair colors encompassed the entire spectrum. Red, orange, and yellow were often to be found on the same head.

Clothing was adorned with everything from chains to safety pins to razor blades to Nazi paraphernalia. The boys had the most elaborate earrings, while the girls favored short skirts, black tights, purple lipstick, and hot-pink rouge.

But what unnerved the cops the most was the number of people who were carrying weapons. Nightsticks and saps and knives worn at the belt. Lengths of chain wrapped around the waist.

The uniformed Dunmore police in attendance seemed unconcerned.

"It's all show," one of them told Grant. "We had one of these concerts before. The kids get rowdy and blow off steam and then they go home to Mama and Daddy. Don't worry."

Grant and Jeffers hadn't worn uniforms in years, but in

a crowd like this, Grant, in his rumpled leisure suit, and Jeffers, with his spit-shined shoes, might just as well have been wearing signs that had COP printed in big block letters. The looks they received said plainly that everyone knew who they were.

Laughing hysterically, one boy offered Jeffers a hit off a joint, but Jeffers turned it down. He looked helplessly at his buddy, but Grant reminded him that they weren't there in any official capacity. It was up to the locals to make police decisions.

Ten minutes before the concert was due to start, some Brisbane teenagers arrived. A whole gang of them. With their modest haircuts and sport clothes, they stood out like neon against the general metal backdrop.

Four of the visitors from Brisbane had been among those attacked at Lynch Sycamore.

Grant immediately alerted the Dunmore police, but they reassured him that anyone was welcome to attend the concert, anyone at all.

"Jeff," Grant said to his partner, "you getting the feeling I'm getting?"

"You know it," Jeffers said. "I believe we in for one long night tonight. Them Dunmore cops don't know the HIVe from the ladies' bless 'em ogzillarary."

The Brisbane detectives continued to watch the arriving crowd closely. But there was nothing to see except the waves of spiked hair and sneering faces.

Then the houselights went down.

The concert was starting only twenty minutes late, which for this type of show was phenomenal. Grant and Jeffers stood at the back of the auditorium. If there was anything else to see this night, it was going to happen onstage.

Five minutes passed, and what happened was nothing. Some roadies came out and checked equipment. One of them sat at the drum kit and beat out some rhythms, but he obviously wasn't one of the Skulls. Some members of the audience hooted and threw things at him, and he retreated backstage.

The delay was of course part of the stage act. And the crowd either knew that or didn't care. As the minutes passed, they simply worked themselves up to a higher level of rowdiness.

Grant glanced at the nearest uniformed Dunmore cop. He thought he saw the beginning of concern in the man's face.

Dusty Rhoades and his friends couldn't have timed it better. They entered the auditorium seven minutes after the lights had gone down. Had Grant and Jeffers seen them, they would surely have alerted their Dunmore counterparts that these people didn't belong. But the vigilance committee slipped in unnoticed and groped their way to their seats.

Ten minutes gone, and still nothing. Then, almost inaudibly at first, the beating of a single drum. It was as if it were in the far distance, on the other side of the mountain. It beat on incessantly as the tape loop played over and over. Before they knew what had happened, the kids in the audience were vibrating to its insistent rhythm. Even Grant and Jeffers weren't immune to the drum's tugging at the pulse of their blood.

Around the time the drum broke through the subliminal level, the HIVe walked into the auditorium. Grant and Jeffers didn't see them, but would probably not have noted them if they had. Because Glorio the actor had been at work. Every member of the HIVe had been transformed. They were going to a costume party and they were in costume. Their own parents would hardly have recognized them. When the lights came up, they were going to blend in perfectly.

It had been Glorio's idea, a symbolic offering to their brothers, the Skulls.

They too found their way to their places.

The audience was now complete, and as if on cue, the stage went completely black. At the same time, the drumbeat increased in volume until it threatened to tear bodies apart with its vibration. The crowd was on its collective feet, screaming and stamping its approval. People had begun to bump one another in the patterned violence of slam dancing.

It was a hot night, but Grant knew he was sweating from more than just the heat.

And then the stage exploded.

Literally.

There was a flash of light, sparks flew, smoke billowed out into the audience.

Under cover of darkness, the Skulls had come onstage. They seemed to emerge from the explosion as the special-effects director skillfully brought up the spotlights, one after the other.

Blood red for Death Aims, the lead singer. He stood at stage center, clutching his cordless mike, staring upward. Then blue for Trance, the lead guitarist, his hands poised over his classic Telecaster, one leg slightly lifted. Then yellow for Speed, the drummer, his sticks raised as if in supplication to whatever gods were in control of this performance. And finally sea green for Bloat, the grotesquely obese bassist, sitting cross-legged on the floor as if it would be too great an effort to stand up.

They were all dressed in skintight black costumes with white skeletons painted on them. In the show's careful lighting, the skeletons appeared to dangle unsupported from the heads of the musicians.

The audience went berserk. They screamed and gyrated and flailed.

"Death *Aims*! Death *Aims*!" they chanted.

Grant felt as if his own skull had cracked and his life was leaking out through the fissure. He looked at his partner. Jeffers was staring at the stage, his expression completely blank.

For a moment the stage show hung suspended in some space far distant from the crispy rice and white sugar of everyday reality; then Trance let his pick hand fall. The sound of a single power chord reverberated through the auditorium. If anything, the crowd screamed louder.

The chord reverberated on and on, prolonged electronically, and then Trance hit the guitar strings again. Drums crashed, the bass picked up the rhythm, and the song began.

It was the irresistible throb of "Virus."

The crowd thundered its approval. It moved as if it were a single multicelled organism, its components bouncing off one another in the random movement of molecules.

Death Aims leapt and whirled and shrilled the lyrics into his mike:

Rotting bodies on the sand
Fission-activated glands
It walks upon this hallowed land
Watch it spread

Ahhhhhhhh THE VIIIIRUS

The audience sang along, screamed along. Grant felt
the hairs all over his body rise from the skin, as though
the air had become electrically charged beyond resistance. His partner looked at him, and Grant knew Jeffers
was feeling the same things.

The song's lyrics hammered on half-deafened eardrums,
and then there was an instrumental break. Death Aims
jumped and spun and cakewalked over to the seemingly
comatose Bloat, who was somehow able to keep his
fingers flying up and down the neck of the bass guitar.

Death Aims leaned over and stuck out his tongue.
Bloat, without missing a beat, raised his head and stuck
out his tongue too. The two tongues entwined, and the
kids loved it. Then Death Aims danced away.

He whirled his way over to his lead guitarist, who
ignored him. Death Aims shook his whole body, especially his pelvis, in a mute attempt to capture Trance's
attention. Still he was ignored. He pointed a finger at
Trance. Sparks leapt from his fingertip.

Trance shook as if he was sitting in the electric chair.
His guitar wailed in disbelief. He and Death Aims stood
toe to toe, shimmying their pantomime of electrocution.
The guitar screeched its way into its highest register.

And then there was silence from the stage. The band
members froze and held their positions. It was a moment
of caesura in the song, calculated to build audience ex-
pectation to a still higher peak.

The crowd knew the pause was coming. Its screaming
ceased on the last note of the guitar.

Grant couldn't believe his ears. The unbearable ca-
cophony of a moment before had vanished and a pin
could have dropped in the hall and been heard.

But it wasn't the sound of a pin dropping that broke
the silence.

It was a human voice, yelling, "*Kill* the bastards!"

At the same moment, the first missile was launched. It was a foam-rubber ball with spikes embedded in it so the points protruded everywhere. Someone threw it at the stage. Someone with the arm of a seasoned relief pitcher.

The ball hit Death Aims in the head. It glanced off and fell to the floor, but blood ran down Death Aims's face. Death Aims stood there as if nothing had happened. And then he smiled. The smile, perched above the skeleton costume, was like the grinning face of death itself.

"You *want* it?" he shrieked into the mike. He wiped the blood from his head and smeared it on the crotch of his stretch pants. "Come on down and *get* it!"

And all hell broke loose.

The Brisbane teenagers, one of whom had thrown the original ball, loosed a volley of missiles against the band. Stones and lengths of hard locustwood and balloons filled with acid.

Someone had the sense to bring up the lights.

The Dunmore police, finally realizing this wasn't part of the show, began to move. They came down the aisles, hands on nightsticks or aerosol cans of Mace, ready to contain whatever violence was about to erupt.

But they were completely outnumbered. The crowd surged toward the stage, swallowing them whole. Those who had harbored long-standing ill will toward the cops had their moment of revenge.

The Brisbane teenagers tried to storm the stage but got caught up in the general melee. Everyone was fighting everyone else. There was no sense to it.

Members of the vigilance committee were stunned. They had come with the intent of disrupting the concert, and they'd been upstaged. They looked from one to another, realized they were way, way over their heads, yet there was no escape. They were a small group of middle-aged men and women trapped in the midst of an enraged mob. There was no choice but to fight for their lives.

The Skulls were hanging tough. They fought with their fists and their musical instruments. They held the stage and didn't give an inch. Even as he found himself at the center of the storm, Death Aims was thinking: *Far* out! *This is the best concert* ever!

Grant and Jeffers joined up with some of the Dunmore cops. They formed a phalanx and pushed their way toward the stage.

As they did, there was another group, one row over, that was trying to get out. It was the HIVe, although in the confusion no one could have positively identified even his nearest neighbor.

And yet, there was one moment. Jeffers looked to his left, and there he saw a group going in the opposite direction from his own. A motley gaggle of painted people with Day-Glo hair. Indistinguishable from the rest of the crowd, and yet . . .

Jeffers zeroed in on one of the men. A tall bearded man. *I should know him*, Jeffers thought.

He tried. In the midst of the chaos around him, he tried. A familiar face, and yet with the wild hair and the beard and the makeup he couldn't put a name to it. It was a face that belonged to a person who should not have been there. A face for which he knew he had a name, but the name would not come.

There was a wound high on the forehead of that face, a wound that looked real.

Then the person was gone, lost in the crowd. And Jeffers' attention returned to his most immediate need, to keep himself in one piece while the phalanx worked its way toward the stage.

He acquitted himself well. Both he and his partner did.

41

The HIVe assembled in the entertainment room. Its members had washed off their makeup, changed out of their concertgoing costumes.

They'd been lucky. They were far enough back in the auditorium that they'd been able to make it to the exits without becoming involved in any serious fighting. They were well on their way back to Brisbane before reinforcements arrived at the college and mass arrests began to be made. No one from the HIVe would be spending long hours the following morning being processed by the undermanned Dunmore Police Department.

The mood of the group was, however, definitely down, and Glorio was aware of this.

"Tonight was not a setback," he was telling them. "We will eventually make contact with our brothers in the Skulls. The time was just not right. But there is still much to do. We need a public statement. Let us draft one now."

That got the HIVe buzzing. There was much talk back and forth about what the statement should say. In the end, though, consensus was reached, and Glorio printed the statement on a sheet of plain paper, in simple block letters. It read:

> People of Brisbane—We are the future. Only through adaptation to the virus known as HIV-4 can our race evolve. Do not fear it. Join us. Welcome to the HIVe.

After writing the message down, Glorio read it out to the group in his beautiful tenor actor's voice, wishing only that he could deliver it to the people of the world in the same way. When he'd finished, everyone in the room applauded wildly.

"This," he said, waving the paper, "will be delivered tonight. The whole of Brisbane will see it on the front page tomorrow."

There was more cheering.

"And we must draw yet more attention to our cause. We must select those who are to receive the seed, and we must select them well. The more prominent and well-known they are, the more recognition will come to us and, ultimately, the more successful we will be. We must expect that those in the public eye will take steps to isolate themselves from us, but we must not let that deter us. My own feeling is that we should next turn our attention to those who now most strongly oppose us."

"Mayor Davis!" someone suggested.

"Kip Kyser!"

"Lieutenant Grant!"

"The district attorney!"

"That woman reporter!"

The names were shouted out. Each was greeted with general approval. Someone suggested Edna Clint, the registrar of voters, while someone else thought it fitting that Dusty Rhoades should follow the lead of his partner, Wes Thomas. The list grew, as the names of judges, political officeholders, business persons and socialites were added.

"Excellent suggestions," Glorio said. "I will think on who suits us best. But in the meantime, we must consider our supply of blood. It must be continually refreshed."

"I think I have the answer to that," Husch said.

"Brother Clayton," Glorio said.

"The viral seed works quickly," Husch said. "Or it doesn't work at all. Thus the recipient becomes, within a few weeks, the next donor. All we have to do is wait for that to happen." He paused, savoring the moment. "The latest word around the hospital is that it has taken with Wesley Thomas."

There was silence.

Then plans were made. There was no point in waiting. This night would be a glorious one after all.

42

Wesley Thomas lived in a home that had been occupied by members of his family for generations. It was a four-thousand-square-foot story-and-a-half white Colonial on the Squier River, half a mile upstream from the proposed site of the Gustavia brewery. The family-owned property surrounding the house had dwindled steadily in recent years, but it still amounted to over three hundred acres.

It was a large spread for a single man, but Thomas had clung to it with the tenacity of someone who realized that his real estate was the only thing he had that suggested he continue to be included among the town's elite.

He required help, of course. A groundskeeper and a housekeeper and a part-time cook. None of them lived in; in fact, they already cost him more than he could really afford. But appearances were kept up, and few bothered to wonder what it must be like to live in such a place all alone.

Now that he was dying, it was purest hell.

At first he'd walked from room to room, picking things up and setting them down, blasting the TV and the hi-fi at the same time to keep away the silence, loading himself with liquor so he might eventually have a few hours' merciful sleep.

And he'd hired a woman to come to him, but that had been a disaster. He knew he could pass the virus on, and his guilt had rendered him impotent.

In the end, there were tranquilizers. If he took enough of them, he could sit for hours, unable to move. At the end of the day he could put himself to sleep. And there was always the possibility that he might overdose, letting death overtake him without his knowing.

Thomas passed his nights fully drugged, and his days in as much of a stupor as he could induce. He learned this about tranquilizers: they might immobilize you, they might chain you to your chair, but they could not turn off your mind. So while his body was inert, the demons continued to rage inside his head. And that, he thought, was as close to hell as you might come on this earth.

Dusty Rhoades had been in to see him earlier in the day. Dusty was so transparent, Wes wondered how he could have gone so many years without seeing what the man was really like. He used people. That's what Dusty was about, using people to get what he wanted.

Yeah, he'd been oh so sympathetic. His partner *was* dying, after all. But soon enough he'd gotten around to what was actually on his mind. Death be damned, the Gustavia brewery had to go through. Otherwise, Dusty would be out a lot of bucks.

Rhoades had tried to dress it up by saying that that was what his partner would want, wasn't it? Life to go on. Brisbane to profit from the influx of beer money. Window dressing was all it was. Dusty was desperately trying to cover his own ass, and he couldn't do it without his dying buddy's help.

Screw Dusty Rhoades.

Thomas felt the pain rising again. Bodies cannot turn upon themselves without a lot of pain. It was more than he'd ever known. It felt as though something was chewing on the raw ends of his nerves. Maybe something was.

The doctors didn't have any firsthand idea what the pain was all about, of course, but they must have reckoned it was going to be bad because they'd prescribed as much painkiller as he could possibly use.

He dropped some Demerol on top of the tranquilizers he'd taken earlier.

It was bad enough to suffer the anguish of the mind that came with the certainty of imminent death. There was no need to endure the physical pain as well.

Except that the drugs only took the edge off. They didn't make it go away.

And then there was the cold. He was so cold all the time. Cold enough that he would turn the heat on at night and keep all the windows closed in the middle of one of the most torrid Augusts on record.

He shivered in front of the fire he'd built. The temperature in the house was close to a hundred, and still he was cold. The cold penetrated so deeply that he might just as well have been curling up in an alpine snow to die.

To die.

That's what it was. Millions of people walked the streets of their lives without the moment-to-moment awareness that they were dying, just as certainly as he. The difference was in knowing when. So long as that was concealed from you, you carried on. But once you knew for sure that there were only days or weeks left, it was all you were able to think about. It turned your mind into mush, blotted out your soul. The only sound you ever heard, the *only* one, was the ticking of the clock. And it was so loud that your eardrums screamed.

The line ends here, Thomas thought as he stared into the fire, his limbs heavy as sand, his muscles slack and useless. Wesley Thomas the Third. Without heirs. In the final hour, as useless as his drugged muscles.

And how had it come to this? That was hardest of all to accept. For it had been blind, ignorant chance.

What if he'd been celebrating the brewery deal a day earlier, or a day later? What if he'd gone to the Kit Kat Club instead of the Inferno? What if he'd gone home before ordering the fifth toasted almond? What if the guy on the other side had been quicker to light the woman's cigarette?

What if, what if. You could look at a sequence of events closely enough that there was an infinite number of points at which it could have branched off in an entirely different direction.

But this one hadn't. *He* had been the one to go with the woman to the Green Brae Inn. *He* had been the one to awake to the message on the mirror. *He* was the one now living the horror whose end drew ever closer.

The fire flickered six feet from where he sat. The various drugs coursed through his bloodstream. He couldn't help but wonder what they did when they met up with the virus.

That almost made him smile.

No. He never smiled anymore. There could be no greater indignity than to be this inert lump of matter huddling close to the fireplace in August.

Or could there?

The sound, when it came, did register in his mind, but just barely. His hearing was dulled by the drugs, but, perhaps equally important, he never *listened*. What was there to listen for?

Still, the sound registered. It was out of place. There should have been only the crackling of the burning logs and the random creaks of a very old house. This sound was neither of those. It was the small sound of someone coming in.

Thomas didn't respond. Why should he? Anyone who wanted to enter could do so. What did he possibly have to lose?

And even if he feared the loss of something, his weight was far too great to permit him to rise from his chair.

The three people walked into his room as quietly as possible. They wore dark clothes and plastic gloves and stocking masks over their faces. They couldn't have anticipated that they could have arrived with the Brisbane Marching Band and it wouldn't have mattered. Thomas would have been no more capable of stirring from his seat in front of the fire.

They came around in front of him, and then they knew.

He looked from one of them to another. Two men, one woman behind the masks. *What foolishness*, he thought. *Our faces are masks enough.*

"Who are you?" he was able to say. "What do you want?"

The woman had a leather bag over her shoulder. She had green eyes, Thomas noticed. Such beautiful green eyes, and what difference did that make?

The woman opened her bag. She took out a plastic pouch attached to a long plastic tube. She took out a needle which she fixed to the end of the tube. Then she gave the whole apparatus to one of the men, a tall lanky fellow.

"What do you want?" Thomas repeated, though he didn't think he really cared what they wanted. They could take his car, his stereo, his rare coin collection. Of what use were such things to him now?

Then the woman and the other man took hold of his arms. The woman rolled up his sleeve.

The tall lanky fellow approached Wes Thomas with the needle, and suddenly he realized what they wanted. The realization came in a rush that cut straight through the drug haze that enveloped him.

They were going to take his blood.

He tried to scream and he tried to fight them, but his arms and legs merely shifted position. The only thing that came from his throat was a sound like the mewing of an abandoned kitten in the night.

The lanky man moved in closer and Thomas smelled the garlic on his breath. Then he felt the cold plastic hands on his arm. They made his skin crawl. He tried to scream again but couldn't.

Then the needle punctured his vein, and what was left of his life began to run out of him.

43

Wednesday, August 22

Dabney Layne was putting the finishing touches on her second story for *AmericaNews*. It was due in at noon and she was just going to make deadline. Thank God for lap-top PC's and modems.

She was calling the piece "Portrait of a Town at War with Itself":

> The people of Brisbane are a people under siege, a siege not from without, but from within. They wait and wait, never knowing when or where the killers will strike next, for the HIVe plays no favorites. And the horror of it is that, while anyone might be the next victim, anyone might equally well belong to the HIVe.
>
> The town's citizens have responded in a manner ages old, by arming themselves and retreating behind the locked doors of their homes, trusting no one who isn't blood kin.
>
> As the levels of violence and fear rise steadily together, one thing remains clear. In a town at war with itself, there can be no winners, only losers. This thought must be uppermost in the minds of Brisbane's leaders as they struggle to prevent that war from breaking out all over.

Layne paused for a moment, then added some notes to her editor:

> Sam, I think this story's good for at least one more feature after this one. Now that Wesley Thomas, the first victim, has come down with the full-blown dis-

ease, the stakes have gone up. The HIVe's spreading of the virus has worked. There is a real human being dying because of them.

This makes the whole thing a lot less abstract, and of course it focuses attention on the little girl. Is she going to get it—the answer is almost certainly yes—or will she be miraculously spared? The human-interest aspect is intense there. People everywhere are going to want to know about her.

There is also bound to be interest in the idea of a town full of gun nuts with itchy trigger fingers. Brisbane has become like something out of the Old West. Make a wrong move, pardner, and you're dead. "We shoot first and ask questions later hereabouts."

And then I think there's a good possibility that there'll be a break in the case in the near future. Everyone is so on guard that it's only a matter of time before one of the HIVe people screws up and gets caught in the act. When that happens, I believe we may see a flat-out race between the law-enforcement people and the nearest lynch mob.

I'm continuing my relationship with Lieutenant Grant. He's still most likely to be at the center of things when they break. I like him. He's one of the few people in authority I've met here who doesn't seem like he's one hundred percent out for himself.

I've had a couple of drinks with District Attorney Sleeth too. He wants to get into my pants, though I don't think he's really that attracted to me. I must represent something of a conquest. Big Time Media Bitch. In any case, I lead him on a little bit in order to get him talking.

There is apparently a good deal of friction among the various city departments, as you might suspect. The cops don't trust the people in the D.A.'s office, and vice versa. Both have their own ideas about how the investigation should be proceeding. Sleeth thinks both Grant and Chief Kyser are incompetent and that *he* should be running the show. But as of now, tradition rules and the cops still hold the upper hand.

Mayor Davis is caught in the middle. He's running for reelection in the fall and he badly needs everything to turn out all right. He's backing Kyser at the moment, but that could change if the cops continue to come up empty. Davis might be forced to do something visible in order to prove to the public that he's doing anything at all.

You'd love it, Sam. It's a fascinating study in small-town politics and there's absolutely no way of predicting what'll happen next. By the time this is over, I'll probably have enough for a book.

Layne looked at what she'd inadvertently written and deleted the previous line.

"You don't want to know that, Sam," she said to herself.

Okay, I've got to go [she wrote]. Meeting my boyfriend. See if you can get a nice placement for me for this story, will you? Front cover, maybe? There's a love. Take care, Penny.

Quickly Layne proofread her article. Then she sent the contents of the file to New York over the telephone lines. Up-to-the-minute photos had already been sent by overnight mail.

Layne stretched, took a long, hot shower, then called Will Grant. He was still reasonably friendly, though this week's edition of *AmericaNews* wasn't out yet, of course. She invited him to lunch and he said yeah, he could use a break.

They met in a small home-style restaurant near the Block. Grant ordered up some ribs and hopping John, the staple Southern side dish concocted of rice, corn, and black-eyed peas. Layne ordered chicken, and was talked into trying the hopping John as well.

"No offense, Lieutenant," Layne said after the waitress had left, "but you look about half-dead."

"Long night," Grant said.

"I heard a little. What happened?"

"Goddamn idiots out to Dunmore College had this concert planned. The *Skulls*, for Christ's sake. Their big hit is called 'Virus,' would you believe it?"

"I've heard of them. They're heavy-metal Satan types, aren't they?"

"Beats me. They never got through the first song."

Grant was drinking beer with his lunch and appeared capable of handling it. On the theory that people don't really like to drink alone, Layne decided to allow herself one glass of wine. Any more than that and she'd be facing the possibility of an afternoon headache.

Grant knocked down half a beer without pausing for breath.

"Stupid asses," he said. "You'd think with all the shit going on around here that the damn band would've been invited not to come. I even called the college up and *told* them that no good was gonna come out of it. But no, the show must go on. They can handle it, they said. Sure, you just try to handle it when you turn out every loon for thirty miles around."

"You went?" Layne asked.

"Yeah. I thought . . . I don't know what I thought. Maybe that the damn HIVe theirselves would show up. And maybe they did, for all I know. Who could tell? Everyone in the place looked like a killer to me."

"How'd the riot start?"

Grant sighed. "You know," he said, "one way or another there was gonna be trouble. If it didn't come from the punks and the skinheads, it woulda come from someplace else. Like Dusty Rhoades's group you told me about."

"They were there?"

"You bet. They looked like warts on Miss America, they was so out of place. Couldn't've been any reason they were there except to start some trouble. But they never got their chance, 'cause somebody else beat them to it. Them teenagers that the HIVe attacked last weekend. They was there too. They started throwing things at the stage, and then all hell broke loose. People started hitting they didn't know who."

"Jesus. You okay?"

"I got a few bruises," Grant said, "but I'll live. I'm just tired. I don't know how many arrests they made up there. Right many. And I stuck with them the whole time. It wasn't the kind of night I want to have a lot of."

"Then I suppose you saw the HIVe's press release in the morning paper," Layne said.

Grant groaned and drank off another half beer. "Ain't that about the last thing we needed?"

"What do you think it means?"

"Who the hell knows? It's the craziest thing I read in all *my* borned days. They expect people to *join* 'em? Commit *suicide*? It don't make any kinda sense."

"It sounds like they believe spreading the virus is some sort of holy crusade. If they do, you're dealing with the most dangerous kind of people there are."

"That's what I know," Grant said. "I just wish the damn paper wouldn't have printed the thing. Begging your pardon, but I don't care if it *is* news. All it does is get people more worked up than they were before." There was a pause; then he asked, "How about you? Come up with anything yet?"

"Nothing you can use," Layne said. "But if the HIVe is a quasi-religious group out on a crusade, *some*body has to have an idea who they might be. They had to have come from somewhere. They can't be *that* invisible."

"I hope you're right."

"That vigilante group, are they going to get charged with anything?"

"Nah. Respectable business people, you know. They weren't the ones incited the riot. And a couple of 'em got banged up pretty bad, besides. They never even got booked."

"I suppose you'd better keep your eye on them, though."

Grant looked at her carefully. "I don't want any crap about vigilantes coming out in your magazine," he said. "You do that and we'll have copycats all over the place."

"Will, do you think I'd do that to you?"

There was another pause; then Grant said, "I guess I'm not sure when you're . . . working and not."

"You can trust me."

"Okay. Good."

Grant had finished up his ribs.

"Look," he said, "I've gotta get back to the office."

"I'll be talking to you," Layne said. "I'll buy today."

Grant had his wallet out. He hesitated for a moment, then dropped a ten-dollar bill on the table.

"Can't do it," he said. "It don't look right. I'll see you later."

Layne watched Grant as he turned and shambled out of the restaurant. She shook her head slowly, a small smile on her face.

An honest cop, she thought. *Snow tomorrow for sure.*

When Grant got back to his office, Jeffers was there. Grant immediately noticed the look on his partner's face.

"Let me sit down first," Grant said, and he did. "All right, what now?"

"Wes Thomas just got in touch with us," Jeffers said. He paused, as if having difficulty getting it out, then continued haltingly. "The . . . the HIVe made him a visit last night. And they . . . well, they took his blood."

"Ah, shit."

"He's got the disease now. Don't that mean his blood can . . . can be *used*?"

"Yeah, that's what it means. Damn us, but we shoulda thought of that."

"What're we gonna do, Will? Put a guard on everyone gets theirself shot up by these people?"

"Christ if I know. There's McKey too. He's got it. We better put someone on him for the time being. But you're right. Pretty soon we ain't gonna be able to keep up with it."

"Chief might have our asses now."

"No use thinking about that," Grant said. "We got work to do. Okay, you get a statement from Thomas. You able to turn up anything on that note that was delivered to the paper?"

"Uh-uh. Anybody coulda did it."

"Well, stick with it. See if they can't lift some kind of prints off it. It's one of the only things we got. Check the stationery stores. Try anything."

"Okay. What're you gonna do?"

"I'm going over to Dunmore. They held the Skulls overnight and I want to talk to them before they're released. I still got a funny feeling about them being here at all."

Grant hadn't said so, but his circuits were suffering from serious overload. He wanted to make the drive to Dunmore alone, just to *be* alone for a little while.

Since the night he'd punched Treat Richards, he'd
been able to keep his temper pretty well in check. But
the pressure on him had continued to mount. For virtu-
ally the first time since he'd become a Brisbane policeman, Will Grant did not believe things were going to
work out in the end.

He'd begun to think that either the fabric of his
hometown was going to be shredded beyond recognition
or that the case was going to drive him stark raving mad.
In his darker moments, he could envision both.

And he had doubts about his abilities as an investigator. Perhaps he didn't have the right stuff for this particular job. He was a patient man, and he worked hard, and
he was persistent. That was good enough most of the
time. But maybe not here. Maybe only a brilliant detective could solve this one. Maybe he just wasn't smart
enough.

The drive was very pleasant in the daytime. It took
him west, roughly along the course of the Squier River,
which rippled and glinted in the afternoon sun. Grant
tried to focus on the moving water, to let it work some
calming magic on him.

He thought about the family farms he passed along the
way, envisioning life going on there at its normal, season-
determined pace, oblivious of what was happening in
town.

He tried a lot of things, but relief was only temporary.
Time and again his mind returned to the central focus of
his life. There was no escaping it. Like it or not, the
immediate fate of Brisbane lay to a large extent squarely
across his shoulders.

Too heavy, he thought as he arrived at the Dunmore
police station. *Too heavy a burden for a man*.

The station was still a madhouse, as those arrested the
previous night continued to be processed. But Grant's
fellow officers were most courteous; he was given immediate special attention. They knew what was happening
in Brisbane, and they'd do whatever they could to help
keep it from spreading to Dunmore.

The lieutenant was given a private interrogation room,
and a few minutes later Death Aims, the lead singer of
the Skulls, was brought in. The young man was still

dressed in his skeleton costume. He'd gone directly from the stage to a cell.

"Who are you?" Death Aims asked. "Are you here to get me out of this fucking hole?"

The first thing Grant noticed was how much smaller the singer was than he'd appeared.

They look so big up there on the stage, Grant thought. *Larger than life, but then, that's the point, isn't it? In the flesh he's no more than five and a half feet.*

"No," Grant said.

The two men sized each other up over the small, aged wooden table whose top was an intricate network of carved initials and burn marks from long-ago cigarettes.

Grant offered Death Aims a smoke. He didn't have the habit himself, of course, but he usually carried a pack for occasions like this, when a friendly gesture might work wonders.

"That a tobacco cigarette?" the musician asked condescendingly.

"Yeah. It's all they allow me."

"No, thanks."

Grant shrugged and put the pack back into his jacket pocket.

"I'm a cop," Grant said.

"No shit, Dick Tracy."

"You've probably had your fill of cops the past twelve hours, I know."

"The man's a bloody genius. Look, let me out of here and I'm gone. I'm back to New York and I hope I never see this hick state again. *We* haven't done anything, cop. It's not our fault if the local kids are a little rowdy."

"I'm not with this department."

Death Aims folded his arms and said, "Then what am I talking to *you* for?"

"I'm a detective in the Brisbane Police Department. You know where that is?"

"Never heard of it."

Grant had asked the question casually, but he'd had his cop's sensors turned up high. He wanted to believe that the Skulls had some connection, however slight, with the HIVe. If they did, it was a lead. But the young man had answered without hesitation or any of the little physical twitches that tipped off a lie to the trained observer.

It was very, very difficult to lie to an experienced cop and get away with it. Psychos could do it. So could accomplished con men. And so could someone who had talked himself into thinking a lie was the truth. But for most people, the odds were too heavily stacked against them. The hostile environment, the authority figure across the table, the strong cultural bias against falsehood, and of course the interpersonal skills of the police officer, all operated in the cop's favor.

Grant didn't think the Skulls' lead singer was a psycho, at least not in the clinical sense of the term. And he didn't think he was a master con artist, except perhaps where his "music" was concerned.

No, Grant's instincts were saying the guy was probably telling the truth.

"You know what's been going on in Brisbane?" he tried.

"Brisbane what? Bloody Australia?"

"No, Brisbane *bloody* next door."

"Look, man, I don't know what in the hell you're getting at here. But if you're trying to get me to play your freaking town, you want to talk to my agent, not me."

"Uh-huh," Grant said. "Perhaps I'll do that. And who would your agent be?"

"Adam Kronsky. He's in the book."

Grant had the name spelled for him, then said, "And that would be the New York phone book?"

Death Aims looked at him like he was a moron. "Where else would an agent be?"

The singer's tone was as patronizing as could be, but Will Grant was far, far beyond the point where a kid's sarcasm could possibly bait him.

"Mr. Kronsky," Grant said. "He got you this . . . is 'gig' the proper word?"

Death Aims rolled his eyes and raised his hands in supplication to whoever his gods might be. "Oh, brother," was all he said.

"He did arrange it?"

"Of course, Mr. Detective. You think a musician has

the time to be hassling with promoters, lining up his own dates?"

"I suppose not. Do you know why he chose Dunmore? What's so special about here?"

"What's special about *here* is that you *arrest* people. We just *love* to get arrested."

There was a pause. The kid leaned back in his chair and regarded Grant with a sullen look. His behavior, Grant was forced to conclude, was quite consistent with someone who'd come to a place he'd never heard of and was as anxious as could be to leave it forever.

And if the Skulls' lead singer didn't have the slightest idea where he was, chances were the rest of the group didn't either.

This had been a trip down a blind alley. Unless . . . There was still the agent. It was a real long shot, but maybe he knew something. Grant made a mental note to call him.

Then he made one last stab in the dark. He always did that, even after he'd made up his mind about something. You never knew.

"Your song about the virus," he said, "what's the point of that?"

"You mean you actually listened?" Death Aims said.

"I have ears. I use them occasionally." Grant smiled.

"Ah," the boy said, "it's just a song. This country's going to hell, in case you hadn't noticed. People are becoming robots. They don't dare *do* anything for themselves anymore. It's like, 'Well, the government will take care of us.' It's like some damn virus. Bull fucking shit, we say. Take control of your *own* lives, especially you kids. There's *no* future for you if you don't. But what would you know about that?"

Well, that explained the virus. Grant thought about the young man's question, then decided to be honest. Come down to it, the guy was probably closer to the truth than he even knew.

"More than you might think," Grant said. "You get to be my age, it don't necessarily mean you can't see what's wrong anymore."

Death Aims looked at him, and began to chuckle.

"Hnnh, you're a funny cop," the singer said. "I answer all your questions?"

Grant nodded.

"Then you suppose you could prevail upon your buddies to let us out of this place? We ain't criminals."

"I'll see what I can do," Grant said.

Only after Grant had left did Death Aims think of the strange letter he'd received the previous week. Maybe that was something the lieutenant would have wanted to know about.

But then the singer thought: *Ah, fuck it. We don't owe the cops nothing.*

44

Martin Jeffers was at the office late. It had been a depressing day.

Not only had the note to the newspaper not yielded anything, but then he'd had to interview Wes Thomas. The poor bastard was dying, and the same people who'd killed him wouldn't leave him alone. They'd come and stolen his blood.

It gave Jeffers the creeps. It was like vampires now.

He shook his head and concentrated on completing the paperwork. Today he'd learned nothing new, but he had to write a detailed description of the things he'd done. Sometimes that was the hardest part to this job. He was much more comfortable in the field than he was behind his desk.

It was ironic. The higher you rose in the department, the more desk-bound you got. He wanted to be promoted, but he sure didn't like where that led.

The phone rang and Jeffers answered it.

"Officer Jeffers?" a woman's voice asked.

"Yes," Jeffers said. "Can I help you?"

"I don't know," the voice said. "Maybe so. This is Sarah Terry. Mary's mother?"

"Yes, ma'am," Jeffers said.

"Mr. Jeffers, my daughter hasn't . . . been *well* since, ah, since the . . . incident. I'm sure you can appreciate that."

"Yes, ma'am."

"She's sort of been in a state of shock, I guess you'd say. But today she . . . she indicated to me that you'd asked her to call if she remembered anything further. Well, she *has* remembered something, but she wouldn't tell me what it was. She wanted to speak with you personally."

Jeffers felt the slow prickle of possibility. "I'd be happy to speak with your daughter," he said. "Let's see, I was just about to go out to eat. How about if I come over your house after that?"

"All right," Sarah Terry said. "I suppose that would be fine."

"I'll see you in about an hour or so."

"Make it two if you would, Mr. Jeffers. I'd rather not interrupt Mary's dinner. It's been difficult enough to get her to eat since . . . since it happened."

"Of course. Thank you for calling, Mrs. Terry."

After he hung up, Jeffers thought, well, what the hell, it probably wasn't anything, but it *could* be. He thought about writing Will Grant a note about the phone call, but then he decided not to bother. They could discuss whatever happened in the morning.

Besides . . .

Jeffers felt that his personal investigation was going well. He'd interviewed Clayton Husch's neighbors and found that the hospital technician was something of a man of mystery. No one seemed to know what the man did with his spare time. Of course, no one *cared* either, but what the hell.

If Husch had a secret life, it could just as well be with the HIVe as not. And if it was, Martin Luther Jeffers was going to be the one to make the connection.

Clarice might not like it, but Martin was about to begin his own private stakeout. Trail Husch after the man got off work. Do it for a few days and see where it led. It couldn't wind up in more of a dead end than every other lead they'd had.

And then there was Mary Terry. Hadn't he told Grant he'd had a hunch about her? He looked at his watch. Two hours. He took his time with the paperwork.

An hour later he called his wife and told her he'd be home late. She took it as well as could be expected. Then he went out to dinner. He decided that, under the circumstances, the department ought to cover it. He ate well, and he didn't rush.

Two hours and twenty minutes after the phone call, Jeffers knocked on the Terrys' front door.

Sarah Terry greeted him.

"Mr. Jeffers?" she said.

Jeffers showed her his identification and she let him in.

"Mary will see you in the sitting room," she said. "I'd, uh, appreciate it if this didn't take too long. She's still, well, you know . . ."

"Short as I can, ma'am."

Jeffers had no idea what a sitting room was, but in a house this size there were a lot of extra rooms and he supposed you had to have names for them. The woman led him down a long hall to a room with windows on three sides and spotless furniture that looked old but unused.

Mary Terry was waiting for the policeman.

His image of her from the interviews immediately after the HIVe's attack was of the kind of girl white boys would invariably be attracted to. Petite and cute and obviously from a wealthy family.

On that grim Saturday, she'd come to the police soon after making a run for her life through the woods, not knowing if she would escape the clutches of the HIVe. She'd still been cranking along on pure adrenaline. The reality of what had happened to Brian and her friends hadn't yet sunk in, Jeffers had thought. She was still bright and bubbly and full of life. She had talked and talked, no doubt using the flow of conversation to keep her thoughts at bay. Despite all the words, they'd been able to get very little of value from her about what she'd actually seen.

In the four days since the incident, Jeffers hadn't seen the girl, though he'd kept in touch by phone. Now he was shocked by what he saw. Mary Terry had aged about twenty years. She looked as though she'd permanently stopped eating. Her face was pale and gaunt and framed by lifeless clumps of hair. Her eyes were sunken and there were deep dark circles under them.

She was wearing a bulky cable-knit sweater, and hugging herself. The central air conditioning was on, true, but it wasn't blasting away. Jeffers was even a little warm in his summerweight suit. Mary Terry was cold.

Lord, she looks like she's *the one with the virus*, Jeffers thought.

"Miz Terry, thank you for calling," he said as he took a seat next to her.

"Have you caught them yet?" Mary asked.

"No, ma'am. But I think we're getting close."

It was a lie but, oddly, it didn't feel like a lie. Maybe his instincts were telling him that they *were* close.

"I understand you had something you wanted us to know," Jeffers said.

"Yes."

There was a long pause. Mary hadn't looked directly at the policeman since he'd first entered the room. Her eyes were fixed on something only she could see.

"Ah, what did you want to tell us?" Jeffers prompted.

"I'm trying to see it," Mary said. Her words came out slowly, evenly spaced, without inflection. "It's so hard. I remember everything up until . . . They were making them lie down, the people in the masks, and then they . . . Brian couldn't stand to watch. He was always the leader. He was the quarterback. If he didn't do something, nobody would. . . . I told him not to go down there. I begged him. They had guns. But he did it anyway. He ran and he was screaming something. And then . . ."

There was another pause.

"Yes, Miz Terry," Jeffers said gently.

"He . . . threw something. He threw a stone. And it hit one of the men . . . in the head. He hit someone in the head. But it didn't knock him down. And then he was . . ."

Jeffers felt as though an electric current had suddenly been turned on inside him. It was only with difficulty that he kept the excitement out of his voice.

"Where, Miz Terry?" he said. "Where did Brian hit the man with the stone? On what part of his head?"

Slowly Mary raised her arm and pointed to a spot on the right side of her forehead.

Bingo.

The man at the concert, Jeffers thought. The one with the gash on his forehead. It had to be. And he'd *seen* that man before. But where? He was so close to breaking the case. So close. He almost couldn't breathe, his chest was so tight.

"Thank you, Miz Terry," he said. "I know this is tough for you, but everything you remember is useful to us. I got to go now. You think of anything else, you just call."

Mary didn't acknowledge his departure.

All the way back to the station, Jeffers thought and thought about it. He *knew* that man, his shape, the way he moved. A disguised version of someone he'd met, maybe even talked to. Who *was* it? He kept substituting different faces for the one he'd seen at the concert. The man's identity was there, just inches away. He'd get it. He knew he would.

Dammit, come *on*.

Grant wasn't at the Block and no one there knew where he might be. A call to his home went unanswered as well. So Jeffers decided to leave him a note, on the off chance that, wherever he was now, Grant might stop here before going home. Otherwise, he'd keep phoning Grant's house every fifteen minutes until he got hold of his partner.

The note read: "Seen a man at the concert with a recent wound on his forehead. Mary Terry now remembers that Brian hit one of the HIVes in the forehead with a stone before he was shot. I think it's the same guy. If you come here first, call me my place."

He set the note in a prominent spot on Grant's desk, with a paperweight holding the edge of it down. Then he left.

It was on the drive home that it came to him.

Husch.

Had to be.

He'd been suspicious of the man from the start, had been quietly investigating him for days, but had met him only that one time at the hospital, last Friday. A lot had happened since then.

Carefully Jeffers reconstructed the image of the tall man at the concert. Then he took away the wild dyed hair, the makeup, the beard. He was left with Clayton Husch, no doubt at all.

He was left with the next-to-last person to handle the original pint of Andrew McKey's infected blood.

Finally the case was broken. Now, if only Will Grant would get home, they could plan their next move—how to get from Husch to the rest of the HIVe and nail them all.

Jeffers couldn't contain his excitement as he parked the car and hurried into his house.

"Clarice!" he called.

The way his voice echoed back to him, he knew the place was empty, but he looked in every room anyway.

"Damn you, woman," he muttered to himself. "Where you at?"

The note was on the dining-room table. It was a night for notes. Jeffers picked it up as if it were something dangerous in itself. He read it, and reread it. Then he sank slowly onto a chair. There was a ringing in his ears, and his legs no longer seemed capable of supporting his weight.

The note was printed in the plain block letters he'd seen before:

> We have your wife.
> Stay by the phone and do nothing further
> until you hear from us.
> Welcome to the HIVe.

45

Rhonda Jo Rhoades was in the Skyview Lounge, working on her third White Russian. *Only* her third, she would have said. She was making a deliberate attempt at pacing herself for a change.

It was another slow night at the dear old Skyview. Wednesdays usually were. But Dusty was with that stupid "concerned citizens" group of his, for all the good they'd done. She hadn't fancied sitting around the house by herself all night.

So far, only one guy had tried to hit on her. And he'd had a manic laugh and garlic breath. No, thanks.

That was it. That and the Atlanta Braves on cable. They were having their usual mediocre season. Here was a club with all the world's money to spend, and year after year they did nothing. Who could get behind a team like that?

A man came to the bar and sat a couple of stools down from her. She glanced once in his direction, took a sip of her drink, then checked him out more carefully out of the corner of her eye.

He was a stranger, not bad-looking. Dark hair and a beard. Casually dressed. Around her own age, or a little younger. Seemingly in good shape, if not a tad on the jock side, which could be bad news.

She reminded herself not to jump to conclusions. She'd done that with Dusty, and look where it'd gotten her.

The guy ordered a rum and Coke and caught her looking at him. She didn't mind. She gave him a trace of a smile and he smiled back more openly. She tried her best to look coy, but she'd never been very good at it.

As soon as the man got his drink, he carried it over and stood next to her.

"May I join you?" he asked.

"Line forms at the rear," she said, gesturing at the uncrowded bar area.

He chuckled and took an adjacent stool.

"My name's Jim Teague," he said, offering a hand.

"Rhonda Jo."

She took his hand and it was cool, pleasant. His grip was just right for the situation, not tough-guy, not overly friendly, not too lingering, but enough to indicate interest. A familiar tingle ran up her arm, then down.

"Haven't seen you here before," Rhonda Jo said.

"Yeah," Teague said, "I'm just passing through, actually. Business."

"Salesman?" Rhonda Jo asked, and held her breath. That was a type she couldn't use, and God, the time she'd have getting rid of him.

Teague nodded. "Fuller brushes," he said solemnly.

"Oh. That must be interesting work." She put on what she called her *interest face*. "You must have had a great number of fascinating encounters."

They looked at one another for a moment, then burst out laughing.

"Can I buy you another of whatever the hell that thing is?" Teague asked.

"Only if you'll tell me the one about the housewife and the upholstery brush."

Teague ordered another round of drinks.

"So what do you really do?" Rhonda Jo asked.

"You mean for a living?"

"Ha ha. Yeah, for a living. If that's what you call what we're supporting here."

"Ouch. Well . . ." He leaned over and spoke in a conspiratorial tone. "I'm a writer."

"So what's the big deal, Mr. Michener?"

Teague shrugged. "No big deal. It's just that I don't want too many people to know. A lot of the time people talk to you differently if they're aware that you're going to be writing about them."

"Don't worry. I just know all kinda writers, and frankly, I'm not that impressed. You intend to write about me?"

"What do you do that people would want to read about?"

This could be an interesting man, Rhonda Jo thought, and she gave him one of her more seductive looks.

"I have my talents," she said, leaving her lips slightly parted. She let the words hang there for a moment, then said, "And what do you write? Books?"

Teague cleared his throat. *Getting a little dry in there?* Rhonda Jo thought to herself.

"Sometimes," Teague said. "I'm, ah, a free-lancer. Mostly I do articles for magazines."

"And you're here because of the HIVe killers."

Too bad. Rhonda Jo was long since tired of those people. She'd tried one early on, a network cameraman from Washington. He'd been in entirely too much of a hurry for her taste.

"No," Teague said, "actually I'm not. If you can believe it, I'm doing a business article. On the Claymore-Perkins plant, for *American Business.* The weekly magazine. You know it?"

"I've heard of it. I'm not what you'd call a regular reader."

"I'm not either, but I take what I can get. You know, to tell you the truth, I hadn't even heard of these HIVe people until I got down here."

"Where you from," Rhonda Jo said, "East Jesus, Nebraska?"

Teague laughed. "I work out of D.C.," he said. "I just don't read the papers and I don't watch a lot of TV. I'll probably miss my own wedding."

"Not married?"

"Nope. Never could see the point. You?"

Rhonda Jo shrugged. "I've tried it. So what do you think of our city so far?"

"It's pretty country," Teague said. "Though with the situation right now, the people seem edgy. Which doesn't surprise me. What about you, aren't you wary of strangers?"

"Should I be?"

"Sure, don't you . . . ? Oh, I see what you mean." Teague flushed. "No, I'm just a guy who still thinks a hive is what you keep bees in. How about another drink?"

They had another round, and they talked. It was light, easygoing bar talk, designed to create the illusion of a growing intimacy while avoiding the risks of the real thing. Teague had to be especially careful to not give away what he was actually doing in Brisbane. And Rhonda Jo deftly steered the conversation away from her personal life whenever it seemed headed that way.

In the end, Teague invited her back to his hotel room and she accepted.

"On one condition," she said.

"What's that?"

"Don't draw no blood now. I don't like that stuff." She winked at him.

God, he thought, it's really on their minds, isn't it? As well it should be. For a fleeting moment he wondered if *he* was taking too much of a chance. Some of the killers were women, and he hadn't really learned much about this "Rhonda Jo." But then he put the thought away. Nah, not this one. She wasn't the type.

He grinned broadly, indicating his teeth.

"Look, Ma, no points."

Rhonda Jo thought that was funny as all get-out.

46

The Brisbane Arms Hotel was only a short walk from the Skyview Lounge.

"I'm surprised you could get a room," Rhonda Jo said. "We're pretty full up with the TV people and whatnot."

"I probably couldn't have on my own," Teague said, "but *American Business* called in some favors. I guess they have a fair amount of clout."

"Uh-huh. Must be some kind of goodly."

The lobby of the hotel was much busier than usual, what with the out-of-towners coming and going like the world couldn't turn without their help. Rhonda Jo was reasonably sure she wouldn't run into anyone she knew, but there was always the chance. She'd come to regard the risk as a somewhat spicy part of the game.

If in fact there was a risk. Surely Dusty had accepted that she occasionally . . . Lord knows she went out alone enough. Or had he? Since that one time, when he'd liked to gone nuts, they'd avoided the subject. Rhonda Jo preferred to think he'd mellowed out about it. But who knew? With that feisty temper of his, there was no telling what Dusty might do next time around. Rhonda Jo kept her head down, more out of habit than anything else, until she and Teague were in the elevator and heading up.

She never saw her husband, way back across the crowded lobby. He'd kept plenty of people between them. And he'd made sure his left hand—the bandaged and plaster-casted hand that he'd broken defending the others at that stupid concert—was always held out of sight behind his back.

She hadn't seen him, but he'd surely seen her. He

stood there motionless for a long moment as the elevator
doors closed and his wife disappeared with the bearded
stranger. His good right hand closed around the cold
lump of steel in his jacket pocket. The anger and the
shame rushed up and down his arms like hot flashes. He
watched as the lights above the elevator flashed up to 8
and stopped.

So it's true, he thought. He'd never followed her before, but since he'd caught her that once, he'd heard the
persistent whisper of rumor and he'd finally wanted to
see for himself. At least he thought he had. Faced with
the reality, he wasn't so sure. He found himself asking:
For how long, and how many times? And he felt the
humiliation, wondering if, as the saying went, the husband was always the last to know.

Did the whole town laugh at him when his back was
turned?

He started forward, stopped, turned, and stopped again.
A man hurrying for the door bumped into him when he
did. The man started to say something, but reconsidered
when he saw Dusty's face, and went about his business
without a word.

"May I help you, sir?"

It was a moment before Dusty realized the question
had been directed at him. The speaker was a man in a
brown uniform with satin piping.

"May I help you?" the man repeated. "You look a
little lost, sir."

"No," Dusty said quickly. "I was . . . I was just looking for the bar."

The uniformed man pointed. "Right through there, sir.
Have a nice evening."

"Uh, thank you."

The man moved away, still watching him, and Dusty
made for the bar. *Sure*, he thought. *Let 'em get nice and
cozy first. Besides, I could use a drink.*

Teague and Rhonda Jo got to his room without incident. The décor was standard Brisbane Arms, made up
to look more posh than it really was. Rhonda Jo wondered idly whether the writer or the magazine paid for it
all.

Then Teague was kissing her. He was a mighty good kisser. Rhonda Jo slid her tongue into his mouth and gave as good as she was getting. Teague ran his fingernails down her back and grabbed her buttocks, pulling her hard against him.

By the time the kiss ended, the chilled air of the room seemed as hot as outside and they were both breathing heavily.

A lot of times you lose, Rhonda Jo thought, but sometimes you win.

They kissed again, taking their time, savoring the pleasant fit of their bodies, each privately screening his or her own fantasy version of what was happening.

When they broke, Teague said, "Hi, there."

"Hello, yourself," Rhonda Jo said huskily. It wasn't entirely put on.

For a moment, neither knew quite what to do next. Then Teague detached himself from her and went over to the dresser. He opened the bottle of champagne he had bought at the Skyview and poured it into the hotel glasses. That was one thing about the Brisbane Arms. The glasses were glass and not plastic.

"To . . . what?" Teague asked.

Rhonda Jo shrugged. "To better relations with Washington," she said.

They laughed and drank.

Then Teague said, "You know, I've had a long hot day, Rhonda Jo, and I didn't expect to meet *anyone* like you tonight. You mind if I take a quick shower?"

"Long as it's not a cold one."

"Thanks," Teague said, grinning like a fool. "Make yourself comfortable. Have some champagne. I won't be long."

He went into the bathroom and closed the door.

Rhonda Jo sat down, but then, as she heard the water come on, began to feel restless. *What the hell?* she thought. *He's invited me up here and left me alone. Who cares if I take just a* tiny *look around?*

She set her glass on the table next to a hotel menu. Then she walked casually around the room. She looked in the closet. Jim Teague had a couple of extra summer suits, a light jacket, and that was it. Nothing looked like it had cost him a great deal of money. She closed the closet door.

From the bathroom came only the sound of the water. Not a shower singer, Rhonda Jo thought.

She walked over to a long dresser with a gilt-framed mirror above it. She examined herself for a moment, turning slowly. Not bad, she decided. With no kids, she had managed to maintain the body she'd had back in her competition days. Maybe not *quite* as good, but close. There was no gray in her hair yet. And her makeup wasn't entirely a cover-up.

Not bad.

The dresser top was bare except for the champagne. She ran her fingers along the wood, through the cool puddle of water the sweating bottle had left, drawing circles with her wet fingertip. Then, peeking over her shoulder even though she could still hear the shower, she quietly opened one of the drawers. Inside was a tape recorder, a box of tapes, and a stack of notebooks and thick manila folders.

Tools of a writer's trade, she supposed. What must it take to do that kind of work? Rhonda Jo shook her head. In school, the essay had always been her downfall. She pushed the drawer back in.

Then she opened another.

And nearly jumped at what she saw.

What . . . ?

Oh my God, she thought. Oh, my *God*! It couldn't be. No, he was a *writer*! It *couldn't* be! But it was.

In the drawer were rows of little bottles. And each bottle was filled with dark reddish-brown fluid.

She almost screamed. But her head had snapped back, and just before her mouth opened, she caught sight of herself in the mirror. Her face was white and her eyes were gaping. But she was okay. She was *all right*. The worst thing would be to bring him running out of the bathroom.

She bit down on the scream and the drawer rolled shut as if on its own. Without a second's hesitation, without a glance backward, she grabbed her shoes and purse and fled from the room in her stocking feet.

Down the long corridor. If only she could get out of the building before he . . .

As she approached the elevator, its door began sliding open.

Oh, thank God, she thought. Thank *God.*

The door opened fully and Rhonda Jo Rhoades ran headlong into her husband.

She bounced off, started to push her way past him, then realized who it was. The two looked at each other, then Rhonda Jo collapsed toward him, her arms spread.

"Dusty," she sobbed. "Oh, God, Dusty—"

Before she could get her arms around him, Rhoades slapped her, hard. The sudden blow stunned her, and she dropped to her knees.

"Bitch!" he said. "Miserable, cheating *bitch!*"

"No," she cried. "Please. Wait."

Dusty looked at his wife coldly. "Why don't you get your friend the beard to help you?" he said. "He tough enough to fight for you?"

He raised his hand to hit her again, but she scrabbled over to him and clung to his legs.

"No," she said. "Please, Dusty. You don't understand. I've made a terrible mistake. The HIVe—"

His hand stopped in mid-swing.

"Huh?" he said.

Her words came out in a rush. "Dusty, we've got to do something. That's why I was *running.* I was wrong, but God, I never suspected. He seemed nice enough, we were just going to have a drink together, but he's one of them. He told me he was a writer but, Dusty, God help me, he's *one of them!*"

"Rhonda Jo, what in Christ's name are you *talk*ing about?"

"The *HIVe!* He's one of the killers! He's got a drawer full of bottles of *blood!*" She began to sob heavily. "I don't want to die. I could have died . . ."

Rhoades bent down and loosened his wife's grip on his legs.

"What room?" he asked.

"816," Rhonda Jo managed to say.

Rhoades started down the hall, the thick carpet absorbing any sound his footsteps might have made. There was no other sound. No one coming out of a room. No one going in. He took the pistol from his pocket and held it loosely in his good hand.

Eight-ten. Twelve. 816. Fourteen.

The door to 816 opened and the man with the beard appeared. He was wearing a towel around his waist and his dark curly hair was still dripping water. He looked up and down the corridor.

"Rhonda Jo?" he said automatically.

And then a man was rushing at him. A burly man with a mustache and muttonchop sideburns and one hand in a cast. A man he'd never seen before. A man with a gun in the other hand and pure murder in his eyes.

It was a terrifying sight. Teague tried to escape into his room, but Rhoades crashed into the door and sent him sprawling to the floor. The heavy metal door clicked shut behind them.

The two men were about equally matched in weight, but Rhoades had the advantage of the first blow. When Teague raised himself a little from the floor, Rhoades kicked him hard in the ribs. Teague flopped down again. He covered his head with his arms just in time to deflect a kick aimed at his head. He rolled and managed to get out a couple of words.

"*Wait* a minute!" he cried. "Nothing happened! For God's sake, nothing *happened*!"

Rhoades growled at him. "Murderer!" he said.

"Wh—"

"Goddamn murderer."

Teague had cowered into a corner, his hands held in front of him as if they'd be some use in stopping a bullet.

"No, wait!" Teague cried hysterically. "This is a mistake!"

"There's no mistake," Rhoades said. "That was my *wife* you were fooling around with. She saw the blood."

"*What blood*?"

Rhoades spread his feet and held the pistol out in front of him, the wrapped hand steadying it.

"Forget it, HIVe bastard."

He cocked the hammer.

"*HIVe*!" Teague screamed. "For Christ's sake, I work for the *government*!"

Rhoades hesitated. The hammer was cocked, his finger was on the trigger, the anger was boiling in his blood. He was going to blow the scum away. He was going to take all of his rage and frustration over the HIVe and the brewery and his marriage, and channel it all into a single bullet at his tormentor's heart.

But he hesitated. There was something in the guy's voice, something about this big muscular man huddled in the corner of a strange hotel room begging for his life. Something that asked a question he couldn't answer.

Keeping the gun trained on Teague, Rhoades moved to the dresser and began opening drawers. Nothing in one, a tape recorder and some notebooks in the next, and then there they were. Rows of little bottles. Rhoades looked the bearded man in the eye.

"My wife said she saw blood," Rhoades said.

"*Blood*?" Teague said, and finally he understood. "Oh, Jesus . . ."

And then the strangest thing happened. The bearded man began to laugh. He laughed until the tears were rolling down his cheeks. Rhoades found the emotion of the moment draining away. He couldn't shoot a man who was laughing like that. He tried to hang on to his rage but he couldn't.

"God damn you, what are you *laughing* about?"

"It's not blood," Teague said, gasping for breath, "it's water. Just . . . water."

Rhoades looked back at the bottles. At a glance they sure looked like blood, but . . . He picked one of them up, shook it, examined it. It *was* awfully thin. Maybe it wasn't . . .

"Please, mister," Teague said. "Put the gun away. I'm sorry about your wife, but nothing happened. We just drank a couple of drinks. Really. And I don't have anything to do with the HIVe. Look at that stuff. Does that look like blood to you?"

Rhoades didn't know what to do. For one highly charged moment he'd been an avenging angel, and tomorrow's hero to the whole city of Brisbane, and now . . . now what? He looked from the bearded man to the bottle and back again. His gun hand relaxed a little.

"Just who the hell *are* you?" Rhoades asked, his suspicions not entirely at rest.

"I'm a U.S. government agent," Teague said as he wiped the tears away. "I'm here undercover to check pollution levels in the Squier River. If you'll just let me show you my identification."

Teague got to his feet.

"Slow and easy," Rhoades said.

Teague kept both hands in the air as he walked to the bedside table. Then, still keeping one hand aloft, he opened the drawer, reached inside, and pulled out a slim leather billfold. He flipped it onto the bed, near where Rhoades was standing.

"In there," Teague said. "You take your time and look it over. I won't move until you're satisfied."

Rhoades opened the billfold. There were a number of plastic-laminated cards inside. Prominent among them was a photo I.D. of the bearded man. It identified him as James A. Teague, of the Environmental Protection Agency. Rhoades stared at the face of the man he'd nearly killed, and he felt ashamed. He was no better than that fool Treat Richards. Shoot first, ask questions later.

Rhonda Jo had been standing outside the locked door of Room 816 for what seemed the longest time. She'd heard the scuffling and the yelling inside, and now she was aware of the ominous silence. Dusty had a gun, she'd seen that, but it hadn't been fired. What was going on in there? She wanted to know, yet she was afraid to find out.

Finally she couldn't take it anymore. She screwed up her courage and knocked timidly at the door.

"Dusty," she called softly. Then, worried that she wouldn't be heard, she said more loudly, "Dusty. Are you okay?"

Rhoades uncocked the pistol's hammer, and Teague felt some of the tension finally flow out of him. Rhoades went to the door and opened it. Rhonda Jo shrank back, the terror and panic still shrilling inside her. She looked beyond her husband, into the room, but Teague was over by the bed, out of sight.

"Dusty, where—?"

"Come on in, Rhonda Jo," Rhoades said wearily. "He's not HIVe. And he's not a writer. You made a mistake."

"I what?"

Rhoades motioned her in, and cautiously Rhonda Jo entered the room. She saw Teague standing there, wet hair plastered to his head, the ridiculous towel wrapped around his waist.

She cleared her throat. "Uh, what's going on?" she asked.

Rhoades threw Teague back his billfold. "James A. Teague," he said to Rhonda Jo. "Environmental Protection Agency, Washington, D.C. He's collecting water samples, which look a little like blood if you don't look too close. For which I almost killed him."

Rhonda Jo looked from one man to the other.

"Oh, God," she said. "I thought—"

"We know what you thought," Rhoades said with disgust.

No, he thought. *She's not to blame. I am. I'm the one with the gun.*

"It's all right," Teague said awkwardly. "I'm sure the . . . situation in Brisbane is hard on all of you. It's a mistake anyone could have made. Tell you what, I'll be going back home tomorrow. Why don't we just pretend it never happened?"

"Jesus, I'm sorry," Rhonda Jo said.

"Let's go," Rhoades said to his wife.

They were silent as they rode the elevator down and walked out of the Brisbane Arms. But on the drive home Rhonda Jo spoke.

"Dusty, I'm . . . really sorry," she said.

"Forget it," Dusty said.

"No, I can't. I . . . I didn't realize how much this was all getting to me. I think we must all be going a little crazy."

"We'll catch the bastards."

"I know, I know. But the important thing tonight is that nothing happened, and nobody got hurt. And I realized something else, too. When you went down the hall to that man's room, it was a . . . a very brave thing to do." She paused, then added coyly, "I watched you do that and you reminded me of someone."

"Huh? Who?"

"The man I married."

Dusty glanced over at his wife and saw something there that he hadn't seen in a long time. He felt a warmth spread outward from his belly and drove fast the rest of the way.

47

Martin Jeffers was praying.

It was something he hadn't done since his mama used to drag him to the Baptist church when he was a boy. He liked the screaming and hollering, but didn't see where the praying did anyone much good. No one black, anyway.

Clarice was a religious girl and always would be. She'd tried to get him back to it after they were married, but by that time he'd already been a cop for a while. He'd seen too much to believe there was a God of goodwill who could allow such things as happened.

But he was praying now.

He'd waited by the phone for the longest hour of his life, desperately torn. As a cop, he *had* to report that he was in contact with the HIVe. It was not only his sworn duty, it was what must be done for the larger benefit of Brisbane. How many lives would be saved if he called? The proper course would be to get as much backup as he could, immediately, and go after the sons of bitches with all the firepower they could muster.

Yet, if he did that, there was an excellent chance Clarice would be killed. And, of course, the baby with her. They were probably watching, even as he waited, to make sure he was alone when they met him.

The agony was such that, more than once, he almost began screaming out loud at the four walls of his home. But somehow he kept the lid on, focusing his anger, planning what he was going to do when he got his hands on them. And he waited. And he didn't call in.

When the phone finally rang, it literally shocked him out of his chair.

It was them. They were very clear about what he was

to do. Drive out the Old Dunmore Road to a crossroads
a couple of miles west of town. Then turn south for a
mile. Stop in the parking lot of an abandoned gas station.
Bring no weapons and, above all else, come alone.

Jeffers knew the place. If he brought any help, they'd
know it, and he'd sit in that parking lot all night while
they did whatever they were going to do to his wife.

He'd followed their instructions to the letter. He'd
waited for fifteen minutes next to the shell of the station.
Two cars had passed during that time, and neither had
shown any sign of stopping.

Then, apparently satisfied, they'd come for him. When
they did, his heart immediately sank to his shoes. There
were lots of guns in evidence, but no masks, no disguises.
He recognized Husch, of course. And one of the others
looked vaguely familiar. But that didn't matter. The important thing was that they were making no effort to
conceal their identities.

That could mean only one thing. Martin Jeffers was
going to die.

So now he was praying to the God he no longer believed in. He didn't really expect to be saved himself, but
he spoke to Clarice's God on behalf of her and the child.
Spare them, at least. Please spare them.

He was bound to a chair, in a room inside the large
house to which they'd taken him. The house was part of
an estate, he knew, that belonged to Dante Glorio, the
TV soap-opera actor who'd once been plain old Bobby
Drew of Brisbane. He didn't know much more about
Glorio, except that it was now clear the man with the
scarred face was the leader of the HIVe, and that he had
at least half a dozen followers, most of them armed with
pistols or shotguns.

Clarice was there too. Clearly terrified, but still alive.
The baby, Lord, Jeffers thought.

"Let my wife go," Jeffers said to Glorio. "She won't
tell anyone. Please. You can have me, but let Clarice
go."

"Noble," Glorio said. "The noble black man, always
ready to put his head in a noose if that's what massa
wants."

Husch smirked and Jeffers knew he'd been right about

the racist lab technician. Why couldn't he have moved against the man sooner?

"Just let her go," Jeffers said through gritted teeth.

"My man," Glorio said, "you don't seem to be in any position to tell me what to do."

"I ain't telling. I'm asking. You got no quarrel with her."

"Hmmm," Glorio said. "Perhaps you're right. But we do have one with you. What's the matter with you, didn't you read our message in the paper?"

"I read it."

"Then didn't you believe it?"

"I . . . I don't know what it meant."

"Well it *meant* exactly what it said. We are the future. In time, everyone will be a part of the HIVe. It's pointless to oppose us, and yet you did. Do you recognize your mistake now?"

"I guess so," Jeffers mumbled.

"Speak up!"

There was a young girl with dark hair. She seemed to be attached to Glorio more intimately than the others. His girlfriend, Jeffers assumed. Yet she also seemed not quite as much of the HIVe as the rest. Jeffers sensed at least a trace of doubt in her.

"Yeah, I made a mistake," Jeffers said to Glorio, while looking at the dark-haired girl. "I'll join. I'll do whatever you want me to do."

"Good," Glorio said. "Well, why don't we let you do just that."

He made a sign to another woman and she brought him a blood-filled syringe. Glorio held it up to the light and gazed fondly at it. The dark-haired girl looked on neutrally.

Jeffers' spirits sank. *No*, he thought, *I was wrong. They're all on the same side.*

"This is our sacrament," Glorio said, "as you know. It is also the agent of change in this world, bringing us our future. That has been revealed to those chosen to create the HIVe."

Glorio, smiling, walked over to the chair that held Jeffers. Clarice, who had been steadily sobbing, began to scream.

Jeffers struggled against the ropes that bound him. He knew it was futile, but he wasn't going to become infected without a fight. He kicked and thrashed until the chair toppled over and he lay on his side, still securely tied.

Glorio knelt beside him.

"Now," Glorio said, "welcome to the HIVe."

He jabbed the needle into Jeffers' arm and pushed the plunger. Clarice was screaming and crying and babbling incoherently.

"Fuck you," Jeffers said to the actor. "They're going to find you. And when they do, they'll fry your—"

The policeman's words stopped as though cut with a knife. His body went rigid and his eyes bulged out. There was a little strangled sound in his throat. And then he died.

Clarice collapsed in hysteria.

Sandy Fraim rushed over and said to Glorio, "What in hell is going on here?"

Slowly Glorio stood up and faced her.

"He had to die," Glorio said. "I added some cyanide."

"Goddammit!" Fraim said. "I thought we agreed no more killing!"

"No, we didn't agree. The only thing of importance is the preservation of the HIVe. You know that, Sandy. And you know that we couldn't be safe as long as this man was alive. He knew too much. He'd identified brother Clayton. It was only a matter of time before he discovered who we were. I could not permit that, and neither could you."

"Dammit, it isn't right. We're supposed to be spreading the seed, not becoming cold-blooded murderers!"

"Sandy, don't—"

"And what about *her*?" Fraim gestured at the crumpled figure of Clarice Jeffers. "Do we kill her too?"

There was a moment of silence as all the HIVe members looked at Glorio.

Then Husch said, "I don't think we should."

"Why not?" Glorio asked. "She knows as much as he did now."

"Yeah, why not?" Fraim said. She looked at Husch as if he was of less importance than she. "We going to draw the line at women?"

"No," Husch said with exaggerated patience. "She's the cop's wife. If they both disappear, too many people are gonna ask too many questions. The rest of the cops are gonna start looking hard, and they're not gonna stop until they find out what happened."

Glorio folded his arms across his chest. "I don't know," he said. "What do you suggest?"

"Look at her," Husch said. "She's a wreck. I think we should let her go."

"Just let her go? I don't know if I like that idea," Glorio said.

"Let her go," Fraim said wearily.

"It makes sense, Glorio," Husch said. "She's pregnant. She's not gonna risk her life and the baby's by telling anyone what happened to her husband."

Glorio thought about it, then walked over to where Clarice was huddled. Husch followed behind him.

"Look at me, woman," Glorio commanded.

Clarice raised her head. She looked up at the man with the scars through her terror and her grief. To maintain even a shred of control was the hardest thing she'd ever done.

"What about it?" Glorio said. "Should we let you go?"

"Please," Clarice said, cradling her stomach, "my baby."

"You've got to do exactly as we say," Husch said. "You go home and you pack your bags. Then you leave town. But before you do, you make sure your husband's friends know you're gone. Maybe you got a sick cousin or something. Martin's going with you, and you don't know when y'all will be back. You got that?"

Clarice nodded dumbly.

"You don't get it right," Husch said, "and I'm gonna personally see to it that that baby never gets born."

Clarice stared at the tall skinny man and knew he meant it. And she knew when she nodded again that she'd do anything he asked. Martin was dead. She must save the baby.

"Should we inject her first?" Glorio asked.

"I don't think so," Husch said. "If she gets sick, she might talk. I say we leave her alone."

There was a pause as Glorio thought it all over; then he said, "All right. Get her out of here."

48

Thursday, August 23

As Will Grant drove to work, he considered the fact that it had now been almost two weeks since the HIVe had made its first attack. He shook his head sadly. In all his years on the force, there had been no other instance in which someone committed a continuing series of crimes over a two-week period without leaving *some* kind of trail behind.

These people were smart, they were ruthless, and they were damned lucky.

All of which left the lieutenant feeling tired and depressed. So much so that he'd decided to pack it in for a little while, to just switch off all the circuits, in the hope that he'd have a fresh outlook the following morning.

So, after interviewing Death Aims, he'd driven to his parents' place, a modest farm in the hills thirty miles south of Brisbane, and spent the night. He owed them a visit, but in truth it was more for him than for them. He had a good home-cooked meal, some old-fashioned family conversation, and several hours' more sleep than he'd lately been accustomed to.

It had worked, and it hadn't.

On the one hand, he was refreshed. His energy level was higher than it had been in over a week. On the other hand, the case, with all its horror and dead-end leads, was still there. It stared him full in the face, a mocking, grinning skull.

Grant parked his car in the police lot and went out of his way to enter the Block by the back entrance, which was locked to the general public. He just wanted to get to work this morning, without having to run the gauntlet

City Plaza had become. Press coverage had slackened a bit, as the story got older, but there would still be people out there who would recognize him and hound him.

When Grant got to his office, Worth was there, resting on his more-than-ample butt, filling the air with second-hand cigarette smoke.

Grant took off his jacket and hung it up. The department air conditioner wasn't working hard enough for anyone to be comfortable except in shirt sleeves.

"Martin in?" Grant asked Worth.

Worth fished something out of his nose and flicked it on the floor.

"Nah," he said. "Ain't signed in yet."

"He call?"

"Uh-uh."

Grant looked at his watch. He was late. That made Martin even later. And Martin, who wanted so badly to get ahead, was never late for work.

So Grant went to the front office and checked with Dot Pritchett. No, so far no one had heard a thing from Martin Jeffers today.

If Dot was a little more than casually interested in Grant's question, she didn't show it. Not that Grant would necessarily have noticed anyway. He was feeling very uneasy, very concerned about his partner now. This was unlike Jeff. There were so many crazies—and normal people driven crazy by the tension—out there that anything could be happening, and sooner or later it was going to happen to cops too.

The detective walked quickly back to his office. Worth, thank goodness, had left. Grant was just reaching for the phone when he saw the note.

He read it and knew intuitively that something was wrong. God *damn*, why had he picked last night to be away? He searched his memory, trying to bring up a picture of the man with the wound on his forehead, the one at the concert, the one who, according to Jeff's note, belonged to the HIVe.

No picture came. Jeffers had seen the man and he hadn't, Grant was sure. But it was a lead, maybe a big lead if Jeffers had been able to follow it up.

He called his partner's house. Clarice answered.

No, she told him, Martin wasn't there. His sister, who lived down South, had took sick of a sudden and Martin had left to be with her. Yes, he'd told Clarice to let the lieutenant know, but what with the packing, she hadn't got round to it yet. Yes, she was about to leave to be with her husband. No, she didn't know when they might be back.

Grant thanked her and hung up. He thought about the conversation. There was something in Clarice's voice. His instincts had been correct. Something was very, very wrong.

Hurriedly he left the Block and drove over to Jeffers house. He barely made it in time. A few minutes later and Clarice would have been gone.

"I done told you, Lieutenant," Clarice said as she continued to load the car, "Martin left last night."

"How?" Grant asked.

"I took him to the airport m'self."

"This is pretty sudden, Clarice."

"That's how it happen sometime. You don't know when you gonna take sick. Nor either did his sister."

"He didn't leave any message for me?"

"No, he didn't."

Grant was following the woman around as she went into the house, picked things up, and carried them to the car. His exasperation was building. There was no way he could force Clarice to talk to him. And she *could* be telling the truth.

No, he just didn't believe that.

"You look like you're hauling enough stuff to take you clear to next July, Clarice," Grant said.

"Could be," Clarice said.

"Well, you got some number I can reach Martin at?"

"I don't know yet. I give you a call."

Grant finally grabbed her by the shoulders. "Goddammit," he said. "What the hell is going on?"

"Take your hands off'n me, Lieutenant," she said coldly, and when he didn't she wrenched herself away. "What you know about my life, anyway? Nothing, that's what. Or Martin either. You don't care about us."

If Grant thought that the case had made him feel

helpless thus far, there were always deeper levels of meaning to the word.

"No, Clarice," he begged. "Please . . . You're wrong. Why can't you tell me?"

"I don't have to tell you nothing," she said. "Now, you mind?"

She'd opened the car door and turned back to look at him one last time. Their eyes held for a moment, Grant's pleading and Clarice's just as strongly resisting.

Then she said, "I got a long drive, Lieutenant. I gotta go."

She got into the car and slammed the door, started the engine, and was gone without another word.

And Martin was gone. Grant didn't need proof; he knew it.

Unable to move, Grant watched her go. He felt abandoned, as solitary as a man stranded on a rock by the incoming tide. And there was something else too, something hardening inside him even as he stood there.

He was going to find the man with the gash on his forehead. And when he found him, he just might kill him.

49

When Grant got back to the Block, he went directly to Kip Kyser's office. Kyser was standing behind his desk. Grant decided there was no point in delaying, so he took a deep breath and came out with it.

"Chief," he said, "Martin's disappeared."

Kyser's permanently florid complexion had always suggested high blood pressure. And his hard, protuberant belly had suggested an alcohol-stressed circulatory system. The two together suggested a prime candidate for heart attack.

Lately, with Kyser under the continuing pressure of the HIVe case, the heart attack seemed a near-certainty. The chief's nerves were raw, his rage bottled up with nowhere to go. His coloring had become almost scarlet.

"*Now* what?" he roared at his lieutenant.

"Please, Chief," Grant said, "sit down. No use getting worked up."

Kyser sat down as if the weight of the entire Block was on top of him.

"What?" was all he said.

Grant sat down too. "Well," he said, "there ain't no putting a pretty face on it. I believe the HIVe got him."

Kyser just stared, so Grant went ahead with what he knew and what he'd guessed. When he'd finished, Kyser was angry and whipped at the same time.

"You find him," the chief said, referring to the mystery man with the head wound. "I don't care what it takes, you find him. Everyone's on triple overtime until we nail him."

"Yes, sir," Grant said, and left.

After he'd gone, Kip Kyser thumped his forehead methodically against his desk blotter, over and over until it really hurt.

Grant went to his office. The chief was right, of course. They had to find the man from the concert. But how? He couldn't walk the streets looking for a man with a Band-Aid.

The concert.

He couldn't shake the feeling that it somehow tied in.

And he had one minuscule lead. He phoned New York City Directory Information. They gave him the number for the Adam Kronsky Talent Agency, and he gave Kronsky a call.

Kronsky was "in a meeting."

"Would you have him call me back as soon as possible?" Grant said to the man's secretary. "It's important police business."

He told her who he was and she agreed to pass on the message "directly."

After that, Grant went through his notes, and Martin's, with a fine-tooth comb, searching for something they might have missed. He could find nothing.

Then he drove out to interview Mary Terry personally. She was obviously still a very distraught girl, and he regretted having to put her through this a second time. But it was important that he know exactly what Martin had known.

The girl cooperated as best she could, but all she could tell him about the man Brian had hit with the stone was that he was maybe a little taller than Grant, but thin. She'd never seen his face, only some blood staining the stocking mask, before she fled into the woods.

The description probably fit a thousand Brisbane men, and who knew how accurate the girl's memory was? The guy might be short and squat. There was nothing in Martin's note to corroborate what Mary Terry had said.

Although . . . If the guy Jeffers had seen at the concert had differed radically in appearance, except for the wound, wouldn't he have said so in his message?

Pointless to speculate. Martin had written a brief note because he expected to talk with his partner later in the evening. He might have left out a whole host of stuff.

Back at the Block, Grant ran into Durwin Sleeth in the corridor.

"Anything new?" the D.A. asked.

Try as he might, Grant just couldn't bring himself to trust the guy.

"No, nothing," he lied.

But Sleeth pressed him. "Where's Jeffers today? Haven't seen him around."

"His sister's sick. He had to go be with her." For all he knew, it might be the truth.

"Too bad. Hope he'll be back soon. We need him here."

"I hope so too."

"Well, keep me posted," Sleeth said. "Whatever comes up, I need to know."

"Yeah, I'll do that."

Grant returned to his office to find a note indicating that Adam Kronsky had called back. He'd almost forgotten about the New York agent, but he phoned him immediately. This time the secretary put him through.

"Lieutenant Grant," Kronsky said. "I understand you were very helpful in getting my boys out of that rotten little jail. You have my thanks. What can I do for you?"

"I didn't do all that much," Grant said. "There just wasn't any reason for holding them. Anyway, there are a couple of questions I'd like to ask you, if you don't mind."

"Shoot."

"How long have the Skulls been your clients?"

"Two years or so. A while."

"Any trouble before?"

"Well, ah," Kronsky said carefully, "you know the kind of audience that's attracted to the boys. Some of them are a little unruly, shall we say. There have been one or two . . . incidents. But nothing like Dunmore, of course. The Skulls are a sophisticated stage act, not some bunch of punk *provocateurs*."

Grant remembered how the Skulls deliberately whipped their fans into a frenzy. *Yeah*, he thought. *Sophisticated*.

"All right," Grant said. "Who decides where the group is going to play?"

"Well, mostly I do," Kronsky said.

"And how do *you* decide?"

"I go where the money is. Though I must admit that at this point in their career we take most of what's offered to us."

"And how exactly did Dunmore come about?"

"Let me see, that *was* a couple of months ago. Yeah, I got a call from the Dunmore College Festival of the Performing Arts. Whatever in hell that is. They offered a decent amount of money for a one-night performance, we had no conflicts on that date, so we took it. Nothing unusual I can remember. What's this all about, Lieutenant?"

"I don't know," Grant said truthfully. "I just don't know. Thank you for your time, Mr. Kronsky."

"No problem. Thanks again for *your* help."

Grant then put in a call to Dunmore College. Or rather, he put in several calls. The Festival of the Performing Arts turned out to be a student-run group that organized concerts and other events, and the students had not yet arrived for the fall semester. It took a while for him to make contact with someone who knew anything. He ended up talking to a woman in the music department who was pretty much the sole summer staff.

She knew about the concert. Traditionally, she explained, they scheduled one at the college just prior to the beginning of the school year. It was used to generate seed money for the upcoming semester's activities. The summer concert was always slanted toward teenagers, she said. This was because a large part of the audience was drawn from the youth of the nearby towns, Brisbane among them. Some of Dunmore's students did come back for it, of course, but the concert was primarily put on for the townies.

The person who'd actually gotten the Skulls to play at Dunmore was a Festival committee member who was attending summer school and had agreed to handle the details. His name was David Bourne. The woman gave Lieutenant Grant Bourne's local phone number.

Grant tried it. Bourne wasn't in but, fortunately, his roommate was. The roommate agreed to have Bourne call the police as soon as possible.

Grant sighed wearily as he hung up. That probably

wasn't going anywhere. He held his head in his hands as he attempted to figure out what to do next.

There were so few choices, so many potential blind alleys. He got out his long list of people contacted so far and read it through once again. Four names stood out from the rest: Andrew McKey, Janet Willen, Clayton Husch, Joanna Feene. The ones who were known for certain to have had access to HIV-4-contaminated blood.

If the first batch had come from a local source, then one of these people was involved. Either directly or indirectly. Didn't that follow? Maybe, maybe not.

Grant decided that, in the absence of any other, it was a theory worth testing. More extensive interviews with these four would have to be conducted.

50

Edna Clint sat in front of her dresser mirror and loosened her hair.

She was a youthful-looking woman of forty, her face only slightly lined, her jet-black hair completely free of gray. Seen from the waist up, she still appeared as slim as she'd once been. Only from the hips down, where she'd inevitably thickened over the years, was there a concession to age.

Her unbound hair fell free. It was quite long, though few people knew that. During her working hours at the Block, as registrar of voters, she always kept it severely pinned back.

The reason had nothing to do with notions of personal attractiveness. That she didn't think much about. She tried neither to attract men nor to discourage them. If she was involved with someone, fine, and if not, that was fine too. She'd long since learned that the only person worth depending on in this life was herself.

Once upon a time, she'd had a go at marriage. The net result of that experience was that she'd ended up divorced with two children to raise. Which she'd done very well, thank you. While at the same time completing her education and then launching the career in local government that had led to her current position.

Her life plan wasn't going badly, she thought as she brushed her hair out. The kids were teenagers now, good well-adjusted kids untroubled by drugs or any of the other problems that seemed to plague the young. Before long, they'd be off to college and her home responsibilities would lessen that much more.

Then she'd be ready to make her next move. She was

already the highest-ranking female in city government. But it was not nearly high enough. There was no reason why Brisbane shouldn't have the first woman mayor in its history. There was no reason why a woman shouldn't represent the district in the state house.

Edna wanted to be that woman. She'd paid her political dues, doing anything and everything to help the party. She was an excellent organizer, and was respected and even liked by the people she worked with. She was a conservative in an area of the country where that meant a lot. Perhaps most important, she really had no skeletons in her closet.

All things considered, she was the natural choice to succeed Brad Davis.

She frowned at her image in the mirror. Brad Davis had been thought to be a strong incumbent this time around, so she hadn't gone for her party's nomination. Let someone else be the sacrificial lamb.

Only it hadn't quite worked out that way. Suddenly, with the HIVe killers on the loose, Davis was looking shaky. There was even the possibility, if the situation in Brisbane deteriorated further, that Davis might be ousted. And that would set her own career back quite a bit. She couldn't challenge a member of her own party. If he won, she'd have to twiddle her thumbs until he was ready to step down.

Damn the bastards, she thought. Not only were they terrorizing her town, they were interfering personally in her life. They had to be captured, and as quickly as possible. That was one of the reasons she'd gone along with Dusty Rhoades and his group, though without taking an active role. That and the simple fact that they were solid, influential people. Of course they'd have to be very, very careful.

She got into bed. Before settling in for the night, she performed her new nightly ritual, checking the gun she now slept with under her pillow. It was a small Beretta semiautomatic. Edna knew nothing about such weapons, but the man at the store had said it was a good one, and had shown her the basics of its use. She checked it to make sure the little safety lever was on. That meant it couldn't be fired accidentally. She checked the clip, mak-

ing certain there were bullets in it. Then she put the
pistol back in its spot beneath her head.

In actuality, Edna hated handguns, and everything they
represented. She would never have thought that she would
end up owning one. But like a large percentage of the
population of Brisbane, Edna no longer felt safe in her
own home. She had herself and her two children to defend, and there was no man around to help her do it. So
she had bought the Beretta.

It had never been fired and she dearly hoped it never
would be.

Thoughts of the HIVe killers, as always, made Edna
nervous. She got out of bed and padded quietly down the
hall to look in on her children. They were both asleep.

All was as well as could be. Edna returned to her
bedroom and, finally, switched off the light, using the
new switch that was right next to her hand as she slept.

When she awoke an hour later, she knew immediately
that something was wrong. She could sense the presence
of someone in her room, someone who didn't belong
there.

The slimy taste of fear was in her mouth. What she
really wanted to do was scream. But that was wrong,
absolutely wrong. She must not panic.

Not panic.

As the terror rose in her throat, she clamped down
hard on it, forced herself to maintain the gentle breathing
rhythm of sleep.

There is an intruder, she thought. An intruder. A
burglar or a junkie or . . . worse. She set her teeth
against the chill that threatened to make her shiver.

If I don't do this right, she thought, *I may die. And my
children . . . My children . . .*

No.

Slowly, without betraying that she'd come awake, Edna
slid her hand under the pillow and got a grip on the
Beretta. With her other hand she found the light switch.
When she moved, she moved very fast.

She turned on the light, whirled around so that her
back was to the headboard, and pointed the pistol out in
front of her.

There were two people in her bedroom. Two strangers. A man and a woman. They were wearing stocking masks and the woman had a leather pouch slung over her shoulder. *Oh, God . . .*

Edna didn't even think about it. The intruders had frozen when the light came on, and were just standing there. Without a moment's hesitation, she flipped the safety to "off," aimed the gun at the man's chest, and pulled the trigger.

Nothing happened.

Her mind raced. What had she done wrong? It was loaded, the safety was off. Why hadn't she learned more about guns? What *was* it?

The man began to move toward her.

The *slide*! She had to get the first round into the chamber! She pulled back on the slide, but it slipped. It was awkward, trying to do this sitting in the bed.

She pulled again and the man grabbed her wrist. *No.* She fought, jerking on the slide, trying desperately to get that bullet in there. But he twisted her wrist. She was losing. The gun was going to drop out of her hand. It was going to fall to the floor.

No. She couldn't let this happen.

There was a soft thud as the pistol hit the carpet.

Edna was just beginning to scream when the man clubbed her into unconsciousness.

The woman opened her bag and took out a hypodermic.

"I'll get the children," the man said.

51

Friday, August 24

Ellen Greene took the other half of her five-milligram Valium tablet.

For the past week and a half, that was the way she'd gotten through her days, taking Valium two and a half milligrams at a time until she found that state somewhere between sleep and waking where the horror was manageable.

But always, underlying every moment of her life, was the unanswerable question. What was going to happen to Lorene? Was she about to lose her little girl? And why? God in heaven, why?

Ellen had not known there could be such pain, and such uncertainty, and such sorrow.

Until it got worse. Until the moment that morning when her daughter walked up to her and said, "Mommy, I feel funny."

Then, not all the Valium in the world could have cut the dread. It was all she could do not to start shaking uncontrollably right there in front of Lorene. And the poor kid didn't even know, couldn't even have begun to understand what had happened to her.

As calmly as she could, Ellen said, "What do you mean you feel funny, darling?"

"I don't know," Lorene said. "Just funny all over. Like . . . like I'm hot all over. But on the inside. Do you know what I mean?"

"Sure, honey," Ellen said. "It's probably just a little fever. Tell you what, we'll go and see the doctor, okay? He'll make it all better."

"Will they have to stick me again?"

"Probably, hon. But it won't hurt that much. They

need to do it so they can tell how to help you. It'll all be over before you know it, and then . . . then we'll go out to Baskin-Robbins. How's that?"

Lorene hesitated. "Can I have . . . *anything* I want?" she asked shyly.

"Of course, darling," Ellen said, choking back the tears.

"Okay. Let's *go*."

Ellen didn't speed on the way to the hospital. There was no need, she told herself. Getting there five minutes sooner wasn't going to change a thing.

She drove slowly, and despite her drug-impaired reflexes, she made it safely.

At the hospital, everyone seemed to know her and her little girl. And why not? she thought. They were freaks. People loved looking at the freaks.

The routine was familiar. Have a small sample of the girl's blood taken and then meet Dr. Mendez in his office for some words of reassurance. Ellen liked Dr. Mendez, but it was difficult not to transfer some of her bitterness onto him. He was so hopeful when there was so little reason to be. She'd read about Wes Thomas. What did Mendez know about watching a six-year-old, your own flesh and blood, die?

Mendez asked Lorene a few questions, though there really wasn't all that much to be found out. Then he met privately with her mother.

"I'm sorry, Mrs. Greene," Mendez said, "but I really don't know what to tell you. What your daughter is feeling could be anything. It could be related to the virus or it could be some other little bug or it could be nothing at all. It's impossible to say if it's the virus until we get the results of the blood test back."

"And that'll be Sunday?" Ellen said.

"Yes, I'm afraid so."

"If it's the . . . the virus, does that mean this is . . . ?"

"We don't know, Mrs. Greene. Honestly, I'd tell you if we did, but this thing is so new, we have to proceed on a case-by-case basis. No one wants to see Lorene get better any more than I do."

Not even her mother? Ellen thought, but she didn't say anything.

"However," Mendez said, "you have to be realistic. Her chances are . . . not good. You have to be prepared for the worst."

So easy for you to say, she thought. *So easy. No, I am not going to let this man, with his nice white uniform and his fancy title, I am not going to let him see me cry.*

"Thank you, Doctor," she said. "You will let me know as soon as the results are back?"

"Of course," Mendez said. "Of course I will."

"Then I think I'll go buy her an ice cream."

"That's a wonderful idea," Mendez said. He shook her hand and managed to keep from crying himself until she was gone.

52

Edna Clint was furious.

She'd just lived through the most horrible, nightmarish hours conceivable. She'd awakened from her unconsciousness knowing what had happened. There was a note next to her on the floor, but she didn't need it. She *knew*.

She hadn't wasted any time. She'd rushed to the hospital, taking her children with her. They'd taken blood samples from all three victims and requested that the Clints return in twenty-four hours for the taking of a second sampling.

Then she'd talked to the police.

Through the whole ordeal, she'd been emphatic about one thing. She didn't want any publicity about this. She wanted to deal with it in her own way, out of the limelight.

The story had broken on the radio at nine o'clock in the morning, and Edna Clint was furious.

She'd gone immediately to Kip Kyser's office and barged right in without an invitation. She'd demanded to know who had leaked the story to the radio.

The chief of police got a little angry himself. He said that he damn well didn't know, that there were dozens of people at the hospital and in the Block who might have done it, and he resented her implying that he would have had something to do with it.

Clint, however, stood toe to toe with him. She demanded that he find out who the leak was and take action. And while he was at it, she added, he might do a bit more about getting the HIVe killers behind bars.

Then, before Kyser could really blow his stack, she'd stormed out of his office.

height of the Iran-hostage crisis, he'd donated a large amount of money to a commando group that had gone into Cambodia to bring out some American POW's reportedly being held there by the Vietnamese forces of occupation. The commandos had come up empty-handed, but Davis had emerged from the affair smelling like a rose to the noses of a hefty percentage of the local voters.

He'd ridden his popularity to a seat on the county board of supervisors and, after cementing his position within the party, to the office of mayor.

His sustaining hope had always been that once he firmly held the reins of political power, he'd be able to start paying back those who'd slighted him. But it hadn't worked out that way. Four years after being elected, he'd accomplished practically nothing.

There was another photo on his desk, and he gazed at that for a while. Two happy young boys playing in a backyard swimming pool. Gone with their mother and half his yearly income, leaving him feeling like nothing more than another sad statistic.

He sighed. Now, even what little had been left him was threatened. The maniacs spreading the HIV-4 virus were still at large two weeks after they'd first struck. The people of Brisbane were clamoring, and rightfully so, for arrests.

Not only had there been no arrests, but there weren't even, as far as he could see, any solid leads.

The latest victims, Edna Clint and her children, had been a real shocker. Nearly as much as six-year-old Lorene Greene on a personal level, more so in political terms.

Clint was a popular woman in town, a respected and powerful political figure. If she died . . . No, *when* she died, a lot of sentiment was going to shift to her party. Enough to defeat him in the fall? Perhaps.

What a terrible way to look at things, Davis thought. *She's also a colleague and a friend.*

It's the damn HIVe killers. They've driven us all temporarily mad. Temporarily, we hope. But in the meantime, something must be done. The investigation must go better than it's been going.

As if in answer to his thought, his secretary announced Chief Kyser, whom he'd sent for earlier.

"Brad?" Kyser said. The chief was wary. His nerves were as frazzled as anybody else's.

"Kip, I heard about Edna," Davis said. "God, it's awful."

"Yeah, she like to tore my head off, too. 'Bout the radio getting hold to the story."

"Who leaked it?"

"Damned if I know. And I better not hear tell either, if they value their ass."

"You think it could be that girl reporter Grant's been so friendly with?" Davis asked.

"I'd thought of that. She could've been."

"We can't have anything like that happen again."

Kyser looked at the mayor suspiciously. "What're you building up to, Brad?" he asked.

Davis didn't answer right away. Instead, he got up and went to the window overlooking City Plaza. They were all still there, down below, the bored and the self-righteous and the freaks and the ones reporting on it all. If anything, the scene was getting worse. There had now been thirteen arrests right in front of the Block. For everything from disorderly conduct to theft to "incommoding the sidewalk," which meant pissing on it.

The mayor was one of the mob's frequent targets for abuse. Sometimes he felt like a prisoner in his own office.

He turned back to the chief of police.

"The investigation ain't going that well," Davis said.

"We're doing our dead level best," Kyser said defensively. "We can't help it if everything comes up cold-footed."

"Suppose I put it this way. Sometimes a little change can do a deal of good."

"You want to just come out and speak your mind?"

Davis rested his hands on his desk. "All right," he said. "The way I see it, we got three problems. Not counting the HIVe theirselves, which we *got* to catch, and soon.

"One, we need to reassure the public. I'm taking a world of shit over this, and I know you are too. There's those don't think we're doing enough. We need to do something that'll shut them people up.

"Two, we gotta keep the leash on Dusty Rhoades and his gang. That idiot boy burning up was bad enough. But now it looks like they were gonna make trouble at that concert if somebody else hadn't've done it first. And we got Edna Clint attacked, who's one of them. They're bound to be bent for blood from now on, which could be big trouble for me and you and your whole frigging department.

"Three, we got Clint herself. You know what a big deal she is in town. Now, don't get me wrong, what happened to her and the kids is awful. But we can't have her shooting her mouth off, putting the whole blame on us because she's hot about it leaking to the radio station. We need to do something and say we done it with her in mind.

"You with me on all this?"

"I hear you," Kyser said, obviously not too happy with what he'd heard. "You think some changes in the investigation . . ."

"Right. I'm not telling you your job, understand. But Will Grant, well, maybe he just ain't up to it. Maybe you need a little fresh air in there. Especially now he's lost his partner."

Kyser gave the mayor a long, hard look. Whatever was going on behind the chief's washed-out blue eyes, he wasn't about to show it. Finally he sighed.

"I don't know," Kyser said. "Maybe you're right. Okay, I'll move the troops around, see if we can't get something going."

"Good," Davis said. "Glad we agree, Kip."

"Skip it. Just don't you forget you owe me one, Brad."

54

Will Grant was alone in his office, the note lying on the desk in front of him.

Edna Clint had found it next to her when she'd awakened. It was similar to the others, in large impersonal block letters. It said:

Welcome to the HIVe. No one must interfere with what we are doing, especially not those of prominence. The future of the race depends on our work. Do not fight us. Join us willingly in the evolution toward a greater cosmic union.

Jesus, Grant thought as he massaged his temples.

It had been a bitch of a night. He'd been awakened at four in the morning to deal with an attack on the registrar of voters, a member of Dusty Rhoades's little civil vigilance group to boot. And two kids. Two more kids.

Grant was tired. Bad tired. Where would it end?

Already he'd begun to hear rumors that other public officials were demanding special police protection. Sure. Take a bunch of guys working double overtime as it was, and stretch them even thinner.

What an oddball he was, he thought. Here he had twenty years in as a cop and he still believed in the system. He'd seen firsthand how the judges and the prosecutors and the defense attorneys made the sleaziest kinds of deals; he'd seen how the rich got off scot-free while the poor went to jail for the same crimes; he'd seen the contempt so many people had for so many of the laws, taking their cue from businessmen, and sports heroes, and movie stars, and politicians right on up to the President of the United States.

He'd seen it all, yet he still believed. He believed that the system, old and creaky though it might be, was the best one ever devised by men, and that the job he did—if unenthusiastically at times—was a right and necessary one.

He believed in addition that most people were basically honest, though most were also corruptible if enough easy money was held in front of their faces.

And he believed that, in the end, the good guys would win and the bad guys would be punished for their misdeeds. That was what the whole idea of justice was all about.

At least, I thought I'd seen it all, Grant thought.

But then there was the HIVe. He'd never seen anything like this case. There was no sense to be made of it. Always, before, there'd been some logic to what people did, no matter how twisted. You looked at their actions long enough and you could see what they were doing. And once you found the thread, you could get in their shoes, anticipate them.

But this? The "future of the race"? "Cosmic union"?

The HIVe was somewhere past crazy, past evil, beyond any categories he'd been able to define in his life. They didn't make *sense*.

How could the system deal with people like them?

He shook his head. He didn't know. And he feared what might happen to his own mind before he found out.

Pound stuck his head in the door and said, "Chief wants to see you in his office."

Grant raised his head from his hands. "Me?" he said.

"No, the peckerwood over there in the corner."

Grant actually looked around.

"Jesus," Pound muttered, and went on about his business.

After a long moment, Grant got up and walked down the hall to Kip Kyser's office. It was a wearisome trip. He had nothing to say to the chief. He had nothing new to report. As Kyser was well aware. He didn't want to be doing this.

Kyser was distant and businesslike, the way he got

when someone was about to eat a very large amount of
shit.

"Lieutenant," Kyser said, "sit down. We need to talk."

Grant sat. *I'm being taken off the case*, he thought.

"Will, you know and I know that the investigation
of these HIVe monsters ain't going that well. I been
thinking about it, and I believe it's time to make a few
changes."

Yeah, Grant thought. *That's it, all right.*

He felt an odd mixture of emotions. He was being
insulted, being told in a roundabout way that he wasn't
getting the job done. There was even the implication,
if he was looking for it, that he might not be *able*
to get it done. All that made him angry. Yet he
couldn't deny that there was also a sense of relief
involved.

He was dog tired. He'd done his goddamnedest and he
hadn't been able to get a thing. Maybe it was time to
take a break.

Screw that, he thought. *No one could have done any
better than I've done.*

"This case has took on a lot of . . . aspects," Kyser
continued. "Now, I ain't saying you ain't done a good
job. You done one hell of a job. Couldn't *nobody* have
given it more than you."

"Then what *are* you saying?" Grant said, feeling himself become defensive.

"Just this. Comes a time when we got to look at the
bigger picture."

"If you're pulling me off the case, just say so, Kip."

"Now, that ain't it, Will. That ain't it at all. I just feel
it'd be best if I move my men around a little. We got
more than one problem going on here."

"Like what?"

"Well, like Dusty Rhoades and this damn group of his.
I don't know what they was doing at that concert Tuesday, but it sure wasn't any good. We can't have people
flying loose, trying to solve crimes on their own. I
think it'd be a good idea if we kept a little closer
watch on them."

"You want me to do it?"

"Yeah. I'd like you to get together with them and persuade them to kind of lay a bit low. Then make sure they stay out of trouble until this thing is over."

"And somebody else is gonna head up the investigation."

"I think that'd be good. Just for the time being. I'm thinking Pound and Worth. Maybe coordinated with someone from the D.A.'s office. What I'd like you to do is get all your notes and files together and give them a full briefing on everything you and Martin did. Sometime this afternoon, if you don't mind."

Pound and Worth, Grant thought. *Dear God.*

"All right," Grant said, "this afternoon." He paused, then added, "You know, I told you a long time ago I thought we ought not to tolerate some damn vigilante thing like Dusty put together."

"Oh, come on, Will," Kyser said. "Their intentions was good. They're just a little out of hand now."

"Yeah, sure. Just a little out of hand. Anything else you wanted to talk to me about?"

"Now you mention it," Kyser said carefully, "there *is* one other thing."

"What's that?" Grant said, feeling immediately defensive once again.

"I guess you know we got us a leak."

"Everyone knows that. What, you think it's me?"

" 'Course not, Will. But Edna Clint was in here this morning, like to have my nuts for breakfast over what she heard on the radio. After asking us all to keep it under our hats. Now, I don't care for a chewing-out, especially from some damn woman. But I got to admit she had a point."

"Of course. But what's yours?"

Kyser examined his lieutenant closely. "Like I said," he went on, "I know it wouldn't be you, Will. But what about your friend?"

"What friend?"

"That girl reporter."

"Layne? Oh, for Christ's sake, Kip, you think I tell her anything I don't want to read in the paper?"

"Just asking, is all."

Grant got up. "Well, I don't particularly like the question," he said. "If stuff is leaking through Dabney Layne, it ain't by way of me. Anything else on your mind, Chief?"

"That'll do her," Kyser said coolly. "You will talk to Dusty and them tonight, won't you?"

"I'll talk to them, if you think they'll listen to me."

"I believe so. This is an important assignment, Will. See you take it thataway."

"Sure."

55

Grant was steaming as he walked back down the hall, passing Worth along the way. Did the man look down his nose at him just a little bit? Grant wasn't sure, but he shot back a look that he hoped was equally hard to decipher.

Worth stopped him. "Ah, Will," he said, "look, I'm sorry about this."

Sure you are.

"But when do you want to, ah, do the briefing?"

"Three o'clock in the office," Grant said. "I should have everything together by then."

"Fine. See you then."

Yeah, you fat smug bastard.

When Grant got back to his office he was, fortunately, alone. He sat in his chair and propped his feet up on the desk, not terribly inclined to go to work.

Up at four in the morning and then stuck in the back of the closet like a Christmas tie.

And what was he supposed to work *on*, anyway?

Oh, yeah, the "vigilantes." Goddamn stupid civilians playing cop. Sure, he'd talk to them.

He called Dusty Rhoades.

"Dusty," he said when he had the realtor on the line, "it's Will Grant. I want to meet with you and your friends."

"Oh. Well, I don't know, Lieutenant," Rhoades said. "We're all pretty busy and—"

"Can it, Dusty. This ain't a social invitation."

"I . . . see. When would you like to—"

"Tonight."

"Tonight? I don't know if I can—"

"Your house," Grant said. "Eight o'clock. See everyone's there, will you? I think that caliber of folks'd prefer it to coming down to the Block."

He hung up before Dusty could protest any more. He didn't care that much for Rhoades. The man had a nicelooking wife and that was about it. Grant wasn't in the mood to listen to a lot of whiny excuses about this and that. God help these people if they ever *did* stumble across any of the HIVe killers.

After hanging up, Grant brooded for a while. He found that any sense of relief he'd felt earlier had vanished. He didn't want to sit around while other people investigated this case. It was his case. Hell, it was the whole town's case. They couldn't afford to have less than a maximum effort.

He couldn't disobey his chief, but . . . The more he thought about it, the more firmly he decided that there was an out. Kyser hadn't actually said he was *off* the case. All the chief had done was remove him from the head of the investigation. He might have implied that he wanted his lieutenant working on other things, but he hadn't come out and said it. Maybe he'd been afraid to.

Whatever, that gave him a bit of slack, Grant decided.

He was doing his assignment, that is, keeping an eye on Dusty Rhoades and his group. Okay. But that wasn't going to be near a full-time occupation. The way Grant saw it, there was nothing to prevent him from pursuing whatever leads might come his way. In his spare time, of course.

He was trying to think of a lead to pursue when the phone rang.

It was David Bourne.

Grant had to think on it for a minute. Who the hell was David Bourne? Then he dredged it up. The kid from Dunmore College who'd done the legwork on the Skulls concert. One of his "leads."

"Hello, Mr. Bourne," Grant said. "Thank you for calling back."

"Is this about the concert, Lieutenant?" Bourne asked.

"Yes, but probably not in the way you think. I'm not

that interested in what happened that night. That's a Dunmore police problem."

"Oh. Well, what, then?"

"Tell the truth, I don't know exactly," Grant admitted. "You read the papers? You know what's going on in Brisbane?"

"The HIVe people?"

"Yes. I'm looking for something that might connect them with the Skulls."

"Well, one of them sings about a virus and the other spreads it. Other than that, I don't know of anything."

"It'll probably come to nothing, I agree, but we're checking every lead we can think of over here. Tell me, Mr. Bourne, how'd you happen to pick the Skulls for your summer concert?"

"Not a very exciting story, I'm afraid," Bourne said. "The Festival got a call from a New York agent saying that a friend of his thought the Skulls might go over pretty well down here, and that we should consider them for the summer gig. It sounded good, so I eventually worked out the details."

"That would be Mr. Kronsky," Grant said. "The New York agent?"

"Kronsky? Yeah, he's the Skulls' agent. He's the one we ended up signing the contract with, of course. But no, he wasn't the one who originally proposed the group. That was a guy named Viktor Laszlo."

"Hnnh. That's interesting. Could you spell that for me, please?"

Bourne did.

"And who was Mr. Laszlo's friend?" Grant asked.

"Beats me," Bourne said. "It sounded like a good idea. We thought we could make some money with the Skulls, so we went ahead, God help us. We didn't realize they were that violent a group. But that's what college is about, isn't it? Learning experiences?"

"Never went myself. Anything else you know that might link the Skulls to this area?"

"Sorry, Lieutenant. Not a thing. And I hope we never see them again."

"Me too. Well, thanks for your time, Mr. Bourne. Can I reach you there again if I have to?"

"Sure thing. Two more semesters, anyway. Then I'm gone. But I can't imagine I'd have anything further for you, Lieutenant."

Grant hung up and looked at the name he'd written in his notebook. Viktor Laszlo. Somebody who knew somebody in Brisbane. It was a lead, no doubt about it.

He got the number from Information and placed a call to the man. This time, he was a lot luckier than he'd been with Kronsky. He was on hold for only ten minutes before he was allowed through to Laszlo himself.

"Just got a sec, Lieutenant," Laszlo said. "What can I do you out of?"

"I'll keep it short," Grant said. "I was wondering what your connection with the Skulls is, Mr. Laszlo."

"The Skulls? Why, none, I'm afraid. I don't handle any rock-and-roll."

"Oh. Well, the reason I ask, I talked to someone at the Dunmore College Festival of the Performing Arts, and he told me you'd helped arrange for the Skulls to play there."

"Not really. I did do a small favor for a friend, but I wasn't involved in any of the details of hiring the Skulls."

"What do you mean, you did a favor?" Grant asked.

"Nothing much. A longtime client of mine asked if I'd look into the possibility of bringing the group to Dunmore. He didn't know who was booking the Skulls and asked if I could find out and then put them in touch with the Dunmore people. It was a simple-enough request, so I did it. I got the two parties together, and that was the last of my involvement with the whole affair. Now, if—"

"Your former client, why didn't he handle it himself?"

"I don't know, Lieutenant. Some things, people deal more readily with an agent. Look, the man has earned me a lot of money over the years. If I can do some little favor for him, hey, as long as it's legal I do it, okay?"

"Sure, fine. Now, this client of yours," Grant said. "What's his name?"

"My friend doesn't like publicity," Laszlo said. "That may be one of the reasons he came to me about this in the first place."

"Doesn't like publicity? In your business?"

"Doesn't like it anymore. He's retired. What's this all

about, if you don't mind my asking? Is he suspected of something?"

"Not at all," Grant said apologetically. "I don't even know who he is. It's just that, well, I'm sure you heard about the riot at the Skulls concert."

"I heard. I don't particularly like the Nazi bastards myself."

"I can understand that. Anyway, the thing is, the Dunmore police are having quite a time sorting the whole thing out, and they asked us if we could give them a hand from over our side. So when I heard from the boy at the Festival that someone here in Brisbane was involved in the concert, I thought I'd look into it. I'm just helping tie up some loose ends."

"I see."

"All I'd like to do is ask your client a couple of questions. Do you think he'd object to that?"

"No, I don't see why he would."

"Then could you tell me his name?"

Laszlo hesitated, then said, "I suppose it can't hurt. His name is Dante Glorio. He's an actor."

"Oh, yeah. Used to been in the soaps, didn't he?"

"Daytime drama, yes. But he's retired now, like I said."

"How come?"

"Look, Lieutenant, if you want to know things like that, you'll have to ask *him*. Now, if you don't mind . . ."

"No, I don't want to keep you, Mr. Laszlo. Thank you very much for your help."

Grant wrote the name Dante Glorio in his notebook and drew a circle around it. He'd heard the name and was sort of vaguely aware that the man was originally from Brisbane, had had a career in TV, and now lived somewhere to the west of town. That wasn't his real name, of course. What was his real name? Grant tried to come up with it but couldn't.

He stared at the name he'd written down. Was this a lead? If it was, it was a damn skimpy one.

"Hi," Dabney Layne said from the doorway. "Got a minute for an old friend?"

Grant looked up, then quickly closed his notebook. That was the last thing he needed, for the press to get hold of his leads before he'd had a chance to pursue them. In fact, he didn't particularly want to see Layne at all right now.

"Withholding information from the public, Lieutenant?" Layne asked as she came into his office.

"Police business," Grant muttered.

"My, we're in a good mood today, aren't we?"

"Look . . ." Grant began, then reconsidered. "This just ain't a good time."

"What's wrong?"

"You know what's wrong."

"Other than that."

Grant looked her in the eye and thought he saw a hint of genuine concern there. He reconsidered again.

"Ah, what the hell," he said. "Kyser's gonna be announcing it to the papers anyway. The investigative team's being 'restructured,' I believe is the term. It's a fancy way of saying they're taking me off the case."

Layne was dumbfounded. "But . . . why? I don't understand."

"C'mon, Penny," Grant said. "You may have been born at night, but it wasn't *last* night. I've been on the case for two weeks and I've pulled a zipper. The town's going nutso. Everybody wants results. We can't give them any, so the chief hands out the next-best thing. Shuffle the players around, make it look like there's big doings. It's the oldest con in the business."

"I don't believe this. You know more about the case than anyone."

"Yeah, that and forty bucks'll get you three hots and a flop. Big deal. The point is, I had my chance and I fucked it up. I couldn't cut it."

"Quit it, Will. No one could have done more than you did."

"Tell that to Kip Kyser. Or the mayor, one. He's got more heat on him, so he's more likely to be behind it."

There was an awkward pause, then Layne said, "Dammit. It just makes me so angry."

"Yeah, lost your best source, didn't you?" Grant said.

"I'll pretend I didn't hear that."

"Okay, but it's true."

"You bastard. You think that's all you are to me, a source?"

Grant shrugged. "I don't know," he said. "What am I to you?"

"Right now you look like someone who's going to roll over and play dead because he got set back a little."

"Yeah? Maybe you best leave then. You don't want to be hanging around with a *loser*, do you?"

"Oh, that's great. Really great. You got your pride hurt and you're going to put it off on *me*? I *care* about this case, Will Grant. I . . . I care about you too. The reason I came down here today is I had an idea that maybe could help you out."

Grant folded his arms. "What kind of idea?" he said.

"I thought we could work together to try to trap the killers."

"What are you talking about?"

Layne leaned forward and spoke as if she didn't want anyone else to hear.

"I spend a lot of time out interviewing people. I go where people are, stores and bars and out front of this place. What I was thinking was, why not keep on going out to bars at night, but not looking to find anyone, looking to have someone find me. You know, sit by myself like I was *available*. That way, if the HIVe people are out cruising the bars I might . . . attract one of them."

"Penny," Grant said tersely, "get the hell out of here."

"Huh?"

Grant felt the anger rising in him. On top of the other frustrations of the day, it was too much.

"I said get the hell out of here! That is *the* stupidest goddamn thing I ever heard of! These people are *killers*, for Christ's sake. And you're gonna make yourself *bait*?"

"Hey," Layne said heatedly, "hold on, pal. You think I wanted to do this on my own? That's why I'm here, remember? I wanted you to know, so you could be behind me."

Grant leveled his forefinger at her. "Don't you *never* do anything like you're suggesting. You start doing police work, and I'll have *your* ass in jail, you understand me? Now, go on. Beat it. I got work to do."

Layne stared at him, her jaw clenched, but Grant ignored her and began sorting through his papers.

"I see," Layne said as she got up. "All right, if that's the way you want it. You have a nice day too, Lieutenant."

When she'd gone, Grant regretted what had happened. He liked her. He *wanted* to like her. But . . . Shit, the principle was the same whether he liked her or not. It was the cops' job to enforce the laws, not anybody's who felt like it. It was just like it was with the vigilantes, no different. You got people out there stalking the killers who didn't know what they were doing, and you'd end up with something out of the Old West. A bloodbath, more than likely.

Layne had been gone for five minutes and he could still feel her presence, smell it almost. If only they could've met under different circumstances, he thought.

Forget it. She was a damn meddler and he had work to do. He had to get his files together to be able to brief Pound and Worth at three o'clock.

He spent every minute of the next couple of hours doing just that. It wasn't easy, but by the time the two fat detectives parked their butts in their chairs, he was ready.

Grant didn't like having these two doing his job. But he was a professional. The briefing he gave them was as thorough as it could have been. *For all the good it'll do*, he thought as he watched them grunt over the notes they were trying to take.

When he got to the last page of his own notebook, it was nearly five. He looked at the name he'd written there earlier in the day and wondered if he ought to tell them about it.

He hesitated, then decided: *No, I'll track this one down myself*.

In truth, Grant had almost forgotten about Dante Glorio. A lot had happened since the phone call to Laszlo.

"That's it, gentlemen," he told Pound and Worth.

There was another half-hour of question-and-answer, and then the other two were gone.

When he was alone, the first thing Grant did was try Directory Information. No number for Glorio.

Okay. Next he called the newspaper. He had a friend

working there who knew more about Brisbane than anyone. Luckily, his friend was in.

"Brett," Grant said, "Will Grant. The encyclopedia working today?"

"Yeah," Brett said, "but I'm not. I'm outta here. I've got a very hot date, Lieutenant."

"Just a couple of quick questions."

Brett sighed. "Yeah, I'll bet. What?"

"Dante Glorio, you know him?"

"Not personally. But I know of him."

"That's what I need. What's his real name?"

"Bobby Drew. You know the Drews, out in the country? Own all that land next to the McCullers place? *Those* Drews."

Right. It was coming back to him now. Couple of years younger than Grant. He'd gone to the same elementary school, but then the difference in family wealth had done its work. Grant stayed in public school, while Drew was off to some private academy.

"He live out there now?" Grant asked.

"Yeah," Brett said. "On what's left of it. The family had to sell a lot of their spread back in the late fifties. Eventually they all died off and Bobby inherited what there was. A hundred acres or so, and the old house. The estate used to be called Windermere, I believe, but he renamed it when he took it over. Calls it Blake Manor now."

"What's that mean? Anything?"

"Uh-huh. Drew, or Glorio rather, used to play a character named Blake on a TV soap opera. Then he had an accident and his face got messed up and he had to quit the business. That's when he moved back here. I don't believe he's hurting for money."

"Anyone live with him?" Grant asked.

"Dunno. I think he's somewhat of a recluse. Because of his face and all."

"Okay, thanks, Brett. That's really all I need. Enjoy your hot date."

Next Grant tried Information again, this time for Bobby or Robert Drew. The operator informed him politely that that was an unlisted number and that she couldn't give it out simply because someone said he was a police officer.

But all that meant was that it would take one more call, to someone else at the phone company who knew who the lieutenant was. In less than a minute, Grant had the number.

He wrote it under Dante Glorio's name, next to the information he'd copied down while talking to Brett, and stared at what he had.

It definitely wasn't much. There wasn't the least bit of evidence that this ex-actor was in any way connected to the HIVe. But that was the way it went sometimes. You worked the flimsiest leads as well as the strongest ones. There was no telling which would yield up something of importance.

Grant glanced at his watch. Speaking of important things, he just about had time to get some dinner before he was due to be at Dusty Rhoades's house.

He closed his notebook. Dante Glorio could wait until morning.

56

They were all there, gathered once again in Dusty Rhoades's living room, as they had been nine days—was it only nine days?—earlier.

Even Rhonda Jo was there. Although she'd opposed the group right from the start, the fears she'd felt the night she thought she'd picked up one of the HIVe had caused her to have a lot more sympathy for what Dusty was doing.

The only charter member missing was Edna Clint. But under the circumstances, Will Grant wasn't about to make an issue out of that.

Grant had known the group's membership since shortly after it was formed. He'd made it a point to find out. But as he looked around the room, he still had trouble believing what he saw. These people should be among the most law-abiding citizens of Brisbane. What in God's name were they doing fooling around with something like this?

Especially Dot Pritchett. He reserved his coolest look for her. She worked for the police, for Christ's sake. She had no business being a part of it.

"All right," Grant said. "You know why I'm here. The chief is shaking up the department's investigation of the HIVe. As I'm sure our representative has told you."

He looked directly at Dot Pritchett, and she looked right back at him without flinching.

"As part of the reorganization effort," Grant went on, "we're asking you to cool it out here. Just lay off. We got some good leads and we're following them up."

"Sure," Rhoades said. "And who's going to protect us in the meantime? You? You're not even on the case anymore, Lieutenant. That supposed to build our confidence?"

"We'll catch them," Grant said. "And we don't need your help to do it. I'm not asking you, I'm telling you."

"Why should we listen to you?" Rhoades said. "You ain't done doodly-squat with this case."

"Is that so?" Grant said.

"If you had, you'd still be on it and we wouldn't be looking at losing the brewery."

There were shouts of assent from the rest of the group.

Grant felt angry and manipulated and helpless. He didn't want to baby-sit these morons. He suddenly thought of Penny Layne. She had her half-cocked ideas and they had theirs. There wasn't much to choose between the two.

I care about this case. I care about you too.

No, maybe there *was* something to choose.

He paused to make sure his temper didn't start leaking out on him. Then he looked around the room, catching and holding each person's eye in turn.

As he did, he said, "All right, that's enough. I'm really only here to tell you one thing, and you best listen up. Y'all leave cop business to us. You see anything, fine, you report it. You hear anything, you do the same. But you *do* anything and you're gonna find yourself on the hub of hell. That about clear?"

Grant got up.

He could feel himself at the center of everyone's contempt, but he was going to leave until Rhoades said, "Clear as a damn incompetent fool could make it."

"What'd you say?" Grant said.

"Good night, Lieutenant," Rhoades said.

And then Grant lost it. Rhoades turned into Kip Kyser and Brad Davis and Penny Layne and all the HIVe killers rolled into one, and Grant went for him.

Rhoades saw him coming and was getting to his feet as the two men collided. They went crashing to the floor, Grant grabbing the other man's shirtfront and shaking it and yelling something incomprehensible at him, Rhoades clubbing away with his cast.

The others were stunned, but only for a moment. Three of them jumped on the lieutenant's back, pulling his arms away from Rhoades. Grant continued to yell and struggle, but it wasn't long before his heart wasn't in it anymore.

The action quickly wound down, then stopped. Grant shook the people off his arms and got up. He walked out of the house without another word.

Behind him, Rhoades was shouting, "Anytime, Lieutenant! Just you and me! Any*time*!"

Grant got into his car and sat there for a moment, his hands gripping the wheel to keep them from shaking.

What's happening? he thought. *What's happening to me? What's happening to all of us?*

There were a lot of questions that he didn't have answers for. But there was one that he did: what to do next.

As soon as he had calmed down, he drove to the nearest bar, where he had a bourbon and water. And then he had another.

And so on. By the time he got home, they only thing he wanted to do was crawl into bed and sleep until all the evil in the world went away.

He was halfway to the bedroom when the phone rang. Any further along and he wouldn't have bothered to answer it.

"Lieutenant Grant?" the voice asked. Male. Familiar.

"Yeah," Grant grunted.

"It's Death Aims," the voice said. "Of the Skulls?"

Grant sighed. "It's late, son," he said.

"Yeah, I know. I tried to get you earlier. Look, I wanted to thank you for what you done for us."

"Don't take it personal."

Death Aims laughed. "You're a funny cop," he said. "Anyway, maybe I can do you a favor in return. There's something I didn't tell you Wednesday."

Grant perked up immediately. The bourbon fumes began to dissipate.

"What's that?" he asked.

"We got a weird letter up here," the Skulls' leader said, "the week before we was coming to play down there. Thought you might be interested in it."

Death Aims read the letter.

By the time he'd finished, Grant was nearly sober. The

letter had to be from the HIVe. They were expecting the Skulls. They were probably *at* the concert.

Jeff's note.

Jeff.

"Can you send me the letter?" Grant asked.

"Sure," Death Aims said. "We don't need it for nothing."

"Thanks."

"Sure thing, Lieutenant."

Grant hung up. A few hours' sleep. Just a few hours' sleep and then things were going to start happening.

57

Dabney Layne had been hanging her ass out for bait for several nights now, and she wasn't about to stop just because Will Grant told her to.

Each evening she made the rounds. The Inferno, the Skyview, the Kit Kat, the cocktail lounge at the Brisbane Arms, and several other upscale spots. A number of men had tried to pick her up, and one woman as well. But in every instance, after engaging in conversation for a while, Layne had decided the person wasn't what she was looking for.

Not that she had a very clear idea of what that was. Who could say for certain how a HIVe member would come on? But Layne trusted her professional instincts. Somehow, she believed, she'd know one when she found one.

Friday was more of the same. She'd done her best, put on a slinky dress she'd bought earlier in the day, a satiny number with slit sides that emphasized her best feature, her legs. And there were more people out, more attempts to hit on her than on weekdays. But zilch had come of it. She'd wound up alone at the bar of the Skyview, approaching her tolerance for white wine.

Layne didn't see the tall, skinny man when he first entered the bar and stood near the entrance, scanning the place.

The man had long hair and a full beard. He was dressed in a gray running suit and had a sweatband wrapped around his head. He looked around purposefully.

There, the man thought as his eyes fixed on the dark red hair. *That's her*.

The thought made him nervous. This wasn't something

he was good at. Unlike Glorio, he'd never had a way
with women. Glorio couldn't know how hard it was going
to be. But it had to be done; he had to take his turn.
There was so much at stake.

The man was relieved that there wasn't an immediate
opening at the bar. It'd give him a chance to collect his
thoughts, decide what kind of things he might talk about.

As unobtrusively as he could, he took a table at the
rear of the Skyview and waited.

The clearing-out process didn't take long. One of the
men sitting next to the reporter, having tried his luck and
failed, gave up. He paid his bill and walked away.

There could be no further delay now. That seat wasn't
going to be there for long. The man in the running suit
got up from his table and went to the bar.

"Is anyone sitting here?" he asked Dabney Layne.

She looked over at him and shook her head.

"May I?" he asked.

"Depends," Layne said. "How sweaty are you?"

The man didn't laugh. He just said, "I haven't been
exercising. I just find this . . . comfortable."

"Be my guest," Layne said.

Nervous, she thought. *No sense of humor. Great.*

"Ah, what're you drinking?" the man asked. "I'll buy
you one."

"Thanks," Layne said. "At this point I think I better
have a lemon spritzer."

"Okay."

The man ordered a Seven and Seven for himself. He
ordered her lemon spritzer as if he'd never heard of one.

When the drinks came, Layne turned to her new companion to thank him again and, for the first time, took a
really good look at him.

And she must have stared, because he said, "What are
you looking at?"

"Oh, just . . . your eyes," she said hastily. "You have
very nice eyes."

Not too hastily, she warned herself.

The man didn't seem to notice.

"Uh, thank you," he said. "I don't know why they're
like that. They just are. A lot of people think I'm on
drugs all the time." He chuckled as if humor came rarely

into his life. "But I'm not," he added quickly and with concern. "I think drugs are terrible. Don't you?"

"Absolutely," Layne said. Her composure had returned. "Ruining the country."

But it hadn't really been his eyes. They *were* unusual, liquid and shiny bright. Under other circumstances, they might have attracted her attention. But not here, not now.

It was the way he was made up.

Back in her college days, Layne had taken a stab at acting. And she'd had talent, she thought, even if not of professional caliber. In any case, she'd gone at learning the trade with her normal enthusiasm and single-minded dedication. She immersed herself in it for a while.

Those days were long behind her, but bits of what she'd learned had stuck in little corners of her mind. Just in case.

It was one of those bits that had pumped the adrenaline into her system when she looked the stranger over. Because he was, unquestionably, made up to look different.

Whoever had done him had done a nice job. The untrained eye would never have noticed. But an actor would.

The man's long hair was phony. So were his beard and mustache. His cheekbones had been artificially emphasized, the shape of his mouth subtly altered.

There might be any number of reasons why someone would want to make over his face. Including . . .

"What's your name?" Layne asked.

"Carlton," the man said. "Carlton Hunt."

Hunt, Layne thought. *Isn't that interesting?*

"I'm Dabney Layne," she said.

"Pleased to meet you. You're not from around here, are you?"

"How'd you guess?"

Again, he took her question seriously. "Well, it's the accent, mostly," he said.

"Yeah, I guess that sort of gives it away."

Over the next hour they made bar talk. Layne played it completely straight. There was always the chance *they* knew exactly who she was, and if she deviated from the truth, it might make "Carlton" suspicious. She couldn't risk that.

He told her that he worked as a clerk in the county tax assessor's office. His office wasn't that popular with the people, of course, but it was a steady job and it sure beat working for the chemical company, like so many of them did.

He'd never known anyone from New York City, he said. Brisbane had kind of been off the main Southern tourist route before the "troubles." And he was very unfamiliar with the workings of a major national periodical. He wanted to know all the details.

Layne didn't find it difficult talking with him. He was friendly enough, in his fashion. He listened well, though she didn't think he was on the bright side.

But the more they talked, the more a couple of things began to bother her. One was the absence of a sense of humor. The other was harder to put into words. It was a remoteness, a coldness at the core. This man, she sensed, was different from other people. She could imagine him doing the most bizarre things without emotion, and without realizing there was something missing.

She'd been alternating spritzers with wine and, though a little light-headed, had managed to keep her wits about her. She'd also been giving him the impression that she was getting tipsy.

" 'Scuse me," she said, swaying on her bar stool. "I don't feel so good. Believe I best go to the ladies' room."

She slid off her stool, stumbled. He caught her arm.

"Thanks," she mumbled, and tottered off.

She stayed in the ladies' room for five minutes. Had to make it look good, but not be gone so long that he was scared off. She splashed cold water on her face and studied herself in the mirror, asking herself some hard questions.

Should she call Will Grant? Should she go anywhere with this man?

And she made her decision.

When Layne returned to the bar, Carlton was still there. She breathed an inaudible sigh of relief and continued with her drunken-lady act.

"Sorry," she told him. " 'M a little sick." She tried her best to blush.

Then she said to the bartender, "Call me a cab, will you?"

The bartender nodded.

"I'll take you home," Carlton said.

She gazed at him with what she hoped seemed like warmth. "Ah, that's sweet of you," she said. She patted his cheek. "But that's okay. Us big-city girls can take care of ourselves."

He looked disappointed.

"I don't mean to put you off," she said. "I really do like you, Carlton. It's just . . . I'm tired and I don't feel good. I wouldn't be much fun tonight. Tell you what. How about having dinner with me tomorrow?"

"Oh," he said. "Well . . . okay."

She grinned. "Great. Why don't we meet here for drinks at seven, and then you can take me to your favorite place. I'd like that."

"Okay."

They drank a little more together and in a few minutes a cabbie came in and called her name.

"The master's voice," she said. "See you tomorrow, Carlton. 'Night."

"Good night, Miss Layne."

Layne went out into a night air made humid by the return of a southerly air flow. She got in the cab and handed the driver a five-dollar bill.

"We're only going a block," she said. "But hurry."

He took her to her own rental car and she rushed back, hoping her plan would work but knowing she had the following night as a backup. She parked on the street, within sight of the Skyview's parking lot. She'd give him an hour, she thought. If he didn't show by then, it probably meant she'd missed him, and she'd give it up. She couldn't very well go back into the lounge to check.

She lucked out. Hunt had apparently finished his drink at a leisurely pace, because it was fifteen minutes before he emerged from the bar. He fetched his car from the lot and drove off.

Layne followed him. She wasn't exactly unskilled at

this. It was one of the little things you picked up if you wanted to be an efficient investigative reporter.

It was easy enough in town. But Hunt kept on driving. Before long they were on a two-lane country road, heading west. Layne had to hang back more than she would have liked. She even let another car get in between them. Fortunately, Carlton wasn't a speeder.

Then, coming up over a rise, she realized she'd lost him. She drove slowly for about half a mile, then turned around and backtracked. There was only woods on one side of the road. On the other, there were two choices. The first was a dairy farm, the second an asphalt road that disappeared into some trees and was marked "Private Drive."

Time to make an educated guess. Layne opted for the private drive. Her bar buddy just hadn't seemed the farmer type.

Then there was the next decision.

Assume that the private drive led to an estate, or at least a large secluded house, back up there somewhere. Was this where Carlton Hunt lived?

Could be, with a nice patrician name like that. On the other hand, he'd said he was a clerk. That might or might not be true. If it was, he certainly didn't live on an estate out here in the country. And, in addition, Layne hadn't gotten the impression that he was a highly educated person. Again, if he were a part of the local landed gentry, one would expect him to have gone to the finest schools.

All right. Suppose, then, he had come here for some reason other than that it was where he lived. If that was the case, then at some point later on he might leave and drive home. And it might be profitable for her to continue following him.

That was a lot of ifs.

Layne took stock of herself. She was facing the possibility of a long night in a hot, cramped car. She was tired and still a little high from the wine. The prospect was decidedly unappealing.

But her investigative instincts were twitching, there was no denying that. She silently cursed herself. It seemed like whenever she went to make a decision, she'd actually already made it.

She went looking for a place to hide.

She had to cruise up and down the main road a couple of times before she found it. It was just the ghost of a track leading into the woods, perhaps an old logging road, and obviously unused for a long time. It was completely overgrown, on the opposite side from the private drive, about a quarter of a mile west. There was a good angle for watching the drive, and anyone emerging from it would be unlikely to spot her, especially since, if they were going to Brisbane, they'd be heading east.

Layne paused, looking at the twin ruts poking their way into the woods. She hesitated, thinking about her rental Ford. It sure as hell didn't have four-wheel drive. If she got stuck . . .

No, might as well chance it. There hadn't been any rain since she'd come to Brisbane. The ground looked solid enough. Carefully she turned the car around and backed down the track. The Ford slid cleanly in among the trees.

Layne switched off the engine and the lights and rolled down the window. After the comfort of air conditioning, the muggy night air seemed like a wet blanket. And she hadn't really considered that there were also bound to be mosquitoes on the prowl. But there was no alternative. If she kept the window up, she'd probably suffocate.

She resigned herself to enduring one miserable night, her only consolation that she'd had to do this sort of thing before and had survived.

It went badly, but her luck held. Only about an hour passed before a car came out of the private drive. At that distance, in the dark, she couldn't be sure. It looked like his.

She made the decision, probably more on the basis of her discomfort than anything else. She started the engine. When he'd passed from sight, she pulled out and began following again.

Country traffic was still light, but they hit Brisbane just about the time the bars were closing. There were a lot of Friday-night fun-seekers on the road. She was able to move a little closer and positively identify the car as Hunt's. Which didn't mean he was driving it, of course.

Layne prayed he didn't live on some tiny dead-end street where it would be obvious what she was doing.

He didn't. He drove to the southeast part of town—a somewhat seedy section that Layne immediately thought more suited to his personality than the country—and turned off one of Brisbane's main drags a block and a half ahead of his tail, onto a smaller street called Sunset Avenue.

By the time Layne made the turn onto Sunset, Hunt had parked his car in front of a two-story white frame house and was walking quickly toward a set of stairs that climbed the house's outside wall. Layne drove past him.

Hunt was on the stairs, with his back to the street, but Layne hadn't dared to turn her head, in case he suddenly looked around. Nevertheless, her practiced eye had seen a lot out of its corner. She'd be able to find this house in the daytime, no problem.

And there was one other thing. She'd been right about the long hair. It was gone.

58

Though she'd never been to his house before, Dabney Layne knew where Will Grant lived. She'd made it a point to find out shortly after she'd first made contact with him. You never knew when information like that might come in handy.

It was a modest little concrete-block house, with shuttered windows and a neat front yard. It looked like dozens of others in the area, except that one of the windows had been broken and cardboarded over.

She wondered if she should have come. It was two o'clock in the bloody morning. He was probably still irritated over what had happened to him. And she was hardly at her best.

Well, why worry about it? She was here.

She got out of the car and went to Grant's door. After only a brief final hesitation, she leaned on the bell. She could hear it ringing as if the inside of the house were far away. It rang for a long time, so long that she almost decided he wasn't there. Then a light came on.

A few moments later the door opened and Grant was standing in front of her. He was barefoot and shirtless, and had on a pair of pants with the fly hanging open. He had a pistol in his right hand, held level with his waist.

He looked at her, bleary-eyed, apparently unable to identify her, before he finally said, "Penny." He sighed and his gun hand fell. "Jesus Christ, what in hell time is it?"

"It's after two," Layne said.

"What are you doing here?"

"Come on, Will. Invite me in. It's hot out here."

He licked his lips. Had a few drinks tonight, she thought, and now he's dry. But who could blame him?

"Look. Can't it wait . . . ?"

"It's important, Lieutenant."

The word triggered the desired response.

"What've you been doing?" Grant asked suspiciously.

"Invite me in and I'll tell you."

Grant sighed again and stepped aside. "All right," he said wearily. "Come in."

Layne looked over the living room as Grant closed the door behind her. None of the furniture matched, but it was sturdy, comfortable-looking stuff. She dropped herself onto the sofa. It *was* comfortable. She felt like going to sleep.

No. She pulled herself up and sat on the sofa's edge.

Grant stood over her. "You want something to drink?" he asked.

Layne found herself smiling. "From the looks of us," she said, "I'd say we both better stick to something nonalcoholic."

"I'll get some Cokes."

"That's fine."

Grant laid his gun on the coffee table. He padded off into the kitchen and returned a moment later with two cold cans of cola. He handed Layne's to her and sat in a chair facing the sofa.

After drinking about half the can in one swallow, he wiped his lips and gave his visitor a tough-cop look.

"You better not tell me something I don't want to hear," he said.

"You don't want to hear it," she said. "But you do, too."

"Goddammit, Penny! You got no business—"

"Will, *look* at me! I'm here. I'm alive and well. Now, you might not like what I've done, but I've lived to tell about it. To tell *you* about it."

There was a softness in her voice at the end that he found he just couldn't resist. Damn her.

He sighed once again. "All right," he said, "tell."

She told him everything that had happened that night. When she was through, he grunted.

"I don't know," he said. "It's interesting, but . . . I don't know."

"I think you should find out who lives in that frame house," she said. "That's what I think."

"You don't even have the address."

"I didn't see a number and I couldn't risk driving by it again. But I can take you there in the morning."

"Yeah, I suppose it's worth checking. What about the place in the country? It have a name?"

"I don't know. All I saw was the sign that said 'Private Drive.' "

"Anything nearby that you could identify?" Grant asked.

"I told you, a dairy farm."

"There a name on that?"

Layne thought about it. She hadn't been paying close attention to her surroundings at that point. Still, she was an excellent observer; she ought to be able to bring up something. She closed her eyes and visualized the road, the sign in front of the farm.

"I see it," she said, opening her eyes. "The name on the sign was McCullers."

Grant shook the cobwebs out of his head. *McCullers, McCullers. McCullers!*

Dante Glorio.

His family estate was next to the McCullers place.

The man who'd wanted the Skulls. The man who'd written the letter? Things felt like they were coming together, but . . . It could so easily be just another dead end.

"You sure?" Grant asked.

"Positive." She could see the sudden change in him. "Does that mean something?"

"Maybe. I know who 'Private Drive' belongs to. His name's come up before."

"In connection with the HIVe case."

Grant didn't say anything.

"Come on, Will. that's not fair. I got all this for you."

He turned it over in his mind one more time. She had possibly done him the biggest favor possible.

"Yeah," he said. "In connection."

"Damn," she said, her excitement plainly visible. She

leaned over and squeezed his knee. "I knew it. This is it, Will. You're going to break the case."

Her touch pleased him. It had been a long time since a woman had done something spontaneously affectionate like that to him. Too long.

No. Forget it.

"Hey, hold your horses, woman," he said. "What we got is a bunch of stuff that could be coincidence. The guy who owns that estate is an actor. Suppose he's giving acting classes and the guy you met in the bar was doing an assignment. Could be."

"You don't really believe that."

"No, I don't guess I do."

There was a pause; then Layne said, "Will, I don't want to spoil things. I really do want you to get credit for this. But would you promise me one thing?"

He groaned. "I knew it," he said. "What?"

"Just that you'll let me know when you get them. If you can. I want to be there."

Grant laughed. "You never do quit working, do you?"

"Yes, I do," she said. "I quit now."

The two looked at one another, each trying to figure what the other was thinking. When Grant finally spoke, he had to clear his throat first.

He got up and said, "Let's sleep on all this. Then we'll see what we can do about it tomorrow."

Layne pushed herself up from the sofa and stood next to him. She was very close to him. Once again, he smelled her presence. It wasn't any cheap perfume. It was her, and she smelled damn good.

"It *is* tomorrow," she said.

There was another long pause, and then, by unspoken agreement, they moved together, sliding their arms around each other.

They stood there while the minutes passed, two bodies in a state of mutual support. The stresses and strains of the recent past seemed to melt away as they pressed chest to chest, belly to belly.

He had nearly forgotten how good a woman felt, Grant thought. No, strike that. What he hadn't known was how good *this* woman felt.

They pulled away from one another very slowly. Grant

had a softer expression on his face than any she'd ever seen there.

"That really was a stupid thing you done," he said.

"It really was," she said, but there was a gleam in her eye.

Then they kissed. The longest, most drawn-out kiss of Grant's life, he thought. All his good-cop resistance crumbled. He moved his lips over hers, traded explorations with her tongue. Her mouth was warm and moist and he was drawn into it.

He became aware that he was standing there with his fly open and that there was something inside his boxer shorts that was now straining to get out. She became aware of it at the same time. She reached down, put her hand inside his pants, and stroked him gently.

When they broke for air, he was hoarse and sweaty. *God, what am I? Eighteen?* he thought.

Layne looked up at him. Kind of shyly, he thought. If that were possible.

"Where do you think we ought to sleep on it?" she said, all wide eyes and innocence.

59

Saturday, August 25

Grant shook the woman lying peacefully next to him. The morning light was in the room. She reached up for him with happy, sleepy arms. He kissed her gently, but then detached himself.

"Penny," he said, "are you awake?"

"Depends," she said. "What do you want to do?"

He grinned. "I want to, but there's something I have to ask you that I should've done last night. Can you remember something?"

She propped herself up on her elbows, fully conscious now.

"Sure, what is it?" she asked.

"The guy you met in the bar, he was what? Tall and thin, right?"

"Not too tall. Maybe six-one or -two."

"Okay. What about his forehead? Did he have a cut on his forehead?"

"I don't know. I told you last night, he was wearing a sweatband."

That's right. She *had* told him, and it had slipped right on past. Dammit to hell.

A sweatband to cover a wound?

"Come on," Grant said. "Let's get dressed."

Layne didn't hesitate. There was an urgency in his voice that immediately got her going. The night had been sweet, but there would be others.

Before they left the house, Grant gave Layne a small semiautomatic pistol. It was loaded.

"Put it in your purse," he said. "If they're after you, I

don't want you to be unprotected. I'll get a permit for
you later. Let's go."

It wasn't far from Grant's house to Sunset Avenue,
and Layne identified the two-story frame house without
any trouble. There was no street number on the house,
but they were able to deduce what it ought to be. Grant
parked his car and radioed the station.

"Give me a cross-directory check on 108 Sunset Avenue," he said.

A few minutes later the response came back. The
building was a four-unit apartment building. One of the
tenants' names rang a bell.

Second floor front.

Clayton Husch.

Hospital lab technician. The middleman in the chain
that supposedly disposed of Andrew McKey's HIV-
4-contaminated blood. A man who apparently knew Dante
Glorio, who in turn was linked to the Skulls and a possibly incriminating letter.

It *was* all coming together. And the first order of
business was to nail Mr. Husch.

"Wait here," Grant told Layne.

Grant walked back to 108 and climbed the outside
stairs. The house was quiet. Like it held some terrible
secret, he thought. No, that was silly. Still . . . he wondered if he should have his gun out. Uh-uh. Everything
so far was circumstantial. But he patted the gun all the
same, making sure it was there.

He knocked on Clayton Husch's door.

*Just want to ask you a couple more questions. Mind
coming down to the Block with me?*

There was no answer. He knocked again, more loudly.
But no one came.

A door opened behind him. He turned to see a sloppy-
looking young woman with dark hair, dressed in a ratty
velour robe. Second floor rear. That would be . . . Tarrant.
Marie.

"You looking for Clayton, mister?" she said.

"Yeah," Grant said. "You know if he's in?"

"He ain't. Went out about an hour ago."

"Oh. You don't know where, do you?"

"You a friend of his?" she asked suspiciously.

"Yes, I am. My name's Will."

"Pleased to meetcha, Will. You're about the first one of Clay's friends I ever seen here."

"Well, you know Clayton," Grant said. "He ain't the real sociable type."

Tarrant rolled her eyes. "Tell me about it," she said.

"You must be Marie," Grant tried.

The suspicion returned immediately. "How'd you know that?"

"Clayton and me are friends. He told me about you."

"What'd he say?"

Grant smiled and looked down at his feet. "I don't know if I oughta . . ."

"Come *on.*"

"Well, just that there was a nice-looking lady that lived behind him, that's all."

"He said that?" Marie shifted her weight and changed her posture as though she'd gotten a sudden transfusion of sexiness.

"Uh-huh. Looks like he was about right, too. But anyway, he left something at my house last night and he's gonna need it today. You don't know where he is, do you?"

"Nah. Could be to work. He works Saturdays sometimes. You part of that group of his?"

"Which group?" Grant asked as calmly as he could with his pulse pounding in his ears.

"That flying-saucer group," Marie said. "He tried to get me to join last winter, but I don't believe in that stuff."

"Me either. He got me there one time, but damn me if it wasn't about the silliest thing I ever saw. Growed-up people involved in that kind of thing. But you must be pretty sharp, not to let Clayton talk you into it."

Tarrant laughed. "He *is* a smooth talker, ain't he? You know, you're a nice fella yourself, and here, first I thought when I looked out my window, was you was a cop. You want to come in for a cup of coffee? Or something?"

"A cop?" Grant laughed. "That's a good one." Then, with a look of concern he asked, "But Clayton's not in trouble with the police, is he?"

"Nah, I don't think so. Some nigger was by earlier this

week, asking questions. Said he was a cop, but I didn't tell him nothing. You coming in?"

Martin. Oh, God, what were you doing . . . ?

"How about a rain check, Marie?" Grant said. "I really would like to, but I got to find Clayton first."

"Anytime, Will," Tarrant said.

Grant's legs were shaky as he walked back to the car, but he pulled himself together. He wasn't about to reveal his fears to Penny.

"Not there," Grant said. "Talked to the neighbor lady, but she don't know much either. I'm gonna drop you back to your car and see can I find him at work. You think you can sit tight today?"

"Come on, Will," Layne said.

"They might still be after you. If this guy really is a part of it." Grant was surprised at the calm with which he was able to say it.

"Sure, I'll hide out in my room all day."

Grant decided to let it go at that. There was no way he was going to be able to control her behavior. She still had a job to do, and she was going to do it. Better not to make a big deal out of it.

"Just keep in touch through the switchboard, okay?" he said.

"Okay."

He dropped Layne off, then went directly to the hospital. Husch wasn't there either.

All right. Next he could do one of two things. Drive to Glorio's and see what he found there. Or stake out Clayton Husch's place.

He decided on the latter. He wanted to talk to Husch before going after the actor. Husch was at the center of this thing. Somehow, Husch had stolen Andrew McKey's blood, and that was where it had begun. Grant was certain of it.

So he went back to Sunset Avenue. He made one pass along the street, looking for the car Layne had described. She had a good eye, had even provided him with the license-plate number. The car wasn't there.

Grant parked a couple of houses down from 108. The day was already coming on hot. He rolled down the windows and stripped to his shirtsleeves. He carefully laid his gun on the seat next to him.

And he waited. An hour passed, then two.

The radio squawked. Grant had turned the volume way down, since he was on stakeout, but the message came through loud and clear: "Code twelve! All units! Code *twelve*!"

The lieutenant had heard a code-twelve broadcast only a couple of times in his entire career. It was a call for every unit to report to the Block. Immediately. It was a code reserved for only the most dire emergencies.

He hesitated.

It was his duty to drop what he was doing and get back to headquarters. No one was going to casually put out a code twelve. But what could be more important than what he was doing? What could possibly take precedence over breaking the HIVe case?

Nothing.

Feeling more than a little guilt, he reached down and switched off his radio. He could hear sirens now, all around him, as mobile units raced back to city center. That made him feel even more guilty.

Basically, he believed that a strong chain of command was the way to run law enforcement. He'd never disobeyed an order in twenty years.

But he'd set his mind on this one. Grabbing Husch was his highest priority.

Early in the afternoon, the lab tech finally showed.

Grant spotted his car first. It came slowly down Sunset Avenue and pulled to the curb less than fifty feet from where Grant was sitting. He picked up his pistol.

Husch got out of the car. For a moment he was facing Grant, and in that moment Grant saw the dark brown scab etched against the pale white of his forehead.

Adrenaline surged into Grant's blood. As soon as Husch had turned his back to the policeman's car, Grant was out the door and running.

Jeff. I've got him, Jeff.

Husch heard the footsteps, but too late. By the time he'd spun around, the lieutenant had him. Grant had assumed firing stance and leveled his gun at Husch's chest.

"Freeze!" Grant said. "Police!"

Husch didn't resist. He followed Grant's instructions to the letter. Hands on the car, legs spread. Grant searched him, cuffed him, read him his rights.

Then he took Husch back to the Block.

The place was nearly deserted. Grant passed only two cops as he led Husch to a holding cell in the basement of the building. Both of them seemed to be in a hurry, but not so much that they weren't interested in the guy he was bringing in. He didn't tell either of them anything.

Grant would have preferred not running into another soul. There were too many leaks in the department, and he wanted to keep the lid on until he had his hands on Glorio. So he'd brought the suspect in through a side door and taken him right downstairs, bypassing the front desk, where he would normally have initiated the booking procedure.

Deana Beere was on duty in the basement. She was a rookie cop and she was alone. Manning this desk wasn't a big job, but still . . .

"What's going on?" Grant asked her.

"You don't know?" Beere said incredulously.

"I've been on a stakeout. Come on, what's up?"

"Jesus. Well, there was an accident at the chemical plant. There was an explosion and . . . didn't you hear it?"

Yeah, Grant had heard the muffled thump that shook the ground under his car. But he'd been waiting for Clayton Husch. Of the HIVe.

"No," he said. "I was on the other side of town."

"Well," Deana went on, "now there's pesticide all over the place. Chief ordered everybody down there to help out. There's I don't know how many people have to be evacuated, a lot of them hurt. And we're trying to contain the spill. It's a mess, Will. You better get on over there after we put this guy in his cell."

"Deana, listen," Grant said authoritatively, "this man is a very important prisoner. I'm not gonna book him right away, but I do need to interrogate him and we do need to lock him up. You can log him in as a John Doe. And, Deana, I'd appreciate it if you didn't tell anyone else what was going on down here."

Beere hesitated. This was definitely against procedure. But then, Lieutenant Grant was her superior. And there was the look on his face.

"Okay," the young cop said.

"Thanks, Deana. Don't worry, I'll take care of it."

Beere opened the door to the cells and they escorted Husch to one of them. Then she left Grant alone with him.

"I got a right to an attorney," Husch said. "You told me so."

"Yeah, you do," Grant said. "But if you talk to me volunteer, it might could go easier on you."

"I ain't saying nothing."

And that was the way it went. Grant worked on him for an hour. Since he didn't have a partner, he had to play both good cop and bad cop. Neither moved Husch in the slightest. He closed his mouth and kept it shut.

He wouldn't talk about anything. He didn't admit knowing Glorio. He wouldn't confirm that he belonged to a group that had something to do with flying saucers. He wouldn't give the names of any of his friends. And he seemed indifferent when Grant threatened to get a warrant to search his house.

The interrogation was a washout. Eventually Grant gave up and went back to his office to try to think things through. He asked Deana Beere to please sit on the prisoner for a couple of hours, and not let anyone in to see him. He'd get the formal paperwork ready for her.

He was still thinking when Durwin Sleeth walked in. "Heard you brought in a suspect," the D.A. said, a smug expression on his face.

Jesus, Grant thought. *One person sees you and in ten minutes the whole frigging Block knows.*

"What's it about?" Sleeth asked when Grant didn't say anything.

"Look, Durwin," Grant said, "I'm trying to work something out here. Just give me a while and you'll be the first to know, okay?"

"Grant, if this is something my office ought to know about—"

"If it comes up important, I'll let you *know*. Now, do you mind?"

"Okay, okay. Ease up on it, Will." Sleeth backed out of Grant's office, holding his hands palm-outward. But once he reached the outer corridor, he walked purposefully down it.

"Goddamn weasel," Grant muttered to himself when the D.A. had gone.

The more Grant thought about it, the more it seemed that the only thing to do was go after Glorio. But how? He got up and paced the room, trying to pull it all together. The silence, not only of his office but also of the whole department, was eerie. He had a hard time concentrating when it was so quiet.

He paced past Pound's desk. The man was a total slob. Papers and notebooks were strewn wherever he happened to drop them. There were forms and folders and files . . .

The HIVe file was right there where Pound had abandoned it when Claymore-Perkins blew up. Grant couldn't resist. He opened it and took a look.

Right on top was a list of things to do, in Pound's squiggly scrawl. Item four on the list was this: *Sandy Fraim, Blake Manor. Wants to meet ASAP. Won't say about what, except it has to do with HIVe. Worth checking out.*

What'd that mean, that Worth was checking it out, or that Pound thought it was *worth* checking out?

Goddamn idiots. In charge of something like this. Wouldn't know an important lead if it bit them on their oversize butts.

And who the hell was Sandy Fraim? Grant thought. But then he realized it didn't matter. Something to do with the HIVe was going on out at Blake Manor, and Dante Glorio was dick-deep in the whole thing. It was time to go get him. If Fraim, whoever he or she was, could help out, fine.

Screw them. He'd break it by himself. With maybe an assist from . . . Grant chuckled. Yeah, why not?

Grant hurried out of his office and across the Block to the office of Wild Bill Pitt. Judge Pitt was very old and a bit on the senile side, but he was a tough law-and-order man. He believed the Supreme Court had gone way too far in its concern for the rights of criminals. Criminals

didn't have many rights to begin with, to Wild Bill's way
of thinking, and the worse their crime, the less concern
they ought to receive.

Half an hour later, Grant had a search warrant for
Blake Manor. Among the things he was empowered to
confiscate were human or other mammalian blood, medical paraphernalia including but not limited to hypodermic
needles and syringes, controlled substances, and any and
all weapons, specifically including but not limited to pistols, rifles, and shotguns.

He was ready.

Durwin Sleeth was just finishing up an entry in *JOUR-
NAL OF A JUSTICE* when his secretary announced the
visitor. He closed the book and locked it away, then
asked that the lieutenant be shown in.

"Durwin," Grant said without a preface, "I'm going to
bust the HIVe. You want to go along?"

For the first time in his memory, Sleeth was at a loss
for words.

"Come on, make up your mind," Grant said. "And if
you've got a gun handy, you better bring it."

Why is he doing this? the D.A. thought.

He stared at Grant. What was going on in that cracker's
mind? He couldn't tell. Well, what if the lieutenant really
was about to break the case open? If he, Sleeth, were on
the scene, God, what a shot in the arm that would give
his career! It might be some kind of trick—he was sure
Grant didn't like him—but then, what did he really have
to lose? Nothing but a little time.

"All right," Sleeth said.

As the two men prepared to leave, Dot Pritchett was
at her desk in the empty police department. She was still
considering the news the D.A. had passed along, about
the man in the basement. She thought about it and thought
about it. *Who to give it to?*

Better check it out first. She went down, talked to
Deana Beere, looked at the log herself.

Afterward she called Dusty Rhoades.

60

Dusty Rhoades was alone in his office when the phone rang. He often spent Saturday afternoons there, meeting with people who couldn't get to see him on weekdays.

Today, though, he was there simply because he was waiting for a call. He'd expected it the previous evening, but it hadn't come. When he'd phoned them, he'd been informed that the board was still meeting and that there probably wouldn't be any word until the following day. They'd let him know then.

Rhoades let the phone ring, afraid to answer it, afraid not to. Then he snatched it up.

"Thomas Realty," he said.

"Mr. Rhoades please," an anonymous female voice said. "Gustavia Brewing calling."

"This is Dewayne Rhoades."

"Hold for Mr. Neir, please."

The call went on hold. Rhoades swallowed a couple of times.

"Mr. Rhoades, this is Wilson Neir," the hearty voice said.

"Mr. Neir, good to hear from you."

"Damn board meeting went on half the night." Neir chuckled. "If we hadn't had some of the home product on hand, I don't think any of us would've gotten through it. Anyway, I'm afraid I've got some bad news for you, son. We appreciate all you've done and everything, but Gustavia's decided to go with Greenville."

"But . . ."

"You had a better package. Yeah, damned if it ain't so. I don't mind telling you *I* did my best for you. But the big boys are right conservative, like I told you. We had to make a decision this week and they decided that things are, well, just too un*settled* in Brisbane right now."

That was all Dusty wanted to hear.

After he'd hung up, he sat there listening to the sound of his life trickling away. He was surprised at what a quiet, insignificant sound it turned out to be.

The HIVe.

It was all the fucking HIVe's fault.

If it hadn't been for them, he'd be the prince of the city. Now he was going to be just another middle-aged guy who'd gambled his money, lost, and come out of it unable to pay his debts. Another fool who'd married for looks and failed to hold his wife when he couldn't keep her in style anymore.

Yeah, Rhonda Jo was gone, that was for sure.

Maybe he could get back on his feet, but it would take years, and even then it wouldn't be the same.

God damn the bastards.

People he'd never even met, ruining his life.

Then the phone rang again. Rhoades almost didn't answer it. What kind of good news could there possibly be? But answering phones was too much of a habit. He picked it up and it was Dot Pritchett.

"Dusty," she said, "I think we got one."

"One what?"

"A HIVe person. Grant brought somebody in this afternoon and locked him up in the basement and he's not saying anything about who it is. He's just 'John Doe' in the log. It's gotta be, don't you think?"

Rhoades didn't know what he thought, only what he felt. A cold, murderous rage that started in the pit of his stomach and flooded his entire body. It was unlike anything he'd ever experienced. Just keeping his hands from trembling was a major effort.

"How'd you find this out?" he asked her in a voice unnaturally calm from the control he squeezed it through.

Dot told him about the conversation she'd had with Durwin Sleeth, and the personal checking she'd done.

"Who else knows about this?" Rhoades asked.

"I don't think too many people," Pritchett said. "The whole damn department's tied up with that chemical spill. And I don't think Grant would've told nobody. But

Sleeth didn't come to me to listen to the sound of his own voice. He wants me to leak it, sure as I'm here."

There was a pause as Rhoades tried to think clearly despite the violent emotions that were churning him up inside.

Finally Dot said, "Dusty? You there?"

"Yeah, I'm here."

"Well, what do you think I should do?"

"I don't think you should do anything. I think we ought to keep it . . . keep it inside the group."

There was another pause, and then Dot said, "Dusty, are you gonna do what I think you're gonna do?"

"Yes. Is that all right with you?"

"Hell, yeah. These people ain't human. They deserve whatever they get."

"Okay, talk at you later. We should all meet tonight."

"I'll pass the word."

After Dot Pritchett, there was no hesitation. Rhoades punched the home phone number of the registrar of voters.

"Edna," he said, "we got one of the bastards."

"I see," Edna Clint said after a moment. "Where is . . . ?"

"He."

"Where is *he*?" Her voice was cold and remote as the outermost planet.

"I'll tell you, Edna, but . . . you've got to promise me one thing."

She waited.

"I want you to take me with you," he said.

61

On the drive out to Blake Manor, Will Grant told the district attorney everything. There was no reason not to. The case was about to bust wide open, on the one hand. On the other, if something went drastically wrong, Grant wouldn't have to take the fall alone. He couldn't be accused of playing the lone cowboy if he took along the highest-ranking member of the investigation available to him at the time.

Grant would have preferred to do it all by himself, of course. He still thought of it as *his* case and that he should be the one to break it. But sharing it in this way was a small sacrifice compared with what might happen to him if he didn't.

Besides that, there was one other thing. These people were scary. He had the element of surprise going for him, along with the cop's built-in authority, but Grant liked the odds a lot better with Sleeth riding next to him. The man might be a weasel, but he was also an excellent shot if it came to that.

For his part, Sleeth heard the story out with a mix of emotions. He was excited about actually being on the scene when the deal went down. Of course. The publicity would be monstrous. And with the kind of character he was demonstrating, no one could ever question his fitness for any future job. His career couldn't possibly receive a bigger boost.

But at the same time, he was afraid. Very, very afraid. People had already died, and more were dying.

It was hard to believe it might all be the work of one broken-down actor with a disfigured face.

Grant stopped the car at the end of the private drive.

dor. Near its end, there was a door to the right. Glorio opened it and escorted Grant and Sleeth in.

The cop and the D.A. gaped.

"It's quite something, isn't it?' Glorio said.

Though the visitors didn't know it, they were in the communications room. The perfection of its seamless dome shape and soft gold lighting rendered them speechless. Grant turned and noticed immediately that the door they had come in by had literally disappeared. Glorio had something in his hand that looked like a TV remote-control unit. Grant took a step toward the actor—

And the room went dark.

Not just dark, black. The blackest black Grant had ever experienced.

Sleeth yelped.

But neither man moved. A few moments passed and then there was a pale golden glow in the dais area at the far end of the room. Both Grant and Sleeth drew their guns. Glorio was standing in the center of the glow.

"You are fools," Glorio said in the beautiful liquid voice. "The future of the race lies with the HIVe. We need not be on opposite sides. You must join us . . ."

Glorio held out his arms to the two men.

"Freeze!" Grant yelled. "You're under arrest!" And he rushed the dais.

Glorio looked at him with pity and the room went black again. Grant continued on in the dark, searching with sweeping motions of his arms, but eventually ran into the far wall. He banged the wall in frustration. For once he regretted that he didn't carry a normal flashlight; the Security Blanket model clipped to his belt was good for only a single flash. If he'd had a more conventional light, they might have nailed Glorio before he could escape the room.

Sleeth was terrified, and couldn't move.

The two men waited in the darkness. Slowly the lights came up again. Grant and Sleeth were alone.

"Come on," Grant said as he inched along the surface of the wall, feeling for the missing door. It might be concealed, but it had to be there somewhere.

Sleeth still didn't move.

"Come *on*," Grant said.

"We're going to die," Sleeth said. "They're going to kill us." And he began to cry.

Grant turned his back in disgust and continued to hunt for the way out. Even as he did, the composition of the air entering the room through the hidden vents was changing. The carbon dioxide level began to rise.

62

Deana Beere had been nervous all afternoon. There had been nothing in her training to prepare her for a situation like this. She didn't know if Lieutenant Grant had the authority to do what he was doing, but there was no one to whom she could turn for guidance. The entire department was still preoccupied with the horrible accident at Claymore-Perkins.

So she sat on her hands, trying to wish the long shift—which was now pushing eleven hours—to its end. She was weary, and getting a little groggy from breathing the stale basement air for so long without relief. All she wanted in the world was a cool shower and a cooler drink and a full night's sleep.

The two people coming into the room startled Deana so much that she jumped up out of her chair. In truth, she'd been nodding off. Embarrassed, she tried to make her sudden movement seem natural.

"Why, Miss Clint," she said to the registrar of voters, "what are you doing here?" She nodded to the man with Edna Clint, a man she didn't know.

"I understand you took in a new prisoner today," Clint said.

"I'm sorry, ma'am, but that's confidential police—"

"I want to see him."

"Ma'am, I can't—"

"*Now!*"

Deana looked from the woman to the man and back again. What was going on? This was even more nerve-racking than the rest of the day had been.

But regulations were clear. Edna Clint didn't have the right of access to . . .

Edna Clint reached into her handbag and took out a small semiautomatic pistol.

What the . . . ?

Deana looked to the man, as if for help.

"Young lady," Dusty Rhoades said, "Edna may have less than a month to live." He shrugged. "I'd do what she says if I were you."

Deana looked back to Clint and found the gun pointed squarely at her chest. The registrar's expression was determined and her gun hand didn't shake in the slightest.

"I, uh . . ." Deana said.

"Take me to him," Clint said.

"Uh, yes, ma'am," Deana said.

The policewoman opened the door behind her. She led Rhoades and Clint down the short corridor between the rows of holding cells. About half of them were occupied. Disturbances were continuing in Brisbane.

Deana stopped in front of the last cell on the left and indicated its sole occupant.

"Open it," Clint commanded.

Deana did as she was told. The three of them entered the cell. Husch was sitting on his bunk. He looked from Edna Clint's face to the pistol in her hand. He couldn't imagine what chain of events had brought her to this moment, but here she was. An involuntary half-smile crossed his lips and he started to get up.

"Don't move," Edna Clint said to him.

He stayed where he was. Clint studied him carefully, then took a stocking from her handbag and gave it to Deana.

"Put this over his head," she said.

"Now, hold on," Husch said. "I have a right to a lawyer—"

"You've got no rights," Clint said, "until I say you do."

Husch sighed. "You're in big trouble, lady," he said, but he didn't resist as Deana put the stocking mask on him.

"Now," Clint said to Husch. "Now, you get up. Walk over to the wall, turn around, and come back here and sit down."

Husch followed instructions.

"Okay," he said when he'd finished, "are we through with this little game now?"

"That's him," Clint said to Dusty Rhoades.

"You sure?" Rhoades asked.

"I'm sure."

And this time I won't forget about the slide.

"What is this?" Deana Beere said.

Edna Clint jacked a live round into the Beretta's firing chamber. The pistol was pointed unwaveringly at Husch's chest. He sprang to his feet, but Clint tracked him perfectly and squeezed off a round.

In the tiny enclosed space of the cell, the noise was deafening. Husch was knocked backward onto the bunk, an ugly red stain almost instantly soaking his shirtfront.

"No!" Deana Beere screamed, and she jumped at Clint, but Edna smacked her with the butt end of the gun and Deana went sprawling.

Husch had clawed his way almost back up to a sitting position when Edna shot him again. His body flopped and jerked on the bunk like someone up above was pulling strings. A high-pitched whistling noise came from his mouth.

Clint continued to fire until Deana Beere finally got her arms wrapped around the older woman and wrestled the Beretta away from her.

People in the other cells were hooting and hollering.

Husch's body twitched and spasmed for a while, even after it was just a lifeless shell. The two women stared at the body, and then, tentatively, Deana Beere went over to confirm what she already knew.

And Dusty Rhoades walked away. Out of the cell, out of the holding area, out of the Block itself. Though he had a rather strange expression on his face, no one paid attention to him. Nor did he notice anyone else.

A hard, bone-deep chill had come over Dusty Rhoades, one that the heat of day didn't even dent. This was not the way he had thought it would be at all. What *had* he expected? Satisfaction or relief or guilt or a sense of completion? Maybe one or all of those, but not this.

He had stood there watching the whole thing go down right before his eyes. He had let a human being be murdered, and not lifted a finger. And the chilling thing was that he had felt absolutely nothing.

63

Dabney Layne had never seen anything like it in all her born days, as they said around here.

Just when it seemed that nothing further could go wrong in Brisbane, along came one of the worst toxic-chemical spills in years. Layne spent the day racing around trying to put together a story that would somehow tie Claymore-Perkins and the HIVe killers into a neat package for her national audience.

Then, on top of that, had come the murder of Clayton Husch.

Oh, the cops—at least the few of them who were still in the Block—were trying to hush that up for the time being, but Layne was so close to events that she was able to piece things together without much effort.

After leaving her in the morning, Grant must have located Husch and brought him in. He'd had the lab tech locked in a holding cell in the basement of the Block, and then he'd gone somewhere. Where? No one knew, but that wasn't surprising, since there was hardly anyone around for him to have told.

Late in the afternoon, someone had entered the holding cell and shot Husch to death. Killed him right there in the basement of the police department. Presumably that person was now being held, but the cops weren't saying who it was.

It was an incredible story, and Layne was on the scene, at the center of the action. Whole careers had been built by lucking into something like this.

Nevertheless, she found herself worrying more about Will Grant than the story. Where had he gone?

The cops didn't have time to be concerned. There was

simply too much going on at once. So she walked over to the district attorney's office. She could probably charm Durwin Sleeth out of whatever he knew.

But Sleeth wasn't there. His staff didn't know where he'd gone, but one of the secretaries said she'd seen him leaving with Will Grant.

When?

Sometime around midafternoon.

And he hadn't checked back since?

No.

Layne left the D.A.'s office and went back to the police department. For the next half-hour she tried as hard as she could to make a case that Will Grant might be in danger and that they should send someone with her to find him.

No one would listen. Grant, she was told, was quite capable of handling whatever trouble he got himself into. Besides, there wasn't any manpower to spare, especially not to follow up some out-of-town reporter's hunch. When Layne persisted, she managed to provoke more than a few tempers.

However, she made such a nuisance of herself that she did finally get in to see Kip Kyser. For about one minute.

"Look," the red-faced chief of police spluttered at her, "you know how much trouble that son of a bitch has already caused today? Running around behind my back! I take him off the case, and what does he . . . ? Ah, forget it. I don't even want to *see* him unless it's to take his resignation!"

"Chief Kyser," Layne said, "he's one of your men and I believe he's in danger."

"He'll be in worse danger when he shows his face back here. Now, get the hell out of my office!"

Eventually Layne had to admit that the cavalry was not going to ride with her. Whatever happened next, she was alone.

So she took stock. She was not a particularly brave person, but she'd been in one or two tight situations before and come through okay. She knew how to use the gun Will Grant had given her.

He'd been concerned for her safety, and now she was concerned for his. It seemed natural. If he wasn't really in trouble, then she wasn't going to encounter anything she couldn't talk her way out of. And if he was . . . ? She wasn't positive where to find the answer to that question, but she had a damn good idea.

Layne left the Block and went to her rented car. Before starting it, she did one last thing. She opened her purse, took out the pistol, and checked to see if it held a full clip. It did.

Then she drove to Blake Manor.

64

When Will Grant woke up, he had no idea where he was. All he knew was that he had a splitting headache and that something dry and fuzzy was in his mouth.

He opened his eyes and tried to focus. There was some green stuff . . . Carpeting. His face was flush against a thick green carpet. He was lying on his stomach. There was lint in his mouth and in his nose. He sneezed.

"Lieutenant Grant," came a voice. "So glad you could join us."

Gingerly Grant pushed himself up to his hands and knees. The pain in his head was excruciating. It interfered with his vision and his sense of balance. And he was dying of thirst.

"Feeling a little woozy?" the voice asked. "It's just the oxygen deprivation. You'll get over it. We need to have you clearheaded."

Grant rocked back so that he was squatting on his heels. The room was spinning and he thought he might throw up. He put one hand on the floor to steady himself. That helped. The room slowed and he was able to swallow.

He squinted and looked around him. It was a good-sized room, with concrete walls suggesting a basement. The lighting wasn't very good, but there was enough for him to put together the general picture.

"That's better," the voice said.

Now he recognized it. It was Dante Glorio's voice. Glorio was seated in a chair perhaps fifteen feet away. A group of people was gathered around him. They were all dressed in yellow shirts and they looked like zombies.

The HIVe, Grant thought, and the thought raised the hair everywhere on his body.

311

To calm himself, he concentrated on getting the details
of the rest of the room. There was a door at the far end,
apparently the only way in or out. There were several
metal pillars supporting the weight of the floor above.
There were a couple of windows set high in the walls.
They were barred.

Grant shifted his weight to see what he could feel.

"If you're looking for your gun," Glorio said, "here it
is."

The actor indicated a small low table in front of him.
On it was a pair of guns, one of them Grant's, along with
his wallet and someone else's, the search warrant, and
various personal effects. There were also half a dozen
syringes, each with a small load of what looked like
blood.

Don't even think about it.

Grant's movement had made him aware of the hard
object at his waist. The Security Blanket flashlight. They
hadn't taken it. They didn't know what it was.

The awful headache was still there, but Grant felt his
wits returning to him. He had a weapon. It wasn't the
most effective weapon in the world, but he had it and
they didn't know that. There was hope.

Grant continued to scan the room and . . . In the far
corner, there was something in the gloom . . . a chair and
. . . somebody in it. He strained to see.

And wished he hadn't.

His head turned away involuntarily and he clamped
down on the overwhelming urge to throw up once again.

"Your friend told us quite a lot before he . . . passed
on," Glorio said. "He regained consciousness first. Fortunately for you, you might say. I suppose he was in
better shape."

The body in the corner was Sleeth's. It was sprawled
supine over the chair as if it had been carelessly flung
there. A syringe protruded from his chest, right over his
heart.

The horror subsided a little, and in its place came the
anger. It was a hard, calculating anger.

*Jeff. And Sleeth. And Brian Sites. And all the soon-
to-be-dead. Lorene Greene.*

This has to end here. I do whatever I have to do.

Grant held on to the cold fire as he put his mind to work on a plan.

"Feeling better?" Glorio asked, and then answered himself. "Good. Now, we know who you are, Lieutenant. We know who your friend is. What else do we need to know?"

"*Is*," not "*was*," Grant thought. *Who your friend is. Maybe he doesn't even know the difference.*

Grant didn't say anything. Better to let Glorio do the talking for a while.

"Like I said," Glorio went on, "your friend told us a lot. But I'd like to hear it again, in your own words."

Grant still didn't say anything.

"Lieutenant," Glorio said, "let me tell *you* something. I don't think you understand what's going on here. We are the new age of mankind. We are in communication with intelligent beings, like ourselves, on other planets. One day we'll all be a part of the greater cosmic family, and these people here in this room will have made it happen."

A flying-saucer group. Grant almost chuckled.

"You can't stop it," Glorio continued, "and you shouldn't want to. The Polarians are glorious beings. It is to our benefit that they have decided to share the virus with us. Now we can only be slowed, not stopped, can't you see that?"

There was a pause.

Nutso. Completely nutso. That makes it tougher.

"No, I guess you don't. Which is too bad. All right, let me put it another way, Lieutenant. If you tell me everything you know about us, I promise you won't suffer. I will shoot you."

The young woman sitting next to Glorio flinched, Grant noted. He figured that would be Fraim. There had to have been a reason she called Pound. Maybe she wanted out. Grant studied her as best he could without being obvious about it. She was at his right hand, close to him. *If she's his girlfriend,* Grant thought, *oh, God, that could be critical.*

"If you don't . . ." Glorio said. And he indicated the syringes on the table in front of him. "You may survive exposure to the virus, in which case you are one of the elect. You will have joined us. Or you may not, in which case I understand it is quite painful.

"Come, come, Lieutenant. What do you say?"

"I don't know what you want to know," Grant said.

"I want to know what you've learned about us. Obviously not the important things, but enough to bring you here. What exactly do you *know*? We must keep far enough ahead of you so the project is not jeopardized by your activities. Surely you understand that."

"I don't know anything more than Sleeth knew. I'm not even on the case anymore."

"Oh, come on, Mr. Grant. You don't expect me to believe that."

Grant shrugged. "Believe what you want," he said. "I've been working on my own. I followed Clayton Husch and he led me here."

"I see," Glorio said. "And do you know where Brother Clayton is now?"

"Yes, he's in jail."

There were shocked murmurings among the HIVe members.

"Jail?" Glorio said.

"I locked him up myself. Then I came out here to arrest you."

"I don't believe you. Where is your evidence?"

"Right on that table in front of you."

"But you couldn't . . ."

"That's what search warrants are all about. Did you read it?"

"I . . . I don't . . ."

"It's over, Glorio. You can kill me, but it's still over. The judge who signed that warrant knows about you, and so will the rest of the force when they read my notes. You're gonna have to go live with your space friends to get away. And if you kill a cop, well, I wouldn't want to be you when the cops catch up with you."

Sandy Fraim was looking at Glorio. Grant tried desperately to read her expression. Was there resignation? Weariness? A desire for it to end once and for all?

He decided to gamble and said, "Not to mention the people of this town. If *they* get their hands on you first, I guarantee they'll tear you to pieces. Give it up, Glorio. It's over. Just ask Miss Fraim there."

Glorio turned his head sharply. He looked at Sandy Fraim, then back to Grant.

"What do you mean, ask her?" he said.

Grant got up. He was a little unsteady, but he had to get off his knees.

"I mean *ask* her," Grant said. "Look at her, for Christ's sake. She's never lied to you, has she? *Look* at her. *She* realizes that it's over. Or she never would've called us."

Grant said it matter-of-factly, as if it were something everyone in the room should know. But Glorio sprang immediately to his feet.

"*Called* you! What are you talking about?" he demanded. He turned to Sandy. "What is he *talking* about, goddammit?"

Sandy couldn't meet his gaze. She looked down. "I don't know," she murmured.

Glorio grabbed her by the hair and yanked her head up. He slapped her hard across the face.

"Tell me what he's talking about!" he shouted.

Sandy spoke through gritted teeth. "I . . . I didn't want there to be any more killing," she said.

"You betrayed us."

"No! I believe in the cosmic family, Bobby. You know I do. But our job is to spread the message, not kill people in cold blood. When we do that, we're not helping, we're harming."

Slowly, very slowly, Grant was moving forward. If he could get within eight feet or so, there was a chance . . .

Glorio grabbed Sandy's hair again, and pulled her roughly to her feet. The rest of the HIVe was transfixed by what was happening.

Twelve feet, eleven . . .

"You've betrayed us," Glorio said to Sandy. "You don't believe in the cosmic family. You're with *them*." His voice choked up. "My best, my first . . . Sandy, I *trusted* you. I would have given my life for you."

Sandy began to cry.

Ten, nine . . .

"*Hold it*!" Glorio whirled and, in the same motion, snatched one of the pistols from the table. Grant recog-

nized it now. It was Sleeth's gun. And it was aimed at the
center of Grant's chest. "Back off, Lieutenant."

Grant kept his hands in front of him and shuffled
backward a couple of feet.

"Sandy, Sandy," Glorio said while looking at Grant.
"We have to talk about this."

There was a long pause; then Glorio chuckled.

"Yes," he said, "I think we'll have our talk now. And
in the meantime, a little diversion for you, Mr. Grant.
Everyone take a needle." He chuckled again. "Except
you, of course, Lieutenant."

He motioned to the group, and each person picked up
one of the syringes.

"Now," he said to his followers, "see that our guest
joins the HIVe." He grinned. "But give him plenty of
time to savor what's happening to him.

"And you, Lieutenant, here's your gun. If you can get
it, you're welcome to it."

Glorio pulled Sandy Fraim out the door. "Excuse us,
we need to be alone for a while," he said as they left.
There was the sound of a bolt being thrown behind them.

The HIVe turned its attention to Grant. The group
moved slowly toward him, moving with a common will,
the same lack of expression on every face, as if it were a
single sexless yellow-skinned animal with ten arms and
legs.

The sight made Grant's skin crawl. He moved in response to the group, circling to his left, trying to set up a
clear lane to the table in case he had to make one final
dash for the gun. But the HIVe kept cutting him off.
Though there was no apparent intelligence to it, it had
purpose, which served it just as well.

And it was relentless, closing on him, closing on him,
the needle ends of its many arms glinting as they poked
at the air, coming ever nearer to pricking his flesh.

Grant kept circling. He realized now that making a
direct try for the gun was suicide. They would be on him
before he got within ten feet of it. There was only one
chance, and for it to work he would have to make himself
totally vulnerable.

He nearly screamed from the tension, and from the
certainty of what would happen if he failed. But some-

how he kept control. The scream came out as a whimper, which was what he wanted.

Slowly, seemingly without plan, he allowed himself to be maneuvered toward a far corner. He was whimpering steadily, begging for his life. The HIVe drew itself closer and closer together as the available space diminished.

Grant's back bumped the wall. He was trapped. Every nerve ending in his body raged against what he was doing. But it was the only way.

He faced the HIVe and it faced him, waving its many pinpoints of death. The scene froze for a long moment and Grant felt the deepest dread of his life. It was all he could do to keep from accepting his fate and rushing madly into the HIVe's midst. Involuntarily he rose up onto the balls of his feet.

The group continued to close in on him. They were packed as tightly together as they were ever going to be. The timing had to be perfect; he had to catch the attention of each person at exactly the same moment. There could be no hesitation, no wasted movements. The moment was now.

Grant whipped the Security Blanket flashlight from his belt and brought it up in front of him, aimed directly at the HIVe. For a fleeting instant it was the point of focus for everyone in the group. They stared at it in surprise. What . . . ?

And Grant pressed the button. The device's bulb gave a single flash, a burst of light of six million lumens' intensity. It was like taking a quick close-up look at the sun.

The HIVe was blinded, but only for a couple of minutes. Grant dived to his right and rolled, scrambling away from the sightless beast with its lethal stingers. The beast, at first stunned, recovered its wits. It began to flail and shriek, stabbing at where it thought Grant ought to be. Its voices blended into a single piercing wail as the needles sank into its own body.

Grant sprinted across the room and grabbed up his gun. His heart was racing and he had only one thought, to get out of the room before these zombies regained their sight.

He rushed to the door and pulled on it. Locked from

the outside. He looked around him. The only other exits
were the high barred windows. Nothing doing there. He
turned back and pounded on the door.

"Glorio!" he shouted. "I've got the gun! I don't want
to shoot all these people!"

He waited, but there was only silence beyond the door.
Behind him, the HIVe had dispersed. Each of its blinded
members was groping toward the sound of his voice. It
was only a matter of time before they could see.

Grant cocked the gun's hammer. As he did, he noticed
something. The ammo clip was missing.

His heart sank. He was trapped in the room, outnumbered, no bullets except . . . There might be one in
the firing chamber.

But if there was, how best to use it?

Grant made a quick decision. He aimed the gun at a
point above the doorknob, where he thought the outside
bolt was likely to be, and he pulled the trigger. The gun
fired. There was a splintering of wood. He yanked on the
door. Nothing. He put his foot against the wall for added
leverage and pulled again. The door refused to budge.

There were HIVe members scattered all about, and
there was enough blood left in the syringes to do the job.
Frantically Grant swept his eyes across the room. He
could use the gun as a club, and maybe the table, but he
had to get moving *now*.

The outside bolt slid back. Grant reacted instinctively,
stepped to the side as the knob turned and the door
began to creep open. When there was enough space, he
grabbed the door's edge and threw it wide, at the same
time launching himself against Glorio.

The two went sprawling.

Grant raised his gun hand and was about to cave in the
side of the actor's head when he realized that the person
beneath him wasn't Glorio, but Penny Layne. She was
staring at something behind him and her eyes were wide.

"Will!" she screamed.

Grant looked over his shoulder and saw a man with a
syringe feeling for a body to stick it into. Grant lashed
out with his foot, catching the man in the midsection.
The man stumbled backward into the basement room.

Two others had nearly reached the door. Grant jumped to his feet, slammed the door shut, and bolted it.

Then he turned. Layne had also gotten up, had retrieved her glasses that had been knocked loose, and was facing him. He slumped, his back against the door, his gun hand hanging limp at his side, his breath coming in deep shuddering gasps. For a long moment he couldn't move. He had to wait until the shaking went away.

Layne reached up and touched his cheek. "You okay?" she said.

Grant nodded. "What are you doing here?"

"It had to be Blake Manor. When you were gone so long, I decided to come. I saw your car out front and I knew you had to be in trouble. So I broke a window and followed your voice down here, and . . . you almost got me with that bullet."

"Jesus. Are you alone?"

She shrugged. "None of your buddies believed me," she said. "Even after . . . Oh, you probably don't know."

"What?"

"Husch is dead. Somebody shot him in his cell."

Grant was unsurprised that he didn't really feel much. The only possible loss was Husch's testimony, but someone else from the locked room would fill in the gaps. They'd get the leader.

"Glorio's not in there," Grant said, indicating the room. "Did you see him on your way down here?"

"Uh-huh, just for a second. On the main floor. He had a girl with him, and he was half-dragging her up the stairs."

"Did he see you?"

"No, I don't think so."

Grant noticed for the first time that the pistol he had given Penny that morning was in her right hand. He took it from her and gave her his.

"It's empty," he told her, "but it might be good for something. Come on."

"Will, are we . . . going after Glorio?"

"Yes. I think he may have decided to kill that girl. She turned against him."

She looked into his eyes, then said, "All right."

Grant headed cautiously for the stairs, with Layne following. Behind them, the HIVe howled and pounded on the bolted door.

65

Dante Glorio was kneeling on the dais in the communications room. Sandy Fraim was lying supine across his legs. He cradled her head in one of his arms. With his other hand he traced the outline of her body.

"Sandy," he said. "Sandy, Sandy. Why?"

But there was no reply. Sandy's head lay at a strange angle, her eyes wide open, unblinking, staring at nothing.

"We were the vanguard," Glorio crooned. "The cosmic family. We could have been heroes, Sandy."

He began to hum a tune over her unmoving form. Softly, almost inaudibly, he hummed along, the stirring theme music from *The Sands of Time*.

Gently he laid Sandy out on the dais, arranging her as if he were displaying a treasured object. Then he sat down on the chair of polished walnut. With the remote-control unit he brought down the general lighting in the room and that around the dais up, until he was highlighted within the glowing golden sphere. He closed his eyes.

"Joseph," he said. "they are trying to destroy our HIVe. Speak to me now. I need your guidance."

He waited, and soon he felt the familiar changes, the stresses and strains on his body as he became a conduit for the interstellar message. When he spoke to the empty room, it was in a voice not his own.

It was an angry voice and it said, "You must persevere, Glorio. Your enemies are nothing. They will pass away and the HIVe will be strong once again. You are being tested and you must persevere."

Tentatively Grant and Layne entered the communications room. Grant had his pistol ready.

Glorio's eyes flicked open, but it was not he who was looking through them.

"*Who are these people?*" Joseph demanded.

"You're under arrest, Glorio," Grant said. He advanced toward the dais. "Don't try anything."

"*Are they those who would obstruct the HIVe?*"

Grant saw the lifeless body of Sandy Fraim. He felt sick. For the first time in twenty years he wanted to kill someone rather than arrest him.

"Come on, Glorio," he said. "Let's go. It's over."

Grant cocked the pistol's hammer. As he did, Glorio raised the hand that held the remote-control unit and pushed a button. The door to the communications room slammed shut. Grant turned to see Layne rush to the wall and stare at its seamless surface. When he whirled back around, he glimpsed Glorio's chair disappearing through a hole in the floor as the room went black. Grant got off one shot into the darkness.

The same trap, Grant thought, and he'd walked right back into it. He was almost paralyzed with fear but forced himself to move. Layne was calling for him. He followed her voice until they touched.

"The door," she said, and she scraped her fingernails along the wall, searching for the seam that had to be there. Grant felt too. It couldn't be far from this spot.

The music came on. The Skulls, at full volume. It was like being without earplugs in a room full of .38's all being fired at once. Instinctively Layne and Grant covered their ears.

And lights began flashing and flickering in a staccato pattern that bombarded the eyes, blasting their vision into a state of complete disorientation.

Grant took his hands away from his ears. The pain was as great as if someone were scratching on his eardrums, but he had to endure it. He knew that there would be something coming in through the vents. Maybe not carbon dioxide this time. Maybe something quicker.

He groped until he got his arms around Penny. He pulled at her hands. She fought to keep them over her ears, but he got his face next to hers and screamed as he pulled her hand away.

"The *door!* The *door!*"

Layne was in a state of total sensory overload, the music threatening to shake her very bones apart and the lights detonating explosions at the back of her skull, but she allowed herself to be pushed against the wall. From somewhere, she summoned up the strength to start feeling for the crack again.

Grant joined her as she scraped hysterically, screaming, crying, knowing that it was only a few moments before the circuits shut down and she collapsed senseless on the floor.

And suddenly, there it was. A tiny crack, no more than a hairbreadth. Layne smashed at it with the empty gun she still held. The Sheetrock dented, then crumbled, revealing the crack more distinctly.

Grant saw what she was doing and began to pound on the plasterboard with the butt end of his own pistol. They worked outward from the crack as rapidly as they could. White dust puffed into the air, choking them, but they didn't stop until they'd cleared a ragged hole the size of a basketball. The smooth wood surface of the door exposed itself, but gave no hint of how to open it.

Grant motioned Layne back and aimed his gun at the wood. He fired four times at point-blank range. The sound of the shots was swallowed up by the music, as was the splintering of the wood.

He'd fired the bullets in a roughly circular pattern and they'd torn the wood up pretty good. Grant backed up a step, then kicked with his heel at the spot, putting every ounce of his hundred and ninety pounds behind the blow. A small fist-size hole appeared in the door.

Too small for Grant. But Layne came over immediately and went to work. She was able to get her forearm through almost to the elbow. She groped left, right, up, down.

Her fingers touched something. Smooth. A knob. She forced her arm further. The splintered wood tore at her flesh, but she felt no pain. There was just enough room to get part of her hand around the knob and turn it a little, hold it with her thumb, rearrange her fingers, turn it a little more.

She leaned her weight forward, turned the knob another inch.

And the door fell open.

Layne fell too, her arm hanging from the hole in the door. Now it hurt. It hurt like hell.

Grant was there to help her disentangle herself. She was bleeding, but not badly. He closed the door to the communications room and the noise level dropped. The walls still thumped, but they could hear one another again. They both blinked to adjust their eyes.

"God," Layne said. It was the only word she could think of. The sound of her own voice startled her.

"I think . . ." Grant said, then realized he was shouting and toned it down. "I think I might have hit him. That trapdoor must lead to the room right underneath here. We got to go after him, Penny. And hope he hasn't gotten to the rest of the HIVe."

Layne nodded. She was too drained to do anything but whatever he said.

Grant hurried down the stairs to the first floor, with Layne following as best she could. He quickly located the door to the room directly below the one they'd escaped from. He hesitated for a moment, then opened it, keeping off to the side.

Glorio was there, in the control room, surrounded by his electronic gadgets and his actor's bag of tricks. He'd taken a bullet in the chest and had lost a lot of blood. He knew he was dying. But he could still manipulate the communications room. He could kill the cop and the reporter. As painfully as possible.

When the two of them came through the door of the control room, Glorio was confused. No, they couldn't be here, they were . . .

Grant stared at the man sitting there in his blood-soaked clothes and for a fleeting moment felt pity for him. Then the emotion was gone. Glorio had only a short time left to live, and Grant knew it was just as well.

He turned to check on Penny, to make sure she was there and that no other members of the group were coming in behind them.

In that moment Glorio somehow found the strength to move. He pushed himself to his feet, lurched forward . . .

"Will!" Layne screamed. "Look *out*!"

Glorio stumbled at the policeman, a beaker of infected blood in his hand. He threw it at Grant's face, aiming for the eyes and nose.

And it all seemed to happen in slow motion. At Layne's scream, Grant spun back around and ducked instinctively to the right. The blood flew across the intervening space and spattered harmlessly against his coat.

The leader of the HIVe continued to fall forward, wrapping his arms around Grant. The two men tumbled backward in a strange embrace, Grant landing hard on his back with Glorio atop him. The breath went out of Grant and his pistol bounced away from him.

Glorio grappled for Grant's throat. Though near death, the disfigured actor was still astonishingly strong. He began to squeeze.

Layne snatched up the gun and aimed it at Glorio's head.

"Stop!" she yelled. "For God's sake, *stop it!*"

There were tears in her eyes and the image of Glorio blurred. Her hand was shaking so much she couldn't hold the gun steady. She moved closer, until the pistol was only a foot from Glorio's head.

"*Please!*" she screamed on last time. But he was beyond the point of control. His fingers squeezed the lieutenant's throat of their own accord.

Layne pulled the trigger, and Glorio's head exploded.

66

Dusty Rhoades had been driving aimlessly for hours, trying to figure how things were going to work out.

They weren't.

In the final analysis, that was the only conclusion.

For openers, his partner was near death. Rhoades might have been the high-energy member of the team, but Wes Thomas, with his old money and connections, had been essential to making the company work. When Wes was gone, a lot of doors would close.

And then, he was broke. No, worse than broke. With the collapse of the Gustavia project, he was so far in debt he would have to declare bankruptcy. Once that happened, he would lose the position in the community he'd worked so hard for, and he would lose it for good. The people who mattered were tough and they were unforgiving.

Throw in that he would always be remembered as the man who somehow blew Gustavia, with all the money it would have brought to the town. Each day of his life he would be judged for that. It would be continuous humiliation.

Which would be more than his wife could take. He knew Rhonda Jo only too well. She still loved him, at least a little; the nights since he'd gone after the EPA investigator had proved that. She might even stand by him for a while. But Rhonda Jo loved her comforts too much. When they really hit bottom, she'd be gone.

Beyond that, the arrest of an actual member of the HIVe signaled that the nightmare was coming to an end. That was the best of news. But it also meant the police would finally have the time to gather up all the loose

threads. When they did, the group's—and his—part in
the death of David Eye was bound to come out.

Then there was the incident at the Block. He'd stood
and watched while Edna Clint shot a man to death. He
was an accessory to murder.

On top of all his financial and social troubles, Dusty
Rhoades was, one way or another, going to jail. That was
something he knew he would never survive.

Somewhere around the third hour of his aimless driving, he made the decision.

Despite her infidelity, he loved Rhonda Jo, he truly
did, and he couldn't do anything that would leave her
holding the bag. *His* bag. The half-million-dollar policy
wouldn't pay out for a suicide. But it paid double in the
case of accidental death.

Rhoades was on the Interstate, driving steadily in the
fast lane. As he neared an overpass, there was a car to
his right, going considerably slower. Dusty let his car
drift slowly toward it. The other driver leaned frantically
on his horn. At the last minute, Rhoades spun his wheel,
as if he'd suddenly seen what was happening and was
trying to avoid the collision.

The other driver saw a man with a cast on one hand
fighting to regain control of his vehicle.

Rhoades's car skidded and headed straight for one of
the concrete bridge supports.

Dusty hit the brake a little, to leave some rubber on
the asphalt, but he was still going over sixty when he
crashed.

He wasn't wearing his seat belt.

67

Sunday, August 26

Dr. Jorge Mendez was depressed.

The blood the HIVe was using had come from the hospital after all. Andrew McKey's contaminated blood had been stolen from under their noses. Procedures had not been strict enough. He blamed himself.

And then the lab called him at home, as he had instructed them to do. When they'd given him their report, he was stunned. For a moment he sat there with the phone in his hand, staring at it like it had come from outer space.

Dr. Mendez was known to his colleagues as an intelligent, quiet, courteous, efficient, but basically dull man. They would never have recognized the Mendez who gave out a wild whoop of joy.

With a shaky hand he placed the call that he had once dreaded and now couldn't wait to make.

"Mrs. Greene," he said, the happiness in his voice unrestrained, "I just got the lab report on Lorene. The virus is gone. It's *disappeared*! Your little girl is going to be okay!"

Ellen Greene tried to say something, anything, to thank this man or whoever was responsible, to give some sort of voice to what she was feeling. But no words came through her sobs.

And the courteous, efficient, but basically dull Dr. Mendez found himself crying too.

68

A low-pressure system, spawned over the Gulf of Mexico, had moved into the area late Saturday night, and by the early hours of Sunday morning it was raining. It rained all day.

Most of the Claymore-Perkins spill had been cleaned up by that time. What was left was going to be washed into the Squier River, and there was nothing to be done about it except hope that the heavy rains would dilute the pesticide beyond its ability to do harm.

Whatever the consequences for those downstream, the streets of Brisbane at least were scoured clean.

As with the streets, so with the spirits of the townspeople. They stayed indoors, listening to the rain beat on their roofs and knowing the horror was finally over. Three key members of the HIVe were dead, and the rest were in custody. All remaining contaminated blood had been seized and stored away under heavy security pending the trials to come.

Brisbane had lost its district attorney and would undoubtedly lose its registrar of voters long before she would ever be punished for what she had done. Some of its children were going to die too. The town mourned them.

It also mourned the loss of the Gustavia brewery, and of the two men who had worked so long and hard to bring it to the city.

But Brisbane would survive. The sun would come out again, the people would go back to their jobs and their lives, the fear would be gone from the streets.

Those who had cleaned and oiled their old guns put them back into boxes and shoved the boxes into the corners of top closet shelves. Those who had purchased new weapons began to place For Sale ads in the newspaper.

The local paper would have stories to run for weeks to come, but the national press had moved on. Flights out of Brisbane were jammed, the baggage compartments of planes stuffed with hard aluminum suitcases. Once again there were rooms available at the Green Brae and the Brisbane Arms.

City Plaza was empty in the August rain. A stack of sodden handbills lay next to an overflowing trashcan. Whatever their message was, no one cared.

Brad Davis and Kip Kyser were sweating for their jobs. Davis was vulnerable because of his knowledge of Dusty Rhoades's group and of the cover-up after David Eye's death. If either of those went public, the reelection campaign was down the tubes.

Kip Kyser had to answer to both of those, as well as to his overall handling of the HIVe case and the fact that a man had been murdered right in one of his holding cells. He hadn't done anything indictable, but if Davis were defeated, a new chief of police was bound to be appointed. Unless . . .

Kyser had a few drinks and then placed a call to Davis' opponent. They should get together, he suggested.

Rhonda Jo was drinking too. She was alone in a house that suddenly seemed way too big for her. She never would have guessed she'd miss Dusty this much.

Jim Teague was at his home in Bethesda, Maryland, working hard on his pollution case against Claymore-Perkins. He hadn't read a newspaper or watched TV since his return from Brisbane. He didn't even know about the spill.

Phil Atherton and Dot Pritchett had met and tried to make love. For the first time since he'd known her, he'd failed. She was gently reassuring, but secretly relieved. Her own lack of physical response, though less obvious to him, had been quite apparent to her. It was over.

The rain continued to beat down on Brisbane, soaking the parched and grateful earth.

69

Monday, August 27

It was still raining, though not nearly so hard, when Will Grant woke up. He immediately turned to his bedmate and slid his arm around her naked waist. He nuzzled her, kissing her neck.

Dabney Layne awoke with a soft hum of pleasure.

"Mmmm," she said, "I could get used to that."

He kissed her some more, and almost before they realized what was happening, he had pulled her over him and slipped smoothly inside her.

She thought how strange and wonderful that was, and then she stopped thinking.

Later, Layne had her head propped on her elbow as she traced circles on Grant's chest with her fingertips.

"We're an odd couple, Will Grant," she said.

"That's what I know," Grant said. "You going back to New York tomorrow?"

"Uh-huh."

"Ever think about getting out of the rat race?"

"No, not really. It's not a rat race to me. It's my career." She shrugged. "It's the only thing I'm good at."

Grant grinned at her. "But one," he said.

"But one," she agreed with a smile. "Though I never thought so before. What about you? What're you going to do? Go back to being a Brisbane cop?"

"Well," Grant said, "I have given it a deal of thought. First thing is to find Clarice. I don't have a lot of money saved up, but there's enough so she can have the baby and not have to worry about holding things together for a while.

"Then, well, I guess I don't need to wait for a full

331

pension. I can get three-quarters now. That oughta be enough to support me in Nashville."

"You're really going to *do* it!"

"Yeah, I believe so. Who should know about pain and suffering but me? All I need to do is set it to music."

Layne smiled at him. "You're some peculiar man, Will," she said. "I've never known anyone like you. It's been . . . it's been a real pleasure."

"Well, I sure wish I would've met you under other circumstances, but I know what you mean. It has been for me too."

There was a pause; then Grant said, "Hey, maybe you could come to Nashville and do a story on the country-music scene."

Layne pursed her lips. "Hmmm," she said. "Maybe I could at that. Maybe I just might could."

Epilogue

"Mama, I had a real funny dream last night," Ellen Greene's seven-year-old daughter said to her.

"What was that, hon?" Ellen said.

"Well, there was this man . . . no, this man's voice, and he was talking inside my head, but talking like right to me, you know? He said, 'Lorene.' He said my name. And then he said, 'Lorene, my name is Joseph and we're gonna become very good friends.' What was he talking about, Mama?"

"Nothing, sweetheart," Ellen Greene said. "It was just a dream. It doesn't mean anything."